For my parents, Bill and Joan.

And for Lolly: my loyal companion. Always by my side with every keystroke . . . or on my lap, or under my feet.

On an icy 5-degree September morning in Orange, New South Wales, four people unknowingly set off a chain of events that would lead to three deaths and a major homicide investigation.

The first person kicked off the event when they broke into Summer Street Jewellery Store, helping themselves to enough fashionable watches and bracelets to keep their drug habit in full swing for the next few months.

The second, the owner of the jewellery store, continued the momentum when they saw an opportunity to cash in on the insurance claim after a poor year of turnover, by stashing away a considerable amount of valuable items before the cops arrived.

The third domino was kicked over when a police officer on general duties weighed up their pending retirement, dismal superfund, long service and holiday leave, and figured a few precious stones and rings would soften the blow of departing the force earlier than planned.

The ripple effect was finally completed by the fourth person, who witnessed the cop filching the items.

Two months later, this would lead to the first recorded death and the formation of Strike Force Oona.

~

Now, on a hot November morning, more than 300 kilometres from the jewellery store, the first body lies naked and partially submerged in a cattle trough.

The air in the lungs has kept her chest floating above the surface of the murky water. Her legs are heavy, wound tightly together with rusty barbed wire, like two needlefish caught in a net. Her ankles have sunk into the soft sludge. The skin on her neck has been scrubbed and peeled away. Two of her fingernails have been removed by force. And while she has only bled a little from her nails, and a few grazes and cuts, the ground around the cattle's drinking trough is soaked in blood. A wallaby has been gutted and its blood and entrails scattered.

It will be another two hours before rigor mortis sets in. Until then, the slim fingers will float below the water's surface, gently bobbing, beckoning Detective Giles to come and find her.

The mother wakes to dust speckled in sunlight. She throws back the bedsheet, stirring the stale air. She needs to put the kettle on. A coffee first. Inject some caffeine into the system and wipe the sleep from her eyes before getting the kids up for school.

She's surprised she's out of bed before her two girls, but perhaps that's because for once she's had a proper night's sleep. Last night there were none of the usual bed-time antics from Kayleen. The bullshit routine of, *Tuck me in, I can't sleep, I need to pee, I'm cold, I'm hot, I'm thirsty, I need to pee again.* And – for the first time in a long time – she's not woken with a dry mouth and a headache. She had put the cap back on the bottle of bourbon after just three drinks.

Atta girl, she tells herself.

The mother stands on the back veranda, where the sun doesn't smash her in the face and the neighbours can't perv on her braless tits under her ratty t-shirt.

She drinks her coffee and sneaks in a ciggie. She doesn't like her kids seeing her smoke, and out here on the back deck she can hear them coming down the hall, giving her enough time to flick the cigarette butt into the garden bed below.

The mother puffs away slowly, making the most of it. There's only two left in the pack, so she needs to space them out until she can get to the shops. She relishes having five minutes to herself; it gives her time to get her head together.

Mornings are normally peaceful, but with the blaring heat, the sound of a distant car engine revving and the relentless barking of the dog next door, the mother knows any chance of dawn mindfulness is fucked.

Recharged, with caffeine in her veins and tobacco on her breath, the mother turns on her bare sticky heels, disentangling herself from the morning clatter. It's time to wake her girls.

Inside, her youngest is already up. She's snuck into the kitchen without the mother hearing a single footstep. At the breakfast bench, Mikaela pours apple juice into a plastic princess cup.

'Mornin'. Is your sister up?'

'Dunno.'

The mother shuffles down the hall to Kayleen's bedroom and finds it empty. She feels the mattress – it's cold. She notices her daughter's school uniform and a blue disposable lab coat, scrunched up in a pile on the floor beside her school bag. The mother pokes the flimsy gown with her toe, then checks the bathroom and her own bedroom.

'Kayleen.'

She looks under the bed and in the wardrobe.

'*Kayleen?*'

The mother feels her chest tighten. She doesn't have the patience or sense of humour for games, but she's hell-bent on not losing her temper. Not this bloody early in the morning.

Back in the kitchen, she asks, 'Where's your sister hiding?'

'Dunno.'

'Kayleen?' calls the mother, but the house is quiet.

Fuck. Where is she?

The mother heads out the front door, letting the flyscreen slam behind her. Other than the endless barking next door, and the shrill of cicadas, the street is quiet. She blinks for a moment into the morning sunlight, lifts her hand to her brow, shielding her eyes from the glaring sun. She looks up and down the street, at fibro houses and half-restored cars abandoned more from lack of enthusiasm than money.

That's Pipeline Avenue for yah, thinks the mother. *The pipeline of shit.*

'Kayleen? *Kayleen!*'

A neighbour from across the road is dressed in her supermarket uniform, her peroxide hair whipped back into a messy bun. As she's about to climb into her car, she pauses and calls out to the mother, 'Can't yah keep control of yah bloody kids?' Her face is a smirk.

The mother says, 'Fuck off and mind your own business.'

ONE

Detective Rebecca Giles first knew a child was missing when an 'all cars respond' call went out. She had just turned onto the New England Highway and begun the tedious half-hour drive back to Muswellbrook. She was returning to the station after wrapping up a brain-numbing interview with Sticky Pete down at Singleton Police Station. The interview hadn't quite gone to plan.

The night before, Giles had rung Sticky Pete's home phone and offered him the opportunity to come into the station for a chat. His missus had been flashing a new ring around town, bragging that none of the other bitches' husbands could afford such a fine piece of jewellery. The truth was, they couldn't – not if they had to pay full price for it – a point that the anonymous caller who'd tipped off Detective Giles was quick to insist on. Pete didn't have that kind of money to splurge, so the ring had to be stolen, and his wife could shut her fat bragging mouth up.

When Giles mentioned the ring, Pete's voice had dramatically shifted tone. He stumbled over his words and stuttered, assuring Giles there wasn't a lot to say. Giles suggested he'd do well to get his arse to Singleton Police Station the next morning rather than waiting for her to show up at his house. That way his better half wouldn't overhear that her birthday bling was subject to the Crimes Act, 193C, and that her husband was being charged with receiving goods expected to be stolen. *Receiving,* Giles had reiterated. *Because I need you to convince me you didn't steal it, Pete. I'm giving you the benefit of the doubt. Be at the station by 9 a.m. I'll be waiting. I'll even put the kettle on for you.*

There had been a spate of break-and-enters in the Muswellbrook and Scone area, and Giles wasn't too surprised that someone in the next town over was responsible. But when Sticky Pete showed up at the station for his interview, he was hell-bent on refusing to cooperate. Once she got him into the windowless interview room, he swore on his rickety heart that he hadn't been up to Muswellbrook or Scone in months.

'Months, for farksake. Got no business being in Scone, and I'm telling ya, even if I did, I ain't got enough fuel in me tank to get there and back. Can't be me. Pissed all me money up the wall buying that ring off some fluoro blow-in down at the Royal.'

Sticky Pete's voice was croaky from forty years of smoking and honest-to-god fear. Giles's voice, on the other hand, was calm and smooth. She was fishing. All she had to do was relax, let her questions drag out, and Pete would do all the work. As long as she asked each question slowly, she'd be ready to reel him in when he stopped moving and buzzing.

'You've got money for beer and jewellery, but no money for petrol?' Giles asked.

'It was the wifey's birthday and it was priced into me budget.'

'Free?'

Sticky Pete had shaken his head and given Giles a pissed off look. 'I swear, I stole nothin'. I don't know the guy who sold it to me. I was just having a beer. Never seen him before. He was a bloody miner or tradie, one of those dumb neon high-vis vests. You know, a fluoro stick on legs.'

'Bloody convenient.' Giles grinned. 'The town's full of fluoro sticks, Pete. It could have been anyone.'

Sticky Pete got his nickname in two ways; aside from his sticky fingers, when you threw shit at him, it stuck. But while he wasn't a big fish to catch, and he wasn't strong, you did need to pump and reel to get him to answer questions.

Pete was an old man, grey and dried out, fatigued with every movement. His teeth looked soft and yellow like baby's custard, with one missing from the top that made his lip curl inward. It gave him a slight lisp, and made a faint whistling sound when he sighed, like a bicycle tyre letting out air. His eyes were blue, blood-flecked, watery, and looked upon Giles with contempt. He'd had a few short stints in jail during his prime and was well known to the cops in the surrounding districts, but his heyday was well and truly behind him now; age, arthritis and a wonky hip had slowed him down. Bar some small, lazy thefts, and the odd call-out to a domestic dispute at his home, he was harmless. He argued that he only broke the law out of necessity; his pension didn't pay much and, with the rising tax on smokes and alcohol, the government was to blame for his petty criminal ways.

Giles had found it hard to be patient or empathetic.

'So did you buy just the ring or the whole set?'

'What? *What set?*'

'The matching necklace, earrings and brooch.'

'There was no necklace, luv, and no earrings or brooch. The guy in the pub was just selling a ring. I don't know nothin' about that other shit. Didn't even know the ring was hot when I bought it.'

Giles laughed. 'If you want to buy your wife a ring for her birthday, Pete, you go to the jewellery shop, not the pub.'

Pete squirmed in his chair when she gave him a stern glare. Giles knew she wasn't menacing looking – she didn't have the face of a Rottweiler, it was more Afghan hound given her long silky dark hair and thin face – but while her bark may have been worse than her bite, her growl caught people off guard and made them feel uneasy.

Although it was hot and muggy in the interview room, Giles had left the jacket of her dark grey pantsuit buttoned up. She didn't want to look casual or relaxed. She wanted to look like she meant business; she wanted to look like she didn't have time to waste and needed to get straight to the point. But Pete clearly hadn't been around many people in suits, and Giles's body language went over his head.

'Thing is, Pete, I've got a lady out at Scone whose diamond and emerald set is missing. Family heirlooms. Turns out she's great mates with the Scone Shire deputy mayor, so I've got my boss breathing down my neck over these bloody missing emeralds and diamonds.'

'I didn't see no fucking necklace or any other shit. I just bought the ring.'

'I don't think I need to tell you, Pete, that it's an offence to be in possession of an item unlawfully obtained. You have a history – a list of tendency-and-coincidence evidence that a judge would jiggle his overflowing midriff at trying to stifle his laugh.'

'What?'

'You have a list of past charges that the court would find interesting reading. A history, Pete – you have a long criminal history. You would have known the guy was off-loading the ring, so that makes you guilty of receiving.'

The legal talk and the stuffy room were making Sticky Pete sweat. He started to scratch at the eczema between his fingers.

'And that ring you picked up was sorely undervalued,' Giles continued, getting ready to reel him in. 'You got it for a steal, so to speak. It's worth well over three grand, which makes this a federal crime that can carry sixteen months to three years. You don't want to go for a holiday at St Heliers, do you?'

Pete had finally taken the bait. Now he was fighting to get himself off her hook. 'I didn't fuckin' steal nothing. Fuckin' cost of petrol, how would I get out to Scone and back, ha?'

Giles knew he had a point. The whole reason she was meeting him at Singleton Police Station was that Sticky Pete was flat broke, with no money for petrol until pension day. All the money he did have, he blew on beers. And a ring for his missus.

She sighed. 'The ring will be seized as evidence before it goes back to its rightful owner. If you're telling the truth, I'll find the crook and, hopefully, he can repay you the purchase price. I've got six months to pin this on you, so you can save me some time and tell me if you took the full set.'

'I didn't, I'm telling the truth. Go find that orange glow-stick from the pub. A fucking walking highlighter. High-vis vest, scruffy fella, big hands and dirty, like he worked in grease.'

Sticky Pete dug his fingernails into his flaking skin and tried to stare Giles down, but she could tell that, really, he just wanted to curl up in a ball and have a good cry. He didn't want to go back to St Heliers Correctional Centre, nor did he want to tell his missus he'd lost her birthday present because he had to hand it in to the police.

'Tops, you'll get two years. Best case, you'll get a community service order. Either way, in the next six weeks you'll receive a future court attendance notice.' Giles could see Pete's eyes beginning to water and his neck turning a ruddy red. The poor bloke's blood pressure was going up. To save him from having a heart attack she added, in a gentler tone, 'I'll tell you what, Pete, I'll ask the pub if there's any CCTV footage. Let's see if we can verify your story.'

'Do you want me to come with you?'

Giles was surprised by Pete's eagerness to help.

'I mean,' Pete stammered. 'I . . . I can ask me mates to be witnesses. Yeah. And if there's footage of the guy, I can point him out to you.'

Jesus. Giles felt a tinge of sympathy for poor old Pete. Any drongo could see by now that he was probably telling the truth.

Giles wiped her palms down her pants, then tucked a wisp of her dark hair behind her ear. She let the quiet between them linger until it turned into an uncomfortable silence. When she felt Pete had wriggled long enough at the end of the line, sweating and gasping for air, she cut him loose. 'I'm sure we can wrap this up quick, within a day or two.'

The moment the old man hobbled out the front door of the station, Giles got out her keys and made her way to her unmarked car. The Royal Hotel didn't open until after ten, so Giles figured she'd give them a call once she got back home to Muswellbrook. She could ask them to hold on to any CCTV footage and then go back down to Singleton after work, look at the footage, and have one of their famous Kobe wagyu scotch fillets while she was at it.

The A15 back to Muswellbrook was monotonous. Aside from the odd semitrailer or grey nomad pulling a caravan, the traffic was light. It was midmorning but she could already feel the heat of the day through the front windscreen of the car.

Giles cranked up the aircon in the Sonata and gripped the steering wheel. She was feeling frustrated with the way her morning had panned out, and the heat wasn't helping. Sticky Pete should be a petty misdemeanour, but those rich Scone bastards with their family fortunes and links to councillors had turned it into the crime of the century.

The call came out over the radio as she hit Rixs Creek. Her thoughts quickly shifted from Sticky Pete to the report of a missing twelve-year-old girl. Was twelve a little too young to run away from home? Giles could think of many reasons why a kid *would* want to run away.

A search would already be in full swing. Officers would be converging to scour the immediate area, and the child's house would be swept from top to bottom. Giles didn't feel too distressed. Normally missing kids were found fast asleep under a bed or at a friend's house, happily bouncing on a trampoline, oblivious to the commotion they'd created. There would be the embarrassed parents, apologising profusely for overreacting and wasting everyone's time, and a sobbing child who knew the real shit would hit the fan the moment the cops left. But it always turned out for the best, and it would make an epic twenty-first birthday story.

Giles figured that by the time she got back to the station, the crew would be working off their frustration at the incompetent parents with a competitive game of darts or table tennis. After a year at Muswellbrook Police Station, she had accepted that working in a country town wasn't going to be as eventful as her ten years serving on the force in Sydney. The liveliest moment she'd seen here was when a brown snake had made a home for itself in the overnight lock-up next to an addict coming down from a meth hit.

The town of Muswellbrook stretched out like a half-crescent moon. On one side was a patchwork of cream, yellow and green paddocks that led up into the Wollemi, Yengo and Barrington Tops national parks – scattered farmlands surrounded by distant mountains. On the other side of the moon were the open-cut mines. Mega-pits with machinery gorging at the surface, chomping

down into the depths and spitting out limestone and slate pips
in search of coal. Excavators so huge, they could be mistaken
for God's Tonka trucks, crawling down the spiralling dirt roads
cut against the walls of the deep pit. A gigantic grey hell to the
environmentalists, but the pot at the end of the rainbow for its
employees and stakeholders.

The town itself was a cupid's bow of homes and businesses,
linked tip to tip by a highway, with its back facing the mines. But
this was purely coincidental – the town would never turn its back on
the mines. They were its lifeblood. The arteries that kept everything
flowing in and out, mostly money.

In the centre of Muswellbrook the main street stretched for
about a kilometre. Everyone had creatively re-named it Main Street
after ditching the name Sydney Street; the city of Sydney was more
than 250 kilometres away and was held in no great esteem by the
locals, so it was easy enough to change.

The street was the heart of the town, but considering it rose over
a hilltop and down the other side like a big belly, it was more like
the gut of the town. Main Street was the town's intestines. As with
all country towns, there was the bakery, RSL, car yards, post office,
grocer, butcher, equipment and supply stores that sold directly
to farmers, fashion and homewares that sold to the women and,
on nearly every corner, the pubs that sold to the blokes' bravado
and sorrow.

Of course, there was a St Vinnie's, which sold cheap donated
items to the lost souls. But the only people who acknowledged it
were those who needed it – everyone else pretended it wasn't there.

As Giles passed the 'Welcome to Muswellbrook' sign, she hesitated,
then swung the Sonata into the McDonald's drive through. She

needed a real espresso, and she needed it now. None of that instant granulated crap she'd been offered down Singleton station. Singleton might be a bigger town than Muswellbrook, but its police station was small, not even staffed overnight.

Giles could have stopped and bought her coffee from the Art Gallery Café closer to the police station, but the cops tended to use the McCafé – it was cheaper – and Giles also liked to check out the tradies that came through there. She was sure one day she would meet a good-looking bloke who'd promise to fix her wiring, and she would promise to protect and serve him.

Normally the parking lot was chock-full with 4×4s and utes, a sea of high-visibility vests in orange, yellow and hot pink. Fluoro sticks, just like the bloke who sold Sticky Pete the ring. Most of them were easy on the eye, and usually Giles would gawp at strong calf muscles and stalwart arms, but it was midmorning and the clientele had already shifted to tracksuit-wearing mums relieved they'd packed their kids off to school for another day and the odd uptight businessman picking up some brekkie.

When she finally walked into the station, the caffeine had kicked in and she had a skip to her step.

Through the glass wall of his office, Inspector Falkov saw her arrive, and he rose out of his chair. He was a tall man with thick grey hair and a long thin nose that leaned slightly to the right, having been broken numerous times in the line of duty. He came out of his office and gave Giles a nod, asking, 'How'd Sticky Pete handle the news?'

Giles raised her coffee cup as a toast. 'Think he had a tear in his eye when he was told to hand back the ring, sir.'

'He's not stupid. He'll be trying to work out which jealous jezebel dobbed in his missus.' Falkov frowned. The creases on his forehead looked like they had been etched on by a child with a 2B pencil.

'Are you suggesting there are grown women out there fighting over a man like Sticky Pete?' Giles coughed a laugh.

'Dunno. You know women better than me.'

Giles was about to retort when she realised no one was about. '*Geez*, sir, this place looks like Singleton Police Station. Where is everyone?'

'They're out canvassing the neighbours, trying to develop some leads.'

'They still haven't found the kid?' Giles felt her fingertips start to burn against the disposable coffee cup.

'Nope.'

'How long's it been?'

'She was already missing for up to eighteen hours when it was called in.' Inspector Falkov looked at his watch. 'That was about two hours ago, so we're clocking up about twenty hours.'

'Twenty hours? That's a big gap. You need to get more resources in.'

'Yep. I am. That's why I'm putting you on it.'

'Me?' A fizz raced through her body.

'The duty officers have been there all morning, but they've made no progress, haven't reported anything. I need to wrap this up, Giles. Find the kid. Get her back to her mother.'

'It's one parent?'

'A single mum, early thirties, slightly older than you. You're a woman, Giles.'

'Thanks, sir. Glad you cleared that up for me.'

'I mean, you can connect with the mother. A sympathetic and tender touch in her difficult time. The blokes here can be a bit rough around the edges.'

'They're dickheads, sir.'

'Yeah, that too. Look, go in soft, extract the info lightly, but do it quickly. Time, Giles. If this is something more serious, more

sinister, then you're going to run out of time. Be supportive, com-
forting, but firm.'

'Like a mattress,' Giles quipped, then cringed at her attempt at
humour. 'No worries, sir.'

Inspector Falkov handed Giles the mother's name and address
and she exchanged her coffee for the piece of paper. 'Latte. You can
finish it.'

'Thanks, big spender.' Falkov flipped off the plastic lid and took
a gulp.

Giles looked down at the address in her hand. If Main Street was
the guts of the town then Pipeline Avenue was the bowels: there was
always shit there.

~

The naked body is now cool to the touch. Lividity and rigor mortis
have started to set in. Pastel bluish and purple colours have begun
to surface under her skin, like the ocean at sunset. Her lips are white
and silent, sewed shut with fencing wire in a figure-of-eight knot.

The muscles in her slim fingers have tightened. They no longer
beckon Detective Giles to come find her. Still, she will wait, floating in the water, her eyes sinking back into her skull. Her family are
waiting for her to return home, and their hopes sink as the minutes
and hours and days tick by.

TWO

It's not unusual for daughters to rebel, to wish to be nothing like their mothers, to take an oath never to dress, speak or even cook like their mums. Detective Giles had taken the same oath when she was thirteen. Only, it wasn't because her mother was critical or controlling, or because her mother thought she dressed like a tramp or would make the same mistakes in life. No, Detective Giles didn't want to be anything like her mother, because her mother was dead.

Instead, Giles was determined that her destiny would not be spun by the same thread as her mother's, measured and cut by tragedy. Giles was resolute; she would not fall to the same fate.

So rather than ending up like her mother, Giles ended up like her father. A cop. And just like her father she drank a little too much, swore a little too often, and laughed his rollicking laugh. She'd also inherited her father's no-nonsense approach, which made her seem cold at times, prickly, a hard nut to crack. So she would have to keep that in check if she wanted to get anything out of the missing girl's mother.

On the other side of town, Giles was about to visit Claire Ellis, who had also followed in her father's footsteps. Just like her father,

Claire had ended up on Pipeline Avenue, slipping between booze and welfare. And just like her father, she struggled to keep a handle on her kids.

Detective Giles did her best to smile warmly, even though she could almost feel the dust mites nibble at her arse as she sat on the lounge opposite Claire, who looked distraught, edging towards manic, and Giles knew she'd have to settle her before facing the press. Local news first, don't send out too much of an alarm, don't go national, just a kid who might have wandered off. Let the Police Media Unit handle that side of it; the PMU was good at getting information out to the media in dribs and drabs when it best served the investigation. Besides, no one wanted to look foolish on national television when the child was found spending their pocket money at the bowling alley's amusement arcade.

Giles tried to give a sympathetic smile. 'Let's start from the morning.'

'This morning?' asked Claire.

'No. Yesterday morning. The morning before. Talk me through the day, from the beginning.'

Claire blinked. 'Why? She didn't go missing yesterday, she went missing this morning. Yesterday she was bloody here.'

The team were working on the assumption that Kayleen could have been missing for up to twenty hours – counting from when she was last seen, not from when she was discovered missing. But explaining that might confuse or panic Claire. Giles cleared her throat and chewed the corner of her lip. She decided not to clarify. Instead, she replied, 'Just in case there's something we might have missed. How was Kayleen yesterday morning?'

Claire took a deep breath. Her throat quivered as she sucked the air down and Giles hoped she wouldn't exhale into a flood of tears.

But she held her shit together, pausing for a moment, collecting her thoughts – or her wits. Finally, she answered. 'Normal.'

'What's normal? Describe your morning routine for me. Slowly, take your time.'

'Same as any other day, just monotonous and *normal*.'

'Aha.' Giles scribbled the word *normal* in her pad.

The mother took the cue to elaborate. 'Kayleen was in good spirits. She belly-flopped on me bed. Tried to find me face hidden under the sheet. It's a game we play. Dumb. Just a game.'

'No judgement, just in your own words each step in the morning. Did your phone ring? Strange car out the front? Anything unusual at all?'

'No. Nothing like that. The girls got themselves ready for school. Kayleen and Mikaela – Mikaela's my youngest, just turned seven a few weeks back – they both had juice and cereal for breakfast. Got themselves dressed.'

Giles watched Claire Ellis as she shifted on the lounge. She looked like she couldn't get comfortable. Giles wondered if the dust mites were getting to her too. Finally, she asked, 'You didn't get the girls ready for school? What were you doing while they were getting themselves sorted?'

'Showering.'

That was a lie. The mother clearly hadn't washed her hair for a few days now, and her feet looked like they could use some soap and a wet sponge. The back of Giles's neck bristled. *Bugger.* Up until this point, she had been on Claire's side.

Giles kept her voice monotone. 'So, they hopped on the bus around eight-twenty?'

'Yeah, about that.'

'Did you see anyone else near the bus stop or in the street?'

Claire shook her head. Detective Giles scribbled again in her notepad. The mother was fidgeting; Giles had been watching her closely for any sign of guilt, remorse, anything that might give her a lead to pursue. She knew they needed to go back and canvass all the neighbours again, expand the search area. Someone must have seen Kayleen. How could nobody notice a child on her own?

'And you can't think of any friends' houses she might have visited?'

'Nope. She doesn't have any friends that live around here. Besides, it's a school day, why would she go visit anyone?'

'Okay, then let's go back to the bus. Nice and slow.'

Claire Ellis nodded. Her breathing was irregular, but that wasn't unusual. Stress and adrenaline do that – guilty or not guilty, their breathing always goes out of whack. Unless they're a psychopath.

'The bus stop. Walk me through what happened.'

'They got on the bus.'

Giles forced another smile. 'Can you elaborate?'

'I've already gone over this with the other officer.'

'I know. But I need to see if they've missed something.' Giles wanted to add: it's not that they've missed something, it's that they've got bloody *nothing*.

Claire's shoulders arched slightly. She slid her palms under her thighs and sat tall. She was still for a moment. 'It's because you're a woman, isn't it? That's why they got you to talk to me. But you're not a mother.'

'They asked me to speak with you to see if I can understand what happened before your daughter went missing. Listen, time is ticking, so I need you to walk me through the events leading up —' Giles caught herself. Only fools let their mouth run. She took a breath and started again. 'Can you walk me through the girls getting on the bus?'

Although Claire had no make-up on and her eyes were puffy, she looked angelic. There were hints that she would have been stunning in her younger days, before single motherhood. Her eyes were a hard caramel colour, the same as her daughters'. Giles had looked over a few of the family photos before entering the house while she was being briefed on the situation. Aside from a missing dad, they were a typical family of three, albeit a poor one.

'I waited with them on the footpath,' Claire answered. 'The bus comes around eight-twenty, it was just after that – the bus was a little late. Me girls were full of apple juice and sugary cereal. Neither could stand still and kill time patiently. Instead, they swung their school bags around and around. Don't know how they had the energy to play in this heat.'

Giles smiled. 'I suspect twelve- and seven-year-olds would have all the energy in the world.'

'Hmm.' Claire sighed. 'Well, they certainly did. Once they hopped on the bus, I stood on the path and waved goodbye until it disappeared out of sight.'

'Nobody else around?'

'Nope. I didn't hang around. Like I said, it was hot. I could feel the sun burning my scalp and see the heat rising out of the grass. With the kids packed off to school, I couldn't wait to get back in the house, into the cool and dark. That bloody dog next door tried to have a go at me as I walked up the drive, went berserk, butting its head into the fence. Neighbour says it'll only be there a few more weeks before it goes back to its owner. I can't bloody wait. That unsettled me a bit, but I was relieved to be in the cool. I got some coffee on and started on some laundry – figured I might as well make the most of the weather. There's not really much to do when the girls aren't around . . .'

Giles wanted to get Claire back on track, so she started again with a supportive statement: 'I want you to know we are doing everything possible to bring Kayleen home. The community has come together and formed a search party to look for her.'

Or her body, Giles thought.

'Where are they looking? Where could she be?' Claire asked.

Where do you *think she could be?* Giles wanted to say.

'All of Kayleen's favourite spots first,' Giles answered. 'The park, the track along the creek you mentioned. Just the places that are in her comfort zone.'

Claire slid her hands up and down her thighs, then held them cupped together as if in prayer.

Giles waited to see if the mother added any more places where Kayleen usually played, but she was silent.

The volunteer search party would be walking the track along the creek, poking sticks into the water's edge and looking through the reeds, praying they were not the one who found a body along the bank. Another group of volunteers had been sent out into the surrounding paddocks and would be calling the child's name. The whole time they, too, would be secretly hoping they didn't stumble across something they'd need counselling for one day.

'Are there any other places you think she might go?'

The mother mumbled something and shook her head. Giles missed what exactly she said, momentarily distracted by the thought of the half-finished latte she'd given Falkov back at the station. She wished she'd glugged it down. She needed to focus.

Giles scribbled notes, but there was nothing in them of any use. A tired mum, annoying kids. Was that anything? Giles thought all kids could be a pain in the arse when they wanted to be, adults too, but kids don't just disappear because they're being an arsehole. Or do they?

Giles breathed in through her nose. She couldn't detect the smell of marijuana, so she concluded Claire Ellis wasn't a pot smoker, unless she smoked her joints outside. Under her feet she felt a crunch and figured it might be a biscuit crumb or peanut shell in the shag of the carpet. It prompted her to ask, 'Is Kayleen asthmatic? Any allergies? Diabetic?'

'Nope.'

That was good. The missing girl wasn't in danger of having an anaphylactic episode. The carpet felt like it hadn't been vacuumed in over a week, so the kid clearly wasn't allergic to dust. Toys were scattered across the living room and there was a pile of washing unfolded in the basket dumped on the armchair. There was a mess on the kitchen bench – browned bananas in a fruit bowl, which had attracted flies, and bottles of medicine.

'Do you often send your children to sleep on Promethazine?' Giles asked.

'What?'

'Phenergan? Or do you use it to help yourself get to sleep?' Giles glanced over the mother's shoulder at the near-empty bottle of cheap bourbon on the kitchen bench.

'Huh?' Claire's cheeks flushed. 'No, the Phenergan was to help Kayleen sleep. Calm her. After the accident.'

'Ah yes, her injury, that was the afternoon before she went missing, right?' Giles checked her notes. 'Four sutures above the brow. That's not normal, is it? Can you explain how that happened?'

Claire glanced at the officers in the kitchen for support, clearly feeling ganged up on.

'Please?' said Giles, softening the edge in her voice. She needed to ease the story out of her, not have the woman clam up. 'In your own words, in your own time.'

But the ticking hands of the clock were not the mother's friend. Every passing second was pushing the child further away from their grasp. Giles wanted to say, *Just get to the point and tell me what happened.* Instead, she gave a patient and encouraging nod.

Claire started to pick at her nails, scratching off the pale blue nail polish. 'I was pegging the washing out on the clothesline. Me pegs are rusted and falling apart. I need to buy new ones. The wood's rotted, and the bastard things stain me linen.' She puffed at a fly trying to suck moisture from the corner of her mouth. There were no screens on any of the open windows, and while they let in the breeze, they let flies in too.

'The accident?' pressed Giles with a smile.

'I was hanging the wash'n and the phone rang. The school said Kayleen hurt herself and that she was down at the hospital. Well, what was I supposed to do? I dropped everything and raced off. It's why half me washing's still out the back.'

'And what time was that?'

'About eleven-thirty I got there. She fell during recess. She said she fell off the monkey bars. I said, "Ever seen a monkey with stitches?" and she said, "Nope," and I said, "Well, then you should leave the monkey bars to the monkeys."'

Giles's smile slipped for a brief moment, but she quickly caught herself and faked it back on.

'I was kiddin' around, you know. It was a joke. Kayleen laughed. What I'm trying to say is, my kid was okay. I walked into the hospital room, and she was sitting up in bed, crisp sheets, a jug of ice water, glass in a paper wrapper and cartoons on the telly. Kayleen's eyes may have been pink and puffy, but she smiled when I walked in. They said to take her home to rest. So, I did. I tucked her in bed, gave her some Phenergan, and when I went back into her room this morning she wasn't there.'

'What time did you give her Phenergan?'

'About two in the afternoon. That was the last time I saw her.'

'How much did you give her?'

'Enough. Enough to get her through the night.'

'You didn't go in to give her dinner?'

'No. She ate lunch. I left her to sleep.' Claire said. 'Can I have a break? And can I sponge a smoke off someone? I just need a fag.'

Giles nodded. She needed a breather too. This line of questioning was getting her nowhere. 'Yeah, sure, let's have a toilet break and a bit of fresh air.'

On her way out of the bathroom, Giles stood at the child's bedroom door. It was still taped off and black smudges lined the door frame, doorknob, window and dresser where forensics had dusted for fingerprints. The first responding officers had been smart enough to set up a protected area, quickly judging the room a possible scene of a crime.

Good job, thought Giles.

Aside from the clear signs a forensics team had been and gone, it was a typical little girls' room. It was ordinary at first glance but had the tell-tale signs of poverty when you really examined it. Giles tore one side of the police tape off the wall and it fluttered to the ground. She stepped inside and picked up a ratty doll that'd had a home haircut and harsh make-up drawn on with texta.

Claire leaned against the doorway. 'That was Kayleen's favourite doll.'

Giles couldn't help but think that the mother had said *was.* Either she'd given up on her, killed her, or she was hoping her own child was dead. Giles's head was pounding, she needed some fresh air.

Claire Ellis had been hankering for a ciggie for the last few hours and was grateful she could bum one off an officer. She felt broken apart and separated from these people who had come into her home. She was numb, empty. A shell of herself. Scared that if a police officer breathed or brushed against her, she'd fall apart into fragments.

She kept her distance on the back porch, lit up, and, as she sucked on the cigarette, considered the events of yesterday morning: the moment she woke, the alarm clock that had been buzzing for nearly two minutes, but her hand couldn't find the snooze button, and instead she'd managed to knock over the lamp. She remembered the sound of her girls' feet as they raced each other down the hall – thumping on the wooden floorboards like bloody baby elephants. She felt a tinge of guilt at how she had tried not to groan as she pulled the bedsheet over her head and faked sleep, or death, before the bedroom door was flung open and both girls rushed into her room.

She felt the gust of air as the bedsheet was whipped back and then her daughter's breath in her face, the sound of Kayleen's bossy voice telling her to get up. She remembered the *bounce, bounce, bounce* of the mattress, the sound of the springs groaning, and how she'd snapped at Kayleen to *stop bloody bouncing!* She recalled how the tone in her voice had been too harsh for the crime. But she was hungover and the noise and bouncing were more than she could take. How do you tell a cop that? That she just couldn't bring herself to face the day. How do you explain that the smell of your own breath and the noise of your kids made you want to roll over and blank everything out?

This morning, however, it had been different. This morning she had felt like she was on top of things. She was free from a hangover; she'd had a decent night's rest. This morning she'd actually got her shit together – until she couldn't find her own kid.

Claire gazed down at the thongs she was wearing. Her feet were filthy, and the top she had on was the same as yesterday. Same stain down the front. She folded her arms over it and dreaded the thought of the detective thinking she was a yob.

She sucked on her smoke and remembered: the white roof of the bus popping over the peak, then the whole bloody vehicle rattling and bouncing down the road. She had told her girls to stand back from the kerb, and they obeyed. The brakes screeched, the bus pulled up at the corner. There were no bus stops in town, it was just a given that everyone knew where the buses stopped, usually near a corner. In fact, they would pick you up wherever you hailed them – just part of the joy of living in a country town.

The door folded open and let out a great puff of air. It smelled of sweaty socks, sweet food, dirt, and vomit. Claire had screwed up her nose. There was the sound of children squealing, laughter and noise spilling from the windows. She watched Kayleen push her younger sister up the steps of the bus. There were thumps of feet and dragging of bags, impatience written all over the bus driver's face as he gave her a nod before closing the door. Claire knew she wouldn't have made for a pretty sight.

She tramped back up the path to the house, navigating between the weeds sprouting from cracks in the hot concrete path, the bottoms of her feet turning dark from the dirt.

The mood in Muswellbrook Police Station was quiet but tense. Inspector Falkov paced in his office. He felt a shiver and wondered if the air conditioning was up too high. Wondered if he had put his best on the case. Detective Giles was relatively new to the team, a cop from Sydney, a city-dweller for more than ten years. But her roots were in the area, her father was a legend here at the station, for goodness' sake, and he was optimistic she'd not forgotten her old-fashioned country charm. He'd cross his fingers she could step up to the challenge he'd given her. *Let's see if she can get this kid home.*

Falkov checked his text messages and emails. His officers were reporting in, but they had no updates of any real use. He'd requested a drone operator, to do a sweep of the creek and the golf course, since an aerial view might pick up something that couldn't be seen from the ground.

What else? What else? He was ticking boxes in his head. A long checklist. The cogs were all turning. Giles was at the family home. The SES were already out in big numbers, searching. Vehicles were being stopped. But the time gap was too big – if it was a snatch and grab, the bastard would be ahead of them, long gone.

Most of the homes on Pipeline Avenue didn't have private security systems; they either couldn't afford one, didn't think there was anything worth protecting, or they owned a Rottweiler, pit bull or German shepherd that was better than any camera system. The two homes that did have security cameras had found nothing on their CCTV footage.

Falkov thought, *That's a worry.*

He shook away the vision of his team digging up the backyard, dreading the media coverage. He'd give Giles a shot, see if her questions broke open a lead.

Falkov pinched the bridge of his nose, fighting back a headache, then looked at his watch and his mobile phone again. The minutes were ticking by too fast.

While Claire Ellis sucked on a ciggie, Giles jumped in the back of the police van to scull a bottle of water and wolf down a chicken and lettuce wrap. Her head was pounding. Claire had been talking in loops; Giles still had nothing. *Fuck.* Her mind was racing. It had been over twenty hours now. Where was this bloody kid?

She massaged her temples. The neighbour's dog with its incessant barking was doing her head in and it was boiling hot in the back of the van. Giles took her suit jacket off, unbuttoned the top of her cream blouse and rolled up her sleeves. The more casual look might be better for drawing information out of the mother. Lower her status a little, more friend than cop. Not like the no-nonsense look she had tried on Sticky Pete.

Her mobile phone rang. Giles tossed the empty water bottle and the paper from the wrap onto the floor of the van and answered.

'How's it going, Giles?' Inspector Falkov's voice sounded dry and tired. 'Where are you at?'

'Working on it. Still searching, sir.'

'I figured that. Look, I got a call from Dubbo station, and they have an officer from the dog unit, a Sergeant Delano. He's twenty minutes from Muswellbrook if you want him.'

'Delano? You know him?'

'No. But he's another resource you can tap into. They heard the media report on the radio and are happy to offer his assistance. It's not a cadaver dog, but if you need a dog to do some sniffing, he's free. I can accept the offer?'

'You saying the kid's dead, sir? Are you calling it already?'

'Nope. I'm just saying it's a resource. It's there if you need it.'

Giles already had one dog driving her up the wall, she wasn't sure she wanted another.

'Thanks, sir. I'll call you if we want the dog brought in.'

Giles hung up. She had to get back to the mother. Too many pieces were still missing. She needed the story, step by step. *Why would this kid vanish? Where has she gone? Who would take her?* If she could work out the why, the where and who would follow.

Detective Turner jumped in the back of the van and sat beside Giles. He was tall and lean and too big for the cramped space. He stared at his hands, turning them over, like the answers were written on them somewhere; he had been one of the first on the scene, and was co-ordinating the officers searching the immediate area and knocking on doors. She was glad to see a friendly face, although he didn't seem to be smiling. He ran his fingers through his ginger hair and gave her a small shrug. His blue eyes appeared dull and un-inspired. He scrunched the front of his shirt in his fist, like his heart was too big for his chest, and asked, 'How are you going, Giles?'

'Yeah, good.'

'Afraid I don't really have an update for you, sorry. No real leads from the neighbours or shop owners. Sometimes there's some shouting at the house, but the friends have given us nothing. There's no estranged spouse or weird uncle to interview. No work done on the house recently, if ever. The principal at Kayleen's school said she was a little unruly, a little wayward – you've got the report. That's probably the most we've got to go on. Other than that, we've put together a list of registered sex offenders and are working through their alibis, but we've not made much progress. You get anything from the mum?'

'Nup. I'm finding it hard to get a read on her. She's wary of me, I can't get her to relax . . .' She thought about it. 'Turner, I'm going back into the house. I want you to stand somewhere out of the way, but where you can see her face. I'm going to ask her some tricky questions and then look away. Do not take your eyes off her. I want you to note every time she swallows. What questions am I asking that make her swallow?'

Turner nodded.

'I want you to see if she yawns, stops blinking, scratches her neck, rubs an eye. I'll look around the room, make her feel like she's free to react without being watched, but you've got to have eyes on her the whole time.'

'You think —'

'Dunno. But I need you to be my eyes.'

'Got it.' Detective Turner's head hadn't stopped nodding the whole time. 'I won't miss a thing, Giles.'

'Just don't stare her down. Don't let her know you're watching. But I'm going for the jugular – we're running out of time.'

Giles joined Claire on the back porch as she puffed away on a second ciggie bummed off a uniform. Claire was drawing the smoke deep into her lungs like a drowning swimmer gasping for their last breath, submerged in her despair.

Giles scanned the backyard. From the tall eucalyptus tree by the house, the loud high-pitched whirr of the cicadas filled the air. The neighbour behind the house had decided it was a good time to trim the hedges, the chainsaw revving, the branches cracking and crunching. Further down the street the distant traffic was loud with semitrailers and V8 motors. Plus the neighbour's dog going berserk all morning had set off a chain reaction and the other dogs nearby had now joined in. It was all making Giles's head buzz.

A second basket of yesterday's washing sat under the clothesline; only half of the load had been hung, the other half was piled in the basket, baking in the sun. *At least that part of her story is true.*

While the mother finished her smoke, Giles watched the dog next door through the steel mesh fence. It was a mongrel that looked part bull-mastiff, part pit bull and lots of other parts that Giles couldn't figure out. It had found a toy and was busy sinking its teeth into a green thong, ripping away at the rubber. The dog tossed it about the yard, chased it and dribbled on it. It ripped off the strap and fought with tearing away the sole stuck between its teeth. The dog then began to bury the rubber, digging up the roots of a geranium in the process.

'You ready to continue?' Giles was feeling time ticking away.

Claire dropped the cigarette butt on the deck, stepped it out and kicked it off the edge into the sparse garden below.

Back in the house, Giles was thankful for the cool and relative quiet. 'Good to go on?' she asked.

Claire Ellis nodded and they sat down opposite each other.

Turner stood just off to the side behind Giles, leaning against the wall, his arms folded, looking aloof and relaxed, but watching everything.

'It took you eighteen hours to call us. You never saw your daughter after putting her to bed at —' She looked at her notes. 'At two in the afternoon, yesterday. And you go back to her room just before eight this morning. You didn't check in on her in all that time?'

Claire shrugged. 'No.'

What mother wouldn't check on their injured kid?

Giles scribbled in her notepad. She needed to take a different approach; grind down and find the weakness. Sometimes you had to muddy the river to find the gold. The words *maternal filicide* kept screaming in her head and making her stomach turn. Claire Ellis certainly fit the profile: single mother, emotionally isolated, lack of resources.

Jesus. Giles flicked to the report from the school principal and cleared her throat. She decided to plunge in, step into that river and get her feet wet, but she also tried to keep the tone of her voice gentle. 'Kayleen is a bit of a handful sometimes? Her principal says she's a great kid – energetic, enthusiastic, sometimes a little bossy – but she has a small group of friends. The school are, and I quote, "implementing strategies to help her deal with challenging situations".'

Claire snapped. 'In other words, those snobs are watching Kayleen like a hawk and making her sit out of group projects.'

'So there *were* some behavioural problems at school?'

Claire avoided answering immediately, wiping her eyes and blowing her nose into a tissue. Eventually, she nodded.

'Your relationship with your daughter?' Giles continued. 'Could you describe that for me?'

'Are you doubting my ability to raise me girls?'

'No. No. But sometimes kids storm off after an argument or want to be alone if they are feeling bullied at school or having conflict with friends. I'm just making sure Kayleen didn't decide to go somewhere to be on her own?'

'No, I don't think she would do that.'

'What about you? How did you spend the evening?'

'Had dinner with Mikaela. Mashed potato, tomato sauce and sausages. Her mash always looks like it's been stabbed to death, but that's the way the kid likes it, smothered in ketchup. With Kayleen asleep, it was quiet. Mikaela wanted to play with her sister, but I said it's better that she sleeps. Let her rest. Sleep off the pain from the fall and the stitches, you know. After dinner, Mikaela and I sat outside on the concrete step. It's the coolest place to sit in the afternoon, under the shade of the jacaranda. I've got no aircon. I had a bourbon and Coke.'

'Nobody else was around?'

'There was a magpie trying to drink water droplets from the garden tap, but other than that, it was just the two of us.'

Giles scribbled the word magpie, for no other reason than it made her feel like she was making some progress. She even circled it.

Claire's posture collapsed a little, her lips thinned. 'Mikaela is a little easier than Kayleen. She's less wilful. Kayleen can be tetchy, difficult. My youngest is more placid. The mood is always light when it's just us two. Do you understand what I'm saying? With Kayleen in the mix, the atmosphere changes. It becomes harder to parent. That's why I didn't go wake her up.'

Giles nodded.

'I only left Mikaela when I went inside to top up me drink. Mikaela stayed outside and played.'

'How long did it take you to fill up your drink?'

'Dunno. Five, ten, twenty minutes? Can't remember.'

'Ah.'

The dog next door began to bark in rapid fire, triggered again by someone bustling in the front yard. Claire and Giles looked towards the back door, both alert, then Claire shuddered and said, 'She pats that dog.'

'Who? Kayleen?' Giles was shocked.

'Yep, like I said earlier. When she's not with friends, she's patting that dog. The both of them do. Crazy, I know. It would rip me bloody arm off if I tried. But it always lets me kids pat it through the fence.'

'Shit, hey?'

Claire flashed a smile for the first time. 'Yeah, shit, hey?'

Giles didn't have any more time to mess about. With Claire softening towards her, she said, 'Your daughter is a bit more than difficult sometimes, isn't she? Pinches stuff from the other kids at school and seems to bicker a lot with the older pupils, answers back the teachers.'

'Like I said, she can be a handful,' Claire admitted.

'I've been informed there's a bit of screaming going on in this house from time to time, mainly the name Kayleen.' Giles looked down at the carpet. She prayed Turner was watching carefully.

'Did that nosy bitch across the road tell you that? This morning she thought it was funny Kayleen was missing. I bet she's not laughing now.' But Claire eventually agreed. 'Sure, yeah, Kayleen pushes my buttons. A lot.'

As best as Giles could tell, her demeanour didn't change at all. She wasn't being defensive, and the crack about her daughter didn't stir her up. She'd been more pissed about her neighbour than the actual comment. She'd have to check with Turner, but either Claire was telling the truth or she had rehearsed all her responses.

Giles felt her fingers tingle, the start of trembling in her hands. *Fuck*. Before the signs became obvious to everyone else, she got up without a word and walked out the front door, letting the flyscreen slam behind her, taking the beginnings of a panic attack with her.

'They've just sent out another media reminder that the child is missing.'

Giles squinted at the two duty officers stationed at the front of the house. 'Thanks.'

The mother had a poorly explained twenty-minute gap. It didn't take that long to pour a bourbon and Coke. You can do a lot to a child in twenty minutes.

'You got any thoughts?' asked one of the officers.

Giles scanned the streetscape. 'Nobody in a radius of 2 kilometres has set eyes on Kayleen. Not a single person. You know why? Because she never left the house. She's here. We just can't bloody find her.'

'Here?' asked the officer. 'Where?'

'Start unrolling shit, opening shit, looking inside shit. What part of the house has this mother avoided the whole time we've been here?'

'You think the mother would —'

Giles swallowed. Her eyes were sore. She was tired. She looked at both officers through blurred vision. 'Why would a mother strap her kids in a car seat and roll them into a river? Why would a mother toss her six-month-old out of a high-rise apartment? Or duct-tape her baby's mouth shut? Or put her kid in a plastic bag and toss it in a bin? Why cook your one-month-old in a microwave? No one really understands why mothers do these things to their children, but they have. Only I'm not here for *why*, I'm here for *where*. The where is my job, and that kid is *here*.'

'Shall we start by looking in the microwave?' quipped one of the officers, but Giles's glare made him curl inwards and drop his head.

'No. Let's bring the dog in.'

The dog in the backyard next door had turned savage. Threatened by the chaos of the people and vehicles coming and going out on the street, the dog had lunged at the mesh fence that separated it from the police. It barked and snapped at the air. Finally, a neighbour two doors down had had a gutful and decided to act.

He flicked off the TV, stormed into the kitchen and glared at his wife. 'Old snarls barkley has gone fuckin' bonkers! Last night and now all bloody morning, bark *fucking* bark! I'm callin' the bloody cops. Get them to sort this shit out.'

His wife looked smug as she folded her arms over her mammoth breasts. 'No need to call, they're just up the road, honey. Walk up the street and speak to them yaself.'

'Bloody oath, just watch me.'

The neighbour walked out of his house and slammed the front door behind him. He stormed up the road, ready to restore peace in his street. Ahead, as well as a bunch of police vehicles parked askew, he could see a media van.

He grinned to himself. *Might make the evening news! Can see the headline now: neighbour shows police how to shut up a mongrel dog once and for all – with a police-issue Glock-23.*

Pipeline Avenue had become a circus, and Giles was the ringmaster trying to control the clowns. The media had arrived at the same time as the dog unit. A German shepherd stood alert beside its handler, ready to track, and the media was treating the police dog like a bloody celebrity. It didn't help that Delano, the handler, was a pretty boy who was loving the attention. To top it off, a neighbour from down the road was gritting his teeth, determined to break the barrier and get to Giles.

'Hey, you!' he hissed, snapping the police tape like an AFL footballer running through the banner to enter the field. 'Are you in charge here?'

Two police officers grabbed at his arms, but he was already in Giles's face. 'That damn dog won't shut up. All bloody morning and last night too, non-*fucking*-stop! Either shoot it or send it to the pound.'

The officers were about to haul him away, but Giles blocked them. 'You're right. Non-stop barking. From late last night into the morning . . . is it trying to tell us something?'

'It's not bloody Lassie, luv.'

'No, it's not.' She looked the neighbour up and down, at his Stubbies shorts and blue singlet top, his black thongs – much larger than the ones she'd seen the angry dog tearing apart. *Those were kids' thongs.* She thought about the timeline of the dog's barking and Kayleen's disappearance. She raised a brow at the neighbour.

'Do any kids live in there?' She pointed at the house with the barking dog.

'Nah. No kids, just a *fucking yapping dog.*'

Giles ignored him, instead bracing herself for the possibility of a heinous scene. She'd seen that dog's fangs, watched it maul a thong.

She turned to the officers and snapped, 'Keep the mother away from the neighbour's backyard.' She waved over Sergeant Delano and his police dog, then ran back into Claire Ellis's house. As she made her way down the hallway, she could hear the click of the German shepherd's paws and Delano's boots behind her.

Kayleen's bedroom window was slightly ajar, open only a couple of inches. Too small a gap for a child to climb through, but what was to say it hadn't been slid shut from the other side?

On the glass pane, highlighted by the dark fingerprint powder, Giles noticed the smudge marks: the girl's forehead and hands had leaned against the glass numerous times. *What was Kayleen looking at? The neighbour's dog?* Claire Ellis had said her daughters liked to pat it.

Giles kicked toys to the side and headed for the window. She forced it to slide fully open and then leaned out, her hips hooking onto the window ledge. She suddenly realised the police dog was there by her side, she could hear it panting, feel its hot breath on the back of her thigh. She knew Delano was probably staring at her arse and her legs tingled at the thought.

She craned her neck. Further up along the side of the neighbour's house, in plain view through the mesh fence, was a flat-roofed dog-house. Giles leaned lower. Inside the kennel, in the dark shadows, she could make out the outline of small toes. *Oh thank God.* The feet and legs of a child bunched up in the corner. No blood that she could see.

Asleep? Still drugged?

The child's toes curled.

Nah. Too afraid to move, too afraid to speak. Or couldn't be heard over the dickhead with the hedger and the mongrel dog.

'She's here!' called Giles. 'She's in the doghouse!'

The girl was hiding behind a black garbage bag, clutching it in front of her body for protection. Poor kid, her furry friend had turned on her for stepping inside its house.

Sergeant Delano squeezed in beside Giles to look for himself. Their hips connected and she felt the heat of his thigh against hers. She could smell sandalwood and tobacco on him, and instantly yearned for a cigarette.

The plastic bag that was hiding Kayleen's face had split open, and a few watches and an expensive-looking leather wallet had toppled out onto the ground, beside the second green thong.

Delano called to the kid, 'Kayleen, it's okay! Detective Giles and I are coming to get you.' He smiled at Giles, an inch from her face, and slapped her on the back. 'Irony, Detective Giles. I love it.'

Giles blinked. Delano was staring at her with cartoonish moon-eyes and a broad smile.

'The neighbour must have got that stupid dog to protect his stolen gear, and it's just given him away. You've solved two crimes with one boofhead. Missing girl, found. Muswellbrook thief, found.'

Giles forced herself to nod, but she knew she'd got it all wrong.

It hadn't been poor old Sticky Pete who'd been doing the break-and-enters in town. And Claire Ellis had nothing to do with her daughter going missing. Giles felt a flush of shame for her assumptions based on unconscious bias. Pete's history and demeanour. The state of the Ellises' house, the booze, the parenting style. Her chest felt restricted and she forced down the swelling embarrassment.

'Good work, Detective.'

'Yeah, ta, Delano.'

She could think of nothing else than her desperate need for caffeine, and nicotine.

~

Ava Emmerson has patiently waited all day for Detective Giles. Her limbs are now stiff. Her sunken eyes, partially open, stare up into the sky. The blowflies have laid their eggs and are making way for fresh flies, which are attracted by the increasing odour. They crawl over the skin, tasting it with their feet.

No longer alive to shoo the insects away, Ava's slim fingers point to the barbed wire tightly binding her legs together. *Come find me,* she would plead to Giles. Instead, the currawongs call to each other. They too have picked up the scent of death and the prospect of a feast.

THREE

It took fifteen minutes for someone from the council to arrive and remove the vicious dog. The ranger nearly shit himself when he first looked at it. 'Strewth,' he said, 'might as well just bloody shoot the bastard,' and received a round of applause for his suggestion from the rubberneckers on the street. Still, he managed to capture and secure the animal without having his arm ripped off.

With the dog whisked away to the pound and an ambulance taking Kayleen to hospital to treat some cuts and scrapes, dehydration, and for observation, Giles and Detective Turner just had to wait for the next-door neighbour to return home so they could begin charging him with possession of stolen goods and breaking-and-entering. Giles was sure they could probably add a few more offences once they got into the particulars.

They seized the contents of the garbage bag for DNA testing, and Giles paused when she spotted an emerald earring. She pulled on a pair of latex gloves and searched inside the garbage bag until she found its match. The earrings were from the same stone set as the ring Sticky Pete had purchased at the Royal Hotel. Giles smiled. Delano had been right, they'd found their guy. The fluoro stick on legs. Sticky Pete was definitely off the hook and free to go on swimming in his murky little pond.

———

The next-door neighbour wished he'd never come home. After an afternoon smoking weed at a mate's place, he'd returned to a street full of cop cars, his dog and stolen stash confiscated.

Kevin Eddy. Daytime pot smoker, part-time sludge cleaner, night-time thief, full-time knucklehead. That's pretty much how the cops had summed him up, *to his face.*

In the interview room at Muswellbrook Police Station, Giles and Turner were taking turns speaking to Eddy. Detective Turner explained, slowly, that if he cooperated, the judge might view his case with a kinder eye, this being his first criminal offence.

'Let's make this easy,' said Giles. 'I'll go down the list of what we found in the bag, and you just name the place you pinched it from. Let's start with the Louis Vuitton wallet.'

Kevin Eddy shrugged and took a moment to think. 'Pinched it off the dashboard of a parked car with the window open, outside Woolies. The dickhead deserved it. Nice wallet, shitbox of a car.' As an afterthought, he added, 'I guess the wallet's probably fake.'

Giles grinned at him encouragingly, then continued to rattle off the items on the list. Kevin recounted where he'd pinched each from – the street, a house – and even offered some self-congratulatory commentary on how easy it had all been.

'The emerald earrings?'

Eddy was staring at Giles, waiting for her to finish her sentence; when she didn't, there was a pause and the thief looked from Turner to Giles.

Giles sighed. 'We know about the emerald ring. You sold it to a guy in Singleton while you were at the pub. We know that, it'll be added to your list of charges, but where'd you get it?'

Eddy rubbed at his forehead. 'Big house out on a property in Scone. Found it in the main bedroom, top drawer. Heard a vehicle coming back to the house, so I pissed off. Was going to go

back next week . . .' He trailed off and let his shoulders drop in
defeat.

Giles could see in his face that he was realising the cops had him
pegged correctly; he was a fucking knucklehead alright.

For dinner, Giles chose a six-pack of beer and a seat at nature's
dining table, along the Hunter River. A beer and a view, that's all she
needed.

There wasn't a lot to do in Muswellbrook. Often, on the way
home from the station, Giles would grab some booze from the
drive-through bottle-o and spend the evening by the river. A map
would show the Hunter River meandering like a drunken snake
from Denman to Muswellbrook. Depending on the season and the
amount of rainfall, the river either flowed or trickled, flooded or
dried out. In some places it was narrow and cut in tight around the
bends, the bank walls steep drops, elsewhere it was wide with sandy
banks that looked like private beaches.

Under the shade of the willow and tea trees, Giles sat on a large
boulder looking over the cooling water. The drop down was a few
metres, and the river was peaceful, trickling slowly. She wasn't sure
if she kept coming here to unwind or to wind herself up; this was the
place where her mother had died.

Thirty years ago, her mother had been swept away in a flood,
dragged under the torrent. She was found further downstream, spat
out, snagged and wedged in the undergrowth on the other side of
the bank. This place swallowed up lives. It had made her father a
widower, and Rebecca Giles the child of a single parent.

Her mother would have known the rains were coming. She'd
have been warned to prepare, along with the rest of the community.
She would have known the estimated rise of the flood waters, the

predicted millimetres of rain. The thing was, Giles had traced her fingers along a map that outlined the edge of the flood zone. Their house had been safe.

Safe.

Plentiful food and water would have been stored, ready. Her father, Benjamin, would have made sure they were prepared for the coming rain. There had been no reason for her mother to leave their house. So what had propelled her mum to step out of the shelter of her home and into such treacherous conditions? That was always the question that stuck in her mind when she came here.

Giles's skin prickled. It felt like a ghost was blowing on the nape of her neck. She rolled up the sleeves of her cotton shirt and reached for another bottle. The beers were still cold, that's how fast she was getting through them. She pried off the top with the bottle opener on her keys and pocketed the metal lid, then raised the bottle in the air as a toast to the river. She wanted the beer to cool her, to ease her shoulders, relax her body. She looked forward to the numbness.

The early evening was dry and hot. The sun had spent the day warming the muddy bank and pockets of stagnant water made the air smell putrid. Further downstream the skeletal limbs of a fallen tree peeked out of the river. A darter bird was perched on the highest bough with its black wings outstretched; a fallen angel; a vulture happy to find death. The devil's bird drying its feathered rags.

It's Beelzebub's bird, Giles thought.

The bird ignored Giles and flicked its glossy black body, then dived into the water below.

Giles grinned. *Hocus-pocus.*

The water rippled and the bird vanished beneath.

The heat, the beer and the events of the day were all starting to catch up with her. Her shoulders still ached, and her head felt foggy. The hours spent searching for Kayleen and dealing with Kevin Eddy had zapped her emotionally, and she couldn't seem to stop her body from humming.

Giles sculled the beer, then tossed the empty bottle into the grass alongside the first, then reached for another. She knocked the top off, but this third one she sipped. They were finally starting to relax her. She closed her eyes and the shade from the overhanging tree flickered across her face.

As a small child, alone at night, wrapped in the warmth of her bed, she used to feel a tingle that felt like fingers; like a mother touching a child's brow. The lightness of fingertip tracing the arch of fine hairs. This feeling would wrench Giles from her sleep – make her body jolt, her legs kicking and her arm snapping skyward to bat away the hand floating above her. Her mother had been dead for years. Wide-eyed and blinking, in the empty room, Giles would snatch the blanket and pull it up over her head, repeating *Just a dream, just a dream, just a dream.*

Coiled tight under the prickly woollen blanket, she'd cry until she was sore and aching. Because she knew she was the only kid in the world who wished her mother would go away and leave her alone.

Giles's dreams in the dark had been melancholy, but a dead mother and an absent father were the demons that followed her during the day.

The cold beer pressed against her forehead cooled her emotions. She tried to visualise what her mother would look like if she were alive today, then she began to imagine what her life might have been like if she still had a mother.

She was haunted by all the unanswered questions. *What was Mum doing at the river? Why did she leave home when the floods came?* The answers lay with her father, but when it came to talking about his deceased wife, he was impossible to pry open.

Benjamin's health was steadily deteriorating. Time was drying up. If Giles was to get to the bottom of her mother's death, she would have to act. She had procrastinated too long since returning home to Muswellbrook a year ago. Now she would have to pull the past up to the surface like a noxious weed: grab the centre, get to the core. She would have to not only examine the roots but also the earth that had allowed it to grow. The only way to dig up dirt was to get your hands dirty.

FOUR

The next morning the police station was abuzz. The criminal investigation unit was in high spirits, recapping the events of the day before. Picking at the details, the turning point, the kid in the dog-house, the stash of stolen goods, and of course the battle to remove the bloody beast. They all agreed that the look on Kevin Eddy's face had been golden, but the look on the ranger's face when he was told he had to remove the mongrel had been priceless. Even Eddy had seemed relieved when the dog was gone.

Before coming into work, Detective Turner had stopped off at Hunt-A-Book in Scone and bought himself a book on the power of body language. Giles figured it would be Turner's new niche, and that from now on every time she folded her arms, he would read her as being defensive or disengaged, when she was probably just cold.

Inspector Falkov had stopped off on his way in too, at the Art Gallery Café, and bought an avocado cake – his wife had recently put him on a diet. He'd left it on the kitchen bench for his team to share with a cuppa, as his way of saying *good job*, but it remained untouched. A pack of Monte Carlo biscuits, on the other hand, had been almost demolished.

'That avocado cake looks inviting,' joked Turner. His blonde-ginger hair was slicked back with styling paste and it made his face look like a round dinner plate.

Although there was only two years' difference in age between them, Turner seemed like a kid to Giles. She still looked at him like she would a junior officer just out of Goulburn Academy. Sure, he had set his sights on becoming a detective and, six years later, here he was reaching his goal, but he still strolled around like a naive country boy. A few years in Sydney would have turned that stroll into a purposeful stride.

'Are you going to try some?' Turner asked her, nodding at the cake.

'Sure, can't wait. Looks delicious.' Giles smiled as she hit the latte button on the Nespresso machine.

'You're lying,' said Turner. He slapped his newly purchased book against his thigh to underline his point.

'Eh?'

'You need to learn how to give a Duchenne smile. If you squeeze your eyes to make crow's feet, your smile will look more genuine, more believable.'

'Ha! You got me. Yeah, I'll skip the cake, thanks. Looks shit.' And she smiled.

'That's it, there you go, just like that.' Turner shoved the last Monte Carlo biscuit into his mouth and tucked his book under his arm.

Giles didn't officially interview Kayleen, but early in the morning she popped in to see how the kid was going. Although she was a little stiff, the overnight stay in hospital, along with the attention of the nurses and her mum, had definitely pepped up the girl's spirits.

From what Giles could piece together, Kayleen had heard the dog whining in the early hours of the morning and so had gone into the yard next door to comfort her furry friend, thinking they both needed some attention, especially after Kayleen's sutures in her head. Soon enough the kid had realised the dog was upset about its doghouse being used as storage for stolen goods, and then somehow, as Kayleen was inside the doghouse trying to move the garbage bag out, the dog had just turned on her and bailed her up. The dog might have been happy about her visit and willing to share its yard when she'd first jumped the fence, but it had not been happy for her to leave.

Kayleen gave her explanation through tears and a snotty nose. Giles had brought her a doll from the same range as the one Claire Ellis had pointed out as her favourite, but still, it took a cup of hot Milo and two KitKats to extract what Giles felt she already knew.

Kayleen chomped on the chocolate wafer while sobbing, and her mother looked tired, almost bored, when she asked Giles to leave.

Yesterday, Kevin Eddy had also sobbed and wiped snot from his nose, when the charges were read to him ahead of his pending court date. Maybe Giles should have given him hot Milo and a KitKat biscuit too.

Back at the station, Giles sat slumped at her desk, looking down at her in-tray and then back up at the cursor flashing on the computer screen, wondering where to start. She had looked over the photos of Kayleen's bedroom more than a dozen times. The toys on the floor, the open window, the ruffled bedsheets and the popstar posters stuck to the wall, the bedroom of a tween.

Giles yawned. Her jaw was tight and she rubbed her eyes. While she had slept eight hours solid last night, she still felt drained, though also relieved that she had the case pretty much wrapped up. Still, her head was foggy. Her mind kept ticking over.

On the edge of her desk sat *The Hunter Valley Town and Country Leader*. Yesterday's events had made the morning's front page. The PMU had done their work nicely, the media report was glowing, with the Muswellbrook Police Station coming up trumps. There was a photo beside the story, and front and centre were Delano and his bloody police dog. Giles was a fuzzy blur in the background, leaning against a police car looking more aloof than triumphant.

Giles didn't feel too annoyed. Kayleen was alive. Safe. Back with her mother. And it wasn't a sordid tale of malice or maternal filicide, just a kid who'd seen an opportunity and didn't have it pan out the way she'd planned. Of course that's not how the paper reported it, with the 'small misadventure' turning into a 'surprise find', but Giles knew the girl hadn't stumbled across the garbage bag by accident: Kayleen had had a perfect view of Kevin Eddy's comings and goings. Her window looked out onto the neighbour's doghouse and up the side of the house to the driveway. Kayleen could have watched Kevin Eddy trot back and forth with goods in hand. There was also the girl's own reputation for pinching property from schoolmates to consider. But you can't accuse a twelve-year-old in a small town – not without proof.

The article praised the discovery of stolen goods and the charges levelled against Kevin Eddy. Giles could almost hear the town sigh with relief. People would no longer have to double-check the locks on their front doors or make sure the house alarm was set every time they left home. Country folk were never good at locking up.

When Giles had searched through Eddy's bag of stolen property, she found a few wallets, watches, expensive-looking jewellery, and the set of emerald and diamond earrings. The vibrant green stones were cut in squares and edged by diamonds – the exact same design as Sticky Pete's ring. The ring that had landed him in trouble.

Before looking in the police database, Giles made a quick search on the Jewellers Association of Australia website to see if the items were listed as stolen for dealers and the public to see. She found the heading *Scone NSW. Category: Stolen from private property. Date of Incident: 14th November. Police Report Number: 3762570. Police Station Reported To: Scone.* There was a brief description of the lost items, including a brooch, a necklace, a ring and earring set. What was missing was a photograph. Most of the listings on the webpage had a picture, either of the item itself or at least of the owner wearing the item. There was no accompanying photo for this listing, though. That was a little odd. Nevertheless, Mrs Pruitt from Scone would be pleased, grateful even, to have her earrings and ring returned, and now she could stop yacking in the deputy mayor's ear and leave Giles and her team the hell alone.

In the first minute of Giles's call, Mrs Pruitt went on a rant about the rising drug problem and addiction in the area, kids high on ice and throwing furniture at their parents and breaking into homesteads to pinch valuables to support their habit. Parties in the bush, *raves* she had stressed, way out in the Wollemi National Park, shindigs with MDMA, and, *and* on private properties in shearing sheds. A disgrace to the shire, to their parents and to that generation as a whole.

Mrs Pruitt made it clear, 'If I hadn't been up at the stables tending to my thoroughbreds, I would have grabbed my shotgun without a second thought.'

'Mrs Pruitt, we'd prefer it if you leave the policing to us,' said Giles.

'Let me remind you, Detective, the necklace and brooch are still missing. I hope you can complete your job.'

'Can I just ask, Mrs Pruitt, do you have any recent photographs of the jewellery in question? Did you take any for the insurance?

Or just of you wearing them at a function? I just don't seem to have any pictures, just a sketch.'

'I've never worn them.'

'A family heirloom and you've never worn them?'

'Family heirloom? Who told you that?' Giles hesitated and madly flicked through her notes. 'They were a sixtieth birthday present from my sister a month ago, I just never got around to storing them in the safe. I may have said they would be put away and bequeathed to my grandchildren *as* a family heirloom, but they're brand new.'

'Quite the gift, Mrs Pruitt. You must have felt cherished.' She had no doubt Mrs Pruitt would have told the deputy mayor that they were a family heirloom to bump up the status of the stolen goods.

'I did feel loved when I was given the *complete* set. Now, is there anything else?'

'No, thank you for your time. The pieces will be returned to you once our investigation is complete.'

'Well, I would like the full set returned, not half a set and half the job done. Good day.'

The phone clicked in Giles's ear before she got another word in.

On the writing pad, Giles scribbled, *Necklace, brooch????? Still missing.*

Eddy's doghouse had been thoroughly searched after the event, and the contents of the garbage bag were photographed and diligently itemised. Giles knew Eddy wasn't smart enough to grow or otherwise acquire his pot for free, so it was possible Sticky Pete had also purchased the necklace and brooch, or Eddy had sold them to someone else at the Singleton pub.

Giles picked up the pencil and scribbled, *Pete? Kevin? Another customer at the Royal?* She hesitated for a moment, then added to her list of suspects: *Kayleen?*

There were two more calls Giles needed to make: one to the Royal Hotel, asking them to hold on to any CCTV footage, to be used as further evidence against Kevin, and one to Sticky Pete. She had to inform him he was off the hook for stealing the ring, but she also needed to make sure that was all he'd purchased. She picked up the phone and dialled.

'Hello?' The voice was abrupt and not nearly as articulate and refined as Mrs Pruitt's. These two women lived worlds apart.

'I was wondering if I could have a word with Mr Peter Nolan, please?'

'He ain't 'ere.'

The phone clicked again and Giles chuckled to herself. Both women did have something in common: they'd both hung up on her with the same level of shittyness.

Perhaps if Giles had asked for 'Sticky Pete', the phone would have been handed straight over. Even Giles could hear a hint of tele-marketing or debt collecting in her tone. She figured she'd leave it an hour or so and try again. Only the next time she called, she'd be less formal.

The mood in the station was playful, everyone was buoyant, and Giles had received so many slaps on the back that her shoulders were starting to ache. But there was a tonne of paperwork to fill out and reports to write up, and with the constant interruptions and back-and-forth banter, progress was slow. Still, Giles managed to get through a good chunk of the correspondence, and by mid-afternoon she felt blurry-eyed, but satisfied.

She was flicking through her in-tray when Falkov sat on the edge of her desk and handed her a piece of avocado cake on a plastic plate. 'Here. I got this for you, Giles, so I'd like to see you try a piece.'

'Sure, thanks, sir.' Giles picked up the slice of cake and took a bite. 'Mm, yummy!' She squeezed the corners of her eyes.

'Okay, okay. Next time I'll get chocolate.'

'Just get something that's made with sugar, sir. It's not a big ask.'

'It's a big ask for my wife.' Falkov patted his stomach, making a thick and hollow sound. 'Stress and cholesterol have her insisting on some major changes. Think of it as her looking after us all.'

The cake wasn't as bad as Giles had thought it would be. She took a second bite and smiled sincerely.

Falkov grinned back, but his face quickly turned serious again. He said in a low voice so the others couldn't hear, 'Listen, I heard you gave the kid a present this morning?'

'Yeah, I just popped into the hospital and dropped off a toy that was better than the crap she had lying on her bedroom floor.'

'Don't cross boundaries, we still have a few questions to ask. Let the kid re-hydrate, recover and return home before you start pushing. There's no rush on this. We've got our man. We need the kid's statement to be handled neat and clean – it all has to hold up in court. That toy could be misconstrued.'

'It was just a check-in, no questioning. Her mum was there the whole time, sir. Just a friendly how-yah-doing. Showing some country hospitality, that's all.'

'Yeah, well, you can be friends once the kid's story is beyond doubt. Signed and sealed. That girl isn't squeaky clean. I want no missteps on this, understand?'

'Yes, sir.'

'Anything else?'

'I've tackled most of the corro, sir. The important stuff. I'll head back to Singleton tomorrow morning and view the CCTV footage at the Royal Hotel. Mrs Pruitt's brooch and necklace are still missing, so I think Sticky Pete wasn't Eddy's only buyer on the day.'

'Good. See you tonight at the pub. Celebratory drinks, six o'clock. Don't be late.'

'Can't wait, sir,' said Giles. Over Falkov's shoulder she could see Turner squinting at her, madly pointing to the crow's feet in the corners of his eyes. She scrunched up her eyes and said, 'Eaton Pub, six o'clock.'

Turner looked less than impressed with her effort.

'Enjoy the cake,' said Falkov.

'Thanks, sir.'

Falkov stood up and returned to his office. Through the glass wall, Giles watched him pick up a slice of cake from his plate. He studied it for a moment, took a bite, then tossed the rest of it in the bin.

FIVE

On the way home Giles took the long detour out to Denman. Every chance she got, she popped into Merton Court to visit her father. The small aged-care facility had been his new accommodation ever since his motor neurone disease had become more aggressive, and it was the reason why Giles had asked for the transfer from Sydney to Muswellbrook.

Two years earlier, Benjamin Giles had been diagnosed with Amyotrophic Lateral Sclerosis, a big fancy name for *you're losing control of your muscles, so quit your job and brace yourself for twitching and cramping and an early death*. ALS would eventually affect Benjamin's speech, swallowing and breathing, but until that happened, he'd twitch and quiver, get the shakes, and wobble around on his crutches fitted with forearm braces. On bad days he'd reluctantly deign to recline in his wheelchair and let the nurses push him around. But he had a group of mates that he continued playing poker with, one of whom was Falkov. Her father still had all his wits. His mind was sharp as a tack. To both Giles and Benjamin, that was a good thing. The best thing.

Denman was a little under a half-hour drive from Muswellbrook through open farmlands mostly scattered with cattle, stock horses and eucalyptus trees. The odd willow tree dotted the paddocks, showing where the creek cut through the flats, and galvanised silos sparkled in the afternoon sun.

Giles hit shuffle on her car's Bluetooth controls and cranked up the volume. She slid the elastic from her ponytail, felt the tension release in her scalp, and, with all four windows rolled down, she cruised a tad over the speed limit as the wind whipped through her hair.

'Look what the cat dragged in!'

'Hello, Dad.'

Giles kissed her father's forehead and then shoved a plastic shopping bag into his lap. On Ogilvie Street, she had popped into the Baerami Olives store and picked up green olives stuffed with whole chillies, then grabbed a sourdough loaf and some Brie from the IGA.

'Let me take you back to your room.'

'Oh, good-o.'

Benjamin Giles had already started squeezing the bag on his lap, feeling the hidden bounty as Giles wheeled him out of the dining room and down the hall.

Once in his room, she shut the door and her father handed back the bag like it was his gift to her.

'Do you want me to help you out of your wheelchair?'

'Nope. My legs and hips are pretty good today. I was just feeling a little lazy, that's all. I've been walking a bit lately. I'm wobbly and the bloody staff think I'm an OH&S risk, tap-dancing and waltzing about the place, but I've got it under control.'

Benjamin eased himself out of his wheelchair and flopped into the armchair beside his bed. The room was small, modest but cosy.

'There's half a bottle of red hidden behind the television,' said Benjamin. 'If you want a glass?'

'Nah, thanks. Do you?'

'Sure,' Benjamin winked. 'Go on, luv, pour yourself one while you're at it. I hate drinking alone.'

Giles grinned and snatched up the bottle. She poured two generous tumblers and handed one to her father. 'Cheers.'

They clinked glasses and both gulped the cheap shiraz like it was red cordial. Giles dragged a footstool to the other side of the small coffee table that sat between them and emptied the contents of the plastic bag.

'Brie? I like Camembert better.'

'You get what you're given, Dad. Or you can take a walk up the shops yourself.'

'And I could!'

'I know. Best you don't though, footpath ain't that flat. Don't want you taking a tumble on account of cheese.'

Benjamin nodded his head, then peeled open the plastic takeaway container. He shoved an olive into his mouth and mumbled, 'Saw your mugshot in the paper this morning.'

'Did you?' Giles smiled as she sliced through the loaf of sourdough with a pocket knife.

'Yep.' His chin dripped with juice and oil. 'Who was that ugly prick with the dog?'

Giles tossed her head back and laughed. 'Delano. Delano from Dubbo.'

'You're taking the piss.'

'Nope, Detective Delano and his dog from Dubbo.' The two of them filled the room with rollicking laughter.

There were no armrests on the sofa, and Mrs Nolan and Pete were used to leaning into each other while watching the telly so neither of them fell off the edge, their shoulders pressed together and the TV remote more than an arm-stretch away on the coffee table. Only now Sticky Pete sat side on, weeping into the arms of his wife like a child. He was inconsolable. Just the thought of returning to jail made him want to neck himself. Mrs Nolan stroked the back of Pete's bristly head like a small injured puppy, hushing and cradling, rocking and soothing.

If Pete had taken an interest in the local news, he would have read the jewellery thief had been arrested yesterday and realised that he was already off the hook. But Sticky Pete didn't read much, he had never purchased a newspaper in his life, and not all gossip travels as fast as one would hope in a country town.

'I'm telling yah, she never came down yesterday or today for the CCTV footage. Barman swore on his ute that no cops've come into the pub the last two days. She's got it in for me. That bitch is trying to bury me.'

'There, there. No more of that, Pete. Stop your snivelling, it's going to be alright.'

'I'm fucked, I tell yah. Fucked.'

'No, Pete. You go and talk to that officer, sort it out. Drive on up to Muswellbrook tomorrow mornin'. I've got thirty bucks in me wallet for petrol, I can cut back on the ciggies for a couple of days. You go up first thing and have a solid word. But don't lose your cool. Have a shower and a shave, put on a clean shirt – show that officer you're respectable. Be adult and sort it out.'

'You're right, that's what I should do. Of course.'

'Of course fucking of course. I wasn't asking, I was telling,' said Mrs Nolan, and she squeezed Pete tight into her bosom.

Kayleen sat on her bed, legs crossed. In her lap were all her sticky stolen things, swaddled in a disposable nurse's gown. The lab coat that she had sworn blind that she'd not stolen: the nurse had given it to her for being so brave when they stitched her head up. She'd even pointed to the gauze taped to her forehead. Her mother had seen through her bullshit, of course, but decided not to say anything. She knew she had to pick her battles.

Carefully, Kayleen began to unwrap the tissue-like material to reveal her treasures. But not all her treasures were there. She had given her mother the necklace, watching her mother's fingers caress the green stone and the diamonds around it. The brooch, though, Kayleen had kept for herself. She wished she could have taken more from the garbage bag, but the brooch and necklace were all that she could hide in her knickers.

Giles had stayed at Merton Court longer than she'd planned and was now in a hurry to get home. She had just enough time for a quick shower and a change of clothes before hitting Eaton Pub.

The visit with her father had been light, jovial, but she hadn't broken any new ground on the topic of her mother. She knew the moment she decided to raise the ghost from her past, the darkness would begin to creep back in. This visit hadn't been the right time to open up old wounds. It was nice just to break bread, so to speak.

Nevertheless, since returning to Muswellbrook so they could be together for the last of her father's time, she felt compelled to dig a little deeper. She burned with questions, and while she had accepted Benjamin's brief explanation when she was a child, as an adult the inconsistencies and gaps in his account were glaring.

Neither had ever opened up an honest dialogue about that day. Her mother, Emilia Maree Giles, was the space between father and daughter.

∼

As the sun starts to leave another day behind, out on the edge of town the wallabies venture down from the mountains. They welcome the setting sun as they spring through the gullies to the edge of the gum-tree line, where the national park ends and the farmland begins.

The wallabies have become adventurous, courageous. Against their instinct, they move slowly out into the open paddocks. They need to feed. They need to drink. The long months of heat and dry wind have left little to scavenge in the hills. Now, in the late evening, under the protection of the growing darkness, they move into the fields. Boldly drinking from cattle troughs, daring to nibble along the edge of the road, where the grass is greenest.

On a property nearby, where things are worse than grim, a small wallaby moves away from its mob and tentatively inches towards a cattle trough for a drink of water. It twitches its nose, points it to the sky, sniffing. The smell of death is in the air. It would flee at the smell of a wild dog, but not another dead wallaby. Still, it registers the scent.

Floating in the water trough, the body of Ava Emmerson is now bloated. Her chin, nipples and hip bones break the water's surface. Her head and limbs are the colour of lavender. The barbs of the wire pierce her waxy skin; from the hips down, her bound legs look like the ridged scales of a fish's tail.

The wallaby bows its head to drink but stops – the water is putrid. The corpse bobs up and down, the barbed wire scratching against the galvanised steel, startling the animal. The wallaby leans back on its tail and kicks out at the drinking trough. The blow makes the metal clang like a musical note. A semibreve rings solo in the air.

The wallaby springs away and the rest of the mob scatters, heading back into the safety of the dense mountain scrub.

The corpse floats. Bobbing listlessly in the water. Still waiting to be discovered. Still waiting for someone else to ring the alarm and come find her.

SIX

Detective Giles, of all people, should know how to build a profile. *Bloody hell,* she thought to herself. Back when she'd tried online dating, the site matched the profile she'd created for herself with habitual, disciplined, emotionally stable, excruciatingly boring white-collar men. She had been reluctant to be totally honest in the questionnaire and played it safe with her answers – clearly too safe.

Profiling was everywhere: marketing, politics, town planning. And dating apps. Only, right at this moment, Giles would characterise herself as a thirty-year-old trying to dress like a stripling teenybopper.

The spaghetti straps on her floral dress seemed too thin, more angel hair than spaghetti, and the hem only just touched her mid-thigh. This was not her style, and she was simply having a drink with her male co-workers – they had never seen her in anything other than a tailored suit, with neatly pressed slacks and beige button-down shirts. But she wanted to change up her image, be more feminine; she wanted them to see she was more than just a suit. The dress had seemed like a good idea, but now that she was actually walking up to the pub she felt self-conscious. She had missed the mark by a long shot, and it was too late to change.

Giles held down the hem of her skirt and bounced up the warped timber steps two at a time, onto the stooped veranda of the Eaton. Over the years the pub had been revamped, repainted, re-roofed, re-managed, re-bloody-everythinged, yet the whole building still looked unfinished.

As dingy as the pub seemed, it was the best place to drink, and tonight was a celebration. Yesterday she had cracked two cases. The missing child and the local thief. She would get at least two free beers, one for each case, and maybe a plate of steak, chips and gravy. All on the government dollar.

Giles had only been back in Muswellbrook for a year and in that time, aside from her workmates, she hadn't made any new friends. So when she stepped through the doorway and looked around at the patronage, it wasn't to see if she recognised anyone, but just to get a quick read on the atmosphere of the room.

The bar had a few stragglers from the mines who had popped in before heading home. The pokies room had its usual retirees or drilling operators with too much money to burn, as well as the odd hardcore gambler. A family with small kids was out in the beer garden sharing a platter of fish and chips and a plate of spring rolls; the parents looked keen to find an escape in the bottom of their wine glasses. Other than a loved-up couple and the low-key music, the pub itself was relatively quiet.

In the corner, Giles spotted her work colleagues and was even more surprised to see Delano from the canine unit buddied up beside them. She felt more relaxed once she saw a lager waiting for her, warming on the table.

'Here she is, the man of the hour,' Falkov muffled, his long nose stuck deep inside his own schooner glass.

'Just an hour? Is that all I get, sir?'

'You get two,' Turner quipped, holding up two fingers like he was flipping her the bird.

'Nice,' smiled Giles, with no squint of the eyes.

'Sorry I missed all the action yesterday,' said Detective MacCrum. 'But I'm happy to help you celebrate.' MacCrum was tall and blond, and he always looked like he dressed in the dark or was slightly colour blind, with black pants, navy jacket, grey socks and mismatched ugly ties. He was a family guy with three kids. His children probably chose his ties for Christmas and Father's Day gifts, and his wife was forever breaking his balls to put in a swimming pool, renovate the kitchen or add a rumpus room to the house.

'It's okay, she didn't need us, she wrapped this one up on her own,' said Detective Sergeant Bray. Bray was the opposite of MacCrum. He was a stocky guy, broad shoulders, more like a cube on legs. His eyes were a dark brown with bushy eyebrows. He was pleasant and witty, though sometimes his jokes were borderline sexist. He'd been divorced once and his second marriage looked like it was heading the same way. It wasn't that Bray was a bad husband, it was just that his job was his mistress.

'Is that for me?' Giles asked, pointing at the brew.

'You should get more than a warm beer,' said Delano, raising an eyebrow. 'I'll go find something more top-shelf. How about some Kraken? Yeah, I'll grab us a bottle of Kraken – for Kraken the case!'

Two junior officers at the end of the table were clearly taken in by Delano's charm and wit, and they both laughed. While Falkov knew he'd be stuck explaining the bill to the petty-cash tin, he didn't stop Delano from heading to the bar.

Giles slipped into Delano's seat and could instantly feel the residual warmth left in his chair; the heat of his thighs was now on the back of her own legs. She shifted, trying to get comfortable. 'So? Are we going to eat before we hit the rum?'

Falkov nudged Turner. 'Giles needs food in her stomach to keep up with the blokes. Go grab a menu, or slip in an order.'

'What goes with spiced black rum?' asked Turner.

'Salt and pepper squid?' said Detective Sergeant Bray.

The table laughed. Turner said, 'Good one,' but it was clear from the expression on his young face that the joke was lost on him.

'Geez, Turner, you've never heard of the Kraken?' asked Bray.

'Nope.'

'The Kraken was a giant squid before it was a rum,' Bray explained, frowning and looking at Turner through his bushy eyebrows. 'It was a great big octopus, a beast of epic proportions! It would take down ships and cover its prey in black ink.'

'And salt and pepper,' added MacCrum, and the table roared with laughter again.

Turner nodded, but he still missed the joke. 'So, get the squid then?'

'Yeah, get the squid,' laughed Bray. 'And chips, and a few chicken wings, and some onion rings for starters.'

'And nachos,' added MacCrum.

Falkov tried not to wince at the mounting food order.

Bray raised his glass to Giles. 'You did good yesterday.'

'Thanks.'

Bray never said much to Giles at the station besides respectful greetings, but she always got a strange thrill when they were teamed up together on the job cycle; he would never shut up about his good old days in the highway patrol, busy on the A15 writing speeding tickets, looking for infringements on hotted up cars and springing surprise roadside breath tests on tradies in expensive utes.

It was a NSW Police policy not to give detectives permanent partners; having someone different to team up with every day made it harder to turn dishonest or even corrupt. Each morning they were assigned to a job cycle car and paired up with a different partner. There were six detectives at Muswellbrook Police Station:

Giles, Turner, Bray, MacCrum, Callahan, who was off for a week having a respiratory issue checked out, and Hebbar, the only other female detective, who was away on maternity leave.

Bray never missed a social event that involved free booze, or an audience for his stories. Giles smiled across at him and then took a sip of her warm beer. She knew he'd be the life of the party.

On the wall behind Falkov and Bray were framed black and white photos. People who once lived in the town, or who were now too old to party late at the local drinking hole. A collection of Anzacs, women's guilds, owners of prize bulls, Legacy and Lions members, victorious footy teams covered in mud, prize racehorses alongside their owners holding trophies, the women's croquet club. They were all up there. A community shrine. People who at some point made the town, lived in the town, or drank at the town's pub.

'You up there?' asked Delano, as the bottle of Kraken hit the table along with a tray of bulbous rum glasses filled with ice cubes.

'Me?' asked Giles. 'How old do you think I am?'

'Barman told me all the local heroes made it up on the wall. Gave me a bit of local history the other day. Chatty bloke, full of stories. I've popped in for a few frothys – they do a good lunchtime burger here, generous serving of fries. Anyway, after yesterday, I thought they might have stuck your picture up.'

'I'm not a hero. And it's the older generation up there, locals. You have to live in this town for thirty years straight to be considered a local, and another ten to have any chance of getting your photo on that wall.'

'But your dad's up there, right?'

'The barman doesn't know my dad.'

'Aah, that was Falkov who showed me. He's there, right? The guy in full dress beside the assistant commissioner?' Delano leaned over Giles's shoulder and pointed at the photograph.

Geez, this guy is a furnace. Giles clenched her lips. The heat of his chest and arm, the smell of sandalwood and tobacco. The back of Giles's legs tingled again.

'Yeah, that's him, looking dapper.'

Delano read the label under the photo. 'Benjamin Giles, District Superintendent.'

'That's Dad alright.' Giles smiled and looked down at her short skirt and shuffled up in her seat a little.

'So you're not a local,' affirmed Delano. He pulled up a chair and sat beside her, his thumb gently massaging his knee.

Giles noticed the size of his hands and felt childish for her racy thoughts. 'Nope, I lived on the outskirts of Muswellbrook until I was twelve, then I was shipped off to Sydney. Private boarding school. After high school, I went straight into the force. I'm far from being a local.'

'Sydney has seeped under her skin,' said Bray, overhearing. 'It'll be years of living in this town before that Sydney grime is scrubbed away.'

Delano ignored Bray, smiled at Giles, and said, 'Private boarding school, eh? That's a bit posh.'

Giles could feel the eyes around the table fall on her. She shrugged. 'Nah, the one thing worse than being a reverend's daughter on a school discount is being a copper's daughter on a full scholarship. I wasn't popular at school.'

'No way,' said Delano. 'I would have guessed you'd be in the cool crowd.'

'Nope. Dad made the students and teachers nervous. And this was a school where most of the parents were judges, barristers or lawyers.'

Falkov laughed and nodded, as though he could picture the scene in his head. 'That's probably *why* they were nervous.'

———

After an hour or two, the pub was full of a second wave of customers. The music was louder, a different beat, and groups at tables had to raise their voices to make themselves heard. It was taking longer to have glasses cleared, and the empty glasses stacked on their table were proof of a good night.

Giles's colleagues had spent the evening drinking to her brilliance. She stared blurry-eyed at the giant sea-monster on the bottle of Kraken, then back up at the old black and white photos on the wall. Returned vets. Ravaged land and livestock after bushfires and floods. Her father in full dress uniform. It was all documented up there – the people the town loved, the trials and trauma they had endured together. It was a shrine to what made the place great.

In the dark light of the pub, Giles couldn't help thinking that not only did Delano look half decent, after a few beers and rum chasers he didn't sound nearly as obnoxious. She drowned out the talk with shots of spiced rum, feeling a lot better for choosing to wear her spaghetti-strap dress.

~

The naked body is cold now that the sun is down. Her neck is a greenish blue, the colour of the ocean after a storm. Her youthful face is almost unrecognisable. In the cattle trough, the water is greasy, and the smell of death is strong in the still air.

In the moonlight, the body waits another day to be discovered.

SEVEN

Sticky Pete had cut himself shaving, twice, and Mrs Nolan had sponged out the blood specks on his shirt collar, twice. He had slicked back his hair with an old tube of Brylcreem and combed it flat against his scalp with a near toothless comb. His shirt was ironed with Crisp starch and his pants wiped over with a lint brush. So when he walked into Muswellbrook Police Station that morning, smelling of a generous splash of Proraso aftershave, he had a small bounce in his step.

With its wraparound veranda and grey galvanised roof, the police station looked more like a quaint homestead. If it weren't for the bold silver signage stating it was, indeed, a police station, you would almost think they'd be serving tea and scones, that you could pop in and have coffee with a cop. But behind the old-world building there was a two-storey complex equipped with the latest technology – it even had a gym.

At the service desk, Sticky Pete asked a young constable if he could speak with Detective Giles.

'Sorry, mate, she's not in at the moment. Went out on another matter early this morning. Not sure when she'll be back.'

'I'll wait,' said Pete, looking at his nametag. 'Constable Griffin.'

'I can take your name and number, save you the wait?'

'Nope. I said I'll wait.'

'You want a newspaper to pass the time?' offered the constable.

'Nup.'

Sticky Pete took a seat in the reception area and Constable Griffin shrugged. Pete wasn't much of a reader. Nor did he want to waste the battery on his ancient phone. Instead, he sat and watched the police move about behind the counter, practising his speech to Detective Giles in his head, making sure he wouldn't forget a word of it.

~

In the cattle trough the water is still. The body is inflated like a balloon, covered in vascular marbling. Layers of skin have started to lift from the hands like those of an old washer woman no longer busy with life's chores. And while the morning is hot, Ava is still cold to the touch. But at last, she has been found.

EIGHT

It was midmorning and Giles wished she'd had an early night: the sea-monster was still swimming backstroke around her skull. Too many shots of Kraken and too little sleep. Her ears were ringing and her head felt like it was a tightly wound ball of elastic.

Giles was supposed to be down in Singleton, looking at the Royal Hotel's CCTV footage, obtaining solid evidence of Kevin Eddy selling stolen goods, hopefully including Mrs Pruitt's necklace and brooch. Instead she was 14 kilometres out of Muswellbrook on a cattle property, watching cows milling around a water trough containing a dead body.

Beside the trough, a concrete water storage tank stood by a towering windmill. Whenever the wind picked up and the blades spun, it groaned for want of oil. Under the windmill and around the trough, some of the cows stared, others snorted at the earth, their wet nostrils caked in the grey dust. Others still stomped their hooves and scratched at the dirt, bellowing. The cattle were thirsty, but something foreign had invaded their waterhole. They knew the scent of death. Death was soaking into their water like a teabag.

Giles had found her at last.

Judging by the state of the body, Giles guessed the young woman had been there maybe two, three or even four days. There had been no attempt to conceal her corpse, instead it was openly on display, stripped of clothes and dignity. Her top and bottom lips were clamped shut by two pieces of wire looped and pulled together; Giles recognised it as a figure-of-eight knot used in fencing.

It was a vision that, at first, made Giles flick her head back, both repulsed and shocked. She had never seen anything like it, not even during her ten years in Sydney, and she had seen plenty of rotten crime scenes there. Even though she took some photos on her mobile, Giles already knew she didn't need to look at the scene anymore – she would never forget it.

Mr Rickard, the owner of the property and the person who had first discovered the body, looked like he'd not shaken the image either. The seventy-year-old was hunched over against the passenger door of Giles's police car, his thin frame crumpled. He was rubbing his face with the palms of his hands, crestfallen, probably trying to wipe away the sight of her.

An animal had been gutted and its intestines were splatted around the drinking trough in a quick and messy attempt to spread gore, a scene staged to create either shock or fear. She wondered if it was satanic, a ritual of sorts. The barbed wire coiled around the girl's legs was a mystery. What was the point of that? Was it a statement? A macabre joke? It seemed to serve no purpose in the act of killing. Was it a signature, a message? If all that had been done purely for shock value, it hit its mark – it took Giles a moment to re-focus and calm her nerves.

Giles was almost certain the gutted animal was a wallaby; there was grass in the stomach chamber. Judging by the size it could have been a calf, but it wasn't calving season, and the entrails were too small to be from a rabbit or wombat. She knew it wasn't human, so not the intestines of the victim.

A few metres away, an old quad bike was parked next to a clump of slaty gums amongst the Scotch thistles. Parked in shade so its rider wouldn't burn her arse on a hot black vinyl seat. Only, the rider had never made it back.

There wasn't anything Giles could do aside from call it in, tape off the area, and wait for the Evidence Recovery Unit to make their way from Newcastle, and for her own team to arrive. ERU would take proper photos and collect evidence, and Giles would make sure all the correct procedures took place. Until then, she wanted to stay away from the body to prevent any further contamination at the scene, and she wanted to stay downwind to avoid the smell.

She returned to her vehicle, where Rickard was sheltering from the sun. Giles's feet were beginning to swelter in her black boots. She sniffed at the heat and wiped away the sweat beads forming on her top lip, then peeled off her dark grey suit jacket, tossed it on the back seat of the car and rolled up the sleeves of her cotton shirt. Her mouth was dry. Just like the cows, she yearned for a drink to quench her thirst.

'Do your cows charge, Mr Rickard?'

'Do you know much about cattle, detective?'

'No.' Giles wiped her sweaty palms across her arse and took a breath. She could almost chew on the air, it was that thick with heat. 'So, do they?'

'Nope.'

Giles stretched out her arms and tried to shoo the cattle away from the trough. She knew they weren't going to step up for a drink when there was a dead body in the water, but she didn't want them stomping their hoofs all over the crime scene.

Around the drinking trough, where the ground was blood and mud, where the entrails of the wallaby had been scattered, Giles had noticed a partial footprint and what looked like drag or scuff marks. *A scuffle?* The footprint was from a work boot, size eleven or twelve as best she could judge. There were also hoof prints from the cows, a set of wallaby prints, and a paw print that could have easily been mistaken for a scrub wallaby, except the paw pads weren't long enough – it was definitely from a dog.

'What size boot do you wear, Mr Rickard?'

'Eleven. Them's big enough boots to fill.'

'Aha, I bet they are. Did you step over that way?' Giles flicked her hand towards the partial print at the end of the trough.

'Nope.'

Great. Now she just needed to keep herself, the cows and Rickard clear so the ERU could get the boot print intact.

Bloody ERU, where the hell are they?

She tipped her head towards the cattle inching up to the trough. 'Mr Rickard, I need to secure the scene. Do you mind if we push this lot into the next paddock?'

'Nope.'

Giles rolled her eyes. 'Will you give me a hand pushing your non-charging cattle back through the gate?'

Mr Rickard was not happy about moving the cattle into the next paddock over, where there were already some horses, but it only took a few minutes to hustle the handful of heifers and steers through the gate. The herd was too hot and bothered to resist.

As soon as the animals were in the next paddock, Mr Rickard latched the gate and watched the mares bristle up, annoyed with the intrusion. The horses began to tramp their resentment across the barren field, their nostrils flaring and snorting. Giles couldn't understand why the mares were wasting so much energy protesting, it had to be thirsty work showing their offence, and the air was juiceless. Everywhere around her, the ground had cracked open and seemed to be gasping. The willow trees down in the dry gully looked sullen. Even the birds in the gum trees were quiet. The place was as dead as the girl floating in the water trough.

After inspecting the scene, Giles had started gathering as much information on the victim as she could from Mr Rickard. Ava Emmerson. Somewhere in her mid-twenties. Freelance jillaroo. Paid to check on water levels, fix pumps, mend fences, a bit of branding and drenching cattle. Odd jobs and contract work. Work that Mr Rickard's old hands, arms and back could no longer do.

Giles had asked Mr Rickard a bunch of questions and he'd answered them short and to the point as best he could. Hard worker. Reliable. Never spoke of a boyfriend. Thinks she lived with her parents in town. Not overly chatty about her personal life. Good with the horses. No bloody idea why she ended up dead in his cattle trough, in that state.

'Was she on the books?' asked Giles.

'Huh?'

'Ava. What did you pay her?'

'Few bob, couple of pineapples.'

'Cash in hand?'

'Yeah, cashie. But she's reliable, knows her stuff. No trouble.'

Was, thought Giles. *She* was *reliable*.

'How long has she been working for you?'

'On and off for about three months. Knew what she was doing. Quiet, respectable. I gave her access to the quad bike and the key to the shed where I keep the tools and gear.'

'You didn't question why she hadn't shown up for a few days?'

'Nope. She comes and goes. She knows what needs to be done and when. I don't give her a list of jobs; she makes her own list.'

'How do you know what to pay her?'

'She tells me.'

'That's very trusting of you.'

'Is it?'

Mr Rickard squinted his cloudy eyes at Giles, one more milky white than the other. He may have been trusting of the jillaroo, but Giles could tell he was not very trusting of her.

'So, this morning. You find her floating in your cattle trough. You ring triple zero and you say,' Giles quoted from her notes, '"I might have someone on my property that's drowned, can you send someone to take a look."'

'Yep.'

'Bit of an understatement.'

'Look at her. Tell you the truth, I didn't know what to bloody say. Figured it was best you came out and looked for yourself.'

Giles grinned and dropped her head. 'Did Ava drive here each time she came to work?'

'How else would she get out here?'

Giles felt her neck stiffen. 'What type of car does she drive?'

'White Toyota Hilux.'

'Year?'

'Old model, from the early nineties at a guess.'

'Where is it now?'

'Parked behind me shed.'

'And you never noticed it sitting there for two, three days?'

'Can't see behind the shed from my house window. She parks up under a jacaranda, in the shade. Leaves the windows open and half the time she finds one of me chooks trying to nest on the front seat.'

It was the most Mr Rickard had said in one go, and Giles was relieved the old bugger was finally talking.

'When was the last time you saw her?'

'Dunno.'

'At a guess?'

'Maybe three, four days. Only, I never saw her, but the salt licks were out, so I knew she'd been on the property. The licks weren't out the day before.'

'Licks? What are they?'

'Where are you from?'

'Sydney.'

Mr Rickard nodded and then spat at the ground.

'So, what are licks?'

'Lick blocks.' Rickard pointed to a light brown cube on the ground in the adjoining paddock. 'It's a mineral and protein supplement for cattle. Helps in the drought. Cows *lick* the block. They were put out a few days ago. Like I said, I never saw her, I just knew she'd been. Why would I walk round the back of the hay shed to see if her ute's there? She just comes and goes.'

'How does she communicate with you? Tell you what to pay?'

'We catch up, have a coffee when we cross paths. She tells me what she's done and I pay her.'

'On the spot?'

'Most of the time, if I've got the cash. Or I fix her up the next time I see her.'

Giles thought it a bizarre way to do business, but her opinions didn't matter, just the facts.

A couple of bull ants scurried over a log they'd made their nest under, and Giles stepped away from the entrance hole visible in the dirt. She didn't want ants up the leg of her trousers. With not much else to do aside from wait, Giles strolled along the barbed-wire fence that now separated the cows from the windmill, storage tank and drinking trough. Small yellowish-brown crickets sprang away from her boots with each step and burrowed deep into the grass as she ambled along the fence line. Giles ignored them, focused instead on avoiding the cow shit, circular pats of dark green, wet and pasty, and a fucker to wipe out of the tread of a boot.

It wasn't just the heat and her hangover that were bothering her. *Why did Mr Rickard call it in as a drowning? Why be vague about the situation to triple zero? Clearly, this is a murder.*

Giles ran through the details she knew: the victim was naked, her clothes and any possessions had been removed, reducing the evidence. The body appeared to have been floating in the water for well over forty-eight hours, so it would be difficult to find any DNA. Plus, every time the wind had blown over the last few days, the windmill blades would have spun and pumped more water into the tank and trough, further diluting any possible evidence. When she'd first arrived, Giles had gestured towards the mechanism and asked Mr Rickard to stop the windmill from pumping water. That risked further fingerprints and footprints at the scene, but she took the gamble that it was better to stop the water flow, and she documented his movements and what he touched in her notebook.

Giles continued rattling through the details in her mind. The cause of death looked like drowning, but she couldn't rule out strangulation or blunt trauma, with the body being placed in the trough after the act. She'd have to wait for forensics and then the autopsy to be sure.

She followed the wire fence further along. Strands of horse hair were caught and tangled in the barbs. The animals liked to scratch their hides on the fence posts, but the barbed wire caught their fur and hair now and then. As Giles walked on, there was a clump of short black hair hanging from another barb.

Black? Mr Rickard's cattle were Herefords – a rusty brown, deep rich red and white – and his horses were chestnut. There were no other animals on the property that were black that she could see.

'Did Ava own a dog?' Giles called out over her shoulder.

'What?'

'A dog. Did she own a dog?'

'Yep.'

It's like pulling teeth.

'What kind of dog?'

'Border collie.'

'What colour?'

'Black and white.'

'Did she bring it with her on her rounds?'

'Not really. Sometimes. Not seen it for a while.'

'Hmm.' Giles looked over the fence. The buffel grass on the other side had been flattened as if something had pushed its way through it. Had something come through the fence, its fur getting caught on the barbs? Running up from the gully, or carted down into it? Giles looked back to the splatter of guts around the mill. Maybe some were from Ava's border collie?

She pulled out her phone and fumbled with the screen, then took a few snapshots of the hair in the barb.

She was speculating, re-imagining how the crime might have taken place. In the heat, waiting for the other units to arrive, she had the time to muse and ponder. Maybe the dog got in the way of the murder? Tried to protect its owner? She left the fur caught in the fence for the ERU to bag and seal. They had all the equipment, no point risking it – it wasn't going anywhere.

Giles wandered back towards the windmill, where Mr Rickard now stood under the tower, trying to steal some shade while rolling a smoke. 'Want one?'

Do I ever!

'Nah, I'm good,' Giles said, as she tried to hide the disappointment at her near lapse of willpower. 'Thanks anyway.'

Mr Rickard rolled the smoke slowly. Giles watched. She could almost taste the nicotine hit and craved a whiff of tobacco, though she knew his cigarette would blow downwind. *Gawd, I'd love a smoke.* Mr Rickard searched his hip pocket for his lighter, then stooped and rubbed his calf.

Giles spotted dark specks next to a tiny tear in the cuff of his pants. Was that dried blood? The hairs on her arms bristled.

'What happened to your leg?'

'Caught it on one of the fences a few days ago. I was climbing through.'

'Don't always come through the gate?'

'Nope.'

'Hmm.'

Yeah. What if the dog tried to take a bite out of his leg. Maybe he kicked it? Or killed it, gutted it, then dragged it through the fence and dumped it down in the gully. Would fighting off the dog have given her enough time to start scrambling up the road to get away? Or get back on the quad bike and tear off to safety? Maybe she was knocked out already? Or dead? That would explain the signs of a scuffle and drag marks she noticed earlier at the edge of the mud. After getting rid of the dog, maybe Rickard dropped her in the cattle trough and held her under the water to make sure she was dead. But then what? He tried to make it look like some crazy maniac was wandering around the property? Out here? Fourteen kilometres from town? On *foot*? *Pig's arse.*

'Any visitors the last few days? Anyone passing through the place?'

'Nope. Got an empty biscuit tin, detective. Been empty for thirty years.'

Giles wanted to say, *Yeah, I know your miserable story.* Instead she asked, 'How'd you find her again?' She'd heard his account already, but she was killing time until the ERU arrived. It shouldn't be taking them this long, not with their sirens blaring.

'Eh?' Rickard still hadn't lit his smoke, and Giles was aching for a drag. Just a sniff of nicotine would help her aching head and give peace to her hangover.

'The girl, how did you find her? What made you look in the water trough?'

'Saw me cattle standing around the windmill, pawing at the ground, bellowing and not drinking. These beasts drink a lot of water a day, especially in this heat. So I came over to see what the matter was. Thought it might be a brown snake in the grass, or a broken pump. But nope, found the girl floating on top of the water.'

That understatement again. Not many people find a dead woman with rusted barbed wire around her thighs and knotted between her crotch and call it a 'possible drowning'. As soon as Giles had seen the girl sewn up like a blind grandmother's cross-stitch, she'd called the station and asked for immediate assistance of a suspicious death, and then called in the Evidence Recovery Unit.

Giles flipped open her notebook, making sure she hadn't missed anything. She noted the weather – hot, bloody hot. On the morning radio, there was an extreme fire danger warning given the occasional gust of high wind, meaning there was a total fire ban. The wind was starting to pick up and the blades of the windmill spun, but the pump rod stayed stationary. With the high humidity the wind was far from cooling.

Giles had scribbled down a quick diagram of the scene, labelling Rickard and cattle as possible prints, the wallaby and dog print, the drag marks, the scuffle marks near the thistles, and her own prints close to the metal frame of the windmill. She noted what she'd touched, what Rickard had touched, and what she believed to be dog hair in the barbed-wire fence. She desperately wanted it bagged,

but she had to let ERU process the scene from the ground up. She'd
have to be patient.

It wasn't quite midday. The heat felt like it was cooking into
Giles's skull. She'd do anything for a hat on her head and a bit of
shade.

'Well, it wasn't a brown snake that spooked your cows.' Giles
kicked at the ground and grinned, trying to keep the mood light.

'Nope,' said Mr Rickard. 'Found her looking like a mermaid.'

'What?' Giles's ears pricked up. 'What did you say?'

'The way she's tied up and floating. Like a mermaid.'

'That's an odd comparison, Mr Rickard.'

'No more odd than finding a corpse in your bloody cattle trough,
detective.'

Giles kicked at the ground again, only harder, like one of the
cows. She watched the dust puff under her feet. Then she spotted
something. On the ground, a few feet away, close to a small stack
of rocks was an ash-pink rose and a sprig of baby's breath. Leaning
over them, she could see they weren't real but rather made of plastic and silk.

Geez. Why did that feel familiar? She couldn't quite place the
feeling, but she could have sworn she'd seen this artificial rose
before. But how could that be?

Giles went to her police vehicle. From the boot of the Sonata
she grabbed a small fluorescent orange traffic cone and dropped it
over the fake flowers. Close by, under the pile of rocks, a section of
woven straw was poking out. It looked like the brim of a hat, but
she was reluctant to draw attention to it in front of Rickard.

'What's the cone for?'

'Just left my own print, so I'm marking it,' Giles lied. 'We'll need
your shoes too, when the Evidence Recovery Unit arrives.'

'When will that be?'

'Got somewhere else you need to be?'

'Just hot standing out here, that's all.'

'Yeah. It is bloody hot,' said Giles.

'Yep,' said Mr Rickard.

'I could toast out here in the sun.'

'Could,' said Mr Rickard.

'I guess we could do with some rain.'

Now there was something the town hadn't seen much of for a long time. And the less they had of it, the more it consumed their thoughts and talk. But Giles was searching for a different reaction. It was a loaded comment – she was looking for a response. A glint in the eye.

'Could,' said Mr Rickard again, and he started to scratch his neck. Giles couldn't help but smile. *Got yah!*

'Yep,' Giles continued. 'Guess some rain'll come soon.'

'Maybe.' Rickard looked over at Giles and scrunched up his face. It was a smile of sorts, but there was something hidden behind it. It felt like she was back at the pub, drinking rum, her head starting to spin.

Rickard shooed away the flies buzzing about his face.

To the farmer, Giles would have been just another blow-in. But *she* knew *him*. She knew him alright. Because Mr Rickard and Rebecca Giles shared the same miserable story.

Every country town has its disaster, a catalyst, an event that becomes the yardstick to measure just how bad things really are. For the country town of Denman, it was the 1955 floods. Fourteen people died, and more than five thousand homes were lost. Then, in 1984 and 1992, the floods hit again, with waters rising nearly to the same level as 1955 – nearly.

In the following years, when the rains came and washed away roads and bridges, the people of the town would say, *Could be worse – could have been like the floods of '84 and '92.* It was only the older generation who would say, *Could have been like the flood of '55.* In 1992, the heavens had seemed determined to set a new benchmark, but the people of the town thanked God it was not broken.

Giles was just a newborn baby when the downpour hit the town for days on end, the Hunter River and Muscle Creek swelling up. People along the river evacuated while their homes filled with water. The deluge turned the main road of Denman into a flowing river, and in the most unbelievable and unfortunate circumstances, it also washed away Mr Rickard's wife and Giles's mother.

Muscle Creek had been a torrent and the Hunter River a lake. The flood gouged out the surrounding farmland, stealing territory. It plucked up fence poles, tore down trees, horse stables and hay sheds. It discarded Mr Martindale's wheat silos 7 kilometres downstream and deposited Daisy Noel's cows, bobbing like corks in a thick stream the colour of tawny port.

Everyone in town remembered the night it rained cats and dogs, and chooks, and wheat silos, willow trees, barbed fences, and fucking cows.

Two days later, Mrs Rickard had been found dead and bloated amongst a dozen Poll Herefords, twisted up in barbed wire and fence posts. The crasser locals had commented that Mrs Rickard had been a bit of a cow herself, so maybe she had bobbed up and down in the creek with the rest of Daisy Noel's herd and simply gone unnoticed.

After the rains, the familiar smell of the town slowly returned. Barbed fences were replaced, so cattle once again knew their boundaries. The debris flowed away, or was hauled to the dump, and the riverbanks were restored. The town readjusted and a new order was established.

Mr Martindale never re-erected his silos. Daisy Noel quit cattle and switched to goats – she figured they'd have more brains to jump to higher ground next time the rains hit. Mr Rickard and Benjamin Giles became widowers.

Rickard went on managing his farm, alone. He never held a funeral for his wife. Or if he did, nobody was invited to the service.

Benjamin Giles *did* hold a funeral for his wife, and the town pitied the local cop who had just become a single dad.

Neither Benjamin nor Rickard ever found new wives.

Christ, that was thirty years ago. Giles remembered the stories well.

Years later, in primary school, the older kids spoke of the day they woke up to find the landscape around them changed. Giles always thought it must have been frightening for a child to find their whole environment instantly unrecognisable.

The townsfolk whispered, too. About Mrs Rickard. They were afraid to utter the word *murder* aloud.

Mr Rickard had testified that, as the flooding began, he saw his wife leave the farm in the ute. She had raced off to get to higher ground. Maybe she turned around to get something she'd forgotten? Maybe, when she did, she had struggled to get back out or reach safer ground. Then the water had gushed towards her from all directions, the banks spilled over, and a landslide of farming material and machinery tumbled straight towards her.

Some suggested she may have heaved herself up onto the top of the hay shed, standing wobbly-legged on the pitched roof. A witness attested to that, but their story was discounted, because how could anyone see anything through the white sheets of rain that fell? If she had called for help, her voice would have been drowned out by the sound of water tumbling from the sky and the cracks of thunder.

Rickard was not there to save her. Mr Rickard was . . . *where?* Where was he when all this happened?

Giles often wondered if Mrs Rickard had seen Daisy Noel's cows float by. Seen the whites of their eyes, the horror on their faces, before the hay shed folded up like a wet cardboard box. Mrs Rickard would have been dragged down in the undertow, along with the cows and farming equipment, and simply been swept away.

When the water levels subsided and the farmers returned to drag the dead carcasses of cattle out of the creek, that's when they'd discovered her body caught up in barbed wire.

Giles knew all this because it had been an epic story in her youth. At night she would sip her Milo and shiver, not because she was cold, but because one of the things that scared her most was the creek at the bottom of the property behind her house. Every spring holiday, when pools of water formed deep enough to swim in, no kid in town would venture in for a paddle. The kids all said the ghost of Mrs Rickard walked the creek.

'She'll grab your ankle and hold you under.'

'Her face is a rotting skeletal smile.'

'Yeah, a walking stiff.'

'She was murdered, you know.'

'Yeah, murdered, it's true. That's what you do to wives you don't want no more.'

'What do you do?' a nine-year-old Giles had asked.

'You drown them.'

'Yeah! Like cats. When people don't want cats no more, they drown 'em.'

Giles had listened carefully to the childish banter and thought,

That can't be right. A wife isn't a cat. There must be a law about drowning your wife.

Over the years Giles had heard all the stories of the ghost of Mrs Rickard. Suburban kids might have had a witch living in an old house on their street, but the country kids around Denman and Muswellbrook had invented a wife-killing farmer and a ghost that walked the riverbanks. Even the adults didn't help quash the rumours. They'd whisper, *He always was a cantankerous old geezer; she was always beautifully put together, so involved in the community – but him! Couldn't spare an egg!* Those who weren't too fond of Mrs Rickard said, *If she was my bloody nagging and interfering wife, I'd hold her under the water too.*

Once, Giles thought she may have seen her. She'd noticed a woman on the creek bank lacing up her shoes. At first the young Giles paid her no attention, as bushwalkers often stopped along the Hunter River to yank off their shoes and rest their feet by the edge of the creek. Only this woman stood and then stepped deeper and deeper into the water until she disappeared. Giles had convinced herself her eyes were playing tricks on her. What else could it have been? It was the limbs of the willow trees, the shadows, maybe even a kangaroo. It was too far away to be certain. Except she could have sworn that, before the woman disappeared, she had turned to Giles and smiled.

The town all talked about the drowning of Mrs Rickard, but not once did anyone mention Giles's mother, who had been taken that same night, by the same rains, the same flood. It was as though Emilia Giles had never existed.

As she grew, Giles had asked her father *why* her mother had died. She had accepted his vague description, that it was simply 'a terrible tragedy'. But by the age of twelve she began to ask, *How?* That's when she was shipped off to boarding school.

Bugger, isn't life a laugh. Now here she was, all these years later, back where she grew up, trying to police the place.

Bloody Falkov knew Rickard's history, he knew *her* history. Surely he would have known this would be a trigger. Falkov was great mates with her dad; they had worked alongside each other for thirty years. But he had sent her out to a drowning, on her own. A bloody drowning. On Mr Rickard's property, of all places. Was he testing her? Maybe pulling her down a peg or two after cracking two cases the other day, then walking away like she was a bloody hero? Except she hadn't cracked either case – the next-door neighbour's savage dog did.

Giles wondered if Mr Rickard was getting bored waiting for the rest of the team to arrive or if he was starting to fret. She also wondered about the possibility of him wanting to see how his wife was found all those years ago, and maybe, just maybe, he'd tried to re-create the scene with Ava Emmerson and the barbed wire.

Or had he really murdered his wife and then dumped her amongst the cattle and debris, and he was re-creating *that*? Rickard only had to make people believe it happened the other way – it would be easy to say that he'd seen his wife leave in the ute and that she must have turned back. Easy enough to start a rumour that his wife was seen standing on the roof of the shed. Giles had witnessed how you can start any rumour in a country town, then stand back and watch it spread.

Giles still needed to think through her theories – she didn't want to jump too quickly to conclusions, she wanted all the evidence laid out in front of her first. The facts. Not just speculation, or a story she had made up to distract her from the hangover pounding in her head. The ERU and her team from the station would be arriving soon.

It would take days for the scene to be processed, but she wanted to make sure they were pointed in the right direction when they got started.

And what about the fake flowers and that hint of a straw hat under the rocks? It troubled Giles like a dull headache, in the background, but still there nevertheless.

Giles thought about the jillaroo. She knew how quickly someone could get heat stroke. Ava might have poked around and found a straw hat in the tool shed.

Giles sniffed. In the heat her head swam with possibilities.

Ava would never have had a chance to run away, she probably wouldn't have even seen the blow coming. Rickard probably hit her from behind, then dealt with the dog. To make sure she was dead, he went back and held her under the water. Then, to hide his crime, he made it look like some psychopath had done it, some nutter with barbed wire, a dead wallaby and a sick imagination, not an old man with arthritis in his hips. Then he'd sewed her lips shut in a figure-of-eight knot to . . . what? Keep his secret?

Something about her hypothesising wasn't right. Something was niggling at her. Maybe it wasn't anything to do with Mrs Rickard, maybe Giles was imposing her own theory about her mother onto the Rickard story?

She shifted her feet, looked at her watch. *God, how hard is it to follow a GPS? Come on, guys, move it. Fifth gear all the way here.*

'Ever marry, Mr Rickard?'

She already knew the answer, but she was trying to stall.

'Once. Wife passed away.'

'I'm sorry to hear that. I lost someone too, when I was young.'

'Now I'm sorry.' Rickard picked up a piece of slate rock and ran his fingers down its edge before tossing it back onto the pile of stones stacked up against the side of the water tank's concrete wall.

'I'd rather you not touch anything. Crime scene and all that.'

Rickard shrugged, and Giles made a mental note of which rocks he touched. She pressed on with her conversation, trying to chip away at the old man, trying to fill in the blanks, scratch a little deeper. She sighed. 'It's hard to lose someone you love.'

'Who'd you lose?' Rickard asked.

'My mother. I was a baby at the time.'

'Sorry, again.'

'Yeah, lots of sorry. The world is full of sorry.'

'I guess.' Mr Rickard crouched down and picked up another stone, a larger one, only thinner and with a smooth edge.

'Yeah, grew up without a mother.'

'Shame.'

Rickard kept returning to the pile of rocks. Giles let him – he was becoming chattier.

'Must have been hard, not having a mother.'

Giles looked back at the fence and then down at the dirt under her feet. The sun was making her drowsy. She drifted away. Last night's piss-up was really starting to catch up with her. *The pub.* That was it – that's where she'd seen that rose and straw hat! Trying to visualise the scene, she squinted her eyes for a moment against the scorching sun – then, *crack!* Her world turned dark.

NINE

When Giles opened her eyes, she was flat on her back. The first thing she felt was immense pain in her scalp. Rickard had her by the ponytail and one arm. He was dragging her behind the police vehicle and near dislocating her shoulder. With her free hand, Giles reached for her Glock-23, but her gun was gone. She groaned and Rickard let her go.

'Son-of-a-bitch came from behind the water tank!' Rickard was panting, pointing and blubbering. 'That prick was here all this time. I fought him off. I think he took off, up the gorge maybe. I don't know where the fuck he's disappeared to. We have to get somewhere safe.'

Giles blinked, dizzy and confused. 'What? Who?'

'The bloody mermaid killer. That bastard must have crept up on us. I think he ran up over there.' Mr Rickard pointed to the other side of the paddock, behind the windmill and up the gorge. 'Up there – he might have gone up there. Get a search party out here, detective! Your guy's right bloody here!'

Giles sat up in the dirt and swayed. It was an effort to get off the ground, and she wobbled on her feet. Suddenly the landscape around her tilted and she had to grab onto the side of her vehicle to

steady herself. Through the car windows she thought she saw something move, but Mr Rickard was still babbling and pointing, so she
turned away and glanced in the direction he was facing. Big mistake.

As Giles scanned the paddock and squinted into the sun, she
felt another crack to the back of her skull. The rest was a blur.
Her aching head, her ponytail yanked, the buffel grass and thistles
whisking by her face, her arm almost wrenched from its socket, the
slate stones under her back, the sound of screeching cockatoos,
Mr Rickard's lined face, years of dirt pushed deep under the skin
and bubbling up to the surface. His milky brown eyes, all gooey and
cataracted. It was hard to know if she was looking into them or only
the chalky film covering them.

Mr Rickard was yelling at her. 'Get up! Get the fuck up,
detective!'

She swung her fist. Her arm flailed in the air. The face of
Mr Rickard waned.

Giles blinked, but all she could see was a dark fuzzy outline of a
face, silhouetted against the sun. A voice whispering hot against her
ear, 'I've got you now, bitch.'

And then water. She was being held under the water.

The Kraken had her by the throat, its tentacles slimy. Choking
her. Her head ached. As she went under the water again, she wished
for sleep.

TEN

When Giles woke this time, it was to the feeling of bristly whiskers on her top lip. That made her eyes fly open. She felt her lungs fill with hot air, and then her chest cave in under a palm pressed between her breasts. Detective Turner was above her, his face serious and bouncing up and down, counting, 'Six, seven . . . eighteen, nineteen . . .'

Then he put his lips to hers and more hot air filled her aching lungs. Her ribs hurt.

Get off me!

Giles turned on her side and vomited sludge and water. It tasted like mud and cow shit and death.

'Christ, Giles, are you okay? You with me? Can you hear me?'

Turner sounded panicked. If Giles could only get enough air back into her lungs, she'd laugh at him.

She flopped on her back. Unable to move. Closed her eyes.

Turner's mouth was over hers again, and her lungs inflated. With what little strength she had left, she lifted her knee and pushed him away.

Dizzy and disoriented, she tried to suck in the clear air. She struggled again to sit up, managed it, then, leaning forward, head spinning, she choked and coughed up more sludge. Her throat felt ripped to pieces.

She croaked, 'You got him? Rickard?'

'Yeah, he's just here. Out of the sun. Taking shade in my car.' Turner looked at Mr Rickard sitting in the back seat with the door open and his legs dangling out of the vehicle. 'We got to you just in time.'

'Good. Have you cuffed him?'

'What? No.'

Giles looked up at Turner. She had to blink and squint to focus on his face. 'Arrest him. That prick hit me over the head with a rock, twice, and then tried to drown me.'

'*What?*'

'He's got my gun.'

'Load of bloody bullshit,' spluttered Rickard from inside the car.

'Giles, your gun is somewhere in the mud. Sergeant Bray is searching for it now.'

'Rickard tried to drown me, Turner! I want that man cuffed.'

'Steady on now,' said Rickard.

'I . . . but . . . Giles, you need to relax and wait for the ambos to arrive, okay? Just take a breath.'

'Don't give me orders, I said cuff him.'

Turner frowned at her. 'What the hell?'

She coughed and wiped the taste of Turner off her lips. 'You fellas might just owe me another bottle of Kraken. While you bastards took your time getting here, I think I may have cracked another case.'

'Giles?'

She rolled over and got herself back on her feet. She felt unsteady. As her body swayed, her arms waved about in the air, her finger dabbing at locations around the property.

'Down in the gully, over there, is the victim's dog. Her name is Ava Emmerson. The victim, not the dog. There's a hat under that pile of rocks by the well. That needs to be bagged. And a flower. In the fence over that way there's some fur, I think from the dog. Bag that too.'

'Giles, I'm not following. I think you need to sit down.'

'Nah, I'm good. I'll meet you back at the station. I'll explain then.'

She clutched her ribs and staggered in a zigzag towards her Sonata, stopping briefly to vomit more murky water onto the dirt, and her own boots.

Turner called out to her, but she waved him off as she climbed into her car. 'Rickard's a murderer, he tried to fucking drown me!' she shouted back. 'And find my fucking gun!'

She kicked the engine over and did a U-turn, nearly wiping out the ERU, and headed back to town. As she stomped on the accelerator, she switched off the police radio and refused to look in the rear-view mirror.

Giles clambered up the timber steps of Eaton Pub. She looked like crap: her clothes were still wet and sodden, covered in vomit, dirt and mud; she had cow shit caked on her thighs and crusty blood in her scalp and hair. But she felt elated. Adrenaline was racing through her body. She could feel the thrill of finding the next piece to the puzzle.

In the corner of the pub, Giles scanned the framed photos of past town residents. And there she was: Mrs Rickard in black and white. One picture of her with the women's guild, another as a winner of a prize bull. And there she was again, looking smug, a member of the women's croquet club. In all three images Mrs Rickard was wearing the same straw hat, trimmed with artificial flowers – roses, hydrangeas and baby's breath.

Giles yanked the photos off the wall and, before the publican could protest, she yelled, 'Evidence in a criminal case.'

What dumb luck, coming to the pub last night.

As Giles headed towards the doors, she called over her shoulder, 'See yah tonight, fill up the ice bucket and get another bottle of Kraken. This time it's on me!'

She rushed down the timber steps, feeling like she was seeping in between the cracks of the wooden planks, her legs turning to jelly. She began to fade, and the world around her turned dark again.

Sticky Pete's patience had just about run out. The waiting room chair seemed to be getting firmer under his arse as the hours ticked by. His legs and hips were numb and starting to throb. He kicked out his feet and stood, stretched a little to soothe his aching hip, then hobbled up to the service desk and asked, 'How much longer?'

'For the tenth time, I don't know. Leave your number and I'll get Detective Giles to call you once she's back. Or pop in next door to the Shamrock, have a beer and burger, then come back after lunch. I should know by then when she'll be in.'

Sticky Pete looked hard at the young constable. He wanted to say, *Buy lunch? With what, yah mug?*

'Nah, I'm happy to wait, mate.'

'Then *be* bloody happy about it,' said Constable Griffin.

'No need to be a dick,' mumbled Pete. He hobbled out of the front door of the police station.

Outside, on the footpath, it felt like 60 degrees. The sun-blasted concrete glared in Pete's face and cooked his feet. With the constant changes in smoking laws, you never knew where you could light up in public, so rather than smoking out the front of the police station Pete decided to walk up the side of the cop shop. He didn't want to get halfway through a cigarette and be told to put it out, he couldn't afford to waste smokes. It didn't hurt that the footpath there was in the shade of the police building.

As Pete neared the corner, he could hear voices around the back, in the police car park. He paused, stopping at the corner, leaned against the wall and lit up his cigarette, letting the smoke drift away downwind. He sucked back on his cheap Pall Mall Blues and listened to the cops' banter.

'Said she's been dead a few days,' said the first cop.

'Jeez,' said the second.

'Wrapped her legs together in a coil of fencing wire – pulled up to her hips like a skirt.'

'Surely the killer would have cut himself on the barbs? They'll get DNA.'

'Nope, dumped in a water trough. Water fucks up forensics. Glad I wasn't the first responder.'

'Jeez.'

'Young girl, too. In her twenties. Brutal. This kind of shit doesn't happen around here. Gonna be hell for the family.'

'Jeez.'

Pete hurriedly sucked on his smoke. While he desperately wanted to ring his wife and fill her in on all the gruesome details of a reported murder, he couldn't face telling her he'd yet to clear things up with Detective Giles. But it would be a good story to tell her once he returned home with some positive news.

Pete dropped his smoke, stamped it out and wondered if it was worth going back inside – to the hard chair in the air-conditioned police station – or if he should see how much a burger and a beer was in the Shamrock Hotel. He opened his wallet a few times, as if the next time he looked inside he'd magically find an extra note. After the fourth time, Pete decided he'd just go have a nap for an hour or so in the back of his car.

ELEVEN

Giles sat up in the hospital bed. Startled. Blinking.

An ambulance had scooped her up from the puddled mess at the bottom step of Eaton Pub a few hours earlier. She'd been assessed and treated on admission by the doctors, and her clothes bagged for analysis by the Evidence Recovery Unit. Photos had been taken of her injuries; her left eye was swollen and a deep purple, and there was bruising around her neck, though no fibres had been found.

The medical staff and the ERU team had got in each other's way as they vied for status and priority over her body. Giles's ears had been ringing, and she'd been too fatigued to help them sort out a pecking order as they bickered over who would examine her next. She knew any DNA sample they collected would bolster the database and increase their chances of finding and convicting her attacker, but she was dizzy and nauseous. She just wanted them all to bugger off.

'Chin up, kid,' one of the ERU officers had said.

Giles thought he was being supportive, but then realised he meant for her to literally lift her chin so he could get a better look at her injuries.

By the time everyone had stopped prodding and poking at her, and she'd answered all of the questions fired at her by the ERU, her head was throbbing. She had been taken to a private room and told to keep sipping her fluids, to rest for the night, and someone would keep checking in on her.

Now it was past 9 p.m. and, after dozing on and off all evening, she woke to find a man in a navy-blue suit and a classic check Burberry tie sitting in the visitor's chair. He was staring at her.

'Are you my doctor?' She blinked again.

'No. I'm a barrister. I'm your legal representation.'

'Legal representation? For what?' Giles pulled up the bedsheet to cover her flimsy white hospital robe.

'Apparently you punched Mr Rickard in the face, then accused him of trying to drown you.'

'I *punched* him? I don't remember doing that. But he did try to drown me. Do you even know what I've been through today? He hit me over the head with a rock, twice.'

'I've been briefed.'

'That old fucker tried to kill me.'

'Well, he's saying otherwise. I'm sorry for your ordeal. The attack and the scene would have been distressing. Confusing, even. Mr Rickard left the police station a few hours ago threatening to lodge a complaint about your conduct with the Law Enforcement Conduct Commission.'

'They didn't arrest and detain him?'

'For what?'

'Attacking me! Attempted murder!'

'Apparently *you* attacked *him*. Hence the threat to go to the LECC.'

'Fine. Let them investigate me.' Giles rolled her eyes.

'You're not worried?'

'Nope, happens all the time. I think the bigger issue here is the young lady found on Rickard's property, and the reason why I'm in a hospital bed.'

'Inspector Falkov is taking this threat very seriously.' Giles scoffed, but the barrister didn't look amused. 'Detective Giles, you failed to have your dashcam on during the investigation.'

'There's no dashcam on a Hyundai Sonata.' Giles prickled. 'Only on Highway Patrol. You can't turn on what you don't have.'

The barrister shifted in his seat, frowned and nodded, taking in what Giles had said. 'But you left the scene without instruction. You were the first responder and you left. It's a matter of investigating and concluding that extreme force against Mr Rickard was warranted under the circumstances. You assaulted him, and he's not happy about it.'

'I was sent to investigate a drowning. I didn't know it was a homicide until I got there. I was already a bit hungover, and then the whole morning turned into a shit-show.'

'You were intoxicated on the job?'

'Hungover, not inebriated. If you're supposed to be on my side, then pretend you didn't hear that last comment.' Giles sighed. 'Look, don't start twisting my words, but, yeah, the night before I was at the Eaton Pub. It was a big night. My team and I were celebrating another case we had wrapped up. I was a bit drowsy in the morning . . . and the heat, that damn heat.'

The barrister straightened his fancy tie, patted it down, then picked off a miniscule piece of lint. 'It's Mr Rickard's word against yours. He has bruising to prove the punch.'

'And I clearly have evidence of fingers around my throat, a black eye, and two bumps on my head. Look, he was drowning me. That old bastard cracked me over the head twice, took my gun, and then tried to drown me in a cattle trough. I think getting in a right hook to save my life was *warranted*. Fair call?'

Dismissive in the face of Giles's rising emotion, the barrister said flatly, 'He was resuscitating you when the other officers arrived. So, as I was saying, we have two different versions of events.'

Giles looked away. *Boorish, pompous prick.*

'Detective Giles, it's your integrity that's at stake. On paper it will look like one of you is lying about how the situation unfolded. As a detective, any question about integrity is career-destroying. It could get you fired. I'm here to help you get your story as close to the truth as possible, without you throwing yourself under the bus. Your statement needs to be accurate. We don't want you having to withdraw anything later on. Your integrity as a cop is paramount.'

Giles had never met this man before, and in her thin robe she felt exposed. He was questioning her policing skills, her honesty. But while it was rubbing her up the wrong way, she knew that he was right. There was no witness to corroborate her version of events, and being labelled a dishonest cop could end her career.

The hospital bed felt cold. Giles pulled the sheet up higher. She mumbled, 'I'm not a liar,' but voice sounded weak and distant, without any of her earlier conviction.

'Look, I believe the doctors will discharge you in the morning. When that happens, go home and get some more rest. Then, if you feel up to it, meet me in my office that afternoon. I don't want you making any comment to anyone, especially about hangovers, until we go over your account of events together.'

'Sounds serious,' said Giles.

'The LECC *is* serious. You may think it's something that happens all the time, but I promise you'll want the best lawyer you can get.'

'And that's you?'

'That's me.'

The barrister dropped his business card on the side table, beside an enormous bouquet of seasonal white flowers. His name was David Hemmings; she'd never heard of him. Without saying goodbye, he left her room.

Nice to meet you too. Giles gazed at the empty doorway. She knew she might soon need the barrister on her side, but she had enough on her plate without dealing with the LECC or Mr Rickard bringing legal action against her. That was just a ruse to make himself look innocent. No, the most important thing for her to worry about was Ava Emmerson.

The image of Ava's body came flooding back and Giles gave a shiver. If it wasn't Rickard who had brutalised the young woman, then who else would want Ava dead? And what type of person could commit such an act? Who was she dealing with?

Giles knew the Evidence Recovery Unit would be collecting everything they could find at the scene; the pathologist would be examining the body; the coroner would no doubt find it beyond suspicious and it would be declared murder. There was nothing she could contribute to the case until she was discharged from hospital and got her story straight.

The ward was quiet and Giles was grateful for the private room. Even though she'd already slept for hours, she was dog tired. Her head felt thick and her body burdened. She needed to rest. She needed to be left alone. She needed to fully recharge so that, first thing in the morning, she could see what the team, the newly housed rural crime investigation unit had found on Ava Emmerson, and then she could either arrest Mr Rickard or start hunting down the real killer.

TWELVE

Turner arrived to collect Giles from hospital after her breakfast of watery orange juice, cold toast, soggy scrambled eggs and a packet of rice bubbles with a tiny jug of milk. The painkillers had been tastier than the breakfast.

Turner handed her a plastic bag with a police navy-blue track-suit set and some slip-on canvas sneakers that looked two sizes too big. There was no bra or underwear in the bag, and Giles restrained herself from grumbling.

'Spin round, Turner. Eyes to the wall.'

Giles was slow getting dressed; her shoulder and ribs ached. She still felt giddy, fragile.

'Are you doing okay?' Turner asked the wall.

'Yeah. They said I had a bit of concussion. Still can't see well out of my left eye.'

'You passed out on the steps of Eaton Pub.'

'Concussion can do that,' said Giles. 'But the doctors had me under surveillance —'

'Observation?' corrected Turner.

'Yeah, that. They reckon I'm okay to be discharged, so long as I go home and rest. But I've been sleeping on and off since yesterday afternoon, and right now I'd rather get back to work, while my memory's still fresh.'

Turner was cringing as he turned back to face Giles. The tracksuit was too tight, and it struggled to cover her midriff.

'Falkov said to take you straight home. He doesn't want you in today, he wants you rested so you can be on top of your game.'

'Hmm, that's thoughtful of him.' Giles thumbed at the white bouquet by the bedside. 'Did the troops all pitch in for the flowers?'

'They're not from us. Were you expecting us to get you flowers?'

'Never mind. It's the thought that counts.'

'None of us thought about getting you flowers.'

'Thanks.'

'You just don't seem like a flowers type of girl, that's all.'

'Thanks again.'

Giles wondered briefly if the bouquet was from Falkov or Benjamin. They couldn't possibly be from David Hemmings, the barrister.

'Has my dad been told what's happened?'

'Yep.'

'Flowers must be from him then.'

'No card?'

'Nope. Definitely Dad then. He's not into sentimental words. If he did write a card, it would read "get up".'

Turner smiled and held out his arm. Giles took it and stood up gingerly. She didn't want to slink back down into a jelly puddle like she'd done on the steps of the pub.

'You sure you're okay?' he asked.

'Yep.' She tested her wobbly legs. Her body was sore and aching, her lungs felt dried out from coughing up sludge and water, but she was pleased to be getting out of the hospital. 'Shoes are a little big. I look like a clown.'

'Nah, you look like someone who came second in a fight.' Turner flinched, realising his comment sounded more like a swipe at her – he'd intended it as a joke.

Giles's face fell. 'Yeah, I guess I do.'

Sticky Pete also woke up sore and aching in the morning. In the car park of a nearby playground, he had slept on the back seat of his old Hyundai Getz. He didn't have enough petrol in the tank to drive home to Singleton and back, and he certainly didn't have the money to get a room for the night.

It had been an uncomfortable night. He'd had to sleep crooked, and he'd forgotten to crack a window, so by morning he'd almost been baked alive. Plus he'd parked under a river red gum – all night he had listened to gentle rain, only to find in the morning that it had been the gum tree's nuts falling onto his car, which were now stuck in the grooves of his windshield, boot and bonnet.

Pete had difficulty straightening his neck out. His shirt was wet with sweat and his neatly ironed pants were now wrinkled. The Brylcreem made his hair look greasy, and his breath was putrid. He had no deodorant, toothbrush or toothpaste. Yesterday he'd looked respectable when he went into the police station – it all seemed so sensible and rational when his wife had explained it – but Detective Giles still hadn't been there when he went back in the afternoon. He'd have to try again today, despite how he looked.

When Pete walked up to the front desk, he noticed it was staffed by a different constable than the day before. The young officer seemed to be taking his role as the first point of contact with visitors seriously, and gave Pete a look of pity that he wanted to smack off of his chops – he didn't really want to admit to himself that he looked almost derelict.

When he asked to see Detective Giles, he could almost see the constable's balls squeezing at the mention of her name. Something big was going on – Pete could hear about a dozen phones ringing in different parts of the station, and the young officer looked flustered at having to man the front desk all on his own. It must have been to do with the murder he'd heard about the day before. Maybe there *was* some nutter on the loose, drowning young women and wrapping them up in barbed wire.

'Look, mate, she's not going to be back in the station for a while. Go home, have a shower and relax. I'll tell her to make you a priority the moment she's available. She can give you a ring as soon as she's in.'

'But the CCTV footage might be wiped by then. Shit, mate, can't I see her now?'

The front desk's phone started ringing – the constable looked as if he was about to pop a blood vessel. Pete sighed, smelled his own rank breath, saw the constable take in the great waft and reel back. 'Look, go home, mate. Clean your teeth. Leave your details and I'll get Detective Giles to call you. It'll be all good.' The constable picked up the phone.

'Don't look all that bloody good to me,' snarked Sticky Pete as he turned and left the station.

Sticky Pete couldn't help thinking that the news about the murder must have been dire for the young constable to be so distant and dismissive. *Shit, I'm going to end up back in jail.* They had no time for the likes of him. Why did life just keep fucking him over? Why turn over a new leaf when the world was out to get you? It was just a bloody ring for his missus's birthday – he was just trying to do something *nice*. Now it was going to get him sent back to the clink. All because Giles wouldn't take five minutes out of her day to speak to him. He sighed. 'That fucking bitch.'

Claire Ellis and her two daughters stepped off the train at Hamilton Station. She had let the girls wag school for the day, giving the events in the doghouse time to die down a bit before they faced their teachers and peers.

Already the heat of the day had kicked in. Before it really ramped up and drained her motivation, Claire pressed on quickly and headed straight for the pawnshop. Mikaela and Kayleen were in tow, trying to keep up. Mikaela was skipping, elated that both she and her sister had been promised brand new pushbikes. Kayleen, however, was brooding; the necklace was pretty and she wished they could have kept it a few days longer. Still, she had the brooch to look at, hidden deep in her own pocket.

The walk felt like a long trek for little legs, made more difficult by the scorching heat, and Kayleen's bubbling temper wasn't helping either. She shuffled along, frowning at Mikaela, envying her enthusiasm and energy.

In the palm of Claire's hand, the green stone and diamonds of the necklace were warm – she'd been clenching it for the whole train journey. Claire was scared she'd lose the damn thing, and she didn't want to risk it falling out of her pocket or getting her handbag nicked, so she held it tight in her fist. She couldn't stop wondering how much she'd get for it. It looked bloody expensive.

As they scuttled down Beaumont Street, Claire paused outside an op-shop and stopped to glance in the window, giving her girls time to catch up.

'Can we get dumplings for lunch?' asked Mikaela.

'Yep,' said Claire. 'Let's get dumplings and sit under the fig trees in Gregson Park.'

'And ride our new bikes?'

'Yep,' Claire said. She turned swiftly on her heels and made a beeline for the pawnshop. The girls again trotted to keep up.

THIRTEEN

'My place is just up here on the left,' said Giles, pointing to a coffee-coloured house. The driveway was lined with camellia trees and standard rose bushes ran along a white panel fence. A weeping cherry tree stood in the middle of the yard. On the veranda, a wisteria vine trailed along the decorative trim under the eaves. Two comfy wooden rocking chairs sat on the front veranda, and hanging baskets were filled with a chain of hearts and begonias.

'Not a flowers type of girl?' smirked Turner. He didn't switch off the car's engine, leaving the air conditioning running. Giles had the bouquet from the hospital in her lap.

'Okay, let's cut the bullshit,' said Giles. 'Rickard is going to lodge a complaint with the LECC.'

'Shit!'

'Yeah, shit. I had a visit from a barrister last night.' Giles handed Turner the card. 'David Hemmings. Do you know him?'

'I don't know him, but I know *of* him. You hear stuff around the station. Is he on your side?'

'Yep.'

'Gosh, that's a relief.'

'But you don't know who sent him to me?'

'Nope.'

'Listen, Turner – when you arrived at the scene, what did you see?'

'Rickard was giving you CPR. You were out cold on the west side of the water trough. The victim's body was in the mud on the east side. Look, that old geezer wouldn't have had the strength to move two dead-weight bodies.'

'What do you mean?'

'I'm not saying we thought you were *dead*, Giles, but you *were* dead weight. Rickard is all skin and bones. The man must be in his seventies.'

'What the hell is going on, Turner? You were there, you would have seen Rickard drowning me.'

'Seriously, Giles, he was trying to bring you back to life. The guy was a wreck.'

'What do you mean, "a wreck"?'

'Trembling, scared. Said some guy just appeared out of nowhere, whacked you over the head, second time round he'd crept up from behind your police vehicle and cracked you again with the rock.'

'*Rickard* had the rock. It was in his hands when I was talking to him. I saw him pick some up and look at them – probably choosing which one to knock me out with.'

'No, he said those rocks weren't from his property. Farmers know their land like the back of their hand. He said he was looking at the rocks because they were volcanic, and that type of rock is way up in the mountains, in the national park, not down on the flats. On the plain, it's all limestone and slate. He thought the jillaroo must have brought them in to use as stepping stones, so she wouldn't get mud caked on her shoes when she stood around the cattle trough or the storage tank, but it confused the hell out of him. He said those rocks weren't there before.'

'And under them?' asked Giles.

'Yeah, a straw hat, like you said. Artificial flowers. Rickard couldn't explain those either.'

'I bet he couldn't.'

'He was genuinely shocked. Recoiled from them, even. Said he'd never seen them before on his property. To be honest, I think the flowers and hat disturbed him more than our victim. I watched his body language, like you taught me.'

'They belonged to his wife. The pub – at the Eaton, there were photos on the wall of Rickard's wife and she was wearing that hat and those flowers in every one of them. That's where I went yesterday.'

'We know, Giles. The ambos pointed them out to us when they picked you up.'

'So why did you let him go!'

'They were planted, Giles. The hat and the flowers. It looks like Rickard was set up. ERU bagged them up and will get an estimation on how old they are – they're being tested for prints, DNA, the whole lot – but I think someone just smeared a bit of dirt on them. To tell you the truth, that hat didn't look like it was more than three days' old, let alone thirty years. I don't believe it was his dead wife's original hat.'

'So, what? You think Rickard was set up to look like he committed the murder?'

'Yeah, I do. Or at least that the hat and flowers were planted to distract us and direct suspicion elsewhere. To waste our time. Make the case weird. Just like that gutted wallaby – whoever killed Ava Emmerson did their best to muck with the scene and fuck with our heads.'

'And I fell for it all.' Giles turned and looked out the window. She could feel her ears burning. 'Like Hansel and Gretel, I naively skipped off into the woods and ate up all the candy. And then the witch got me.'

'Could have been any of us,' said Turner.

'But it wasn't, it was me.' He gave her a sympathetic look. Giles looked away; she didn't want sympathy, she wanted answers. She toyed with the white petals from the bouquet, racking her brain for more. 'Wait, but then – explain why Rickard had my gun?'

'He could have shot you if he wanted to, Giles. Seriously. ERU swabbed him, we interviewed him, but there was no direct evidence linking him to either crime. Ava's murder or the attack on you. He said you went down, he grabbed the gun from your holster and held the perpetrator off. He was trying to get you back on your feet.'

'By my hair? So, he saw this person then?'

'Yep. The description he gave was tall, dressed in darks, bala-clava, black leather gloves.'

She blinked, shook her head, and plucked a petal from a flower, crushing it between her fingers.

'Rickard says he was trying to drag you to the back of your police vehicle, so he could get you in it, drive off to safety. But the perpetrator came back up from behind, hit you again, and pulled his own gun on Rickard. Told Rickard to grab your arms and made him help carry you to the cattle trough.'

'Well, that was nice of Rickard.'

'He had a gun on him, Giles.'

'Where was my gun then?'

'On the ground, in the mud. The guy ordered Rickard to toss it.'

'So now I'm in the water? Then what?'

'Black balaclava man holds you under, only you fight back and knock his own gun in the mud. While he looks for it, Rickard retrieves your gun and fires two shots at the perpetrator. Both hit the water trough.'

'You're kidding.'

'The old geezer has cataracts, Giles! He's almost blind. Ballsy of him, though.'

'Silly prick could have shot me instead!'

'Well, I guess he missed you both.' Turner flashed a smile. 'But the bullet holes drained most of the water out of the trough. But between that and the splashing around from dumping you in and the girl out, the surrounding animal prints are . . . well, contaminated. Ruined. They found cow prints, but not the dog print you'd spotted, and only a partial wallaby print. The fight to dump you in the trough wiped out a lot of the previous evidence.'

Giles punched the window of the car with the back of her hand. The case was a complete shambles. She realised she'd need that barrister more than ever. She turned to Turner, snatched back the business card and slipped it in her pocket.

'But it also added new evidence,' Turner continued.

'Like?'

'I believe black balaclava man is real. There's proof there were more people present than just you and Rickard.'

'*Was* there?' Giles raised her brow, still sceptical.

'There were prints everywhere in the mud. Rickard's, but also unidentified prints. Not yours. Patience, Giles. Just wait for pathology and the ERU to get back to us, then we can start doing our job.'

'Is Falkov pissed at me for leaving the scene?'

'A little,' said Turner. 'But he also feels bad that you were attacked. So does the rest of the crew. Bray said you looked beat up at the hospital. He was clearly rattled.'

'Bray was at the hospital?'

Turner nodded. 'He did a quick interview with you about what happened. You don't remember him being there?'

'Nope.'

'I wouldn't tell him, might hurt his feelings. He was seriously concerned.'

'Bray? Concerned?'

'We all were, Giles. We do believe there's someone out there that did this, and that they're possibly still in the area. There is no way Rickard could strip a girl naked and bind her up in wire like that. He's old, in poor health – his hip, his eyes. He couldn't catch a wallaby to feed himself.'

'Yeah, he does look like a baked beans man. So no charges have been laid?'

'Nothing we *could* charge him with at the moment. We'll question him some more, confirm his version of events. And then we'll need yours. When you're ready to write your statement. And the ERU are still processing the site. They're thorough, Giles. If there's further evidence to be found, they'll find it.'

'And the girl? Ava. What do we know about her?'

Turner rubbed his face and sighed. Giles wondered if they should get out of the car and go inside for a cool drink before they continued this debrief, but she'd never invited anyone from work into her house before, and she felt raw and exposed enough as it was.

Turner flicked open his notebook and scanned his scribble. 'Twenty-three years old. About 160 centimetres tall, approximately 68 kilos, slight build. Former local, had been living in Orange for about eight or nine months until she split up with her boyfriend. She returned home to Muswellbrook just over three months ago, moved back in with her parents. She was a good kid. Stable life, nice friends, liked horse riding. Jobs in cafés, sales assistance, but her main experience was on various cattle stations. Apparently she liked working for Rickard. There's no obvious motive for her murder.'

'Does Rickard have any connection to her family?'

'Nope.'

'Owe each other money?'

'Just income from the work she does on his farm. Not the kind of thing she was writing up invoices for.'

'This isn't a tax evasion case, Turner, it's a murder.'

'I know, I know, I was just saying.'

'She'd clearly been there a while, why wasn't she reported missing days ago?'

'Parents said she liked to sleep out in her swag at the Washpools at Towarri National Park, or out at Lake Glenbawn. She would have a night or two under the stars, then a few nights at her parents'. They said she came back to town because the break-up with her boyfriend had been bad. She liked the peace, sleeping out. Her parents only started to worry when she didn't come home for three nights in a row – normally she was gone one, maybe two nights at the most.'

'A girl alone sleeping in the bush? Don't you think that's odd?' asked Giles.

'Apparently she was a Girl Guide. And she was a jillaroo, after all.'

'What about the boyfriend? Was the break-up mutual?'

'Dunno yet. We've started looking into all her social media. Facebook, texts, emails, Instagram. Setting up a timeline, her last known sightings, who she hung around with.'

Giles nodded.

'We are waiting for the pathologist to give us cause and time of death. We believe a few days, but I'm still waiting to hear.'

'Have her parents identified the body then?'

'Yeah, it was ugly to watch. We only showed them the tattoo on her wrist. Too distressing otherwise. They confirmed it was her. We took a DNA from them to be safe.'

'The tattoo – what was it?'

'Two bluebirds. On her right wrist.'

'You saw her? Fully laid out?'

'Yeah. Giles, I've seen fatalities at accidents, but . . . Ava was off the scale gruesome. Worst degradation the team said they'd ever seen. The way she was humiliated – the particular attention to detail, displaying her body. I had to sit down – it made me dizzy. Falkov seemed more pissed at me than at you.'

'Was that your first time attending an autopsy?'

Turner couldn't meet her eye. 'Yeah.'

'You won't ever get used to it. But that's a good thing. Did you find her dog? The border collie?'

'Safe at home, with her parents. She left it with them before heading out.'

Giles frowned. She hadn't expected the dog to still be alive and in the picture. 'Then did the ERU get the animal hair in the barbed-wire fence?'

'Ah, shit, nope.' Turner raised a brow. 'I don't know, I didn't point it out to them. Sorry.'

'Then go back and get it. Show it to Michael at the veterinary hospital, see if he can tell us something – what animal, what breed. We can give it to ERU later, but let's fast-track this.'

'The vet?'

'I know him, he'll look at it quicker than the lab. Tell him I sent you.'

'No worries, Giles. I'll go back to the scene right away. But let me help you inside first.'

'Nah, I'm all good. Turner?'

'Yeah?'

'Thanks for saving me.'

'No worries.'

'And Turner?'

'Yeah?'

'Next time you're on duty, shave before you come in. I've got stubble rash on my top lip.'

'You got a concussion, dehydration, you nearly drowned, there's a murderer on the loose, the LECC is after you – and your problem is 'stache rash? A bit of beard burn?'

'Just shave, mate. It stings.'

Giles didn't wait for Turner's response as she climbed out of the car, cradling her bouquet of flowers close to her chest. The heat outside the car consumed her, making her stop and feel it sink into her skin, into her shoulders and arms. She nudged the car door shut with her knee, nodded goodbye to Turner as he drove off, and then walked up the driveway to her home.

In one of the hanging baskets, she fished around for her spare key and opened the front door. She looked past the entry, across to her lounge room and then down the hallway, feeling the pull of her bedroom. There she could curl up, pull the doona over her head, and let her emotions seep out.

FOURTEEN

The pawnbroker in Hamilton pulled up the Jewellers Association of Australia's website on his computer and lazily scrolled through the site looking for a photo of the necklace on his counter, not bothering to read any of the posts. Hamilton was a long way from Scone – far enough away that he couldn't really be stuffed reading the entries. The woman seemed believable, and she was happy to give her name and show him ID. With two little girls and her cheap nail polish, she looked like any other early-thirties single mum hocking off the family jewels to help cover the rent.

As he half-heartedly went through the normal procedure of acquiring an item of jewellery, he knew the necklace would sit on display for less than a week before being sold. The diamonds, emerald and gold were all real, and a necklace like that in the window would be a way to draw people into his shop. He wanted the necklace, and the woman wanted to sell it; it was a win–win. He counted out the cash and, five minutes after the woman and kids had left, the necklace was proudly on display, marked up to twice the price he'd paid for it.

———

By midday, Claire and her girls were heading home. On the train, Kayleen and Mikaela ate steamed shrimp and pork dumplings. They were overexcited and noisy. Passengers cringed at their antics and wrinkled their noses at the smell of pork and lemongrass that filled the air. They did their best to ignore the girls – some passengers moved into the next carriage, others simply rolled their eyes and stared out the window.

The girls' new bikes obstructed the entry doors, making it difficult for passengers to step on and off the train. Their new helmets swung on the handlebars. Mikaela's helmet was covered in Disney princesses, while Kayleen's was more boyish: red and black, with flames up the side.

Claire knew she should have been pissed at Kayleen for stealing the necklace, but her anger had quickly dissolved into greed when she looked more closely at the emerald stone and the pavé of small diamonds encircling it.

The devil's luck, thought Claire. The opportunity outweighed the moral dilemma. She didn't remember making a pact with the devil, but she'd still take the astounding good fortune.

In the end, they had skipped Gregson Park, with Claire instead setting up an afternoon playdate with another girl from Kayleen's class. Kayleen wanted to ride with her new friend and show off her bike at Highbrook Park, back in Muswellbrook. Considering Kayleen had been a bit short on friends lately, Claire had relented and arranged for the kids to meet.

Claire popped a hot dumpling into her mouth and smirked. For once in her life things were going well. She had a new top from a real shop, with the brand and price label still hanging off it, and a wad of cash in her wallet – a big wad of cash. That necklace had paid up way more than she'd ever imagined.

She stared at her daughters' new bikes, then grinned. Yep, life just couldn't get any better.

The air smelled of Dencorub. Giles lay on the lounge under a pile of baby-blue throw pillows. She was stiff-necked and sore. The hot water bottle was now lukewarm. She should have gone to bed, but it was only early afternoon and the case was swimming around in her head.

She had three missed calls from Falkov, and three messages from him on her voicemail. She didn't listen to them. Giles wanted him to think she was sleeping the afternoon away – she was worried he might put her on a couple of days' leave, bring her in to answer questions, or ask her to write up her statement. And, right at the moment, she didn't have any answers for him, or at least not in the correct order. Besides, she had a whole bunch of questions of her own to ask first.

Giles's memories of the previous morning remained jumbled. Her timeline was all out of whack. On the coffee table sat a pad and pen with notes in dot points. One dot point for each event she remembered, in chronological order, from the time she arrived to the time she dashed off to Eaton Pub. Half the dot points were scribbled out or had arrows moving them to elsewhere on the page, and the other half had question marks that she had circled again and again until the pen had cut through the page.

She had to write down exactly what had happened, not what she *thought* had happened. But she couldn't get the sequence right. Giles wanted to get back to the scene and retrace her steps, to see if she could get it all clear in her head, but she also wanted to do a bit of homework before talking on tape or writing up her statement.

She knew her version was not the same as Rickard's or Turner's. No one's account of what happened yesterday matched hers. Aside from events out of sequence, there were things she didn't remember at all, like punching Rickard or gunfire. What was troubling her most was why someone would want to return to the scene a few days after killing Ava Emmerson, unless they realised they'd missed something; or left something behind; or wanted to leave something behind – like a hat.

The hat and flowers bothered her. It was definitely a reference to Mrs Rickard, though she could see that it was doubtful it was the original hat from thirty years earlier. But even if Mr Rickard wasn't responsible, it still meant a person who knew his history was. She'd have to get a list of Rickard's acquaintances – people he knew but wouldn't buy a packet of biscuits for.

On her personal MacBook, she started to search online for straw hats like the one Mrs Rickard wore. There was an abundance of them online, in all shapes and sizes. As she scrolled through the results, before long she found a lady's classic raffia hat that looked like a perfect match. Delivery would only take two days. Giles moved the hat to the shopping cart and paid. Typed in Muswellbrook Police Station as the delivery address, and then all she needed to do next was see if the store made good on their 'within two days' promise.

Artificial flowers were easier to purchase. Dozens of online shops offered next-day delivery. Baby's breath, roses, hydrangeas, they were all available. But the hat was a good place to start, and Giles felt satisfied she had got the ball rolling.

Stretching and rolling out the kink in her neck, she picked up David Hemmings' business card. Everything about the barrister looked expensive, even his bloody card had embossing and gold lettering. She feared if she paid him a visit at his office, he'd tell her to step away from the case and not have any more contact with her

team until the LECC debacle was sorted. But lots of police officers were investigated by the LECC while merrily carrying on with
their duties, so why was such a big deal being made out of this complaint? Did Rickard have connections in the force? Or was it her
connection to her father? A blight on Benjamin more than herself?
The thing was, she was telling the truth – they just didn't like her
version of it.

So, calling Falkov back or visiting the barrister didn't seem like
good ideas at the moment.

She did want to know more about the barrister, however. Giles's
curiosity was niggling, and the best person to fill in those blanks was
Benjamin Giles.

Curiosity killed a cat, but satisfaction brought it back, Giles
thought. *Fuck the cat, scratch the itch.*

Even though there was a drought and water restrictions were in
place, Giles took a long ten-minute shower. She needed the hot
water to run down her spine and the back of her thighs, she needed
to feel some relief from the aches in her body. She rubbed the bar
of soap into her calf muscles and tried to massage out the stiffness.
Then she lathered up and scrubbed her neck, trying to wash away
the thought of someone's hands around her throat.

She dried off and pulled on a fresh set of clothes, tossing the
police tracksuit into the washing basket, then wondering if it should
go straight into the bin.

When she tried to pull her hair up into a twisted bun, her scalp
ached, and for the first time it was obvious to her just how hard
her hair had been yanked as she was dragged along the ground.
The thought alone was bringing on another headache. Giles let her
wet hair drop and instead gently ran a comb through it, avoiding

her scalp. Before she left the bathroom, she dabbed a little concealer around her dark, swollen eye and winked at herself in the mirror.

Thirty minutes later, she was walking down the corridor of Merton Court, heading straight to her father's room, the last door at the end of the hall.

'Gee-wiz, what are you doing here, sweetheart? You should be resting up at the hospital.' Benjamin gripped the arms of the chair and tried to lever himself upright.

'Don't get up, Dad.'

Benjamin let his body drop back into the chair and grimaced, more at the sight of his daughter than the struggle with his illness.

'I got out of hospital this morning, was given the all clear. I've been out cold on the lounge all afternoon.' It was a small fib that saved her having to explain herself further.

'Falkov said you took a nasty hit to your head.'

'Two nasty hits, actually. But I'm okay, Dad. Popped in to show you I'm fine. See, I'm up and about. Nothing to worry about.'

'Plenty to worry about, by the sounds of it. You'll get him, luv. But you need to rest up, you don't want to jump back in too quick.'

Giles sat down on the edge of her father's bed and looked around the room. Benjamin wasn't one for nostalgia; there were no personal effects on display, just his slippers lined up by the door. The rest of the room was arranged in a similarly orderly fashion.

'Thanks for the flowers,' she said.

'What flowers?'

'You didn't send flowers to the hospital?'

'Nup. I would have sent a bottle of whisky before sending flowers.'

Giles grinned. Yeah, that sounded more like her father.

'I sent you a barrister instead.'

'So that was you!'

'He can guide you with the LECC, steer you in the right direction.'

'Should have gone with the whisky idea and saved your money.'

'It's off the books. Just some legal advice and some sensible tips on how to answer any questions. You want to solve this case but keep your record clean. If anyone can help you navigate the next few days, it'll be him.'

'Still would have preferred the whisky, Dad.'

'I think I should be sending a case of whisky to your whole team – that jillaroo sounded like a frightful sight. What sick bastard is out there binding girls' legs together with barbed wire and drowning them in cattle troughs?'

'Well, you sure know a lot about the case.'

'Falkov.'

'Hmm. What else did he tell you?'

'Saw the photos. Looked over the list of collected evidence. Saw a picture of the bruise where you punched Rickard.'

'I'm not lying about *not* punching him, it's just that I don't *remember* punching him.' Giles looked down at her hand. She curled it into a fist and rubbed at her knuckles. They *were* tender to touch, but then her whole body was sore. Her hand ached as much as her back, shoulders, ribs and skull.

'Sweetheart, I just want you to be in the clear. We're not saying you're lying, but Falkov wants you to look credible. If you stay on this case, you have to have all your facts clear, correct, and no gaps. That punch – the explanation just needs to be worded in a way that shows your response suited the circumstances. That means you're going to have to remember hitting him.'

'Thinking Rickard was trying to strangle me might be cause for exercising force, don't you think? That punch was both bloody reasonable and necessary. How's that for a defence?'

'There you go. And your barrister will help you word it when the time comes. Look, I'm paying him to give you solid advice on how to tread your way through anything to do with the LECC. Those bastards are thorough. I don't want you getting rattled, that's all. The LECC might look at the Tactical Options Model and take into consideration Rickard's age, size and fitness compared to yours.'

'I don't think that old prick is as frail as everyone says he is. He managed to drag me a fair way and then dump me in a water trough.'

'He had help with that. Didn't do it on his own. And he did it at gunpoint.'

'Did he? Really? Because the only people I remember being there are Rickard and me.'

Giles looked away and out the window. She needed space to think and she didn't want her dad trying to read her face. The barrister was right: if they thought she was a lying cop, that was career destroying. But a cop who couldn't remember things somehow seemed worse.

'Dad, I just don't remember anyone else being there aside from Rickard. It was him I saw holding a rock.'

'You didn't see the other prick because he crept up on yah.'

Giles nodded and turned back to her father. 'But after I went down, when I was on the ground, it was Rickard's face I saw.'

'It's not unusual for memories to not align with the true events. It was a high-stress moment. Give it time, things will come back to you, slowly. Don't force it.'

Giles pulled David Hemmings' business card from her pocket and handed it to her father. 'How do you know him?'

'Same way I know everyone around here – through the force. He's good, luv. He's the best.'

Benjamin handed back the card. Slipping it into her pocket, Giles knew she'd be using it. Otherwise she would have dropped it in the bin.

'Thanks, Dad. Maybe I'll pop in on him. We'll see.' Giles looked around the room for an open bottle of wine, but nothing was in sight. 'Where are you hiding your grog?'

'Under me pillow.' Benjamin thumbed towards his bed.

Giles pulled down the bedcover and flipped the pillow over. They both laughed as she unscrewed the lid off the bottle and started pouring drinks.

'How do you keep sneaking this stuff in?'

'Falkov, again.'

'You two are thick as thieves.' She handed a tumbler three-quarters full to her dad.

'We're mates. We worked together for thirty years, until my body clapped out – but my wits are perfect. We chat about cases and I try to shed some light.'

'I'm sure there'd be a few things you would be able to shed some light on.' Giles meant her mother, but Benjamin didn't hear the shift in tone – or if he did, he ignored it.

'It makes me feel useful. What else is there for me to do?'

'Do you and Falkov talk about me?' Giles took a gulp of red wine and wished it was something stronger.

'You *are* part of this case. So, yeah, you come up in the conversation.'

'Falkov sent me to a drowning, Dad. On my own. Would a mate send your daughter to a drowning?'

'Luv, you're going to come across a lot of ugly shit on the force. You can't pick and choose. You can't expect not to be put on a case because it might hurt your feelings. You're a cop. You've gotta keep your personal life separate.'

'Bullshit.'

'Well, you're going to have to learn how. If not this job, what else would you do?'

'Dunno.' Giles took a measured swipe. 'As a cop yourself, I would have thought you would have had a flood evacuation plan. That when the rains hit you'd —'

'There was *nothing* personal about Falkov sending you.'

'Falkov knew who Rickard was. His history, his backstory. Rickard lost his wife on the same day, to the same flood, and the same river that took Mum. Falkov knew all that.'

Benjamin shrugged.

'Why do you always clam up at the mention of Mum?'

'Geez, did you come back to Muswellbrook in my dying days to comfort me or bloody torture me?'

'What do you think, Dad? I wouldn't be here if it wasn't for you.'

'You know, you put shit on this town, but I built a life here. My friends, my career, my home. Your mother's buried here. I sent you off to boarding school to give you a better education, a head-start in life, but all it's done is turn you into a snob. Don't look down your nose at this place. You can't afford to be snooty, bloody swanning around all high and mighty. Your history is written all over this town.'

Benjamin was shaking, he needed a moment to catch his breath. 'Dad —'

'If you were a better daughter, you wouldn't let me waste good wine.' Benjamin held up a trembling hand and Giles took the tumbler of red wine from it, before it went all over the floor.

A year ago, when Giles had returned to the Hunter Valley, she knew she'd either need to get to the bottom of her mother's death or let it rest for good. After a few months settling in, she ached to clear the air. To get the full story from her dad. No child can sleep soundly when their story's not been read to the end.

Giles had originally thought about approaching the National Archives, telling them the circumstances, requesting her mother's file, but she knew it was best to avoid the police altogether – the news that she was poking around would find its way back to her father eventually. Instead, she had found the coroner who'd had jurisdiction at the time. He was old, retired, but he still had his memory. He loved Earl Grey tea and long, *long* chats.

He'd explained to Giles that her mother's death only looked suspicious in the beginning. Emilia Giles had made no attempt to fight the raging river – there were no torn nails, no sign she had made any effort to reach the riverbank. But then, as a young woman who had only migrated to Australia from Italy two years earlier, she hadn't grown up on Aussie beaches, or swimming in dams and rivers. It was possible she had never swum before. Perhaps she had sucked in the first mouthful of water, panicked, and drowned.

The coroner had explained, 'Your father didn't want your mother's body cut up. We did X-rays and saw lungs full of fluid, ruled it an accidental drowning, so she could be buried intact.'

'You didn't think to question the small cuts on her shins and ankles?' Giles had asked. 'Nobody thought to query why she had fled the safety of her house to begin with? Why she was barefoot if she had planned to leave?' Giles went on to explain her concerns further and hinted that she thought his evaluation may have been a bit iffy – a bit *inexact*? Partly as an apology, partly as a favour, the old man had pulled some strings and requested the full files be taken from storage. He'd handed a copy to Giles, and she had gifted him a Wedgwood teapot to show her gratitude.

Since then, Giles had looked over the police files of her mother's death a million times. The incident report was so neat and clean, it barely gave any explanation. The officer who had signed off the report, still just up-and-coming in the force, had been a young Falkov.

Since returning from Sydney, Giles had realised it was easy enough to *plan* to confront someone, but actually doing it was another thing altogether. She needed to work up the courage to get the conversation going, and with her father's illness, finding the right moment was proving more difficult than she'd imagined.

And, maybe, she was also a little scared of what she would discover. Her mother's death was a Pandora's Box. Was she really ready to look inside?

Giles stayed with her father until his tremors had calmed down. He had that punched-in-the-guts look, and she figured she probably did too. When it was time to leave, they both looked fatigued. She wanted desperately to reach out and hold him in her arms, hug him. Only Benjamin wasn't a hugger, and there was enough discomfort in the room as it was. Instead, she kissed his forehead and said goodbye.

FIFTEEN

The heat silenced the small town of Denman.

Tin roofs clanged as they expanded and gave off a hazy sizzle, like barbeque hot plates awaiting a sausage. Parked cars baked. Tree limbs drooped while birds sat in silence along the other branches, too hot to chirp. Neighbourhood dogs lay sprawled, panting, seeking shade under awnings, trees and backyard sheds. It was too hot to do bloody anything. The last time it had been this hot was back in the seventies. The weatherman should have turned up on the telly in flared jeans and a denim jacket with a peace sign on his lapel.

In the local public school, pupils sat still with the overhead fans whizzing pointlessly above them. Homes had their air conditioners groaning. Barmaids in the only two pubs in town rested their elbows on the counter, watching extra kegs chill, knowing some thirsty buggers would be coming in that afternoon. Volunteers with the rural fire service stared out at the surrounding mountains, looking for smoke. Farmers cursed, watching their crops cook. Cattle rested their snouts in water troughs, but didn't drink. Nothing was moving, but everything was working overtime to make it through the heat.

Denman had a population of less than two thousand, although it had more visitors a year than it ever had residents. With the tourist trade passing through on winery tours, the town had become a must-see on any visitor's map. Ogilvie Street had once been mainly agricultural-supply shops and essentials stores, but now the main street was groaning with cafés, giftware and local artisan produce.

Walking down Ogilvie Street, the Denman Hotel, an old heritage-listed building, beckoned to Giles. Her face softened. While she still felt frustrated with Benjamin, and tormented by the scorching sun, the sight of the pub soothed her. The pub had been one of her favourite places to visit as a kid. She and Benjamin would sit on the wraparound veranda, Giles sipping lemonade while her father drank a beer.

Now, it was like the building was calling out to her, *Hello, old friend.* And when Giles thought no one was looking, she lifted her hand and gave a sheepish wave back as she passed. She had decided to seek refuge from the sun in the newsagency, knowing it would have air conditioning.

Inside, perched upon a stool behind the counter, the owner was reading a romance novel. It was mid-afternoon and there was no one else in the newsagent aside from Giles. The owner hardly raised her head to acknowledge her presence.

So much for country hospitality.

Giles recognised the woman from primary school, but it was obvious the woman didn't know her. Her husband came out from the back room, and Giles remembered she'd kissed him once, a long time ago; his hands had felt like sandpaper as he clumsily tried to slide them under her top. She smirked and looked away, feeling awkward, her face a little flushed, even though she was no longer known to the husband or wife, having been long forgotten.

A stack of newspapers sat beside the greeting cards stand and Giles picked up the top one. Ava's death was on the front page, but it was only a short column, and there was no photo. The jillaroo was not named. It was obvious to Giles that the Police Media Unit hadn't given out the whole story. Probably because there were still two conflicting versions: Giles claiming Rickard was a murderer who had attacked her, and Rickard claiming the actual murderer was still running around in the national park. It was all a bloody shit tangle of a story. The PMU would have given the press only the basics, not least because they didn't know much themselves.

The article reported a tragic suspected drowning on a property outside of Muswellbrook. A homicide investigation was underway, as police had not yet determined how exactly the girl died. A crime scene had been established and forensic crews were investigating. None of the gruesome details were reported.

She clicked her tongue. *God, once they get the full story, they'll make the headline massive.*

She dropped the newspaper back on the pile and left the shop.

Next door to the newsagency was the florist, with buckets of roses and hydrangeas displayed in the window. The tubs of flowers caught Giles's eye and she popped inside. At the counter, a middle-aged woman was curling ribbon around a colourful bouquet.

'Can I help you?'

Giles smiled. What she really wanted to know was if the woman had sent a bouquet of white blooms to Muswellbrook Hospital, and if so, who had ordered them. Instead, she said, 'Pretty colours in that bunch.'

'Gerberas. Not my favourites, but they are colourful. They're a happy colour.'

'Huh, that's interesting. What would an all-white bouquet mean?'

'Normally you'd use that to express sympathy.'

'Ha! That's funny.' Giles raised a brow. 'I was wondering – do you sell plastic flowers?'

'Absolutely not.' The woman screwed up her face. 'But if you tell me what you're after, I'm sure I can offer you a fresh bunch that'd do the job.'

'No, I really was hoping for artificial,' Giles said, then quickly added, 'They're not for me, I'm just looking for a friend.'

'Well, I suppose you could try the gift shop down the road.'

Giles thanked her and made her way down the street. With its heritage charm, the gift shop was a drawcard for both tourists and locals. Inside, the artificial flowers were as expensive as the fresh ones in the florist shop had been. There were roses and baby's breath, but the tub labelled hydrangeas, like the flowers in the photos of Mrs Rickard's straw hat, was empty. Giles grabbed a sprig of baby's breath and a few artificial roses.

At the counter, Giles put on a casual persona and asked the teenage shop assistant if there were any artificial hydrangeas out back, or had they completely sold out?

'You're the second person who's asked for those.' The girl's eyes ran all over Giles's face, taking in the bruising, the swelling, the attempt at covering up the black eye.

'Am I?' Giles ignored her inquisitive expression and pressed on. 'Who was the other person?'

'Some guy. Cute for an old fella. You know, he had swag. Smelled good. He was smexy!'

'Would you recognise this smexy man again?'

'Maybe.' She smirked. 'If I smelled him. Why?'

'Dunno. But if he ever asked me out on a date, I'd know to steer clear of him. I mean, artificial flowers? Yuck!'

The shop assistant didn't laugh. She probably figured Giles for a woman who had plenty of man trouble. Giles made a mental note to put her on the interview list. Turner could get a full description, something more than 'old but cute'. She looked around for CCTV cameras, but was disappointed, although not surprised, that there weren't any.

On the counter were Palm Beach scented candles and for a brief moment Giles thought of Sydney, of Palm Beach and Barrenjoey House at lunchtimes, of the ocean and summer days swimming in the salty sea. Muswellbrook couldn't smell any less of coconuts and lime. Giles picked up the sea-salt fragrance candle and reached for her wallet; it would be the closest she'd get to Sydney for a while.

The last shop Giles stepped into was the chemist. She needed more heat rub and another pack of Panadol – her head was starting to thump again. At the counter, sunglasses, caps and hats sat on a rotating stand and Giles froze.

Jesus.

On the display sat a straw hat that was identical to Mrs Rickard's. Giles now had a second shop assistant to add to her interview list. She didn't want to ask any questions herself that would alert the sales team or implant a memory, nor did she want to let on she was a cop and that her questions were part of a police investigation. She'd leave it to her team to ask questions. Keep it official. Keep it neat and clean. She crossed her fingers they would remember if anyone had purchased a straw hat in the last few days, and wondered, if they did, would the cashier give the same description: 'cute for an old guy'? There had been no need to order a hat online, when it was right there and available to purchase in the store. Giles grabbed the hat, some Deep Heat and a packet of painkillers, and even though her body ached, she couldn't wipe the grin off her face.

SIXTEEN

Sticky Pete sat in his wreck of a car outside the police station, at a loss as to what to do with himself. He couldn't drive around town to kill time – he didn't have the luxury of burning through what little petrol he had left, he still needed enough to get himself back home to Singleton. His phone battery was dead, so calling his missus and asking her what he should do was out of the question. Besides, she'd spit chips when she realised that after two days he still hadn't spoken to Detective Giles and the issue wasn't any closer to being resolved.

Pete scratched at his flaked hands. All this worrying was bringing on a headache and flaring up his eczema. He was hot, thirsty, hungry, and his own putrid smell was beginning to turn his stomach. The inside of the car was hot and smelled like damp cat. He rolled down the window and nearly choked on the fresh air as he gulped it in. He squeezed his nails into his palm where it itched, his skin red and blistering.

The thought of returning to jail filled his gut with despair. He kept telling himself that crying about it wouldn't fix anything, but he couldn't stop his eyes from welling up.

———

Highbrook Park was famous for its giant slippery dip, which was named Larry the Lizard. The structure of the lizard stood over 10 metres tall, and Larry's 70-metre long tongue was a slide that sent kids zooming all the way back down to the ground with echoing squeals. Kids would toss sand down the slide and rip up cardboard boxes to use as mats, which made the slide faster and scarier; it also made a mess that the council had to clean up on a daily basis.

The park was popular, offering bubblers, picnic benches and barbeque facilities. It had other play equipment, including a flying fox, and even a learn-to-ride bicycle track.

When Kayleen's new friend Sara got out of school, the two of them met up and they spent the afternoon riding their bikes along the track, disobeying the miniature STOP and GIVE WAY signs, pretending to drive around town and having imaginary bike accidents and roadside arguments as to who was at fault. Both girls were loud and obnoxious, scaring away the smaller kids with their role-playing of road rage, street races and fatal collisions.

But as the afternoon wore on, Kayleen began to get tired of the game. The pretend crashes were scratching her new bike and the plastic grips on her handlebars were scuffed where they'd grazed the concrete.

'I'm thirsty. Race you to the bubblers,' Sara yelled, and she dropped her bike to the ground. The back wheel was still spinning as she tore off, running towards the toilet block. Kayleen lowered her bike gently, pissed that her friend had got a head start – that was cheating. Still, she didn't want to lose, so she faked a laugh and ran as fast as she could to catch up.

Pete decided to wait it out a couple more hours and then return to the station. Surely Detective Giles would be there by then and he could sort everything out. Until then, he could get some fresh air back at the kiddies' park. Take a piss and have a drink of water. Wash his face and gargle the stench from his mouth. Take another shot at crawling out of the shit hole he had got himself into.

At the bubblers, Sara slurped water in great gulps and let it dribble down her chin and neck. Kayleen felt thirsty just watching and wanted desperately to push her friend out of the way so she could have a turn.

'Move, Sara. Let me have a drink. I'm hot.' Kayleen gently bumped her hip into the side of her new friend.

The girls took turns drinking, making it into a competition of who could keep going the longest, who was the thirstiest, who had the greater willpower to ignore their bloating stomach.

'You're not drinking! You're spitting it back out!'

'Am not!' said Kayleen. She took a mouthful of water and spat it up into the air like a fountain, sending both girls into giggles.

Their full stomachs ached, and as they sat down on a log at the edge of the car park, they tussled for prime position. All afternoon they had been testing each other and their nascent friendship, and yet they still seemed to click. Kayleen wanted desperately for it to last.

'If I give you something, would that mean we'll stay friends no matter what?' asked Kayleen.

'Depends what it is?' said Sara.

Kayleen slipped her hand into her shorts pocket and when she withdrew her clenched fist, Sara looked greedily at it.

'It's precious. Valuable. Like really, really expensive.'

'How expensive?'

'You can buy bikes and clothes and takeaway food.'

'I've got a bike.'

'A better bike.'

'What's wrong with my bike?'

'Nothing,' said Kayleen. 'You can buy whatever you want, or just keep it.'

'What is it?'

Kayleen uncurled her fingers and handed the brooch to Sara. She instantly felt regret.

'It's beautiful.' Sara stared at the green stone and surrounding diamonds. 'Is it real?'

'Yeah, those are real diamonds.'

'Bullshit!' said Sara, and the curse made Kayleen look over her shoulder to see if any adults had heard the swear.

'Shh, my mum will go nuts if she hears you. But it's real, no joking, no . . .' she glanced again before whispering, 'bullshit.'

'I'll keep it. I don't want to buy anything with it. We'll be best friends forever.'

Kayleen was startled at first by the idea of a forever friend, then her face stretched into a broad smile. 'Forever?' A feeling of relief and lightness overtook her feeling of regret for handing over the brooch.

Sara's face was full of promise. 'Forever and ever,' she said.

Kayleen's younger sister, Mikaela, was playing on the nearby flying fox. But her mother's patience had worn out – it had been a long day with the morning train trip to Newcastle to cash in the necklace and then the afternoon at the park, plus the damn heat.

'Ten more minutes, okay, then we'll make a move and head home,' Claire said.

Mikaela huffed but smiled. The sun caught the caramel colour of her hair, the same shade as her eyes. The kid was cute as a button. Little freckles on her nose. Claire smoothed the child's fringe.

She thought, *I love you*. Instead, she said, 'Ten minutes, I mean it.'

The kid melted Claire's heart, but she couldn't help feeling pissed that Kayleen's new friend had turned up on her own. Was she really expected to babysit someone else's child? Claire had expected to sit on a park bench, smoke, and gossip with another adult, maybe show off her new top. But instead, because the other two little cows didn't want to play with Mikaela, she'd been left to push her youngest on the swings and flying fox, watch her slide down the tongue of the giant lizard, clean dog shit off the bottom of her shoe.

'What's for dinner?' the little girl asked.

'Dunno.' Claire shrugged.

'Can we get takeaway?'

The mother frowned. But she realised that, for the first time, she didn't have to do any calculations in her head, weighing up milk and bread and smokes against takeout. Her face warmed in a rare moment of cheeriness. 'You know what? Yeah, sure. Let's get fish and chips for dinner.'

'Can we?' Mikaela was beside herself.

'Sure. Go get the girls, tell them to collect their bikes, we're going home.'

'Can Sara stay for dinner?'

Claire grinned and lifted her hand, gently pinching the chin of her youngest daughter. Even though the girls had ignored her all afternoon, Mikaela still had it in her heart to invite Kayleen's bitchy new friend to supper.

'If she wants,' said Claire, and Mikaela ran off to gather them up.

The girls pulled up on their bikes abruptly, squeezing the brakes tight to make them skid.

'I'm not buying you new tyres, Kayleen,' snapped her mother.

'Mum's taking us for fish and chips,' said Mikaela. She wanted to tell her older sister to stop mucking around or she'd ruin the day and they'd miss out on takeout.

'*Really?*' asked Kayleen.

'Yeah.' Claire turned to Sara, who was starting to get on her nerves. 'Wanna come?'

'Nar, I'll ride home, thanks. Mum said come back home in time for tea.'

Kayleen's mother hesitated. 'You okay to ride there by yourself?'

The girl only lived a few blocks away, but the fish and chip shop was in the opposite direction and Claire wanted to beat the rush – at dinnertime it got packed out with all the miners and tradies buying up the best pieces of battered fish. Besides, the kid had turned up on her own.

'You sure you're alright?' she asked again.

'Yeah, it's all good.'

Claire nodded. She felt better for having pressed Sara once more, but was also relieved. 'Come on then, girls.'

'See yah tomorrow?' asked Kayleen.

'Maybe,' said Sara, non-committal. She scooted off on her bike.

Kayleen instantly longed for her brooch again – she felt bereft. She took her mother's hand and pushed her new bike with the other. Mikaela rode ahead, but she was still trying to get the hang of riding a bike – she was wobbly, her legs out, ready to stop herself from falling. As they headed off towards the fish and chip shop, they didn't even bother to look back at Sara.

Sara had no desire to leave the park. She wanted to keep riding the mini learn-to-ride track, even if she had to do it on her own.

The park was emptying out, and soon she'd have the place to herself.

She also wanted to be left alone to gaze at her new brooch. She wanted to hold it up to the sun, see it sparkle, and she didn't want to share that experience with anyone else.

Pete knew that if the detective hadn't returned by evening, he *could* bear to stay another night in Muswellbrook, sleeping on the back seat of his car, because first thing next morning his pension payment would be in his bank account. He could have a midmorning beer for breakfast, recharge his phone at the pub, and top up his petrol tank for the drive back to Singleton. *Surely* by then Detective Giles would have returned to the police station. He would get everything sorted out and, when he got home, he and his missus could have a good belly laugh about the last two days. It would make for a ripper yarn down the pub, and if he bumped into the prick who'd sold him the ring, he'd thump him one on the nose.

It was late afternoon and the park was near empty. Families were packing up cars, some teenagers were strolling towards the footy field with a rugby league ball. Aside from a jogger and someone walking their dog, Pete was the only one in the park.

The toilet block had already been locked up for the night, so Sticky Pete took a discreet piss by the trunk of a stringybark tree. Some of it hit the tip of his shoe because he kept looking over his shoulder to see if anyone was watching – or, worse, filming him on their phone. Pete had no interest or time for that sort of crap, but he knew enough to be careful, he didn't want to end up on the world-wide bloody web. *Fucking internet.*

On the other side of the toilet block, Pete washed his face and gargled water from the bubblers. He swished the water around in his mouth and spat it back out on the dirt. His mouth felt fresher already. He tried his best to smooth back his hair and straighten out his shirt collar. The breeze had picked up and it cooled him down. He was starting to feel better, cleaner, cooler, calmer. He'd got his shit together and his situation was almost all worked out. Everything was going to be okay.

Taking a leisurely stroll by the giant slide, Pete practised in his head the words he'd say to Detective Giles. He knew he wasn't clever and got muddled up – that was why it was important for him to rehearse. Cops made him nervous at the best of times, but he had to clear his name. He hadn't broken into anyone's home, he'd bought that ring at the pub, and that was not a crime, at least not when you didn't know the item was hot. No matter what the detective said, people bought second-hand stuff all the time off the web-net. Why was a pub any different?

Pete rolled his argument over and over in his head until he felt he could say it calmly, without losing his temper. He wasn't going back down to the police station until he could state his case like a respectable, mature adult.

While rehearsing his argument, he spotted a little girl riding in circles on the bike track. As she weaved around the circuit, riding past him, he caught sight of something on her shirt, glistening in the afternoon sun. An emerald brooch circled in diamonds.

Jesus! Fuck me!

Life wasn't out to get Sticky Pete; it had just dropped the answer to all his problems right in his lap.

He made his way towards her. If he could creep up just a bit closer, he could confirm the brooch was the same design as the ring. He didn't want to spook the girl, but he had no battery left on his mobile phone to call the cops and tell them the bloody thief was riding a pushbike around the kiddies' park.

Should he flat out ask her where she got it? What her name was, where she lived? Did she pinch it? Did her father? Was her dad the one who'd sold him the ring? He wasn't going to let her out of his sight, that was for sure.

As the girl started to leave the riding track, Pete followed her up towards the flying fox. She dumped her bike in the patch of bark and started to climb the ladder up the tower. He took a gamble and approached her. 'Hey, you. I like your bike. What's your name?'

'What would you like it to be?' smirked Sara, looking down at him.

Pete blinked. 'What?'

Sara laughed and reached out for the bars of the flying fox. She kicked off the edge of the tower and zipped along the cable. At the end of the ride, she dropped to the ground, then walked back to where he stood. There was a bounce in her step, a touch of bravado, as if she was ready to give Pete a mouthful if he came anywhere near her.

'I just wanted to know your name,' said Pete.

'Fuck off, that's me name. Fuck – F-U-C-K – and off's the surname. Want me to spell that for yah too?'

Sticky Pete was taken aback, and the girl giggled at his flustered expression.

'Whatever happened to sugar and spice? You should be a lady.'

'Fuck off, paedo. You should be in prison.'

Pete felt his blood pressure rise. His itchy inflamed hands curled into fists. This foul-mouthed little mole was supposed to be his get-out-of-jail card. She could help him, but instead she was a pint-sized smartarse giving him lip.

Pete looked at the brooch pinned to the kid's shirt. Up close, he could see clearly that it was part of the same set as the ring. He asked bluntly, 'Where'd you get that brooch you're wearing? You nick it?'

'I said, fuck off. I saw you with your dick out behind that tree.'

'They locked up the toilet block, I was taking a piss.'

'More like having a wank.'

'I should wash out your filthy mouth.'

'With what? With that?' Sara pointed towards Pete's groin.

Sticky Pete was reaching breaking point. The little shit was mocking him, when he was on the verge of going to jail because of her. Without another thought, he hobbled two quick steps forward, grabbed her by the scruff of the neck and ripped the brooch from her shirt. He was going to take this pocket-sized bitch down to the police station himself. Tell those bloody officers he'd made a citizen's arrest. Let *them* listen to the words that came out of her dirty mouth.

Sara kicked and swore, but Pete no longer gave a shit. He grabbed a handful of material at the back of her shirt, then dragged her towards his car. Though the swollen joints in his fingers burned, he wasn't going to let her go.

'I'm driving you to the cops,' Pete sneered as Sara tried to wrestle free from his grip. 'You can tell them where you got this brooch.'

His old Hyundai Getz was one of the few cars left in the car park. It was still littered with the cup fruit that had fallen off the river red gum trees. His roof was strewn with the small woody capsules, and a bird had shat down the front of his windscreen. The car looked as derelict and as frightening as Pete himself.

He opened his driver's door and pushed the kid towards the car. She grabbed hold of the door, and he peeled her fingers off, pushing her inside the car, forcing her to move over to the passenger side as he climbed in straight behind her, nearly sitting on top of her.

He reversed out of the car park, and then floored the accelerator, eager to get to the police station as fast as he could.

Sara screamed and Pete snapped at her, 'I'm not abducting you, kid, I'm just taking you down to the cop shop. I want to show them this pretty brooch of yours.'

'That's mine!' The child snatched after it in the air, while Pete held the brooch out of her reach.

'No it ain't. If you tell them the truth about where you got it from, I won't say a word about you calling me a paedophile or about the swearing, and then you won't get in any trouble for your filthy mouth.'

'Stop the car! I'm sorry, you're not a paedo. Please, please, *please* give me back my brooch.' Sara was begging through tears. 'Let me *go*!'

But Pete ignored her pleas. He had one hand on the steering wheel and the other firmly on the collar of her t-shirt.

Torn between obeying an adult and fleeing from the stranger, Sara was both confused and frightened. At twelve years old, she'd learned *don't talk to strangers,* but she had done more than talk – she had let her little gutter mouth run off. It was funny when she did it around her mates, and when she did it to shock old people, people she didn't know. Only now, she was being punished for it.

Sara scratched at the old man's arms. Kicked the glove box, but the grip on her shirt was tight.

'Please. Please. *I'm sorry.*'

The moment Sara saw the roundabout up ahead and felt the car slowing down, she bit down hard into the old prick's knuckles and opened the passenger door. As the car accelerated around the bend, she yanked herself free from Sticky Pete's grip and jumped out.

As expected, the fish and chip shop was busy. Customers were already lining up to order their evening meal. On top of the counter, a small golden cat was waving its left paw, beckoning patrons. The maneki neko figurines were rare in country towns. The owners had taken great pains in selecting the battery-operated plastic toy; whether it should wave with its left paw for customers, or its right paw for money. Eventually they'd agreed: people before wealth. And people they got. The shop was always full of regulars, and the wealth soon followed anyway.

Through the glass countertop, there was too much to choose from and too much to look at. Sweet prawns, bugs, juicy fillets, flat-head, mussels, dory, jew, scallops, cod, gems, trout, barra, crumbed, battered, fried, with chips, with salad, chicken salt with that?

Kayleen stared at the fish laid out on crushed ice and garnished with sprigs of parsley. She was brooding over the loss of her brooch. She wondered if she should tell her mother she'd found it with the necklace, that she didn't say anything because she'd wanted to keep it, but now Sara had gone and stolen it. But she was scared her mum would make a song and dance about it.

She didn't know what to think. She'd told a lot of little lies and skipped away scot-free with them all. Even the detective had seen she was lying about how she ended up in the doghouse, but just like all the other adults around her, she'd just given Kayleen a look of acknowledgment and let her bullshit slide. When the detective had come back to visit her in the hospital, Kayleen had been terrified of what she'd accuse her of – she couldn't stop crying – but the necklace and brooch were never even mentioned. Were they waiting for her to come into the police station and confess? Or had she and her mother actually gotten away with stealing it?

Kayleen watched the little lady behind the counter scoop up three large pieces of battered fish and drop them into the hot oil. The lady gave her a wink and Kayleen brightened. She decided she didn't need to mention the brooch to anyone. Instead, the next time she saw Sara, she'd just pinch it right back.

———

The thump under his car sounded like running over a kangaroo or a dog, maybe a speed hump or a termite mound. But Pete knew it was the child. The passenger door was gaping open, the seat was empty.

His mouth filed with bile. He slammed the brakes and pulled up the handbrake. He prayed that no one was looking out their lounge room window. He was tangled in his seatbelt, struggling with the door handle. Finally he was out of the car and hurrying back to the kid. Part of her twisted body was horizontal across the road, her head in the gutter. She was completely still.

Pete stood over the small body, repeating *fuck* and *what have I done* over and over. He was beyond distraught. But what if another vehicle came by? There was no time. What if someone called the cops or wrote down his numberplate? Panicked, he bent down and scooped the child into his arms. He lurched back to his car and put her in the boot.

SEVENTEEN

Giles woke with the smell of stagnant water and rotting flesh up her nose. It bolted her upright so fast it made her head swim. She looked around the room, suspicious of her surroundings, taking a moment to realise she wasn't anywhere near that fucking cattle trough. With a few slow, deep inhalations, she calmed down. It was the fragrance of her Palm Beach candle, coconut and lime that she could smell.

She had taken a couple of Panadols earlier and fallen asleep on the lounge with an ice pack under her neck, hoping the rest would recharge her. Only now her heart rate was up and her body was pinging. She was checking her phone to see if it was a respectable time for a shot of something strong, when it started ringing. Falkov came up on her caller ID. The time was 5.17 p.m. She tapped the screen – she couldn't avoid him forever.

'Sir?'

'Giles, I know the last two days have been madness,' Falkov blurted in a rush. 'How are you doing, by the way?'

'I'm okay. A little drowsy and sore – bloody sore.'

'Are you resting up?'

'Yep.' Giles was reluctant to let Falkov know she'd woken from a bad dream, or that she had been shopping around for artificial flowers and hats, when she was supposed to be at home recovering. Nor could she tell him to add the shop assistants from Denman to the interview list, because then she'd have to explain what she had been up to. But the only thing she could investigate until she returned to the station was what she knew for certain. And finding the hat was one of the few things she could be sure was a reliable memory.

'Look, Giles, I'm concerned you might be too close to this case. Emotionally involved. The attack on you has changed things. If you end up with the LECC breathing down your neck and looking into the way things were handled, it might increase your level of stress. I need clear, calm heads.'

'I'm fine, sir. Just a few bumps. I can stay professional. I can keep my wits about me.'

There was a pause before Falkov replied. 'You were the first responder at the scene, but you can't be the lead detective on this case. If you come back, all I want you doing is assisting the other detectives. Understood? Ride with them, collect information, put your thoughts on the table. Look, Giles, we all know there is never a real lead detective – we're all in 100 per cent. We're a team.'

'I know, sir.'

'Good. So, are you feeling better? I don't want you rushing back too soon.'

'Yep, feeling better, sir.'

'Happy to have a chat about it, if you like?'

'No need.'

'Counselling?'

Giles hesitated; it was routine to make sure officers were offered counselling after a traumatic experience. It was standard box-ticking to keep the Human Resources department happy – HR liked their paperwork in order. But there were plenty who considered it a weakness if a police officer said yes to counselling. Giles had once taken up the offer to see someone after a case, and was told, 'You're a cop, what do you expect, choosing a job like this?' After that, she had always turned down any counselling.

'Nope. Mentally strong as an ox, and physically I'll come good. It's just a few bumps and scratches, bit of bruising, I'll be ready to return to duty first thing in the morning, sir.'

'Glad to hear it. Then let me tell you a joke, Giles.'

'A joke, sir?'

'A detective, a pathologist, a counsellor, a lawyer, a QC barrister and a police prosecutor all walk into a room. They sit at a round table and the coroner asks, "Did the responding officer do the right thing?"'

Giles slumped. 'That's not a joke, sir.'

'That's right, it's not, and I don't want it turning into one.' Falkov kept talking. 'That meeting is tomorrow morning, 9 a.m. sharp. We know the coroner is going to rule Ava Emmerson's death a homicide – it's beyond suspicious and it was clearly no accident. This will get serious media attention, Giles, so when you sit at that table, you let the coroner decide. You don't embellish, you don't elaborate, you just answer the questions that are put to you. This case is not about you, the LECC or Mr Rickard, it's about Ava Emmerson and the facts on the table.'

'Yes, sir.'

'I need to get an official ruling that it's homicide so we can get cracking on putting together a task force. Bray has been going over the discrepancies in the details you gave him and the ERU at the hospital, and what Mr Rickard has recounted.'

'They don't correlate?'

'You know they don't. You say he attacked you, he says it was someone else. But either way, you were knocked around. So, when you're ready, if you like we can walk the crime scene, see if that jogs your memory. We'll start over with your account. Then you can type up your statement.'

Giles slumped even lower. Her account was being tossed out. Falkov wanted a different version than the one she had given.

'I'm not sure my recollection of events is going to change much, sir.'

'Different day, different perspective, perhaps?'

'Perhaps.' Giles rubbed her temple and wished she hadn't answered the phone.

Falkov had kept talking, '. . . get to the bottom of this. If there is a killer out there, we've got to get him off the streets, fast. The press has now been briefed. All eyes will be on us.'

'Sure,' said Giles, though she felt it was more like all eyes were on her.

'One more thing. Before everything went belly up, did you get a chance to talk to Sticky Pete and tell him he's off the hook? The front desk said he was in and out of the station the last two days wanting to see you.'

'Shit, no. Sorry. I can chase that up now, sir?'

'No worries, that's okay. I'll ask one of the Singleton mob to stop by his house and tell him in person. They know by now we have our hands full.'

'Thanks, sir. And, sir?'

'Yep?'

'Did you tell my dad Rickard was filing a complaint about me with the LECC? He's wasting his money on a barrister to represent me.'

'I told him you were in the hospital. He *is* listed as your next of kin.'

'You could have let him know without discussing the case with him.'

'Giles, he was my mentor for thirty years. I thought he'd want to know if his daughter needed help.'

'Help? With what? Solving the case? Or help with the LECC?'

'Bit of both. Your dad's got a sharp mind, Giles. Can't hurt having fresh eyes looking over what's been collected on the case. He's very discreet, he'll keep everything confidential. I don't need one of my best detectives under investigation. The sooner we can put the LECC to bed, the sooner you can focus on Ava Emmerson.'

Ava Emmerson. Giles repeated the name in her head. *The mermaid in Mr Rickard's cattle trough.* Giles paused, then blurted, 'Why was I the only one sent out to a drowning?'

'There was big collision on the highway. The others were controlling traffic while the fire brigade cleaned up a petrol spill and trying to flip a caravan upright. You were all I had. The ERU were late because the highway was closed. It was a nasty accident, Giles. The road was blocked for a few hours. You were available, so I sent you.'

'Is that true?'

'Giles, please. More respect.'

Giles couldn't help thinking respect went both ways. She desperately wanted to ask Falkov what he remembered about her mother's death, considering he was such good mates with her dad, and they discussed everything.

Instead, she asked, 'You know Rickard's story. You know the history of that river, sir. Did you send me out there alone to ruffle my feathers? Bring me down a peg or two after solving the two cases the day before?'

'Giles, I'll pretend you never asked me that. It's utter nonsense. Get some rest. Next time I see you, I hope you have a clearer head.'

The call ended sharply and Giles was left staring at her phone. She was about to swear when it rang again, no caller ID.

'Hello?' Giles snapped.

'Detective Rebecca Giles?'

The sound of her Christian name gave her a start. 'Yes?'

'It's David Hemmings. We met last night.'

'Oh, yeah, I remember. Sorry I've not had a chance to call you or drop in. I think I may have lost your business card.' It was safely tucked in her pocket.

'That's okay. I understand. You have had a tumultuous few days.'

Giles wanted to laugh at Mr Hemmings' description of events, but he also sounded a little stiff and intimidating. She replied, 'Yes, they have been a bit . . . tumultuous. I'm still trying to get my head around it all.'

'If Mr Rickard wants to lodge a complaint about you, he'll have to submit it in writing, and that hasn't happened thus far. But the threat is real and a concern. So, before we begin, I was hoping we could meet so I have a clear understanding of the events and the attack on Mr Rickard.'

This time, Giles did laugh, but out of surprise not humour. 'It was self-defence! What about *his* attack on *me*?'

'I think this is why we need to meet. That way I can advocate in your interest. If Mr Rickard goes forward with this complaint, it could be incriminating. You don't want a civilian accusing you of lying about this incident.'

Giles rolled her eyes. It was becoming clear why her father had jumped to get her help. 'Okay, tomorrow then? This time I'll show up. I've got a meeting in the morning with the coroner. I can come after that. How about eleven-thirty?'

David Hemmings was silent, and Giles figured he was looking over his diary, trying to find a space to squeeze her in.

'That works. I shall see you then. Do you have any further questions before we meet?'

'Nope.' Giles shrugged. Should she? 'No, I think it all seems clear. I'll let you get back to your family.'

'Oh, right.'

There was an awkward pause and Giles wondered if she had overstepped a boundary. She was trying to be conversational, but to be fair there was no background noise on the phone that gave away signs of a household.

'Thank you for taking my call, Detective. I look forward to meeting you again.' The formality was back in his voice.

'Sure.'

The call ended and Giles tossed her phone down on the coffee table. She lay back on the lounge and held the melting ice pack firmly against her head. She breathed in deep again, just to make sure the air still smelled sweet, then closed her eyes and pictured Palm Beach on a Sunday afternoon.

EIGHTEEN

The two shots of Rockstar Banana Bomb peeled away her panic, but it was the third shot that put a stop to any more thoughts of doom.

A little tiddly, Giles dumped her earlier purchases in a pile in the centre of the coffee table. The artificial flowers looked realistic enough, at least from a distance, but up close the imitation was obvious. Giles's fingers caressed the plastic stem of the rose and the silky material shaped into sharply toothed leaves. The dainty petals of the baby's breath, however, felt real to the touch.

When she was little, she would pick the yellow and pink flowers of lantana bushes, unaware it was a noxious weed, and her father would put the flowers in empty Vegemite jars filled with water and sit them on the kitchen table or along the window-sill. They never used their only crystal vase, which sat in a small display cabinet alongside a pair of ornamental china salt and pepper shakers shaped like Siamese cats. As a child, Giles never dared open the cabinet, fearing something more than delicate kitchenware and crystal would fall out. She knew these pieces would have belonged to her mother, maybe even once sat on the kitchen table, but then they were put away, to be glanced at in passing, looked over later in her teenage years, and almost forgotten in her adult life.

Giles looked over her afternoon purchases. There was no brand name or manufacturer's identification on the fake flowers; they could have been churned out at any number of overseas factories. The hat, on the other hand, had a label inside, its manufacturer easily identifiable.

Giles was eager to find out if the hat recovered from Rickard's property was the same brand as the one in her hand. She also wanted to know if both the girl in the gift shop and the cashier in the pharmacy would give similar descriptions of who purchased the items.

The alcohol had made her cheeks warm, and she had that joyful feeling that she was getting closer. *If* someone else was there, she'd catch them, and *if not,* if it was Rickard, she'd prove it.

She took another ten-minute shower to help soothe her aching muscles; the ice packs and anti-inflammatory tablets weren't doing their job. The bruising on her body was dark, turning from the colour of red wine to deep blues and plum purples. Giles winced as she ran the cake of soap down her body. She gently stretched out her back, allowing the heat of the water to run down her spine.

By her feet, on the tiled shower floor, the hat and artificial flowers sat soaking in the water. Giles kept kicking them gently away from the drain, so they didn't block the water from flowing down the plughole. The drenching had turned the straw hat a dark brown, and the flowers were flat and losing their shape.

The vegetable garden at the back of Giles's house would have been abundant if it weren't for the king parrots and rainbow lorikeets helping themselves to the tomatoes and chillies. And if Giles watered it more often. The heat had wilted the leaves, and most of the fruit had been burned off by the sun.

Giles grabbed a stainless-steel trowel and dug a hole by the rosemary. The soil was soft and dry. When the hole was a few inches deep, she dropped the hat and flowers into the shallow pit and then covered them with dirt and mulch. She reached for the garden hose and watered them in, watching the murky puddle slowly drain into the soil.

As she twisted the nozzle of the hose to cut off the stream, she heard someone walking up the pebbled path behind her. She spun around. Sergeant Delano and his furry bark-alarm were a foot away from her.

'Shit, you spooked me,' she said. 'I didn't hear you coming.' She eyed Delano's guardian, hesitant if she should interact with the dog or be wary of it.

'I rang the doorbell, no one answered. But I saw a car in the drive, so I figured you were home.' He held out a bunch of fresh flowers wrapped in tissue paper. 'Turner said you got all sooky because no one bought you flowers.'

'You're the one who sent flowers to the hospital?'

'Nope, not me. But I did get you this bunch.'

Giles took the yellow roses and smiled. Was Delano interested in her or just being thoughtful? She looked him over. She liked the way he stooped, the way he kinked his neck, squinted his eyes against the setting sun and surveyed her barren vegetable patch. She liked the broadness in his shoulders, too. The outline of his calf muscles wrapped in denim. He was lean and muscular like his dog, which was now locking eyes with her, its black muzzle pointed down. Who knew a dog could be condescending?

'I would have thought you'd gone back to Dubbo.'

'Nah. Still down here. I heard about yesterday.'

'About me having a sook or the incident at Rickard's property?'

'Both.'

Giles laughed and said, 'I'll go put these in a vase.' She hesitated, then on a whim added, 'Do you want to come in for a coffee?' Then to the dog, 'Bowl of water?'

Delano smirked. 'Sure.'

The kettle hadn't even boiled when Giles locked lips with Delano. The heat of his body was too much to resist, so she'd leaned forward and offered him her mouth, and he'd accepted the offer.

He tasted sweet and his lips felt soft. She wanted to latch onto him, grip him tight against her body like a shield. She felt vulnerable and needy as she dragged her nails down the ridge of his back, and then he lifted her up and she wrapped her legs around him, hooking herself on his hips. Delano bit into her neck and she squeezed him tighter against her chest.

'Last bedroom down the hall,' she said into his ear.

Delano carried her into the room, and the dog followed. As they reached her bed, his legs buckled and they both collapsed onto the mattress.

'I'm not that heavy, am I?'

'Must have tripped,' he mumbled, and his lips found her neck and his hands found her chest.

Giles fumbled to pull his shirt over his head. Asked, 'Is your canine a voyeur?'

Delano chuckled. With a click of his finger, the dog left the room, and Delano closed the door behind it.

Back on her bed, Delano was warm and firm, strong and solid, and she clung onto him tight, tasting the saltiness of his skin and breathing in his scent. Her fingers traced the dips and ridges of his back and her thighs squeezed and locked his bulk against her.

She knew he would return to Dubbo and they might never cross paths again, but until then, she didn't want to let go of his body.

Falkov settled back into his leather recliner and chomped down on some of the date and walnut loaf his wife had made that afternoon. He was slowly getting used to the homemade banana, carrot, walnut and date cakes that were a substitute for chocolate biscuits, and the cups of green tea that had replaced his usual nightcap of tawny port. His wife was still trying to nudge the beer or rum and Coke from his evening routine, but baby steps. Falkov wasn't a man who adapted well to change. Not when it came to food and drink.

After dinner Falkov and his wife watched mindless television. The show was his wife's choice, and Falkov nodded off halfway through, stretched out in his chair, snoring up at the ceiling fan. He wasn't much of a reader, and he didn't own a dog, so snoozing in front of the television was the only way he knew to wind down after a day at work.

As he sank back into his chair taking deep raspy breaths, his mobile rang on the kitchen bench. He sprang up, bumping the coffee table, spilling hot tea over his wife's home-styling magazines.

In the kitchen, he tapped the phone's screen. 'Falkov . . . yep . . . yep . . . yep . . . Does the neighbour own a vicious dog? . . . Then leave Giles out of it . . . yep . . . I'll be there in ten.'

Falkov poked the screen again then groaned.

'Is everything okay?' Falkov's wife could tell that everything was not okay. 'Do you want me to wrap your cake up so you can take it with you?'

'Another kid's gone missing. Not come home for dinner. I suppose we won't find this one in the neighbour's doghouse.'

'Are you worried?'

'Nah, but what are the odds of a second child going missing in less than a week?'

'Inspired by the first, perhaps? Your first kid made the newspapers.'

Falkov walked over to his wife, bent down and kissed the top of her head. 'Don't wait up. I'm sure we'll have it sorted in a few hours. You watch your show and save my tea. I'll drink it cold when I get home.'

After, Giles felt defenceless and exposed. She and Delano were lying on their backs, catching their breath, dry-mouthed and sweaty, their hearts still pounding in their ears. Giles was praying that Delano wouldn't say anything stupid like *thank you* or, worse, *I really like you.*

When Giles could no longer stare at her bedroom ceiling, she rolled onto her stomach, rested her head on the pillow and stared out the window instead. The last rays of sun lit the sky a dull blue-green. She gazed at the outline of the wisteria trailing under the eaves and considered whether she should ask Delano to stay for dinner or tell him and his dog to leave.

Behind her, Delano wrestled with the bedsheet. She felt the mattress dip and then his hot breath on her shoulder. He began to trace around the bruising across her back.

'Does it hurt?' he asked.

'Yeah, a little.'

'Were you scared?'

'Yeah, a little.'

Delano's fingers lightly danced over her shoulder and down her spine, until he paused at an old scar under her shoulder blade.

'What happened here?' He stroked the scar with his thumb.

'My father crucified me.'

'What?' Delano laughed with surprise. 'Crucified?'

'Literally nailed my back to a block of wood.'

'Benjamin Giles? *The* Benjamin Giles? The great superintendent?'

'It was an accident. I was just a kid.'

'What happened?'

'He might have been a brilliant cop, but he wasn't a brilliant father.'

'No parents are brilliant,' said Delano. 'I spent most of my childhood at my mate's place to get away from mine.'

'I was usually at my aunt's house being babysat while Dad was on duty. He was absent a lot. Work. I spent my high school years away at boarding school. At least Dad could skip the period and sex talk.'

'What about your mother?'

'She died when I was a baby.'

'You're kidding? No way!'

'It was just me and Dad. And I guess my aunt, too.'

'Did you like her?'

'Yeah. She was more like a grandmother, though. She wasn't a cool aunty. Very old-fashioned. I spent more nights there than I did at home, eating dinner and doing homework and sleeping over. Don't get me wrong, I'm not saying Dad was a bad person; he was a single parent, doing his best.'

'So why did he crucify you?'

Giles shrugged. She felt Delano's thumb circle the scar again.

'Tell me,' he urged.

She gave in. 'I was in sixth grade. One weekend, I had a friend from school over to play. I didn't have many friends as a kid.

I studied a lot, kept to myself. My father instilled a good work ethic in me and good manners, but this weekend, I was allowed to have a friend come over. I was eager to impress, overexcited.' Giles played with a thread that poked out from the edge of the pillow. She swallowed, unable to roll over and look Delano in the eyes as she recounted her story. Instead she ran the cotton thread through her fingers. 'It was a disaster from the beginning. We played around the house for a while, then ended up mucking around in his tool shed. I guess kids are naturally inquisitive, or just not very tactful. My friend asked me pretty directly how my mother died, and I told her that she drowned in the Hunter River.'

Giles could feel Delano rise up on his elbow.

'I had no idea.'

'It was a long time ago.'

'What was her name?'

'Emilia. Emilia Maree Giles. She left her family in Italy and came to Australia on a short working visa. Met my father while picking fruit and, after a few months of courtship, they married.'

'Sounds romantic.' Delano's breath blew across her back again. 'That explains your dark hair and eyes. She must have been beautiful.'

Giles pinched the cotton thread and yanked it from the material. 'I guess. All I have is a few photos. One of their wedding photo and one of my mother a month before I was born. Another with her leaning against a car, her head tipped back laughing, and one where she's with the friends she picked fruit with, other seasonal workers. But that's all I have.' Giles didn't mention the pre-autopsy photos.

'So, the scar?' She felt his fingers on her back.

'Because my father and I never really spoke about my mum, I told my friend, "She drowned. I never really think of her, it's no big deal." But as I swallowed down the taste of that lie, my father stepped into the tool shed. He pushed me back into a pile of fence posts and snapped, "It is a big deal – you nearly got swept away with her." I had never known that. No one had ever told me what had really happened, and not once did I think, *Where was I when she was swept away?* I watched my dad leave the tool shed and stayed silent, listening to his gumboots crunch away through the dead grass. I said to my friend, "My old man's crucified me," and she said, "Nah, it wasn't that bad. I've copped heaps worse." But when she held out her hand and tried to pull me back to my feet, she realised Dad *had* crucified me. One of the old fence posts had three inches of nail sticking out. It pierced my shoulder blade, straight into my back. My friend grabbed the plank, jiggled it a bit, and slid the nail out. She mopped up the blood with an old grease rag. I didn't say a word but I had to fight back tears, thinking this new friend would never come back to my house again.'

'Did she?'

'Nope. But that's when I started asking questions about my mother and the flood. I wanted to know more than 'it was an accident'. I wanted *details*. I wanted the part of the story with me in it. The next year I left for boarding school. On my last day in town, that same friend awkwardly wrapped her arms around my neck and hugged me goodbye. Aside from my aunt, I don't think anyone else had ever hugged me in my life. That hug made me feel more lonely than ever.'

'What did your father have to say about your back?'

'I don't think he even knew it happened. I never told him. I tossed the bloody rag in the incinerator. But after that, I started questioning why I was at the river with my mother. I would have been just a newborn baby at the time. My father told me to let my mother rest in peace, to accept the past. And with the gap between school holidays, my own social life, discovering boys, joining the police force – before long, I stopped asking questions. And then I stopped mentioning my mother altogether. We've not talked about her in years.'

Delano rolled Giles onto her back and looked over her face. There was an ease to his sudden smile. She thought he was about to say his goodbye. Instead, he tilted his head, kissed her breast, and began to make love to her again. Only this time, he was gentle.

Giles buried her face into his chest. She breathed him in, drew him in close, clung onto him with her thighs again, hoping he could simply seep into her skin.

NINETEEN

There was the familiar sound of a distant rooster crowing and Giles knew the sun was on the rise. For a second she had forgotten about the events of the night before, but then the image of Delano came flooding back, and the memory of his hipbones pressed firmly against hers. She reached out her hand and ran it across the cotton bedsheet; it was still warm where he had slept.

She could hear the clanking sound of drawers opening and closing in the kitchen. She hoped Delano would find the eggs in her fridge and spot the bread by the toaster. She was starving – last night had left her with an appetite. She wondered if the woofer also liked eggs, because Delano would have Buckley's chance of finding anything that resembled dog food in her kitchen.

The morning after sex always felt problematic to Giles. The conversation was graceless and uncomfortable, the air lingering with the unspoken question, 'What next?' On her back, naked, she stared up at the ceiling. In her head she ran through how she would say the awkward 'good morning' so she didn't sound tongue-tied or self-conscious.

Delano didn't seem like a keeper or boyfriend material, but the words *casual sex* made her chest feel knotty. Plus, sex made you do dumb stuff, like run your mouth off about personal moments from your childhood. Of all the stupid stories she could have told him, she had to pick that one. But sex made you whisper aloud all your secret things. It made you vulnerable. It made you open up, and Giles preferred to keep herself closed and private.

As she thought back to last night's conversation, she cringed and pulled the sheet up to cover her body.

Her phone rang and Turner's name popped up on the screen.

'Hey, Giles, I've just got off the phone with the pathologist.'

Giles pulled her mobile away from her ear and looked at the time. She had slept in. It was almost eight o'clock, the sun had long been up. 'And?'

'He said judging by the decomposition, Ava Emmerson had been dead at least eighty hours, three to four days, when we found her. But there was still evidence of redness in her cheeks and eyes from haemorrhaging, so he is suggesting cause of death was strangulation rather than drowning. He also thinks that the bruising he found on her neck is a sign of someone squeezing their fingers around her throat.'

'Close the throat, silence the voice.'

'Hey?'

'Strangulation reeks of domestic violence, a crime of passion. Or wanting to shut someone up. Either way, it's close to the victim, it's personal, most probably eye to eye.'

'You're thinking the boyfriend?'

'Are you?'

'Yeah, but the manner in which her body was left suggests something more sinister. Crazier. Weirder.'

Giles searched for her t-shirt and underwear as she explained to Turner, 'I think someone wanted to stop this girl from talking. We just need to know what she knew, or what she had to say. Have you got in contact with the boyfriend?'

'Still chasing up Jezza.'

'*Jezza?*'

'Jeremy Liddle. Or Little Jezza, which is what his mates call him. Apparently he's away shooting pigs. Left a few days ago with a couple of mates, few cases of beer, gun box and camping gear. We're looking into it.'

'Handy that he's out of reach right after his ex-girlfriend is found dead. Anything else?'

'Pathology said there were a few patches of hair missing, so it's suspected that Ava was dragged by the hair.'

'So was I. Rickard grabbed me by the hair, by my ponytail.'

'Yeah, first trying to get you to safety, then at gunpoint. Giles, let's just collect all the evidence, and then we can look at the facts all together.'

Giles pulled her t-shirt over her head so hard that her ears stung. 'What if Rickard set it up to look like he was being set up?'

'It's a theory.'

'It's genius. Plant the hat and the flowers in a deliberately sloppy way to make sure they're found by us, get us thinking it's all been staged – and it has been, but by Rickard. It would work a treat.'

Turner was silent on the other end of the phone. Giles struggled to pull her pants on and snapped, 'Are you still there?'

'Yeah, I'm still here. That seems extremely risky. Rickard doesn't strike me as a big risk-taker. His mind doesn't really tick like that.'

'Turner, I'm not dropping Rickard as a suspect. Not until you can categorically prove someone else was out there.'

'We *can* prove it, Giles. Rickard's shoes are a size eleven, Ava Emmerson was a size eight, you're a nine, and we have unclaimed prints of size eleven and a half. A man's hiking or work boot that doesn't match those of anyone else at the scene. That's the print of our killer, I'm sure of it.'

She was silent, rolling the information around in her mind. 'Fresh prints? You think there's no way Rickard slipped on some shoes that were half a size too big for him?'

'Come on, Giles. They were fresh prints. Fresh. Was he swapping around his shoes while you were out there with him? No, he's telling the truth. Someone else *was* there.'

Giles rubbed the base of her palms hard into her eye sockets. *Fuck*. The sun that morning, her hangover, her bloody childhood fear of the ghost of Mrs Rickard, then the knock to her head – it had all jumbled up her reasoning. She squeezed her eyes shut; she felt like she was losing her mind.

Turner was still talking. '. . . said there was a dog print in the mud, did you mean a dog's paw print or an image of a dog's head?'

'A paw print. What would a dog's face be doing in the mud?'

'There was an image on the heel of that boot print we found, a logo. It was a dog's head.'

'Fuck, this case just gets creepier.'

'MacCrum is chasing up the shoe and looking into the logo. I know the last two days have been crazy, but I believe Rickard is telling the truth. Look at him. He couldn't possibly do all that to the victim on his own.'

'An accomplice?'

'It's a possibility. But the old geezer doesn't have any friends. And why would he be in cahoots with anyone? Rickard has no motive for the girl to be dead – he'd benefit more from her being alive and working his land. My gut says this other person is solo. But someone else *was* on that property. Bray said he thinks they've found fresh motorbike tracks up in the gulley. That would explain how the perpetrator got on and off the property so quickly: through the bush by trail bike.'

'Someone local, then,' said Giles. 'With access to a trail bike.'

'Kinda scary, but possible.'

'I really should get back to that crime scene. I need a good topographic map of the area, the national park. If a trail bike came through, we'll be able to work out their path in and out. I'm sure somewhere along there we can link up with that national trail trekkers use.'

Turner laughed down the phone. 'Bray is one step and one Yamaha FJR1300 ahead of you. He's like a kid with a new toy, looking for a way out through the national park.'

The idea of the bulky detective on a trail bike made Giles perk up. 'Well, maybe I'll go to the scene just to see Bray pop a wheelie.'

She pulled tight the string on her pyjama shorts and then made her way down the hall to the kitchen. Delano, and his dog, were gone. On the kitchen bench, he had lit her Palm Beach candle and made her a cup of coffee. An empty plastic container was in the sink. Delano had found her stash of carrot sticks, and they'd probably ended up as the dog's breakfast. A white flower plucked from the mystery bouquet sat beside the coffee cup. Giles wondered if Delano knew white flowers were for sympathy, and he was feeling sorry about having had sex with her. She was also disappointed she wasn't getting eggs on toast for breakfast, although he had made her a cup of coffee. She touched the mug and found it still too hot to drink.

Turner was still speaking on the phone, and Giles refocused on the conversation. '. . . we're on it, believe me. We are going over every blade of grass on that property. Pathology still wants more time; they're not done with their report yet, but they're wrapping up what they've got so far for the coroner's meeting this morning. We've started compiling a list of possible suspects – friends, friends of the family, the ex-boyfriend, and yes, Rickard's name *is* on the list.'

'Good. I also need you to add some people to the interview list: the girl that works at the gift shop in Denman and the chemist.

They sold a straw hat and some flowers a few days ago. I want to track that person down. But the ex-boyfriend, Jeremy, he's a strong lead. And we also need to have a chat with Ava's parents.'

'I was on my way to the Emmersons' home now.'

'Do you want to wait just a little bit and I'll come with you? I've got the coroner's ruling at nine, but after that I'd like to chat with her parents too. I want to know why she came back home from Orange. And I want to make sure we can strike the parents off our suspect list. If I meet with them in person, it'll help me get a feel for them.'

'They do have an alibi for the three days since she was last seen, and I think it stands up,' Turner said. 'Look, Falkov is doing a briefing at the station later this afternoon. If you and I chat to Mr and Mrs Emmerson, we'll have more to offer him, help us start building the bigger picture.'

'Excellent, I need that briefing – I need to be brought up to speed. If you can pick me up on your way in, I'll do the round table and then we can head to the Emmersons' place together.'

'Are you cleared to return to duty?'

'Falkov cleared me for active duty last night. I want to catch this person, Turner. I want to get whoever did this to Ava, and to me, behind bars.'

'We all do.'

'I'll meet you out the front of my house in twenty?'

'Where are you now?'

She looked at the candle flickering on the kitchen bench. 'Palm Beach.'

'Where?'

'I need a shower. I'll see you in twenty minutes.'

In her bedroom, she peeled off the t-shirt again, scrunched it into a ball and breathed in its scent. It smelled of Delano, sandalwood, tobacco and sweat. The aroma made her feel light and happy. She dropped the t-shirt on her bed and hit the shower.

While her back still ached and the bruising was prominent, she was feeling stronger. The plan for the day was perfect. Coroner first, then an interview with the Emmersons, followed by a full debrief back at the station. By the end of the day she would be back on top of things.

TWENTY

Giles dressed in a dark grey pantsuit and white button-up blouse. She used a silk Oroton scarf tied in a square knot to hide the bruising around her neck, then dabbed foundation onto her face, under her jaw and around her eye, adding eyeliner, a little lip gloss and some mascara to hide the fact that the rest of the make-up was only an attempt to hide bruising.

She looked at her reflection in the mirror, finding a face that, if it hadn't been her own, she almost wouldn't have recognised. The unsettled expression. The facade of make-up that almost highlighted the troublesome lines etching their way around the corners of her eyes. *When did I get this face?* The lines along her forehead trailed in the same pattern as her father's. Only his were deeper and didn't smooth out when relaxed. Still, this harsh new face of hers seemed to have just appeared out of nowhere.

Giles thought back to her father and her years away in boarding school. When she returned home for the holidays, Benjamin would stare at her and study her features when he thought she wasn't looking. Once, as she'd stood on the railway platform waiting to be picked up, he'd looked right past her. Then his eyes had darted back and there had been a look of surprise: it wasn't his child he was collecting, but a young woman.

As she matured, their conversations became more strained. The gap between them expanded. Benjamin knew how to converse with a child, singing silly songs and acting the fool. But having a young lady in his house, that was something different.

Her fingertips pressed at the fine lines in a futile attempt to make them disappear. She turned away, grabbed her hairbrush and plaited her long dark hair, opting for a bun – *good luck dragging me around by that.*

Having washed away the aroma of sex and sweat, cleaning Delano from her skin, she now smelled of deodorant, lavender soap and a spray of Yves Saint Laurent Black Opium. She was more airline stewardess than police detective.

In the garden, she dug up the straw hat and flowers. They were damp, dirty and looked like they had aged overnight. As best as she could judge, she thought they would be almost identical to the hat and flowers found at Rickard's property. She dropped the items into a large zip-lock bag.

With the plastic bag in hand, she went around to the front of the house and waited for Turner in the driveway. Her mind was wandering. The extra set of boot prints confirmed she and Rickard were not alone. *Who else was there? Why can't I remember?*

Turner was right on time. She flicked him a wave and nodded hello as he pulled up. Jumping into the passenger seat, she tossed the plastic bag onto the dashboard.

Turner recoiled. 'Should you have evidence just sitting on my dashboard like that?'

'It's not the hat from Rickard's property,' said Giles, slamming the car door shut behind her.

Turner was shocked. 'You sure? I was at the scene, that sure looks like the hat I saw.'

'That hat there,' Giles pointed to the plastic bag on the dash,

'I purchased yesterday at the chemist in Denman. Last night I took a shower with it on the floor under my feet. Then I buried it in my veggie patch overnight, together with some artificial flowers. Only, I couldn't get my hands on any hydrangeas, just the roses and baby's breath I saw at the scene.'

'We didn't find any artificial hydrangeas.'

'That's the point. In the photos from the pub, you'll see hydrangeas in Mrs Rickard's hat, but the gift shop in Denman is currently out of fake hydrangeas. If someone was trying to implicate her, they wouldn't have been able to get them either. I bet when the hat we found at the scene comes back from testing, we'll find there's not a skerrick of DNA on it. And that it'll be as brand new as this one.'

'So you think it *was* a set-up. A prop.'

'Damn good prop, don't you think? Some thought and effort went into this.'

Turner sucked in his cheeks and put the car into reverse. 'Who would want to set up Mr Rickard for murder? Who's out to get him?'

'Maybe no one is out to get him, maybe he's just a convenient scapegoat. It's all about Ava Emmerson. Who would want a 23-year-old jillaroo dead? Mrs Rickard's tragic death was just a good distraction. Good enough to steer me in the wrong direction. Clever, in fact.'

'Almost perfect.' Turner looked smug. He blinked as he ran his fingers through his fuzzy ginger hair – he'd forgotten to slick it with hair gel. Turner reversed out of the driveway, scraping the undercarriage of the car on the kerb. He cringed, spun the wheel and accelerated fast down the suburban street, pushing Giles back into her seat.

'*Too* perfect,' she said. 'The killer was overthinking his crime, and he went back to the scene three days later to plant the hat. And then Rickard and I showed up before he could get away.'

'Why go back?'

'Fixing some mistake – or reliving the crime? Regret? Set things right? Any of those reasons would point to a kind of narcissism.'

'So, you *accept* someone else was there?'

'Yeah. I do now. It's just that I can't *remember* anyone else being there. But if you have prints and Mr Rickard as witness, then I can't argue with that.'

'Shit, Giles. Rickard is going to crucify you.'

'It's okay, I've been crucified before. I survived.'

The round-table meeting was a no-brainer. The coroner ruled Ava Emmerson's cause of death as murder. Giles was relieved that the meeting didn't end up as one big joke, like Falkov had been worried it might. While there were a few suggestions as to how Giles might have treated the scene a little differently, it was all standard. No one wanted to engage in a conversation about what had actually happened to Giles after the crime scene was established. They skipped that and looked only at the evidence that had been collected, the pathology report, the physical examination, lab tests, X-rays and the ERU's photos. It was all clear cut. Murder.

An hour later, she and Turner pulled up in the driveway of Mr and Mrs Emmerson. She was officially working for Ava's family and friends now. She needed to bring them answers and closure.

Let the real work begin.

David Hemmings held the delicate key in his manicured fingers and carefully wound the gold Franz Hermle clock. Checking his phone, he moved the minute hand back, just a tad, then placed the glass dome back over the ticking, moving wheels. In two minutes, the clock's little hammer would tap the brass and chime sweetly. It would be heard throughout the office: twelve crisp *twangs*. Like tapping fine crystal with a silver spoon. And when it did, he'd know that Detective Rebecca Giles was exactly half an hour late for their appointment. And, after a few minutes more of watching the clock's mechanisms twist and turn, listening to the seconds tick by, he'd realise she wasn't going to show up at all.

TWENTY-ONE

Mr and Mrs Emmerson were not their daughter's killers. They were a mother and father steeped in grief. Mrs Emmerson was in her late forties, an office assistant at an accounting firm, wife, mother, all-round good citizen. She'd never even received a parking ticket.

Mr Emmerson was in his early fifties, going grey and losing his hair on top. He had two red lines near his temples, where he'd normally either wear glasses or a cap propped on his head. He was a plumber by trade, which meant he had access to some interesting tools, but he didn't ride motorbikes and, by the looks of it, wore a size ten-and-a-half shoe. Mr Emmerson liked fishing, but that was about as close to a blood sport as he got. He didn't have a gun licence, nor did he own a gun. He was a broken man – angry and impatient to find the person responsible for his daughter's death. A man who thought it was his job to protect his family, and the guilt was eating away at him.

Mrs Emmerson stood in their champagne-coloured kitchen opening cupboard doors, searching for coffee cups.

'How long have you lived here?' asked Giles.

'Seventeen years.'

Seventeen years and Mrs Emmerson no longer knew what cupboard she stored her mugs in. She looked confused and tired, and was clearly having difficulty concentrating.

'Let me make the coffee, Mrs Emmerson,' said Giles. 'You relax.'

'Relax?'

It had been a poor choice of words. Turner jumped in and said, 'Can we sit in the lounge room? Is that a comfortable place to talk?'

Mrs Emmerson nodded and they left Giles alone in the kitchen.

It was a typical middle-class house. Homely, neat, clean. Knick-knacks were on display, an old tea-towel with a picture of the Big Pineapple hung from the oven door. On the fridge, stuck on with magnets, were a few photos, including one of Ava on a horse, and a utility bill.

The well-stocked fridge told Giles the neighbours were already rallying around the couple. A homemade lasagne and casserole sat on one shelf, while the fruit bowl on the kitchen bench was over-flowing with mangos, oranges, kiwi fruit, apples and pears. Next to it, a tea cake wrapped in clingwrap was propping up a card in an unopened envelope. There were no flowers filling the home, but there would be soon. Giles supposed they would be white.

She carried the cups of coffee into the lounge room and sat down in an armchair. She was grateful now that she hadn't got the chance to drink the coffee Delano had made her earlier that morning, which had cooled by the time she'd got out of the bathroom.

Mr and Mrs Emmerson sat side by side on the sofa. Mrs Emmerson's voice and hands were already shaking, and her husband looked grey and distant. He kept fidgeting with his watchband, like it was too tight and restricting circulation. Giles looked down at the floor. Turner would appreciate her reading of body language.

She waited for both parents to sip their coffee before asking a question, letting them settle in, get comfortable; it was likely to be a long and difficult chat. They had already been asked a million questions, so Giles didn't want to sound like she was going over the same details. She needed them to feel like she was working a fresh angle, but without instilling false hope.

Giles asked, 'After returning home from Orange, Ava had been living here for three months, is that correct?'

'Yes, Ava came back home after breaking up with Jeremy, her boyfriend,' said Mrs Emmerson.

Jeremy. Jezza. It was hard for Giles to imagine. Maybe Ava had called him Jez. Shortening it. Softening it. Her Jez. Jezza to his mates, Jeremy to her parents. She imagined them before they'd broken up. Jez and Ava, a cute couple. Fantasising together, dreaming of the life ahead of them, not knowing it would end up being a nightmare.

Giles asked, 'How was she after the break-up?'

'She was melancholy. Heartbroken.'

Giles kept her voice soft and gentle. 'Did you ever meet Jeremy?'

'I spoke with him a few times on the telephone, when they were together on loudspeaker or FaceTime. They were both coming down to Muswellbrook for Christmas. We would have met him then.'

'How did they meet?'

'Through a friend, Snapchatted, and then she went to Orange for a weekend and decided to stay and see if they could make a go of it. It lasted eight months. She liked him. A lot.'

'Do you know why they broke up?'

'He was busted for drugs,' said Mr Emmerson flatly. 'Ava, she could pick 'em. When they first started dating, she had no idea, but the fella was into party drugs – disco biscuits, she called them.'

'Drugs?' As far as she knew, the Emmersons hadn't mentioned drugs until now, just the break-up. 'Who ended the relationship?'

'Ava,' said Mrs Emmerson.

'Drugs,' said Mr Emmerson.

'It was social drugs,' Mrs Emmerson explained. 'Jeremy was randomly pulled over on the way home from work and tested positive for cannabis. They found a couple of ecstasy tablets in his glove box. He ended up being charged and lost his licence.'

Two pills, then. More than three and the boyfriend would have been charged with supply.

'You didn't mention this before.' Giles took a sip of her coffee to make the comment seem less serious, to help the couple to open up.

'Getting charged was the last straw,' said Mrs Emmerson. 'Ava had given him a few chances before, but this was the tipping point.'

'So she knew her boyfriend dabbled in drugs.'

'When they met, it was just an occasional thing, but recently it was becoming *more* of a thing. More frequent, something to get him through the day. After he was busted, it was the last lick. She quit her job and came back home.'

'I want to bloody strangle the bugger,' said Mr Emmerson. 'I'll kill him if he had anything to do with Ava's death.'

Turner chimed in to calm the man. 'I understand how, as a father, you would feel that way.'

'She was devastated,' said Mrs Emmerson. 'Our daughter would never do drugs.'

Giles nodded and bit her lip; parents always believed the best of their children. Most would be horrified if they really knew what their kids got up to.

'Ava didn't dabble in recreational drugs? asked Turner. 'Not even at parties, or when she was with friends?'

'Like I said, Ava didn't do drugs. Not even recreationally. It's why they split up. She was a good girl, Detective Turner.'

Giles thought this was probably the truth, as the pathology report that morning had confirmed there had been no alcohol or drugs in Ava's system.

Turner asked, 'In the three months that she was back here, who did she see? Who did she socialise with?'

'No one. She was withdrawn. She didn't go out with mates. She hadn't even told her friends she was back in Muswellbrook. She wanted space, time. She went to work and came home. Kept saying that men weren't worth it.' Mrs Emmerson reached out for her husband's hand, and he took it. 'Ava was just keeping to herself.'

'She wasn't seeing anyone else these last three months? No new boyfriend or friends once she was back home?'

'No, no one. She wasn't herself. The break-up felt like a betrayal to her. It popped her bubble.'

Mrs Emmerson was doing most of the talking; Giles could tell the woman knew more about Ava's personal life than her husband. But that was common. Girls chatted to their mothers about relationships, and to their fathers about their car trouble.

Ava's social media hadn't been updated in the last three months. No Facebook posts, no Instagram. The ERU had found her phone in the console of her car, out behind Mr Rickard's hay shed, where he said she always left it. There was no reception out in the paddocks, so there was little point in taking her phone with her, unless she wanted to take pictures or check the time. Considering her swag had also been left in the car, Giles guessed that Ava hadn't planned on spending that long at Rickard's property. She was probably just checking on a few things, dropping off the salt blocks, and then she would have hit the road to camp out for a few nights.

Giles drained the last of her coffee and hankered after a biscuit. Her stomach was empty, and she was feeling light-headed. She wished she had cut up and buttered the tea cake on the Emmersons' kitchen bench. She wasn't on her game; her questions were leading nowhere. Aside from the boyfriend's growing addiction to drugs, there wasn't anything new here.

'Can you tell us a little bit about her work history?' Giles asked.

The couple looked at each other and Mr Emmerson nodded at his wife, clearly aware that she knew more about their daughter than he did.

'Ava moved around. When she finished school, she studied farming and agriculture at TAFE, then left home to work on a farm out near Bathurst. She came back home to Muswellbrook during grape-picking season, then went off to Orange. She liked working on cattle stations. After Orange, she got the job on Mr Rickard's property.'

Giles had two things in common with Ava Emmerson: they had both returned home, and they had both ended up in that cattle trough. Only, Giles had survived.

She had just two more questions. She leaned forward and put her empty cup on the table. 'Why would Ava stay out alone in the bush? A girl on her own in Towarri National Park seems a little risky.'

'She loved it out there. She grew up camping. We travelled a lot, family holidays. Fishing, campfires, tents, bushwalking. Our trip to Lightning Ridge when she was ten was one of her favourites. The bush was like her second home. She would have a night out under the stars, two at the most. That's why when she didn't return the third night, we started to worry. We drove out to the Washpools and Lake Glenbawn, but she wasn't there. We figured she might have found a new place and stayed another night. But then the next day the police arrived, and, well, you know . . .'

Giles nodded. Yes, she knew. Last question. 'Can I see her dog?'

Giles ran her fingers through the dog's coat. It was soft and warm, and the animal lapped up the attention.

'She's beautiful,' said Giles. 'Would you mind if I took a sample of her coat?'

'Coat?'

'Hair? Fur? Would I be able to take a sample of the dog's fur?'

'Sure.' Mr Emmerson shrugged, looking back at his wife to see if she'd object.

When Turner tweezered a sample of her coat, the dog hardly flinched. He bagged it while Giles rubbed the dog's stomach and scratched behind its ears.

Back in the car, Turner looked at the dog hair in the clear plastic bag.

'That's not the same as the hair I took from the barbed-wire fence.'

'How do you know?'

'This hair is soft. Fine. The hair I took was coarse – thicker strands.'

Giles clicked her tongue. 'Yeah, that's exactly what I thought.'

TWENTY-TWO

While Turner and Giles spent the morning with Mr and Mrs Emmerson, Bray had spent his morning on the Yamaha FJR1300 in the mountains of the national park, trying to find the track out of Rickard's property. He attempted riding up the spur of the mountain, but the shrubs, undergrowth, rocks and old wombat holes made it dangerous and difficult. He spent more time pulling up to a stop and pushing the bike through the dense bush than he did riding it. It was taking too long and leaving a distinct path. If the killer had gone out via this route, Bray would have spotted it a mile off.

He changed approach and tried the valley. The re-entrant collected water in winter, but there had hardly been any rain this spring and none at all this summer, so the valley was utterly dry.

Following the map, Bray had followed the V-shaped contour lines towards the hilltop and then, when he hit the tree line, he veered off along the edge of the mountain. Within ten minutes he came up the national trail, and – eureka – within twenty he was out of the mountains and onto the open paddocks and farmland on the other side. Forty minutes tops to get out of Rickard's unseen. It was brilliant, but it required planning. Either you needed knowledge of the track through the mountain range or a map of the trail. Bray was almost certain the meeting with Ava had to have been calculated and planned, but there was still no way to know if murder had been the intention or if it had been a meeting about something else that went to shit, with the wire and the wallaby an afterthought.

With Delano still in town, Falkov called on him to help with the investigation. He wanted as many pairs of boots on the ground as he could get, and some paws wouldn't hurt either. The team knew it would have been easy enough for the killer to dig a hole in the bush, high up in the mountains, and use it to hide Ava's clothes. The killer wouldn't make the mistake of keeping them, no matter how much they might have wanted a trophy. There was no murder weapon – he had used his hands – but there had to be a metal-wire brush somewhere, which the killer had used to scrub down the body, and a pair of wire cutters for the wire that he'd used to dress the body.

With no distinct scent for the dog to follow, the officers were hoping to make use of the dog's natural curiosity in the bush. A canine would have better odds of sniffing out the out-of-place implements than cops poking sticks into the ground. Having Delano's dog along for the search made them feel more progressive, but it proved equally useless in the thick terrain and the vast area they had to cover. The Wollemi National Park was over 5000 kilometres square; it was like looking for a needle in a haystack.

Delano never said a word to anyone about spending the night in Detective Giles's bed.

Sticky Pete had spent the early hours of the morning weeping into his hands and the crook of his elbow. His nose was crusted in mucus and his eyes were red and sore. He'd do anything to be back in the arms of Mrs Nolan, his cheek against her bosom, her hand on his head, having her tell him it would be alright. Instead, during the night Pete had punched the steering wheel of his car so many times that two of his knuckles had split and bled.

He had hardly slept. The moment he was overcome with exhaustion and started to drift off to sleep, he'd see the image of the child's body in the gutter and it would snap him awake. He'd bounce up straight in his seat, his heart pounding like he'd been woken by the boogeyman. The park was not safe anymore, and he couldn't bring himself to leave her by the flying fox where she had last been, so instead he spent the morning mindlessly driving around with the volume of the radio up high, as though the blaring noise of talkback radio would block out the fact that he had a dead child in the boot of his car.

Pete was torn, trying to work out if he should hand himself in or hide the body. His seat belt was too tight, the car was too hot, and his guts were aching – he felt like he was going to have a bout of gastro.

He needed to calm down and make a plan. *Should I hand myself in?* How was he going to rock up to the police station and explain himself out of this mess? *It was an accident, the kid jumped, I was trying to do the right thing.* He just wanted to show them she'd taken the brooch and thereby clear his name. He would have just called the cops, but his phone was dead.

No matter how Pete spun it, it all led back to Detective Giles. If that bitch had gone down to Royal Hotel and done her bloody job, the kid wouldn't have ended up dead.

Pete knew he was many things – a liar, a thief, a swindler, a pain-in-the-arse of a husband, a pest to the cops, a moody boozer, and a lazy, worn-out old man – but he didn't hurt kids. He wasn't a child killer.

The best thing he could do was come clean. He might have hurt a few people's feelings in his lifetime, but he'd never hurt anyone physically. If he told the cops how it happened, he might get involuntary manslaughter, ten to sixteen months. Right about now, sitting in a jail cell eating rice pudding felt like a better place to be than driving around with a child's corpse in the back of his Getz.

Pete had made up his mind. He didn't even signal as he spun the car around in an illegal U-turn, heading back towards Muswellbrook Police Station.

TWENTY-THREE

When Turner and Giles arrived at the police station, they could hardly cut through the crowd of people to get to the car park behind the building. It looked like half the community, along with local and national media, had gathered out the front of the station. Mothers stood with toddlers clinging to their hips, the media had cameras perched on their shoulders and journalists were taking comments from the public and scribbling in notepads. The footpath was filled with people, spilling out onto the road.

Turner carefully inched the police car through the crowd and finally pulled up in the parking lot at the back.

'Jeez, I guess the Ava Emmerson story is already on the news.' Turner switched off the engine and tucked the keys in his pocket, but he didn't look eager to get out of the car. Nor was Giles.

'It was in the paper yesterday,' said Giles. 'But only that there was a drowning we were investigating. I guess PMU have let the media know?'

There was a rapid tap on Giles's window – MacCrum's face was an inch from the glass on the other side. His finger twirled in the air, signalling for her to roll down the window. Instead, Giles unclipped her seatbelt and stepped out of the car.

'Welcome back,' said MacCrum. 'It's a shit-show. Did you hear the news?'

'I think I am the news,' said Giles.

MacCrum scoffed. 'It's not all about you, Giles. Another kid's gone missing. About half-past five last night.' He frowned and his brows joined together to draw one straight line across his forehead.

'*Another* kid?' Turner slammed his door shut and made his way around the back of the car to join them. Turner looked as surprised as Giles, and she was glad she wasn't the only one left in the dark.

MacCrum nodded. 'We've had a full-scale search for her all night, but all we've turned up is her bike.' He hooked his finger into the knot of his tie to loosen it. It was the colour of an orange popsicle and it now hung askew from his neck. His face sagged, looking like he'd not slept a wink. He looked over his shoulder at the mounting crowd, then back at Giles and Turner. 'People think this girl will be found the same way as Ava Emmerson.'

'Who's the kid?' Giles asked.

'Sara Milligan. Just turned twelve, and apparently a friend of Kayleen Ellis, the kid you found in the doghouse.'

'What?'

'Yep. Last seen with Kayleen in Highbrook Park around 5 p.m. I know. Nuts, right?'

'Do you think the two of them were up to something?'

'Kayleen, her mother and her little sister left Sara Milligan in the park. There is nothing suggesting these two girls are staging drama for kicks or attention. Sara's bike was found by the flying fox, right there in the park, so it's unlikely the kid disappeared on her own. Sara's mother called it in when she didn't come home last night.'

Turner grimaced. 'Why didn't you call me back in?'

'Your twelve hours were up, Turner. We've had volunteers, RFS and uniforms out all night and morning.'

Giles was way behind the eight ball, and Turner seemed as lost as she was.

MacCrum flicked his head towards the front of the building. 'If you think the media looks like it's about to bite, you should get a load of the public. And I'm telling yah, they don't even know the half of it.'

'Which is what?' asked Giles.

'We asked the PMU not to divulge the details of the barbed wire or the wallaby guts – we don't want to put out stuff that only her killer would know. But people know that Ava Emmerson is a suspected murder, and the media is sweating on the coroner's ruling.'

'Coroner has ruled murder,' Giles confirmed.

MacCrum smirked. Finally his brows separated. He looked happy for a second, then his face dropped. 'The story of Ava Emmerson was released yesterday, before the second kid disappeared. Bad timing. Now Sara Milligan is missing, so of course the whole town is convinced there's a serial killer out there. The phones are going nuts, everyone is offering information. The paperwork is already starting to pile up. Plus Rickard rang to say he was being harassed and that he might shoot the next prick who trespasses on his property. The whole town is scared, rattled. This shit has spooked them. One girl murdered and another missing.' He tilted his head towards the front of the building and said, 'Falkov is about to address the media. So, if you want to enjoy the show, come around the front. Maybe keep an eye on the crowd. Our suspect might have shown up to see the fun.'

As she followed behind MacCrum and Turner, Giles's head was spinning. She couldn't wait to get into the afternoon briefing and have her questions answered. She had a tonne of them.

Out the front, she scooped up a pamphlet from the community mothers' group. She glanced over it. There was a photograph of Ava dressed for her Year Twelve formal. It was a few years old, probably taken from her Facebook page, but it was the first time Giles had seen Ava alive. She looked youthful, with the world ahead of her. She was pretty, happy. The flyer included the hashtags #JusticeForAva and #FindOurSara and urged people to help. It even had the police station's phone number – no wonder the phones were ringing off the hook.

Giles folded up the piece of paper and shoved it in her jacket pocket, just as Falkov stepped out of the front door of the station to an eruption of questions and clicking cameras. He looked calm, centred and in control. He waited for the journalists to jostle into position with their microphones and cameras and only when he felt they were ready did he began to address them.

'Last night, twelve-year-old Sara Milligan went missing. She was last seen at Highbrook Park at approximately 5.15 p.m. We are treating her disappearance and the murder of Ava Emmerson as two separate incidents. I repeat: there is currently no evidence that the two events are related. We are doing everything possible to bring Sara Milligan home safely, and we are also thoroughly investigating the death of Ava Emmerson. If anyone in the community has any information that could assist the police with either case, we ask that you come forward.'

It was the standard speech. Acknowledging the public's concerns but saying nothing.

Giles scanned the crowd. There were journalists, curious onlookers, a few irate locals trying to stir up the crowd and mothers demanding to know if their children were safe to walk the streets. MacCrum was right; it was a shit-show.

Amongst the more vocal group, Giles spotted Kayleen holding her mother's hand. The younger daughter, Mikaela, wasn't with them. Claire Ellis was pale and petite tucked in amongst the crowd, and Kayleen seemed anxious, having been dragged along to an event that she clearly didn't feel comfortable attending. They both looked completely different from the day Kayleen went missing. The mother's hair was washed and swept back in a high ponytail, and her top was bright, colourful, clean and pressed. Kayleen was in three-quarter pants and a t-shirt with a cartoon face with exaggerated eyes and wild blue hair. Giles was curious to read their formal statements once she got inside.

There were a few other kids standing beside their parents, mostly young girls, and a couple of fathers with their arms crossed, trying to look big. At the back of the gathering, Giles suddenly recognised Sticky Pete. His head was down, partly concealed under a flowering crepe myrtle shrub; he had his hand up to his face, scratching at his forehead. He stood out from the crowd because of his derelict appearance, and also because he was the only old man in attendance. Giles knew Pete didn't have any kids of his own to worry about.

She guessed Singleton Police would have told him by now that Kevin Eddy had been charged with stealing the emerald and diamond ring, so either he was there to gloat and rub her nose in the fact that she'd accused the wrong man, or he was there to thank her for finding the real criminal.

He's just picked a shitty time to come and see me.

She made a mental note to catch up with him once Falkov had finished addressing the crowd.

It was all over within five minutes, and once they realised Falkov wouldn't be answering any of their wildly speculative questions, the media didn't hang around. Nor did most of the mothers, who probably needed to whisk their children back off to school. A few locals hung around to give some more comments to the journalists, but the show had ended. Kayleen and her mother were gone. Try as she might, Giles couldn't spot Sticky Pete either.

Giles caught up with Turner on their way inside. 'Did you see Sticky Pete in the crowd?'

'Nah. Why?'

'Did the Singleton mob manage to get onto him?'

'Nah-ah, they tried calling his house and mobile phone, and they even popped round to his place. Pete's wife said he hasn't been home in a few days. He was here two days in a row waiting for you.'

'No one told him that he's off the hook?'

'Once we heard from Singleton, no one could find him to tell him.'

'He was just here,' snapped Giles.

'Then you should have told him,' Turner snapped back.

Shit, thought Giles. *I don't have time for this.*

TWENTY-FOUR

In the briefing room, two walls were being used to display photographs and list the collected evidence.

The front wall was dedicated to Sara Milligan. There were photos of the child: one was a school photo, clear and easy to see her features, the colour of her hair and eyes, freckles, and a small scab under her chin from where she had recently fallen off her bed. There was an aerial map of Highbrook Park, another of the Upper Hunter Valley, the arterial highways in and out of town highlighted. There were googled images of the clothes she was last seen in: an anime t-shirt, whitewashed jeans and canvas shoes. Her mother even thought she knew what underwear her daughter was wearing on the day. All of these reference photos were pinned to the wall.

There was also a family tree that included stepbrothers from Sara's father's previous marriage. After intrusive questioning, all of Sara's family had been ruled out as suspects. They might have been a little rough around the edges, but it was a family that looked out for each other, not one that would hurt each other.

The wall to the right was dedicated to Ava Emmerson. Again, there were photos – one recent, Ava in hiking gear, and one of her year twelve formal, the same photograph that had been used for the flyers. There was another aerial map, this one of Rickard's property, with post-it notes all over it, indicating where events had happened. There were ERU's photos from the primary scene – motorbike tracks, shoe prints – and photos of Ava's body both at the scene and from the autopsy.

What troubled Giles the most about this wall was the photo of Mr Rickard. He looked old and frail. It really did seem unlikely he would have the strength to overpower a woman in her early twenties – or a highly trained police detective. Giles swallowed, her mouth felt dry.

Falkov stood at the front of the room and ran his fingers through his thick mop of grey hair. He looked tired. He was concentrating on some papers in one hand and squeezing the bridge of his skewed nose with the other, like he was trying to re-set it straight.

The room shuffled around. The entire crime investigation team was there: Giles, Bray, Turner, MacCrum and Callahan, back from his short absence. Together with a couple of uniforms to assist, they had assembled around spare desks, empty chairs, spread out, but with a good view of the boards filled with photos and reference images. Each member was working at different parts of the puzzle, so collectively they could piece it all together.

The room had a sombre atmosphere. Giles was sure the uniforms were looking at her differently. While most had checked in with her, asking how she was doing, they looked awkward while doing it, like the check-in was nothing more than standard procedure. When she said she was fine, they quickly left it at that. She wondered if it was the bruising on her face or the fact that she had been so fixated on Rickard being the only one involved, when clearly she'd been wrong about that. She felt the heat in her neck and sank a little lower in her chair.

Falkov began speaking and the room fell silent. 'I don't need to remind everyone that the information shared in this room is strictly confidential. No going home and speaking with the missus. If you need to debrief, off-load or otherwise have an urge to chat about the case: talk it out with me. There is sensitive evidence that we want to keep from the public. Understood?'

The room chimed, 'Yes, sir.'

'Before we start, welcome back, Detective Callahan. I'm happy to inform you all that he has got the all clear on his respiratory issues.'

'Just dumb sinusitis,' said Callahan. 'I'll be back to smelling Turner's cheap cologne in no time.'

There were a few chuckles and Turner playfully punched Callahan on the shoulder. 'More likely the dust piling up in your wallet. You should air it now and then.'

More chuckles, and Callahan looked grim. 'I gave away the family dog because I thought I was allergic. Wife told me to get the dog back, or *I* don't come back.'

'Ooh,' the room rang with more laughter, then quickly settled down again.

Falkov continued. 'We're glad to have you back, your timing couldn't be better. We need you on this.'

Callahan nodded, chuffed to be valued. 'Thanks, sir.'

There were mutual nods from the team and Falkov glanced down at his notes and then back up at Giles. 'And welcome back, Detective Giles. Good to see you up on your feet so soon.' He forced a smile.

Giles knew that Turner wouldn't call it a genuine smile; Falkov had forgotten to wrinkle up the corners of his eyes.

The room gave polite applause and MacCrum mumbled that it was good to see her. Then the room fell quiet once more and Falkov started his briefing.

'As we know all too well, these first few hours in the Sara Milligan case are critical. The leads we collect, the decisions we make – minute by minute, every step will determine the outcome, so let's use our time wisely and make *good* decisions.'

Falkov gestured towards the photo of the child.

'As you all know, last night, just after twenty-one hundred hours, Mrs Milligan of Brentwood Street reported her twelve-year-old daughter missing. Sara had spent the afternoon with a friend playing in Highbrook Park. Mrs Milligan believed her daughter was at the friend's house for dinner but, when she didn't return home by eight p.m., she rang the family to check on Sara. When the family explained that Sara was last seen at Highbrook Park at 5.15 p.m., intending to go directly home, Mrs Milligan called the police. Units were dispatched and have been searching for the missing child ever since. Her bike was found at the back of the park, close to the flying fox. The friend Sara was with, as you all know, was Kayleen Ellis from Pipeline Avenue. The same child Detective Giles found in her neighbour's doghouse four days ago. Kayleen was at Highbrook Park with her mother Claire Ellis and younger sister Mikaela. Sara and Kayleen were riding their bikes. It was an ordinary playdate. But when the Ellis family left Sara alone in the park, we believe something went terribly wrong. We have interviewed both families and, at this point, there is no evidence either was involved.'

Giles swallowed. Was Kevin Eddy a suspect? Maybe he got Sara and Kayleen confused and took the wrong one, intent on punishing her for getting him busted. Or maybe Eddy wanted to hear what statement she'd made to police. All sorts of bad things could happen when an angry man and a child came together. Giles scribbled Kevin's name in her notepad and circled it.

Over her shoulder, Bray saw what she'd written and whispered, 'Cross it out. We went down that path, he's clean.'

Giles raised an eyebrow as if to ask, *Are you sure?* Bray gave her a firm nod, and she scribbled the name out.

'From the information we've gathered, it's likely there are people who know what happened, even if they weren't directly involved,'

Falkov said. 'Witnesses that saw something they may think is insignificant but is of great value to us. Officers have been tracking down people who were in the park at the time and interviewing them, and we have been putting together a list of known vehicles in the car park. MacCrum?'

MacCrum nodded and stood. He looked pleased with himself. Giles could tell he knew he'd done a good job and was eager to tell the room all about it.

'So far, no one we've interviewed who was in the park is a suspect. Nor were many able to remember who else was in the park – except, of course, the dog walker.'

The room snickered. It was a police joke: always ask the person walking the dog what they saw. Dog walkers paid more attention. Mothers were focused on their kids or busy chatting; teenagers were in their own bubble, engrossed with their friends and phones; walkers and joggers were always too busy counting steps, kilometres, listening to podcasts, staring at their Fitbits and Apple watches. But lone dog walkers looked up and around. They spent their time gazing at birds, plants, gardens, everyday objects; dog walkers said *hello* and *good morning*; they seemed to remember nearly every person that crossed their path.

'The dog walker was the only one who recalled seeing a grandfather – an elderly man – in the park. We are yet to locate or identify this person. We now believe we have a full list of everyone who was in the park yesterday, except that elderly man.'

The room shuffled and there were a few murmurs. While they hadn't actually identified the individual, at least they now had a strong suspect.

MacCrum continued, 'As for vehicles, we've asked everyone present what other cars they saw at the park.'

Falkov wiped his hand down his face. 'How reliable is that?'

'People pay a lot of attention to the car they're parking next to if they drive a nice car. People with nice cars don't want to park near a shit-box, so they would have noticed what they pulled up next to.'

Callahan grinned. 'That's true. I don't care what car door adds an extra ding to our family wagon.'

'You don't care about the police Sonata either, mate,' said MacCrum, and again everyone except Falkov erupted in laughter at Callahan's expense.

MacCrum cleared his throat and went on. 'You can't grab a kid and walk away without anyone noticing – you need wheels. So the vehicle is our best lead. We've compiled a list of the cars the witnesses saw and what they drive themselves, matching them all up to see what car is missing its driver. The reoccurring car is a small white vehicle. We think the missing owner of this vehicle is our guy. The car was described as an old, small hatchback – a Honda Jazz or Hyundai Getz. The strongest witness, who knows a thing or two about cars, is certain it was a Getz. They all agreed, however, that its back panel had a rusted dent, about 30-by-30 centimetres.'

Falkov nodded. 'There are a lot of Jazz and Getzes out there, but it's worth keeping an eye out. Unfortunately, the closest CCTV near Highbrook Park is at the servo and a few shop fronts along the main street of town. There is nothing around the park or in the park itself, it's all just residential. This isn't Sydney, guys.'

A few heads turned towards Detective Giles, including Turner. She stared straight ahead.

Turner swivelled back to Falkov and asked, 'Is there any link between Kayleen and Sara, other than that they were friends?'

'None that we can see,' answered MacCrum. 'Unless we find anything else, we have to treat the incident at Kayleen's home and Sara's disappearance as unrelated. At the moment, it's purely coincidental.'

Giles bit her bottom lip; she didn't believe in coincidences. No one on the force did. There had to be a link somewhere – it might not be Kevin Eddy, but there *was* a link. If they found that, they would find Sara. She was certain of it.

MacCrum had nothing else to say. He sat down and let Falkov take over again.

'We're canvassing the area, including volunteers. The press is all over it. As you saw before, the media is running strong on this story being linked to Ava Emmerson's murder. It makes great reading. But we don't believe there is any connection there, so don't get distracted. All our attention needs to be on this white hatchback and the unidentified man in the park.'

Inspector Falkov stepped from Sara's wall to Ava's. Comparing the two, it was clear they had even less to go on to find Ava's killer. Now that the coroner had made his ruling and Falkov had received clearance, the task force had been given the randomly generated name Oona.

Falkov took a moment to look over his notes before raising his eyes to address the team. 'Ava Emmerson. Let's begin. We need to confirm a solid timeline and the circumstances leading up to her death. Before moving to Orange, Ava did not have a falling out with friends; in fact, they celebrated her move and new relationship with a girls' night out. There was no rivalry amongst her peers or former colleagues. She didn't owe anyone money, her previous boyfriend moved to Noosa and his alibi checks out. Her past employers all had glowing things to say about her work ethic and general attitude. Ava left for Orange with no enemies, but once she returned to Muswellbrook, someone wanted her dead.'

The room was silent.

'Look, she didn't just stumble across her killer on a secluded farm. I suspect she was deliberately sought out, targeted. At the moment we have nothing – no witnesses, no weapons, no suspect. No evidence that can connect someone or that would hold up in court.'

Ava Emmerson's case looked cold before she had even left the mortuary. Giles was determined to turn up the heat. She still had to share with the team what Ava's parents had told her and Turner about Jeremy Liddle's drug habit.

Falkov must have read her mind. 'Her death was not robbery or sexual assault. We need to dig deeper into her life. Giles, I've booked you and Detective Callahan into the Motor Lodge at Orange two days from now. These next twenty-four to forty-eight hours are crucial to bringing Sara home, so we need you here to gather as much information as you can. But then you'll both be heading up to Orange – Jeremy Liddle is expected to be back from his hunting trip. While you're there, talk to her former employer, plus any other friends she may have made while living there. I think this murder starts up there.'

At McDonald's, the first thing Pete did was use the bathroom. He filled his palm with a generous pile of foam from the soap dispenser and lathered up his face and hands. By the time he had managed to splash enough water onto himself to get it off again, there were grey soap suds all over the mirror and floor – that would piss off a fifteen-year-old with a mop, bucket and can of air freshener, but Pete was feeling cleaner.

At the counter, he ordered himself a large Big Mac meal and helped himself to the complimentary newspapers. He took a seat in the corner booth at the far end of the restaurant and sat alone with his tray of food and papers. Families avoided him – the soap had done little to disguise his rank smell.

He could tell the staff feared they might have a 'situation' on their hands – a seemingly homeless man mumbling away to himself – but he ignored them. He flicked through the newspapers while munching down on fries, then sculled most of the Coke. He hadn't eaten in twenty-four hours, but today was pension day: he had money to eat, money to get home. Or money to get as far away from the Hunter Valley as he could.

The first piece Pete read in the local paper was about a different girl who had gone missing. She'd been found later that same day at her neighbours' place, but the article also mentioned that the culprit who was responsible for a spate of break-and-enters in the Muswellbrook and Scone area had been caught during the search, with mainly jewellery and watches recovered.

Pete's eyes flicked to the top of the page. The newspaper was two days old. He folded in on himself, felt his jaw tighten; he just *knew* this was the prick who'd sold him the ring. Who else could it be? His troubles had been over days ago, and he hadn't even known.

Pete mumbled down into his chest, snatched up the last of his burger and filled his mouth, chomping on his rage. He gulped more Coke, trying to work out where to lay the blame. He should have read the paper at the police station when it was bloody offered to him. *That dickhead constable at the counter should have told me I was off the hook!* He could have mentioned that Pete didn't need to sit all day in agony, stewing on the idea that he'd end up back in jail. *And why didn't Giles call me?*

Pete continued to scan down the article as it gave some dumb-arse advice on how to make simple and inexpensive changes around the family home to deter thieves, all of which he knew wouldn't have deterred him. His mind was buzzing, still trying to grasp the fact that he was no longer in the shit. All the angst of the last few days had been for nothing.

Fuck. If only he could rewind to yesterday afternoon.

In the national paper, the story of a local woman who'd been murdered took up half the front page. There was a photo of Ava Emmerson when she was alive, a brief history of her love for the bush and her years as a jillaroo, and how she had been found strangled and dumped in a cattle trough. No arrests had been made – it appeared the detectives were baffled. Pete laughed at the word *baffled*. He could think of plenty of words to describe coppers, and *baffled* was not one of them. To Pete, it sounded like that whole police station was as useful as tits on a bull.

Yup. A station full of bull tits.

As he scanned further down the article, he grinned at the description. The national paper had dubbed it the Mermaid Murder, courtesy of the owner of the property where she'd been found. While there was no mention of it in the article, Pete remembered the conversation he'd overheard at the back of the cop station. Ava had been wrapped in barbed wire.

To most people, this article would have been horrific, distressing, but to Pete it was the second-best piece of news he'd had all day. The police were hunting down a killer, and the female officer 'admitted to hospital after being injured at the scene' was recovering. That had to be Giles.

Pete's spirit was renewed and he nodded his head. *Yes, yes!* This was good news! This might just be the way to keep himself out of jail.

From his years dabbling in petty crime, Pete knew the best criminals pinned their crimes on other crims. He was terribly sorry that the little girl was dead, but what was done was done. What was the point now of Pete rotting away in jail for the rest of his life? But if he could make the little girl's death look like Ava Emmerson's killer did it, that sick bastard would go to jail for Ava *and* for the kid in the boot of Pete's car. All he needed was some barbed wire and a watery place to dump the kid's body.

Pete smirked. He might actually get away with it. He might yet come out the other end of all this a free man.

It was hard to sit behind her desk while a killer was out there. But Giles wanted to make sure she had read every detail of the case, so that when she spoke to Ava's ex-boyfriend in Orange, she would be able to tell if he slipped up or contradicted himself. She needed to know more about Ava than he did.

Her shoulders ached. She'd been working at the same speed as the air conditioner: full bore. She'd highlighted key points, taken notes, trying to see if anything in the collected information jumped out at her. She got up and studied the evidence wall, memorising the details; she drank coffee and studied her notes; she googled and scribbled.

She was deep in thought when Bray sat down on the edge of her desk. He was still in his motorbike pants from his morning ride in the national park, but he had put on a clean t-shirt and Giles could smell a fresh application of deodorant. In his hand was an aerial photograph of Rickard's property, wrinkled and well used from that morning. He held it up. 'Got a moment to look at this?'

Giles twitched her lip, then moved the file she'd been looking at so Bray could roll out the map on her desk. He used her stapler and desk phone to hold down the corners.

'This is Rickard's property.' Bray's big fingers dabbed the page. 'Here is the location of the windmill and cattle trough, here is the hay shed where Ava parked her car, here is the tool shed where the quad bike was kept. This is Rickard's boundary, and this is where Wollemi National Park starts. You can't see the house or hay shed from here, but you have a perfect view of the windmill. This morning, I cut up along here, close to the ridgeline, and eventually I hit the national trail. That's not for the casual bushwalker, let me tell you – it's more for the diehard adventurers. So it's not used often, but it's there, and on a motorbike, once you find it, it's an easy ride out.'

'You're sure the killer rode out that way?'

'I took some photos of the track. Old horse prints from long ago in dried mud, but fresh bike tracks and freshly broken twigs off a tree. Must have gotten snagged on the way through. He didn't leave too much behind for us to find.'

'Hence Ava's missing clothes and her skin scrubbed off her neck. Didn't want to leave any DNA either.'

'And the gutted wallaby. He definitely wanted to muddle the scene. Water is a great way to ruin evidence; the water trough was a good call on his part.'

Giles shook her head. 'The thing is, I never heard a bike the whole time I was there, coming or going.'

'You were out cold when he took off to get away.'

'But Rickard never heard a bike either, did he?'

Bray sighed. 'Look, let me talk you through a theory of refraction.'

'Refraction?' Giles frowned.

'If the wind was blowing in the right direction, together with the noise of the spinning windmill, crickets, birds, plus your hangover —'

Giles butted in. 'How do you know about that? Who told you?'

'No one *told* me. But I saw you leave the pub the night before and catch a ride home with Falkov. I'm guessing the next morning your ears would have been buzzing, your head would have been a little thick. I'm not having a go at you, Giles – I was the same. It was a hell of a night.'

Giles didn't answer; the barrister would have been proud.

'I'm just saying, you might have had no chance of hearing a motorbike up in a gully in the national park. It's a long shot, and you were unconscious for most of it. And if you never heard it arrive, it means the killer was already there when first Rickard showed up and then you. Bad luck on the killer's part. He was stuck in the middle of a paddock with his bike hidden up in the gulley and no way to get to it unseen. I think he was inching his way out, hiding behind the water tank, keeping himself concealed.'

'I'm not sure about all that,' said Giles.

'Are you listening?' he asked. Bray still had dirt marks under his eyes and scruffy hair from the motorbike helmet. 'Just go with me on this refraction theory for a second. During the daytime, it's very hot on the surface of the earth, so sound refracts the other way, up into the atmosphere, away from our ears. You with me?'

Giles slowly dipped her head.

'If you've ever seen a thunderstorm come in on a hot summer day, when it's very hot, the refraction takes the sound up away from you, so you don't hear the thunder until it's practically on top of you. But at night time, when it's cold and sound refracts back downwards, you'll hear the thunder from a long distance away.'

'So you're saying it was so hot that the sound of a bike . . .' Giles trailed off, she felt like they were clutching at straws.

'I think you and Rickard just turned up at the wrong bloody time. The killer wasn't finished with staging his crime scene.'

'But he came back – Ava had been dead three days. The scene was staged in a sophisticated way. It's foolish to return to it.'

'Then there was a strong reason for the killer to return. He felt his hand was forced. Our suspect isn't stupid – he's clever.'

'But what was that reason? That bugs me.'

Bray shrugged. 'Forgot something?'

'Wanted to add something?' Giles suggested.

'Like what?' asked Bray.

'A hat? Some fake flowers?'

'Possibly.'

'Has to be local, then. Someone who knows the history, knows Rickard. I think we need to talk to him again.'

'Not you, though,' laughed Bray. 'Rickard doesn't want anything to do with you. Leave it with me, I'll chat with the old geezer. I'll find out if it was personal, someone who wanted to spook him. Maybe it's not about Ava, maybe it was about him? Get him to sell up his farm? I'll see if he has any debts, financial or personal. His relationship with the neighbours, see if he has any enemies.'

'He's a cranky old prick – he might have a few.'

'I've got the time,' said Bray. 'At least it's something to go on.'

'We just need to work out who the guy on the bike is and we've got our killer.'

Bray rolled up his aerial photo and bonked Giles on the head with the end of it. 'We'll find him, Giles.'

As the afternoon turned into the evening, the mood in the office shifted. Frowns, heads down, shoulders hunched. People only spoke when they wanted answers to their questions.

One of the conditions of Falkov approving Giles's return to duty was that her incident report had to be on his desk first thing the next morning. She stared at the blank screen, making up tunes in her head to the rhythm of the flashing cursor, fingers tapping between beats, contemplating Falkov's offer of a walk-through at the scene, but decided against it. Type it up first, see the gaps, then visit the location if necessary.

Her account was bland. Facts only. Arrived, assessed, sealed off the area, interviewed, then – whack! Reached for gun, gone, then – whack again! Opened eyes, bloody Turner's boofhead. It was stale, generic, minimal. It had the same lack of detail as the report on her mother's death, explaining what happened, yet saying nothing much at all. Open to interpretation. A poorly written account of an incident that would have been anything but mundane.

Fuck it. Less is more. That's all I've got.

She saved and uploaded it to the internal system, printed a hard copy and left it in the centre of Falkov's desk. He'd sign off on it – he'd have to. She knew he wouldn't renege on his instruction to have her go to Orange.

A little after seven, Giles signed out of her computer and clicked it off. She returned the printed files, grabbed her backpack and took one last look at Ava Emmerson's wall.

On the way out, she slipped into the ladies' and splashed her face with cold water at the stark white sink. The pressure of the case was starting to hit home. Her shoulder throbbed and her heart seemed to be thumping in the wrong place.

Suddenly she felt claustrophobic. No, not claustrophobic: *panicked*. God, she was having a fucking panic attack. She gasped, struggling to breathe. The air felt like lumps of porridge.

Breathe, just breathe. Just take a breath and calm down.

The self-talk did little to help. Her breath was out of sync: a gasp in, nervous exhale, quick inhale like it was her last. Giles slammed her palms on the mirror either side of her reflected face and hissed, 'Get a fucking grip, girl.' But the conviction fell flat.

With her head resting against the cold glass, she squeezed her eyes shut and took long deep breaths in. When she was finally back in control of her emotions, when her hands had stopped shaking and her chest was sore and her eyes stinging, she splashed more cold water on her face.

She shuffled around the stuff at the bottom of her backpack and found an old herbal relaxant spray. She shoved the nozzle in her mouth and kept spraying until her cheeks tingled and her tongue was numb. At last, she felt calm, or at least calm enough to walk out of the bathroom and hold her shit together. Her breathing was returning to normal. Giles dried her face with a paper towel and left the bathroom.

As she swung the door open, she overheard Turner in the hallway. 'Yeah, she must be pissed she didn't wrap up *this* case in a day. You can't be that lucky all the time, I guess.'

She stepped through the bathroom door and stood in front of him.

'Giles,' Turner stammered. 'Didn't see you there.'

'I did crack the last case, Turner, but the next day I nearly had my own skull cracked. So, yes, I think my luck is running out.'

TWENTY-FIVE

The sky was a joyless blue and the first cluster of stars had begun to glimmer, though it was still a long way from the devil's hour. Pete decided the best time to ditch the kid's body would be under cover of darkness. Until then he'd drive around the quiet country roads outside town, trying to find a good place.

He wondered for a moment about hiding the child in Mangoola coal mine. Perhaps a gigantic coal truck would dump a tonne of dirt over the body and the kid would never be found. But then, Pete needed her to be found – he wanted to point the finger at someone else. That's why he needed somewhere with water, to link it to Ava Emmerson's murder. Somewhere in the middle of nowhere, with no houses or regular traffic, but where she'd be found sooner or later.

He had a pair of wire-cutters in the boot. He'd pinched a toolbox off a tradie's truck in the car park at Woolies years ago. If he could snip some wire from the fence, he could recreate the details of the Ava Emmerson scene he'd overheard at the police station. He was still hell-bent on thinking of what had happened as an accident, but it was a crime nevertheless. Someone else would have to go down for it.

With full darkness descending, Pete pulled up at a barbed-wire fence beyond which he could see a half-empty dam. He waited for fifteen minutes by the road, but no other cars came past from either direction. This place would be perfect.

The idea had sounded simple in his head, but once he opened the boot, he realised it wasn't simple at all. Pete could hardly bring himself to touch her. He was overcome with emotion, racked with guilt. Guilt was a bugger of a thing – it fucked up bravery, he knew. Still, he had to suck it up, stick to the plan and deal with the situation quickly.

Scooping up the body, he tried not to breathe in through his nose or look her in the eye. He hobbled down towards the dam until he could no longer hold the weight, then dragged her the remainder of the way, leaving her partially submerged and sinking slowly into the mud and murky water.

From the nearby fence, he snipped some wire. With the tension released, it flung through the posts and sounded like a whip whistling at speed. Pete ran along the fence and found the end of the wire. It had coiled up in a clump a few metres down the fence line. He snipped the other end and hastily began pulling it free from the post – every minute he spent out here increased the chances someone would stumble across him.

Pete returned to the body, dragging the wire through the grass. On the child's shirt there was a tear where he'd snatched the brooch. He started to gag, forcing himself to breathe in deep and hold his breath, rolling the child over so she was face down. As best as he could, he wrapped the wire around her ankles and thighs.

He couldn't stand the sight, the smell or the thought of it any longer. He was hot and nauseous, and eventually vomited into the dense reeds along the dam. Pete wiped away the spittle with his thumb, then he took the emerald brooch from his pocket and tossed it into the middle of the dam. The water made a *plonk* sound and he watched the ripples in the moonlight until the surface was still again.

If only he could go back to yesterday. Oh, god, if only he could go back and change the day, start again. But it was too late. Too too late. Something had shifted. He was no longer the man he was yesterday.

If only . . .

The dark bush and dead body gave Pete the shivers, but, if he was honest, *he* was now the boogeyman.

At the servo, Pete pulled up at the bowser and topped up his car with fuel – a full tank wouldn't get him all the way to Brisbane, but it would get him close to the border.

In the shop, he bought a sandwich and iced coffee. Aside from the Big Mac, he was catching up on all the other meals he'd missed while he was waiting for his pension.

Pete's mind was muddled. He wondered if he should go home and come clean with his missus, tell her what happened, unburden himself. But that might put her in the shit, too; she might be charged for not reporting it, making her an accessory after the fact. Pete was sure that was a thing.

It was best to play it safe. The fewer people who knew about the crime, the better his chances of keeping it hush-hush. And, as far as he knew, he was the only one weighed down by this secret.

But Brisbane was a long way, plus he had no friends over the border. And he couldn't imagine what life would be like without Mrs Nolan . . .

Maybe I should just head home and pretend like it never happened.

The officers stationed at Sara Milligan's home were looking at their watches – as the hours passed, their vocabulary was shifting from 'missing person' to 'abduction'. Inside the home, they had the televisions and radios turned off. If the kid was found hurt, or worse, they didn't want the family to hear it from the media first.

Time had run out to bring Sara Milligan home.

The egg and lettuce sandwich washed down with iced coffee, Pete's stomach settled.

He was thinking with a clearer head now. He was full of ideas. He scratched the bristle on his chin with his dirty split fingernails. It would be best to burn the car, get rid of any trace of the child, and, instead of going home, wait it out just a little bit longer to see what happened. A night or two in the bush under the stars wouldn't hurt. He'd roughed it before, plenty of times. Slept in worse places. He could stay out of sight, rest and relax, and then when he returned home, he could put it all behind him and get on with his miserable life.

Pete returned to the servo's shop to buy a packet of Panadol and a plastic jerry can.

TWENTY-SIX

Giles slipped her Glock into her bedside table drawer, tucking it under a bunch of bills and old birthday cards. She never knew if she was too lazy to put it away in her safe or too worried she'd never get it out in time if she needed it. She quickly changed out of her work clothes, feeling more comfortable in linen cargo pants and a t-shirt – less restricted, more relaxed. She laced up her white Lacoste sneakers and, in less than five minutes, she was at the Thai restaurant in the centre of town, ordering takeaway for her and Benjamin.

'Well, you've got your hands full,' said her father.

'Yes, I do.' Giles stood at his doorway and raised two bags in the air. 'Thai in one hand and a couple of bottles of Two Rivers' shiraz in the other.'

'I meant the two investigations.'

'I know what you meant, Dad.'

Giles entered the room and dropped the plastic bags on the coffee table. She looked around for a moment, then towards the other side of the room where glass sliding doors led out onto a small balcony with pot plants and two plastic garden chairs.

'Do you want to sit outside?'

'Too bloody hot out there,' said Benjamin.

Giles shrugged her shoulders. Wherever Benjamin was comfortable was fine with her. She hunted around for some glasses, cutlery and plates. She opened one of the bottles of wine, poured the Vignerons Reserve into two tumblers and handed one to her father.

'Cheers.'

They clanked glasses and drank.

'Not bad,' said Benjamin, looking down into the tumbler. 'Why the decent drop?'

'Because it's nice. No reason needed to drink nice wine. You know, you really should get yourself a set of wine glasses, Dad.'

'Ah, well, you can put that on my birthday gift list.'

'Your birthday was three months ago.'

'I'll wait. It'll come around again. Happens every year.'

Giles chuckled at the dad joke. She fished around in the plastic bag and pulled out a stack of plastic containers, peeled the lids back and started dishing up flat noodles, cashew nut and chilli jam stir fry, jasmine rice and massaman curry. Half of the food slopped back into the containers as she served it – she struggled not to splatter the table with sauce.

'There are some coconut prawns.' Giles nodded her head at the foil-lined paper bag.

'You remembered.' Benjamin fished around inside the bag, pulling out a crispy fried prawn and shoving it whole into his mouth.

'You'll choke.'

'Nuh-uh, won't.'

'Will.'

Giles pushed her father's plate towards him, grabbed her own, and sat on the bed, legs crossed, digging in. She hadn't eaten anything at the briefing, not wanting the distraction. It was only on the way home that her stomach had growled, and she realised she was ravenous. She knew her dad would skip sausages and mashed potato in the communal dining room for Thai in his bedroom. Motor neurone disease hadn't affected his taste buds.

They ate in silence. Food first, then talking. There was no point in ruining the meal if the conversation went south.

Benjamin cleaned his plate and helped himself to a second serving. 'So is this a social visit?' he asked. 'Or are you going to tell me how the case is going?'

'Which one?'

Benjamin leaned forward to wipe a few grains of rice from the table, instead smearing a waxy white streak across the surface.

'Start with the child, the one that knows your kid who was in the doghouse.'

'You're looking for a connection?'

Benjamin nodded. With his shaky finger, he was still trying to rub away the smudge on the table. After a moment, he gave up and took another scoop of rice, his shaky hands dropping half of it on the coffee table. He clicked his tongue at the mess he was making. 'Dish us up a little more, will you?'

Giles leaned forward and slopped a little bit from each container onto his plate. She thought her dad looked frail. His hair was more white than salt and pepper these days. There had been a time when he was strong as an ox, tanned and solid, with an intense face and a head full of thick black hair. But now he was thin, with quivering hands, twitching muscles. His mind, however, had not lost focus. His thoughts and words never got muddled. Giles knew eventually they would be affected by his terrible disease, but until that happened, she'd make the most of their time together.

'Got an alert out to stop any white Getzes, plus a vague description of a person at the park we are yet to track down. Elderly guy, grandfather type. It's a lead, not a confirmed suspect. PMU and Falkov are preparing the parents for a press conference tomorrow. As you can imagine, they're extremely shaken by the ordeal.'

'Press conference is a good move. If the person responsible sees it, it could make them panic, could make them do dumb shit that helps you catch them.'

'Yeah, it also makes the public panic, and makes vigilantes do dumb shit,' added Giles. 'Cases this close to home can bring out the worst in people sometimes.'

'And the best.' Benjamin tipped his head towards his daughter.

Giles paused, her spoon of rice and curry still in mid-air. She crinkled her nose and mockingly said, 'Aww, thanks, Dad.'

'Yeah, yeah, enough of the warm and fuzzy. Keep going – what else have you got?'

She filled her mouth with food and mumbled away, 'It's still undetermined if Sara Milligan wandered off, had an unfortunate mishap, or if she's been abducted.'

'What do you think?'

'What the rest of the task force thinks. The bike behind the playground has been confirmed as belonging to her, and her parents are adamant she wouldn't abandon it.'

'Can't help agreeing with the parents.'

'They also said she would never get in a car with a stranger. So we are re-interviewing friends of the family, adults Sara knew.'

'Any of them drive a white Getz?'

'No. But that car does seem to be our best lead.'

'Abduction, then?'

'It's looking that way. Everyone's working around the clock.'

'Except you?'

'Need my beauty sleep, clear my head, look at things fresh. All that shit . . .'

It wasn't about beauty sleep – she wanted Benjamin's take on things. Giles scooped up another spoonful of rice and shoved it in her mouth. Chewed slowly.

'Tell me more about the two girls. Sara and Kayleen.'

Giles took a sip of wine to clear her throat. 'They were new friends. Kayleen and her mother have been interviewed, and they were both distraught. And Kevin Eddy, the neighbour, has a solid alibi – he was meeting his public defender – so we know that stacks up. Sara had never been to Kayleen's house, nor Kayleen to Sara's – this was their first playdate. First time Claire Ellis had met Sara.'

'Why the new friendship?'

'Dunno.'

'You haven't spoken to Kayleen yourself?'

'Nope.' Giles poked at her food, then scooped up a spoonful of beef curry.

Benjamin waved his own spoon at her. 'Go back and speak with the kid. Alone. Take some mints with you or something. Chat to her, then come back and we'll talk some more.'

Giles's cheeks grew warm. She stopped chewing and swallowed the lump of beef whole. It lodged in her throat and she gulped the shiraz, forcing the meat down.

'So, the second case? Oona?' Benjamin had another coconut prawn in his hand.

Giles cleared her throat. 'You know it's gone national?'

'Saw it all over the news on the telly. Don't let the media pressure you. Just stay focused on the job.'

'I guess Falkov has filled you in?'

'Yep. She was strangled, dragged and dumped. Wired up, mouth and legs. I saw the photos, looked at the reports, lab report.

The lot, really. The fencing knot that clamped her mouth shut is an unusual way to *button one's lip*.'

'That's what I said too. Someone wanted this girl to keep her mouth shut. I think Ava knew something. The strangulation, the throat and the lips. Dad, her death – her body – it's one of the worst I've seen. It wasn't just violent, it was angry. Hateful. Some sort of sick joke.'

'Might be something useful in that.' Benjamin waved a prawn at her before popping it into his mouth.

'Might be.' Giles shrugged. 'It was the way she was bound up in the wire. It was creepy, but it served no purpose. Just . . . *strange*. Why dump her in a cattle trough? Why kill her at that place?'

'Convenience?' said Benjamin. 'It's a long way from anywhere. No witnesses. That way he had all the time in the world to stage it.'

'It was definitely staged for effect.' Giles nodded. 'Then re-staged, if my timeline is right. The wire and the gutted wallaby happened in the initial attack on Ava, but the hat and flowers were an afterthought.'

'See! Panic. Panic makes you do dumb shit. Your guy's not as calm as you think. Not as clever as he thinks.'

'True. He left his footprints second time round. Because Rickard and I were there, he didn't have time to clean up his tracks. The prints lifted from by the water trough were a size eleven and a half. We found out the brand was Steel Blue – an Argyle bump cap boot with a side zip. The company's logo was on the heel.'

'That's gotta be a good clue?'

'Not really. It's a blue-collar worker boot, for tradies, miners, farmers; every second bloke in Muswellbrook would own a pair.'

'So no great leap forward in your investigation.'

'You know, the media have dubbed it the Mermaid Murder, even though we haven't disclosed the stuff about the wire around her legs. But Rickard made a reference to mermaids when I was out there, said she looked like one floating in the water. It was jarring.'

'The newspapers just like giving things names. It sells papers. You've got to pare it all back to the basics, luv.'

Giles watched her father again struggle to refill his plate, the spoon quivering in his hand, but she didn't offer to help. 'You know, mermaids appeared in folklore as unlucky omens. Either foretelling disaster or provoking it.'

'I think that's reading too much into it.' Benjamin sighed. 'Go through the details of Ava's death again. Back to basics. Look at the how, work out the why, and that should lead you straight to the who.'

'It's the *why* that has me stumped. This was a good kid. We can't find anything dubious about her life.'

'You'll get there. Just don't overthink it.'

Giles nodded again. 'You're right, Dad.'

As Giles topped up her glass of wine, images flashed in her mind. Mrs Rickard's hat. The shoe imprints.

She asked on a whim, 'Did Mum ever have a favourite dress? Or hat? Pair of shoes she loved to wear?'

'Dunno. She liked the colour green. Lime green. And blossoms, floral prints. But that's about all I could tell you.'

'When the rains were coming, did you talk about how to get out if the flooding reached the house?'

'I told her you'd both be safe. There were bottles of water, candles if the power went out. Plenty of food in the pantry. I said the roads might get cut off for a few days, told her she could stay with a friend closer to town if she felt more comfortable. But she was happy to stay.'

'Then why did she leave, if she was safe?'

Benjamin snatched up the foil bag and fished around in the bottom for the last prawn. Then he scrunched it up and tossed it on the table. It bounced off and landed on the floor. 'I don't know. Panicked. Maybe changed her mind. I was out co-ordinating SES volunteers and evacuations. I was going past the house and thought I'd pop in to see how the two of you were doing. The house was empty, and then I found her down by the river.'

It sounded like Benjamin was giving Giles a dressing-down, not an explanation, but she was having none of it. She wasn't a child anymore. She pushed, 'Why did she go down to the river?'

'Christ, luv, I don't know!' He put the prawn in his mouth and chewed hard.

Giles pressed again, 'What made her leave the house? Was she running away from something? Someone?'

'What are you saying? That she fled from me?' White prawn meat spat from Benjamin's mouth. 'You jump to conclusions, that's your problem! You dig and dig, and then you fill in the blanks with nonsense. I bloody told Falkov to keep the reins on you, and he sticks you right at the top of the two bloody cases.'

'You *what*?'

'You, you . . .' Benjamin couldn't finish – the prawn meat had lodged in his throat and he was choking. Giles jumped up from the bed, upending her plate and throwing rice and noodles onto the floor. She got behind Benjamin and wrapped her arms around his bony frame, made a fist with one hand, grabbed it with the other, and squeezed, thrusting upwards. Prawn meat coughed up and landed on the coffee table.

'Geez, kid,' he wheezed. 'You're going to kill me before this disease, you know that!'

With her arms still around her father's chest, Giles hugged him. She rested her head on his shoulder and held onto him tight. 'I'm sorry, Dad. I love you. I'm so sorry.'

~

At the back of Muswellbrook, the prestigious estate of Ironbark sits with a welcoming sandstone facade. On half-acre blocks are five- and six-bedroom homes with swimming pools and pool rooms, triple garages, each property boasting 180-degree views of the mountains and the twinkling lights of the coal mines.

Behind the estate is vacant land, ideal for trail bikes or horse riders. In the early morning, a father and his daughter, saddled on quarter horses, ride out towards Raymond Creek, near Apple Blossom Flats. The morning heat is already on the rise and has made the horses sweat; their girths are white foam. The father and daughter steer the horses down along the wetlands to let them have a drink.

When they reach the dam, the horses drop their heads, snort at the water and then begin to drink. Before too long, the father detects the smell of death on the wind. Perched up high on his horse, he looks for a bloated wombat, a dead fox or kangaroo, perhaps having been shot and then escaped its hunter, only to bleed out. Whatever it is, the father knows it's only going to smell worse by the end of the day thanks to the rising heat.

Then, at the edge of the dam, he sees the pale blue legs of a child. The legs are still, and awkwardly bent. Immediately he knows who it is. He has been reading the papers. He has been watching the news.

He leans over to his daughter's horse and pulls up the reins. He says, 'Hey, ride up onto the road and meet me there.'

'But Rumball is still drinking,' says his daughter, puffing at the flies landing close to her lips. She is reluctant to cheat the horse out of its drink.

'You and Rumball ride up there and wait for me. Do as you're told, love.'

The daughter clicks her tongue, nudges her heel into the horse's ribs and pulls the reins to the side. The horse turns and trots back up the embankment.

The father is relieved, thankful he has spared her the trauma of seeing a dead body. When his daughter is out of both earshot and view, he pulls his mobile phone from his pocket and calls the police.

TWENTY-SEVEN

Falkov looked like he hadn't taken his own advice to get a proper night's sleep. His hair was scruffy, and he had missed a few spots in his morning shave. The moment he saw Giles and MacCrum entering the station, he pointed at them and beckoned them into his office.

Giles leaned against the frame of his office door. 'Sir?'

'The missing person investigation of Sara Milligan has now been moved to possible homicide. A father and his daughter went for an early morning horse ride and stumbled across a dead girl.'

Giles pushed off the door frame and stood tall. 'It's Sara Milligan?'

'I believe it is. She's not been formally identified yet, and no family have been notified, but I've sent Bray and Turner down there and they think so. They're working on the scene with ERU.'

Giles and MacCrum both took a moment to absorb the immense disappointment and sense of failure. They had been unable to bring Sara home safe and well. Giles thought of the parents, siblings and friends, and the community's reaction; MacCrum was probably thinking of his own daughters and wife.

Once he'd let the news sink in, Falkov continued. 'She was found wrapped in barbed wire. The same as Ava Emmerson. Rickard couldn't have committed both these murders. Some crazy bastard is out there.'

Giles looked out of the window into the station and saw the other officers watching them, curious to see their reaction. Her hands started to shake, her chest seemed like it was collapsing, and her heart felt like it was being squeezed tight. She had stalled the investigation chasing the wrong suspect. She had wasted her own time, and now another life had been lost.

'A serial killer? In this town?' asked MacCrum.

'For the love of god, I hope not. I want you both down at the scene,' said Falkov. 'Giles, gather as much information as you can before you and Callahan take your trip out to Orange – you're still going. And Giles? Your incident report was dry. I had to dunk it in my morning cup of tea to finish reading it. But it will do. For now.'

Giles squirmed but didn't respond.

'Go and see what Turner and Bray have got so far at the scene. And when you get to Orange, make sure you ask the boyfriend if he has witnesses to his whereabouts the last few days. A sober witness.'

'You think . . .?'

'Sara Milligan was found bound in barbed wire. That detail was never released to the public. But it will get out now because it was a civilian who found her. We can't keep it a secret anymore.'

The Evidence Recovery Unit was in full swing by the time Giles and MacCrum arrived. It was midmorning, but the portable LED field lights had already been unpacked – they knew they would be there long after dark.

Giles could see a few locals who had come to the hill to look, some with binoculars in their hands, trying to see down into the valley. She nodded up towards them. 'We should be asking the lookie-loos if they saw or heard anything last night. This area was already swept and cleared when Sara first went missing. Someone might have heard or seen a car.'

'The junior officers are heading up there now,' said MacCrum. He pointed to the top of the hill where a patrol car was parking near the small gathering of locals. Although there were slim odds that anyone might have seen something.

Bray and Turner stood over by the body, in conversation with members of the ERU.

'Feel like we've missed the start of the party,' said MacCrum.

'Hmm, don't send me an invite to any of your parties then,' said Giles.

The two of them leaned against the boot of the police vehicle for support as they peeled plastic booties over their shoes and slipped on hairnets and latex gloves. The senior officer of the ERU and the pathologist gave Giles and MacCrum a welcome wave as they walked up to the body. They only got a fleeting glance from Bray and Turner.

The pathologist was asking Turner, 'Did the horse riders touch the body?'

Turner nodded. 'Just one, the father. He rolled the victim over. After a moment or two of shock, he touched the neck for a pulse. And he thinks he might have poked her in the ribs, to see if she would move. He's still pretty shaken, a bit vague on exactly what he did. Highly doubt he's a suspect. His state of shock seems genuine.'

'He rolled her over?' asked Giles. 'She was face down when he found her?'

'Yep.'

So the murderer couldn't look the victim in the face. A killer with a conscience? Some feeling of guilt? Or empathy? Not a psychopath, then. But Ava Emmerson had been floating on her back. Facing up. He'd had no empathy for her.

Giles stepped forward to take a closer look. The child was lying on her back and staring up into the sky. She appeared peaceful, serene. She was a pretty little girl.

'Okay, well, let me get in there first,' said the pathologist. 'You guys will have plenty of time to look over the photos and evidence once I'm done. Did your horse rider vomit?'

'Not that I know of,' said Turner. 'I can ask him and confirm that.'

'Hand me a marker – I've got vomit here in the grass.'

Turner passed the pathologist a bright orange rubber cone with a number printed on both sides. He took it and dropped it in the grass. 'I'll take samples after I get a few photos. Do we have a confirmed identity for the victim?'

Turner nodded again. 'We'll get a family member to confirm at the mortuary, but we believe it's Sara Milligan, twelve years old, went missing day before yesterday. Last seen alive at Highbrook Park at around 5 p.m., or just after. Last seen dressed in whitewashed jeans and a blue t-shirt with an anime design – exactly what this girl is wearing.'

The ERU officer slipped two preservation bags over the deceased's hands to prevent contamination, then said, 'If it's any consolation, by the look of her clothes, I wouldn't say there was sexual assault. There's a small tear in her top, like something has been yanked off it – a badge, sticker? Iron-on transfer? Could just be a moth hole, too. I'll take a look once we get her back.'

'I'll have the body for two to three days before I can release it, but I'll get everything I can, I promise,' added the pathologist.

Giles asked him, 'First guess?'

'There's grazing up the forearm – gravel and asphalt. The kid has slid along a road.'

The ERU officer interrupted, 'There's a shoe missing, so I'd start searching the gutters and roads in the area for the other one.

Cream canvas shoe. Not branded, probably more like Kmart or Big W. Well worn. Find the missing shoe and that may pinpoint where she was hit.'

'Hit?' asked Giles. 'As in, a traffic fatality?'

The pathologist nodded. 'Yeah, pedestrian traffic fatality. See these marks on her shirt and pants? That suggests she may have gone under a car, or anyway a vehicle of some kind. There's grease, perhaps the print from a coil spring, but now I really am guessing. But the frame of her body and the angle she's in suggests broken bones. I think she was run over. It could be a hit, dump and run?'

The ERU officer looked up at Giles. 'We managed to get a good set of tyre tracks over by the other side of the fence. The boys have taken photos and made a few plaster casts, but don't release the type or the fact that we found it – you don't want your killer changing his tyres. There are some distinctive marks that would make matching them up easier and strengthen your case.'

'Like?' asked Giles.

'Well, first, they're Bridgestone tyres, but hundreds of cars have those. The front-wheel tyres are more worn down than the back – that's common too. And there are traces of an oil leak, but all old cars leak oil. Nothing unusual about that either.'

'So, what is distinctive then?' Giles was feeling impatient.

'Gum nuts,' said the ERU officer.

'Gum nuts?'

'Yep. One of the tyre treads made the imprint of a gum nut. Plus, we've found gum nuts from a river red gum in the grass around the dam, but there are no river red gums around here.'

All the officers looked around at the surrounding trees. Plenty of gum trees and banksias, but none were a river red gum.

'You boys are clever,' smiled Giles.

'Yes, we are.' The pathologist wiggled his eyebrows at her.

'So, we're looking for a common car, with common tyres and a common oil leak that sat under a common river red gum tree that is dropping its fruit,' said Bray.

The ERU officer's expression fell. 'Yeah, something like that.'

'Cheers.'

Giles scowled at Bray and said, 'What kind of attitude is that? Is a white Getz common enough for you?'

'Okay, Giles. Sorry.' Bray smirked. 'I got me knickers in a twist.'

'Didn't happen to get a print off a work boot, did you?' MacCrum asked. 'Picture of a dog on the heel?'

'Nope, but we've been briefed. Don't worry, if we find one, you'll know,' said the pathologist. 'Look, this is going to take a while. You can stand around and watch if you like, if you've not got anything better to do?'

It was a polite way of telling them all to bugger off, and Giles instantly peeled off her latex gloves and headed back to the car. MacCrum followed.

'Let Bray and Turner stand in the heat all afternoon,' she said. 'Let's do some digging around of our own.'

MacCrum shrugged. 'I just want to get back in the car and switch on the aircon.'

At Highbrook Park, other members of ERU were going back over the playground. Now that they knew it was a murder investigation, they were searching for clues they'd missed the first time around, given this was the last location where Sara Milligan had been seen alive.

Word was out. The media and rubberneckers had already gathered. People were coming to see why there was a new surge of police activity at the park.

As Giles walked up the path, she could taste the heat in the air. The car park was lined with river red gum trees for shade, and the footpath and surrounding area were littered with gum nuts that had fallen from the trees. The ERU were taking photos and moulds of the tyre marks in the gravel of the car park.

She yelled out to one of the ERU officers, 'Let me guess, Bridgestone tyres, front tyres worn more than the back, and a small oil leak?'

'You've been chatting to the other crew,' nodded the officer.

'Am I right?'

'Yes, but the prints are difficult to get a mould of. We're not as lucky up this end – the other guys have got mud, we've got dry gravel.'

'Would these tyres fit a Getz?'

'Sure would.'

Giles looked up at the leafy canopy of river red gums. She scooped up a handful of gum nuts from the ground, looked at them, and smiled. 'So close,' she said. 'Almost there.'

TWENTY-EIGHT

The Emmersons had been waiting patiently in the reception area of the police station for Detective Giles to return. Bella the border collie sat panting by their feet, alert and interested in the activity around her. She had been patted and stroked by most of the officers by now.

Giles was surprised to see them. 'Mr Emmerson.' She shook his hand and gave Mrs Emmerson a polite nod of recognition. 'What can I do for you both?'

'We . . .' Mrs Emmerson looked up at her husband for support. 'We wanted to talk to you about Ava's case. Is there somewhere . . .' She trailed off.

'Sure, let's go into the meeting room. Bella can come too.' Giles flicked her head towards the door. 'After you.'

In the meeting room, Giles noticed Mrs Emmerson had made an effort with her appearance, a touch of lipstick, some mascara, clean top that looked ironed, and Mr Emmerson had combed his hair back and shaved since she last saw him. It was a small comfort knowing that the couple were taking care of themselves. Some bereaved parents forgot to shower, eat or even sleep while waiting for answers.

Bella walked around the room sniffing at the skirting along the walls, then the furniture and then Giles's shoes. Giles wondered if the dog was about to piss on the carpet. Falkov would have a fit.

'Thank you for seeing us,' Mrs Emmerson said.

'Absolutely, anytime, Mrs Emmerson. I was planning to check in on you, see how you both were. But the case —'

'We heard another girl has been found. We got a call from a friend. They knew the family – the ones who found her. They said it was the missing girl, Sara. Is it a serial killer?' Mrs Emmerson blurted. 'The Mermaid Killer?'

Both parents locked eyes with Giles.

'I can't discuss any other cases with you, I'm sorry. Are you afraid? Do you feel unsafe?'

Mr Emmerson scoffed. 'We don't have any more daughters left to lose.'

Giles swallowed. Her eyes darted back and forth between both parents. She had no reply. She didn't want them to start the blame game – the normal things that grieving families say to the police during an investigation into their loved one's death. *You should have . . . if you only . . . why didn't you . . .*

Instead, she moved on with a gentle tone in her voice. 'Was there anything else you would like to discuss?'

'We wanted to elaborate on why Ava returned home,' said Mrs Emmerson. She looked uncomfortable. Her head was nodding, like she was agreeing with her inner voice.

'Yes?' pressed Giles.

'She came home because of the break-up with the boy. That was true. We haven't lied.'

Giles felt her back tense. She forced a smile and indicated Mrs Emmerson should continue.

'There were a few other reasons she came home too, but the split with Jeremy was the main one.'

'Anything you can tell us, Mrs Emmerson, helps us find the person responsible.'

'There was a break-in at the shop where she worked.'

'Shop? I thought you said she worked on farms?'

'Yes. Yes, she did. But in Orange she worked as a sales assistant for a jewellery shop. On Summer Street.'

Giles's jaw tightened. 'In your first interview, you said she was a jillaroo. You gave us a rural address outside Orange. So, did she work on farms too in Orange? Or just in the jewellery store?'

'Just the jewellery store. She couldn't find full-time farming jobs, and she liked the change that came with having to dress up for work. She had to stand all day, but that was easy for her. It wasn't physical, not like she was used to, but she enjoyed it.' Mrs Emmerson looked worried. 'The address I gave you in Orange was Jeremy's parents' place, not her workplace. I'm sorry if I confused your officer.'

Giles bit her lip. She would be having a stern chat with Turner about his interviewing skills.

'So, what happened at the jewellery store?' She was impatient for the Emmersons to get to the point.

'Well, there was a break-in. And Ava was there alone at the time. She was often left to look after the store when the owners slipped out for errands, meetings with suppliers, stuff like that. Ava had to go to the bathroom, so she locked everything up and ducked out to use the public bathroom. She was gone all of five, ten minutes, but when she came back the store had been broken into. It rattled her. A lot.'

'Was there a specific reason why she was rattled?'

'She didn't say too much, but she didn't want to work there

anymore afterwards. Said she no longer trusted anyone. Jeremy included. It wasn't just his return to daily marijuana smoking and weekend party drugs; it was the fall-out after the robbery.'

'Did she think her boyfriend did it?'

'They often ate lunch together in the back room. He knew what days she worked, and when she would be there by herself. He knew the layout of the building, where things were kept. I'm not accusing him, but Ava no longer felt . . . safe.'

'Safe?'

'That's what she said. "I don't feel safe anymore."'

'Did the police look into Jeremy Liddle as a suspect for the robbery?'

'No. I don't think so. Anyway, Ava never said anything to them. She gave a few statements, to the police and the insurance company, and the relationship with her employers was strained afterwards. She said dealing with the cops made her edgy. Ava wanted out. The drugs were the last straw. She just left. We weren't even expecting her – she simply turned up at home, said she was back. She had chucked it all in. She was angry, private. As I said, the robbery rattled her. She was nervous, jumpy.'

'Snappy,' said Mr Emmerson. 'You couldn't say a word to her without her going off, telling us to stop talking about it. She didn't want anyone to know she was back home.'

'It was like she was hiding.'

'Hiding? From what?' Giles felt the dog shuffle between her legs under the table. 'Did she think she was in danger?'

Mrs Emmerson paused and looked at her husband, then: 'Yes, I think so.'

Giles couldn't believe the Emmersons had kept this information to themselves. But she couldn't let them know she was pissed – now that they were opening up, she needed to keep them onside.

'Why didn't you mention this earlier?' she said as pleasantly as she could.

'That was Orange, this is the Hunter. We didn't think . . . I suppose we were in shock.'

'Why didn't she talk to the police if she felt at risk?'

Mrs Emmerson didn't meet Giles's eye. 'Police can be scary. To the cops it might have been just another theft, but to her, it was traumatic. Whenever I mentioned the police, she'd fly off the handle. Flip her lid. I just wanted her to calm down. She was my child – I wanted to love her, not upset her.'

Giles nodded, then heard the sound of Bella pissing on the carpet.

Bray sat on the edge of the meeting room table and rubbed his big hands down his face, absorbing the fresh information. 'This throws a whole new light on the case. She worked at a jewellery store someone stole from, and she felt like she was in danger. I can't believe they didn't mention any of that before. We thought we were looking at an everyday citizen, but this – this changes things. A lot.'

Giles glanced up at Bray. 'Think the Emmersons also felt threatened?' She was on her hands and knees, sponging the dog piss from the carpet. The paper towel was turning yellow.

'Dunno.' Bray frowned, clearly running the new facts through his head. 'And how would Sara be connected to a shop in Orange?'

'She's not,' said Giles, reaching up for the roll of paper towel on the table. She snapped off more sheets and patted the carpet again. 'They are still two different cases.'

'So white Getz guy didn't take a motorbike and ride out to Rickard's property?'

'No. I don't think so. I think we have two separate killers. This is a copycat. Do you agree?'

'Yeah, I do. It might not make any sense, but I agree. Just don't know how the information about the water and wire got out.'

'You boys are always talking to your wives.' Giles snorted. 'Everyone loves to be friends with a cop's wife – they tell the best stories.'

'Yeah,' Bray grinned. 'The shit I told my first wife over the years, it's no wonder she divorced me. I think she left me just to get away from the stories. Second wife loves them.'

'See?' Giles wiggled a finger up at Bray like he was a naughty child.

'Get those piss fingers out of my face.' He flicked her hand away.

'But it's true.' She got up from the floor and tossed the soaked paper towels into the waste bin.

'I guess if I kept my mouth shut more often, I'd have made the first Mrs Bray happier. The upside is, there is DNA all over Sara Milligan – fibres, hair. Just have to wait for the lab.'

'But still no DNA from Ava they can compare it to?'

'She was scrubbed clean. The water carried away the rest. They've drained the water trough and are sifting through the sludge in the bottom, but I wouldn't get my hopes up.'

'That's just what I mean. Sara's killer was an amateur – Ava's killer was clever. The wire is what connects the two, but there were no animal guts scattered around Sara.'

Bray agreed. 'So, two different killers.'

'Don't tell Falkov the dog pissed on the carpet.'

'Don't have to, you've left the evidence for everyone to see and smell in the paper basket. You're not much of a detective, are you, Giles?'

Giles picked up the waste bin and rolled her eyes. 'Disposing of the evidence now.'

'And get some air freshener while you're at it.'

TWENTY-NINE

Close to the banks of the Hunter River, the vegetation was different to the adjacent flood plains and paddocks. By the river, there was buffel and spiny mud grass, black roly-poly and old man saltbush. There were different tea-tree species, the odd willow tree, large boulders, jagged rocks, and oversized limbs that had fallen from trees.

Giles stood in the middle of the open flats, behind her the cultivated paddocks, ploughed dirt and fields of grass for cattle to graze on. Nothing grew tall enough that it could whip a person's legs, nothing to scratch at their shins. But along the bank, the thick shrubs, tall grass and sharp rocks were a hazard.

Giles had spent hours – weeks – in her study, poring over reports and old newspaper clippings from the long-ago flood. She had looked at the photos of her mother's body and seen for herself the scratches and small cuts under her feet, around her ankles, across her shins. She had to have been running. And the thicket along the river was the only place she could have got those scratches. Before the river swept her away, wrapping her up like a murky blanket and drowning her under its covers.

She slipped off her shoes, peeled off her socks and rolled her pants up above her knees. She looked back at the river, visualising the path along the bank, trying to retrace her mother's steps.

Giles pointed herself downstream. She took a deep breath and started to run through the paddock. Nothing touched her shins, but the moment she reached the river and tried to race along the riverbank, she stumbled and stubbed her toes on a rock. The spiny mud grass nicked her ankles, the black roly-poly felt like a thousand paper cuts as it whipped her legs. The thicket was like a herd of cats clawing at her bare skin.

A pigeon startled her as it flew out from under a tuft of grass, and two water dragons scuttled down the bank and hit the water, but Giles kept running, her legs thrashing through the vegetation.

A little over 300 metres downstream she stopped, caught her breath and looked down at her legs. Her feet were nicked, her legs were red from grass rash, scratched and bloody from minor cuts. The soles of her feet burned. The scratches on her shins began to itch and sting. Her legs looked exactly like her mother's in the pre-autopsy photograph.

Giles bent down and scooped up a handful of dead grass, crushed it in her fist and tossed it into the wind. She looked over the dry landscape and imagined its opposite: torrential rain, strong winds, the rising river, banks breaking. The Giles family home hadn't been damaged by the flood in any way, not even the shed.

What would make a mother snatch up her baby and flee the safety of her home? What are you trying to hide, Dad?

Flashes of blue bounced across the ground. Small fairy-wrens with their blue-black plumage were hop-searching in the grass for insects; their reeling, high-pitched chittering sounded sickly sweet. She watched the birds flutter about, chasing tiny insects she couldn't see.

When Giles was ten, her father had come home one day with a second-hand slug gun and taught her how to shoot cans off the fence posts. Some days later, she had taken this new toy down to the river, in search of a rabbit. A moving target seemed more exciting than a stationary one. Because of the long drought, there wasn't a rabbit in sight; instead, she took a shot at a wren. As it sat on the tip of a fallen log and chirped to the sunshine, she had lined up the scope with its plump chest and pulled the trigger. As fragile as spun sugar, the bird had fallen onto the dry creek bed like a puff of fairy floss.

A young Giles had felt a cold emptiness. The mountains frowned. The tall gums and willows leaned forward and loomed over her head as if questioning her.

Guilt had made her crack open the gun barrel and then bury the wren. She'd even placed a few dry gum leaves and a sprig of yellow flowers from an acacia tree over its grave.

Once home, she'd packed away the remaining lead pellets in the top drawer of her father's roll-top desk and slid the gun under her bed.

Back at her car, Giles leaned against the bonnet, shoes and socks in one hand, mobile phone in the other. She listened to the voicemail left on her phone. It was from David Hemmings, the barrister, telling her he was available after-hours if she wasn't able to attend appointments during the day. He left his address, explaining he'd be home tonight. 'Feel free to pop on by.'

He'd ended the message by saying he had some good news about the LECC, and Giles needed to hear some good news. But when she arrived at Hemmings' home, she wondered if it was the family's dinnertime and an impolite hour to visit.

She could tell the front door was solid wood even before she knocked on it. It almost hurt her knuckles as she rapped them against the timber. On the front step, she waited in silence and rubbed her hand.

The heavy door locked away any sound from inside, but when it swung open Giles was overwhelmed by music, something orchestral, cellos craving to be heard over violins and brass, pitching and aching. Giles felt the music's sadness seep into her skin.

Hemmings blinked at her. Giles could smell spicy curry and once again realised she was ravenous.

'Detective Giles?' Hemmings stepped out into the dark of the front step.

He was dressed in khaki pants and a white buttoned shirt, rolled-up sleeves, no tie. He no longer looked threatening or intimidating. He'd lost the stern expression she'd been met with in the hospital, and had replaced it with surprise, confusion and concern.

'What the hell happened to your legs?'

It was the word *hell* that now made Giles blink. Then she remembered her pants were still rolled up; Hemmings was looking at the bruises and cuts on her shins and ankles.

'I went for a run by the river.'

Hemmings took her hand and drew her inside, closing the front door. As he led her down the hallway, the music became louder and more dramatic, and the smell of food made her stomach ache. She felt dizzy, tired, and *bloody hungry*.

'Sit. I'll get something for your legs.'

'I'd rather you got me something to eat. Please?'

Giles sat down on a chesterfield sofa and Hemmings disappeared into the kitchen.

She took a moment to look around his living room, rolling her eyes at the artistic buffet lamp – part sculpture, part functional light – sitting on a white marble coffee table. The Persian rug was in mahogany and gold. So predictable. The house looked like it was straight out of *Barristers' Home and Garden Magazine*.

Giles was about to get up and ask to reschedule their meeting for another day, when she hesitated and looked at the paintings on the wall. They were all Renaissance era. Sexually charged. Erotic. Sensual. Voluptuous women overpowered by demon lovers. Scooped up into the arms of men, subdued by cherubs, tossed onto the backs of bucking stallions. Fabric was being torn from their bodies with aggression and passion. There was no denying it, Giles felt aroused by the artwork, by the aroma of the food and by the vibration of the music.

Hemmings made two trips to the kitchen: from one he returned with a hand towel slung over his shoulder and a small bucket filled with warm water and disinfectant, from the second with a bowl of rice and curry. He put the bowl on the table and kneeled down at Giles's feet. He held her ankle and placed one foot into the bucket. The water was warm and milky; Giles immediately felt the sting of the disinfectant.

'Did you do this on duty?'

'No. Just decided to go for a run down along the riverbank.'

'With no shoes?'

'Forgot my joggers.'

'And our appointments.'

Giles leaned forward for the bowl of curry, her shoulder gently grazing Hemmings. They both pulled back, apologising for the bump of arms. He smiled, passed her the bowl and went back to treating her leg.

'What type of curry?' Giles asked.

'Pasanda. Do you eat chicken?'

'I eat anything when I'm hungry.'

'It's coconut cream and almonds. I made it from scratch. Garlic, ginger, turmeric.'

Giles was impressed. Hemmings stopped washing her leg and watched her take a spoonful of curry and rice, waiting for her verdict.

'It's good. Really, it's good. Very creamy.'

Hemmings' slight smile widened as he dried Giles's calf, then he started on her other foot. He splashed the water up to her shin, and she flinched a little as the antiseptic stung again.

'I believe you found the missing child. Tragedy, an absolute tragedy.'

'Yes. It's been a big day. I'm off to Orange tomorrow, still working on the Ava Emmerson case.'

'Are the two connected?'

'Nope.'

His touch was gentle.

'Did you put the flowers by my bed in hospital?' she asked.

'You had quite the black eye. I felt sorry for you.'

'Do you buy flowers for all your clients?'

'No.'

'Then that's stepping over the line, isn't it? A little unprofessional.'

Hemmings grinned. He didn't seem at all annoyed. His sharp edge had gone and his eyes were soft, not searching or guarding or judging.

'I'm glad you stopped by. I wanted to tell you in person: the LECC is no longer a threat to your career. Mr Rickard is dropping the idea of reporting you. I suggested to him that you had just fought for your life – you were confused and in shock. Punching an old man, well, he thinks *that* was over the line. But he now understands that you need to investigate, to find the killer, so he's prepared to forgive the punch and your accusation that he was involved in Ava Emmerson's death.'

Giles laughed with her lips clamped shut. Her mouth was full of food and all she could do was pull a face to answer for her actions.

'I know you were under threat. I know you were being assaulted. Mr Rickard thinks that, considering you have your hands full with the deaths of those two young girls, well, pursuing the matter with the LECC seems counterproductive. Detective Giles, all you have to do is apologise to him. It doesn't have to be on the record, but you do need to make sure it sounds sincere.'

'I'm not the best at apologising.'

'Practise. If you make Mr Rickard happy, it will all go away.'

Hemmings took her foot and wrapped it in the towel, lightly drying her toes and calf.

Giles leaned forward, put the bowl down on the table, again brushing her arm against him, but this time deliberately. She slid her hips forward on the lounge. She shook her foot free from the towel and wrapped her legs around his torso, locking her ankles together in the dip of his back and drawing him into her. She sank her fingers into the back of his neck and pulled his large body on top of hers. And she kissed him. She pushed her tongue into his mouth and silently begged him to become one of the demons in the paintings, for him to tear the fabric from her body.

Hemmings gripped Giles's shoulders, finishing the kiss first, then gently pushed her away. 'I'm sorry, now I *am* stepping over the line.' He leaned back and sat on the edge of the marble coffee table.

Giles chuckled, partly to cover her embarrassment. 'I started it. I should be the one who's sorry. I think the river . . . I've been overwhelmed, emotional. I'm sorry. Really, I am.'

'No, don't apologise, I'm flattered. But you're still my client.'

Giles struggled to hide her amusement. Hemmings was blushing.

'What were you *really* doing by the river?' he asked.

'I was trying to retrace my mother's steps. She was swept away in a flood when I was a baby. The thing is, I've got the photographs from the report, and there were unexplained lacerations on her legs. But the grass down by the river has these tiny saw-like blades . . .'

'What was she doing by the river in flood conditions?'

'No idea. That's what has been haunting me almost my entire life. I have no explanation for her leaving the house. I was trying to recreate – re-enact what happened. I was running along the riverbank and —'

'Running away from the river?'

'No, towards it. I've gone over it a million times. It's the only way she could have ended up with so many lacerations. Up where our house was, the ground is flat and the soil is soft. But down by the river, the vegetation is dense – the buffel grass, tussock and reeds. To get to where we know the river swept her away, she would have had to run from the house down to the river, then along the embankment.'

'You're a detective, Rebecca, you keep asking *why* your mother was running towards the river, *towards* the flood, not trying to get away from it. Maybe ask a different question.'

'Like?'

'Maybe she wasn't escaping but arriving. Looking for something? Retrieving something? Getting rid of something? Maybe you should be asking, "What was at the river that made her go there?"'

Giles face felt hot. *What had been at the river that was worth risking her life for?*

THIRTY

The next morning Giles rocked up to the police station with her bags packed for Orange, ready to hit the road. Under her tailored pants, her shins and ankles were yellow from the antiseptic blotted on her wounds. The cuts on her heels were taped with gauze. It hurt to walk; it hurt to think about walking. She had spent most of the night tossing in her sleep, dreaming of all the evil things both Ava Emmerson and her mother had run away from, or towards.

Callahan was waiting for her. By his feet he had a small overnight bag; it was obvious his wife had left him to pack for himself.

'We should be on the road by now,' he said, tapping his watch.

'Sorry,' was all Giles mumbled, refusing to elaborate. Dressing her wounds that morning had taken longer than she thought.

It would be a four-hour drive; four and a half hours if they had a break in the middle. They would hit Orange a little after midday, and that would give them a chance to check into the motel and visit the jewellery shop to interview the owners, but still leave them plenty of time to make it back to the motel in the late afternoon for happy hour.

'Do you want to cruise straight up the Golden Highway or drive the Bylong Valley Way?' asked Callahan.

'Scenic route sounds nice. We could stop halfway at Rylstone for a pie and swap drivers.' Giles didn't like Callahan's driving or his choice of music. This way she could at least be in control of both for half the trip.

Sticky Pete had spent the night in his car for the last time. Muswellbrook train station was easy enough to walk to, and from there he could make his way back to Singleton by train. With his pension discount, it would cost him all of two dollars.

Pete liked his little white Getz. It wasn't worth much, but it was one of the few things he owned that was of any value. One of the few things he owned that he had actually purchased honestly. It was breaking his heart to destroy it, but he knew it would hold all sorts of clues that could get him arrested.

He had driven the car out to the back of Muswellbrook's open-cut mines. From the highway that led into town, it was hard to see the excavated landscape, or the high-security fencing, because of the dense bush, wattle trees, pines and gums that lined the outer perimeter. But even if the trees didn't block the view, except for the cattle farmers nobody really paid attention to the gigantic hole in the ground, not when there were rolling hills of grapevine trellises and olive trees.

If they did happen to look down into an open-cut mine, the only thing that would come to mind was money. Lots of it. For the town, for the shareholders, for the government, for the employees – everybody but Pete. It was a pit of money. Why had he never tried to take up a job in the mines? Earn an honest living, make some bucks. Why couldn't he have tried to live a life like every other half-decent fella? If he had taken a different path, he'd be a different person altogether. And that child would still be alive.

But that kind of thinking was too bloody late now. That type of thinking just fucked with your mind.

Pete pulled the jerry can out from the boot of the Getz, unscrewed the lid, and doused the front and back seat in fuel. As much as he wanted to watch the car burn, he knew he had to get moving before someone called the fire brigade. With the extreme heat and high fire danger, they'd be there within ten minutes; everyone panicked at the whiff of burning smoke.

Good thing Pete wasn't a complete dickhead. He'd parked the car at the dead end of an abandoned mining road made of bitumen, where it would be surrounded by mounds of dirt and crushed rock. Not a lot around there could catch fire, just a few patches of grass, and it wouldn't spread into the bush. He just had to pray the car burned enough to destroy all the evidence before the smoke alerted someone.

Pete lit up a cigarette, sucked the smoke back deep into his lungs and then puffed it out and up into the air. He stood back for a moment to admire his car, to say goodbye.

That detective had cost him a beloved car. If she had just done her bloody job . . . Again he rolled around the words. *If only, if only, if only.*

Pete was hell-bent on getting revenge on Detective Giles. Maybe he'd light up *her* car. It would be karma to fuck Giles over for ruining his life. She deserved it, she had it coming. It would be easy enough to find out where she lived – he still had his connections with the boys from the last time he was in the clink.

Pete sniffed at the heat. He felt the afternoon breeze reaching his sweaty scalp through his greasy grey hair. It began to cool his head and his temper. He raised his bony shoulders, lifted his arms and allowed the wind to pass under his armpits. He felt his body temperature drop and the nicotine begin to soothe his aches.

Bloody hell, I'd love a drink about now, a cold stubby. Or something a little stronger.

He took one last drag of his smoke and flicked the butt through the open window of the Getz. There was a second when nothing seemed to happen. He clicked his tongue and stepped closer, about to toss the jerry can onto the back seat when, *whoosh*, the fuel caught alight. It felt like his eyelashes had melted. The heat was intense, and the fire spread quickly from the front to the back of the cabin; within four to five minutes it was well ablaze. It went up like a fireball. Pete laughed hysterically, slapped his thighs, then applauded.

That was a fire alright. A hell of a fire.

He could stay no longer – he was almost certain the trucks would already be on their way. He turned and hobbled quickly down the road, then turned off it and disappeared into the bush.

THIRTY-ONE

The fire trucks were lined-up askew, their lights still flashing. Two trucks from Bulga RFS were in the midst of controlling the flames when Bray and Turner pulled up. They parked their car 20 metres away but could smell the fire and feel the heat the moment they stepped out of their car.

One truck was focused on the car, the other was hosing down the surrounding dry grass, where embers were beginning to land.

The tyres of the car had already melted, along with the surrounding bitumen. The white paint on the bonnet had bubbled and started turning black. There were popping sounds from inside the cabin and as the detectives approached, the front windscreen collapsed into the vehicle. Red flames swirled over the roof, orange flames like lava glowed from under the chassis. Thick smoke turned from grey to black, spinning around the car like a small tornado, rising straight up into the sky.

One of the firemen held his hose fearfully close to the fire, and as he moved up and down the vehicle, flames quickly reignited. It looked like the fire would never be extinguished. The firefighter aimed his hose through the car's front grill, and white steam and grey smoke plumed even heavier. It was a battle of fire and water and, for a while, it seemed the fire would win. It took a further ten minutes before the flames were more or less burnt out. Then all that remained was a black shell, and the stench.

Bray and Turner stared at the car speechless. They both knew it was the white Getz they'd been looking for all over the Hunter Valley – they had been watching their evidence literally going up in smoke, and with it their best chance of a conviction.

Bray's face was hot, but he couldn't look away. His anger slowly fizzled out as the flames continued to die down, and by the time there was nothing left to burn, he had got his emotions back in check.

A young firefighter walked up to the two detectives and said, 'Car's cactus. Is this your mess to clean up?'

'Maybe,' Bray snarled.

'Here, wrote this down. Front half of the car wasn't fully alight when we arrived. I memorised the plate.' He handed Bray a scrappy piece of paper that had once been used to wrap a burger. In texta the firefighter had scribbled the licence plate number.

Bray quickly changed his tune. 'Shit – thanks, mate. I owe you a beer.'

'Make it two – there was a jerry can nearby when we arrived. I kicked it out of the way, so it wouldn't melt. It's over there. Thought you might be able to lift prints?'

'Fuck! I'll buy you a brewery!'

'Yeah, no worries,' said the firefighter. 'Not calling us the Evidence Destruction Team now, are yah?'

Bray had no answer for that. As the young firefighter walked off to roll up the hoses, he supposed they both knew he'd never be getting that drink.

In the Sonata, Turner ran the plates. They came up belonging to a Mr Peter Nolan, a resident of Singleton. Turner did a double take. Giles said she'd seen Sticky Pete at the press conference.

He'd been sitting in the station for two days, waiting to speak to her. *Jesus.*

When he rushed back to Bray and told him the news, Bray couldn't believe it. He shook his head and said, 'Go back to the car and look up Mrs Nolan's home number. Ring her and ask her what kind of car Pete drives. We need solid confirmation it's his – I don't want to discover Pete sold this car six months ago and they just couldn't be bothered to change the registration.'

Turner spun on his heel and headed back to the Sonata on another mission, while Bray stood with his hands on his hips, watching the firefighters rolling up their equipment. Some were raking back the dry grass and extinguishing a few more embers that had blown further along into the grasslands, starting another spot fire. If the fire had been started a few minutes later, when the wind was up, they'd have had a raging bushfire on their hands. It could have been a bloody disaster.

Turner returned. 'Yep. Mrs Nolan said that's Pete's car. He still owns it. She's hysterical – says he's not been home for days. Left a few days ago to come to Muswellbrook to see Detective Giles. She confirmed he was driving the Getz. Apparently he hasn't called or come home since. She thinks her husband's dead. I assured her he was just missing and all we had was his car. She reckons the Mermaid Killer has got him.'

'Well, he hasn't bloody been slaughtered by the Mermaid Killer. He's Sara Milligan's bloody killer!' snapped Bray.

'Yeah, but I didn't tell her that.'

Bray nodded at the phone in Turner's hand. 'Call Falkov and tell him what we've found. Then we'll need to ring Giles and give her the news.'

THIRTY-TWO

Callahan was a massive James Reyne fan. The drive to Rylstone was soundtracked by Australian Crawl's *The Boys Light Up*. Callahan was singing along like he was an eighties rock god, playing the songs over and over on repeat, and Giles had to listen. She knew once they reached the service station, filled up with some fuel and grabbed a bite to eat, she'd have the wheel and with it control of the music. She'd change it to something a little less surf rock – something that would allow her to think.

Callahan and Giles had an odd friendship. Neither quite knew where they sat in the unspoken hierarchy at the station. Giles had Sydney status, but Callahan had worked an infamous case where skeletal remains were found in Belanglo State Forest. Neither jostled for rank, accepting their different experiences and respecting their different expertise.

Callahan occasionally talked about his personal life, except he spoke about his wife and kids like they were distant relatives. He spent a lot of time away from home, working cases, plus he liked the travel. If Giles was being honest, it sounded like the household functioned better when he was gone; apparently his presence at home buggered up the kids' routines. It sounded like his wife liked his salary but didn't like his career (and, probably, his taste in music).

Giles stared at the road ahead. There was enough heat rising up from the bitumen to give the illusion that there were pools of water shimmering in every dip. She listened to Callahan sing three more songs before she turned down the music and asked, 'The relationship with the boyfriend – what do you think we'll find?'

'Dunno, have to wait and see when we get there.'

'Seems to me these guys were opposites. Ava loved the bush, he loved partying. Do you think she tried to tame the wild boy?'

'Maybe?' said Callahan. 'She must have liked him. She gave up working on farms for a job in a jewellery shop. She swapped her RM Williams for stilettos.'

'Let's see if this guy was worth it.'

Callahan laughed and jokingly cautioned, 'Now, now, stay professional.' Then his thumb hit the volume on the steering wheel and he turned the music back up.

'Do you know Orange well?' Giles called out over the noise.

'Yep. Real well. I worked at Orange Police Station for three years, but that was nearly ten years ago now. Still great mates with the boys, though. We get together with our families every now and then, catch up and go camping and fishing. Do a bit of trail bike riding, cook damper and steak, drink beer. Watch the wives down chardonnay and let them mock us. That sort of thing. But I'll warn you, those cops from Orange love handing out speeding tickets – love to sting you for seatbelt and mobile-phone offences. Good at the odd motorcycle helmet infringement too. So when we rock up close to town, make sure you cruise in doing the right thing.'

The Sonata accelerated and Callahan turned up the music so that it was too loud to continue the conversation.

The two detectives worked very differently. In a car, Giles was a talker. She liked to nut things out, bounce around ideas, but Callahan liked to clear his mind so he was sharp when he arrived at his destination.

Giles pulled a file from the backpack on the floor between her legs and opened it across her lap. She flicked through the photos, running her eyes over each image. There was a close-up of a collection of the rocks by the water tank on Rickard's property. Another of a rock speckled with blood and hair. Giles's blood and hair. There was a photo of the bullet holes in the water trough, close-ups of the wires around Ava's legs where some of the barbs had pierced through the skin. The autopsy report had ruled out sexual abuse, no interference internally. Giles felt better knowing that at least the girl hadn't been raped.

She pulled the paperclip off the second bunch of photos and began to flick through images of Sara Milligan. Sara's body was not displayed like Ava's. Sara was not naked, and the barbed wire was not taut around her legs. If anything, the fencing wire had just been laid in place. Sara hadn't been interfered with either and, aside from the barbed wire and being found near water, that seemed to be the only thing that connected the two murders.

Bray and Turner stared at the mobile phone, listening to it ring on loudspeaker. They were both dreading the call. Bray more so – he'd lost two rounds of scissors, paper, rock and now he had to be the one to tell Giles that her little ring thief was a child killer.

It was Callahan who answered.

'Where are you?' asked Bray, holding the phone up towards the sky for better reception.

Callahan's voice crackled in and out, but it was still intelligible.

'About twenty minutes from Rylstone, where we'll be stopping at the best bakery and pie shop this side of the mountains.'

'Guess where I am.'

'Where?'

'I've been watching a bonfire.'

'Today? In this weather?'

'I've been watching the fire brigade put out a car that had been dumped and set alight. Out the back of Mount Arthur. It was a ripper of a fire – high flames, black smoke, toxic. Mate, it was like smoking a thousand cigarettes with every breath, and bloody hot as hell. Guess what type of car it was.'

'What?' Callahan's voice was impatient.

Bray paused between each word. 'A . . . white . . . Getz.'

'You found the car?'

'I found the burnt-out shell of the car.'

'Jesus!' It was Giles's voice now. 'You're shitting me!'

'It gets better. The front number plate was still as clear as day when the firies rocked up. One of them had the sense to write it down.'

'The plates were still on the car?' Giles again, but sounding more distant than Callahan. Bray guessed that Callahan was driving, his big head closer to the car's mic.

'Guess who owns the car.'

'Who?'

Bray could tell she was getting tired of this guessing game. He looked at Turner and raised a brow before pronouncing, 'Peter Nolan.'

'Sticky Pete?' said Callahan.

There was no reply from Giles. Bray assumed she was still trying to absorb the information.

Callahan again: 'Then I bet that's Pete's DNA all over Sara Milligan.'

Still no reply from Giles.

'Would Pete's DNA be in the system?' queried Turner over Bray's shoulder.

In 2001, police were given the power to take DNA samples from prisoners deemed serious offenders. Samples were then compared with DNA that had been collected at scenes of unsolved crimes. Matches on the database had led to nearly five hundred new arrests and almost two hundred convictions. But Sticky Pete wasn't a serious offender – he had only been in jail for short stints and small crimes, and that had been in his younger days.

Turner put his hand out for the phone and Bray passed it to him. 'I don't know if Pete has ever been considered a serious indictable offender.' Turner was thinking out loud, answering his own question. 'I'm not sure if he's been convicted of an offence that's had a jail term longer than five years.'

Giles's voice bellowed from the phone, 'Then you guys need to find out if he is in the system! Because right about now, he *is* a serious indictable offender.'

Bray and Turner shot each other a look.

Turner stuttered, 'There would be fingerprints.'

Bray snatched the phone back and barked at the screen: 'Giles, if I could find Sticky Pete, I'd rub that swab halfway down his fucking throat. I'd get a blood sample, too – from the broken nose I'd give him.'

'Help yourself to a hair sample too while you're at it,' said Giles. Her voice had lost its growl.

The phone crackled and went dead. They had lost reception; Bray figured they were driving down the gorge through the narrow valley. He wished Giles was still on the phone, but he was also worried what she would have to say next. Bray was glad it was Callahan in the car with her and not him.

———

Giles was silent as she flicked through the file on her lap one more time, her eyes briefly scanning each photo until she found one of Sara. She leaned in, her finger tapping on a small tear on the girl's t-shirt, approximately a centimetre below her collarbone. Giles lifted her hands as if she was about to fasten an imaginary brooch to the girl's shirt, and her fingers landed in the same place as the tear.

'Shit. Sara was wearing the brooch,' said Giles.

'What brooch?' Callahan glanced over at her.

'Kayleen. Kayleen is the link between Sara and Sticky Pete. I'm certain of it. The stolen brooch and necklace that were part of the same set as the ring – they were never recovered when we went through Kevin Eddy's loot. I think Kayleen may have kept it for herself, then given the brooch to Sara. And then Pete saw her wearing it, recognised it and . . . took it?'

Crusty old bad-tempered Sticky Pete. He'd suddenly become a different person from the geriatric crim she'd interviewed days ago down at Singleton Police Station. Now he'd be described as Peter Nolan, Sara Milligan's killer.

'If Pete has the brooch, that means the necklace is still un-accounted for,' said Callahan. 'You think Kayleen has it?'

'Maybe. Her mother was wearing a really nice top when Falkov was giving his press conference, but I've been in her house and seen the way she treats her clothes. Kayleen's mother isn't the world's best housekeeper, let's put it that way. That top was new, I'm sure of it. And Kayleen was wearing an anime t-shirt as well, similar to Sara's – same style, just a different cartoon figure. Kayleen's trying to keep up with the other kids, and Mum's got money to splash around, so she buys Kayleen a shirt to help her join the pack, make new friends. I reckon the necklace has been sold, and Mum's spending the money.'

Giles looked at her mobile phone – in the top corner it had no bars, just SOS. They were driving through the bottom of the gorge; in a few minutes they'd be back out on the open road and she'd get reception.

'I'll get Turner and Bray to drop in on Kevin Eddy. He's on bail, shouldn't be too hard to track down. They can ask him if he put the necklace and brooch in the garbage bag. If he did, then the kid's taken it and Turner can start calling pawnbrokers.'

'You think the mum pawned it?'

'Abso-bloody-lutely! It's not like any of her friends would be able to afford buying it off her. And she's not stupid, she wouldn't have posted it for sale online, but she's not got the connections or resources to pull some shady deal either. If she did, she wouldn't be living on Pipeline Avenue.'

THIRTY-THREE

At the edge of the road, black crows pick at the meat of a dead kangaroo. They make no sound as they use their beaks to tear at fur. Pull at sinew and muscle. They cock their heads, turn an eye.

As a car approaches, they hop to the edge of the road and wait for it to pass. The wind ruffles their feathers before they hop back to the carcass and continue to feed.

In the midday sun, the dead animal begins to bake. Its legs stiffen, it becomes bloated and stinks. Drivers wind up their windows and turn off air conditioners as they pass.

The kangaroo's whiskers and half its tongue are somewhere in the undercarriage of a semitrailer, making its way to Melbourne.

~

Pete followed the road. He was using the trees and bushland to conceal himself, travelling about 10 metres from the edge of the bitumen. Through the thick foliage he could see cars flickering by. He kept an eye out for the cops.

The mosquitos had been at him. He scratched a bite on his cheek, unable to satisfy the itch. The bite had left a bump and clear pus kept weeping from it.

Pete was hot and bothered, and scared. The heat rising from the dirt was making him sleepy. Droopy-eyed, he looked out across the road, listening for oncoming vehicles. He had seen the firies and then the cops whiz by, lights flashing, accelerators to the floor. He wished he could have stayed to see the car burn. Just to be sure there was nothing left behind for the coppers to pin on him.

He pushed his way through the thick terrain. Ahead he could smell death, and his stomach heaved. The image of Sara's dead body flashed before him. The scent of roadkill made him panic, plus he could hear another vehicle coming. He bobbed down into the scrub and waited for the car to pass, pulling his shirt up over his nose so he could breathe in his own stench and not the dead kangaroo's.

A full-scale manhunt was now underway for Peter Nolan. Police were at Muswellbrook train station, and at both ends of the A15 highway to Tamworth and Newcastle. His name and face were everywhere in the media. The police had reached out to the community, warned them, established a hotline number, and his home was under surveillance. Pete was a murderer, possibly the Mermaid Killer. And he had disappeared into thin air.

The police had established a perimeter in a 4-kilometre radius around where Pete had dumped and burned his car. Hoping Pete hadn't been lucky enough to hitch a ride, they'd calculated that, with his arthritic hip, the old man could have walked about 2 kilometres from his burnt-out vehicle since he'd lit the fire. But they were playing it safe. They didn't know what direction he was headed in, so they'd deployed nearly the full fleet. The cops were going to get him.

———

In the briefing room, Falkov looked like he was about to have a stroke. His face was grey and ruddy as he addressed the small group. His detectives and most of the other officers were already out in the field, but he had pulled in new resources, including a squad from Newcastle, who would be going directly into the dense bush, and a police helicopter unit. He needed to brief the new officers quickly, but the updates were coming in thick and fast.

Falkov's voice was firm. 'Peter Nolan's location is currently unknown. He is now a fugitive. Hopefully the news of the manhunt will reach him and get him moving around, giving us an opportunity to get eyes on him. We are doing everything to circulate his face in the community and put further pressure on him to move. All highway patrol units are on alert. His mobile phone doesn't appear to be in service, so either he's turned it off, his battery is flat, or he's in a non-mobile service area, which in the Wollemi National Park means he could be anywhere. Before you go in, you need to know that the landscape is dense, treacherous, but that also means he can't be advancing fast. I imagine he's hiding. I doubt very much that he is armed, but all precautions are necessary.'

The small team were fresh and bright eyed. They were each given a mugshot of the fugitive and their eyes were set firmly on their target. Peter Nolan had Buckley's chance of evading capture.

Pete tried to press on, but the stench of the dead animal had got a hold on him. He stood still and scanned the surrounding shrubs and roadside for the rotting carcass.

By the edge of the road, he could see the black mound. He walked towards it. The animal's jaw bone was exposed and red guts were hanging outside its stomach.

Pete wrinkled his nose and sneered at the corpse, feeling irrational hatred towards it. His anger began to water his eyes, and a sob rose in the back of his throat. He tried to swallow it down, suck it back, but his throat was choked with a lump. It wouldn't go. He couldn't calm down, his arm was aching again, he didn't know if he was cold or scared, hot or tired, but he was shaking like buggery, and he couldn't get his breath right.

Pete lashed out, kicking the dead kangaroo.

He whispered to himself, '*You're a kid killer, Pete. A goddamn kid killer.*'

THIRTY-FOUR

Giles and Callahan had only just started spreading the files out across the small kitchen table in Giles's motel room when her mobile phone rang. Turner's named popped up on the screen and she hit loudspeaker.

'Hamilton Pawnbrokers.' Unlike the earlier call, Turner's voice was clear and upbeat. It was as though he were in the room with them.

'Did you get a description?'

'A mother with two kids. Claire, Mikaela and Kayleen – perfect account of all three. On top of that, Claire handed over her ID. Her real ID,' he said. 'Owner still has a copy, plus the CCTV footage. Constable Griffin is on his way down to Hamilton now to retrieve it all.'

The room was cramped and, aside from the space leading from the foot of the bed to the bathroom, Giles had little room to move. She started to pace back and forth. The aircon was rattling, but it was more just making noise than actually blowing cold air. Callahan sat in the only chair and watched Giles pace.

'We are putting everything together to charge Claire Ellis,' said Turner.

Giles crumpled, doubling over with her hands on her hips and her head almost on her knees. *Fuck, fuck, Dad was right. Talk to the kid, bring some mints.*

She flicked back upright. 'Turner, I want to be there when you charge the mother. I want to talk to Kayleen. Kevin Eddy spent a few weeks doing the rounds, robbing different places in the area, and Kayleen probably watched it all from her bedroom window.' She was talking a hundred miles an hour. 'She saw where Eddy was stashing his goods. I think she kept the necklace and brooch for herself, then gave the brooch to Sara.'

'Why would she give away the brooch?' asked Turner.

Bray's voice was next, just as clear as Turner's, and she realised they had their phone on speaker too. 'She's a kid. Guilt? Doesn't want to get busted with it? Buying friendship?'

'Buying a friend sounds like Kayleen,' said Giles. 'I'll ask Falkov if charging Claire Ellis can wait until I'm back in town. She's not going anywhere, another day won't hurt. I just need ten minutes with the kid. I think Kayleen will open up to me.'

There was silence on the phone. Neither side spoke. The air conditioning droned, filling the gap.

Then Callahan asked, 'And what's happening with Peter Nolan?'

'We have CCTV footage of him at the servo in town,' Turner answered. 'He bought a jerry can and filled it up.'

'But they haven't found him?' Giles was cursing her luck – just as they had a nailed-on suspect, she was out of town.

'We've got an extensive search underway, nearly all units are out there – we've got the whole perimeter covered. PMU is working with the press and the phones are running wild with tip-offs, although so far they're mostly time-wasters.'

'Any chance he's already hitched a ride out of town?' Callahan called out from the other side of the table.

Turner's voice was softer. 'Anything is possible. Giles, Pete turned up at the press gathering. Why did he do that? He'd already killed Sara.'

'To see what we knew?' Giles shrugged.

Bray's voice now: 'Or he could still be here, watching.'

'Watching what?' Giles asked. 'The police? Media?'

'You,' said Bray.

'Me?'

Turner's voice boomed again. 'He came to see *you*, Giles. He sat at the front desk for two days and then, even after Sara was dead, he came to the station again. There's something he wants from you, badly.'

'Giles, do you think you're safe?' asked Bray. 'You know him better than all of us.'

'I don't think Pete is a conscious killer. I think right now he's a scared and lonely man, running as far away as he can get.'

'He doesn't have much money,' said Turner.

'But he's got sticky fingers,' added Callahan.

'He could have hopped on a coal train?' suggested Giles. 'Are we checking those?'

'Giles.' It was Falkov's voice. Giles stood up straight. *Shit, Falkov has been listening the whole time.* 'Pete's *our* problem. You and Callahan turn your full focus to Ava Emmerson. Right now. Go to Summer Street, talk to the boyfriend, Jeremy Liddle. The moment you're done, brief me. Do that and I'll let you have your ten-minute chat with Kayleen tomorrow morning. Make sure you're up before the birds.'

Callahan wriggled in his chair. Either he couldn't get comfortable being in Giles's room or something was bothering him. He flicked the files on the table like he was sorting through junk mail, then said, 'What connects Kevin Eddy, Kayleen, Claire Ellis, Sara and Pete? Stolen jewellery. Where did Ava Emmerson work? A jewellery shop. And where are we off to? A bloody jewellery shop.'

'Shit! That's the link?'

'Those two roads must cross somewhere, Giles. I think Summer Street Jewellery Store is that intersection.'

Callahan pulled out his laptop and searched through his emails, opening an attachment sent to him by the jewellery store's insurance company. He scanned through the document until he found the list of stolen items. Cheaper goods listed first. Novelty watches, 9-carat gold bracelets, charms. Near the end of the list, he found what he was looking for: an emerald and diamond set.

'Bingo.' Callahan held his hand up for a high five, but Giles was already rushing out the door and left him hanging.

THIRTY-FIVE

It was only a five-minute drive from the motel to Summer Street. Callahan was at the wheel and as he cruised past Cook Park, he envied the kids feeding ducks by the pond, the businessmen munching sandwiches on park benches, the joggers getting a run in on their lunch break. The park was a burst of colour – a short reprieve and a welcome distraction; a glance at how the other half lived.

Giles seemed to be in a different headspace. She was missing the view as the scenery flashed by, the trees, the fountain, the gazebo. She had her head down and her attention was entirely absorbed by the store's insurance claim.

'How many girls have you seen wear emeralds?'

'Huh?' Callahan was distracted, now looking for kerbside parking. 'None, really. More silver, gold, or maybe diamonds. My mother has a pair of ruby earrings, but she only wears them on special occasions. I wouldn't think emeralds were popular.'

'Do you think green is a harder colour stone to sell?'

'I don't know, Giles. I don't wear that shit. What do you think?'

'I'm just bothered by the list here. I've read the reports. The statement reads that the low-value were kept in the storeroom, the high-value in the front of the shop. Why steal a stack of novelty watches and cubic zirconia pieces from the back of the store. Why not steal only the valuable jewels from the shop cases? That's a lot of time-wasting.'

'Maybe the robber didn't know the difference?' Callahan said, as he reverse parallel-parked between two 4×4s with oversized bull bars and rows of spotlights.

The back of the Sonata bumped the bull bar of the 4×4 behind. Callahan swore and put the car in drive, inching forward so the two vehicles no longer touched.

'You're as bad as MacCrum,' said Giles, as she unclipped her seatbelt and stepped out of the car into the scorching heat.

The Leweks were not happy or comfortable with the surprise visit from Callahan and Giles. Mrs Lewek kept herself busy by spraying the display cabinets with window cleaner and rubbing at smudges that weren't there. She let her husband do most of the talking.

Mr Lewek was polite but dismissive. He assured Callahan that he'd put it all behind him – the robbery had been over three months ago, he couldn't remember much about it, statements had been made, he'd already sorted it with the insurance company. He was a looking-to-the-future type of guy. Sorry he wasn't much help, getting old, fuzzy memory.

Giles listened to Mr Lewek ramble away while she looked around the shop. Glass door and windows at the front, roll-down security mesh for locking up at night. Solid doorway with double Lockwood locks that led into the storeroom and a small kitchen area at the rear, where there was another external door.

Giles turned the knob and found the back door was unlocked. She stepped out into an alley. There were dumpsters and other doors, the back entry into more shops, a public bathroom at the end of the alley. There were a few upturned milk cartons at the rear of a café and a clump of cigarette butts littered the step. Giles returned inside and Mrs Lewek shuffled into the back room, locking the door with her keys.

'Is there anything else you'd like to see?' asked Mr Lewek. He was clearly trying to wrap it up.

'So, your security system and cameras were on the blink the week you were robbed?'

'Bad timing. Though no one would have known – the strobe light and cameras were there. How would anyone know they weren't working? I had the guy booked in for the next day to come fix it.'

'Did the officers you spoke to take the name of that guy?' asked Callahan.

'Um, I can't remember. Do you think —'

Callahan cut Mr Lewek off. 'What was wrong with the security system?'

'Rats in the roof chewed through the cables.'

Mr Lewek's memory suddenly seemed sharper.

Giles pointed towards the rear of the shop. 'The report said the back door was kicked in, and that Ava hadn't locked the door between the storeroom and the front of the shop. Is that right? That's how they got in?'

'Terrible what's happened to that young lady, just terrible.' Mr Lewek shook his head.

Giles repeated the question, pulling Mr Lewek back on track.

'Um, she put the "back in ten minutes" sign on the front door. And yes, I think she forgot to lock the middle door. But she did lock the back door. Only, it's pine and often jams – the key gets stuck. We really only lock it at the end of the day.'

'And then you realised, after the police left, that your ring counter had also been hit. You made a second statement adding those items?'

'I didn't notice until later. I just thought the stone sets were gone, and the stuff from the storeroom.'

'For a jewellery store, I'm surprised by your relaxed attitude to security, Mr Lewek.'

'Been in this shop for nearly twenty years – and in this town. Aside from this incident, never been broken into once.'

Giles nodded. 'So, the back door is kicked in, they take stuff from the storeroom. Then they come into the showroom, steal the stone sets from the front counters and the ring counter, and then they exit again via the back door?'

Lewek nodded too. 'Yes, I think so. That seems to be what happened.'

'Hmm.' Giles walked to the ring display. 'Is this where you always display your engagement rings?'

'Yes.'

'Haven't moved the display in the last three months?'

'No.' Mr Lewek was looking a little flushed. 'Same set-up as always. Works for us.'

Callahan shot Giles a look. He was leaning on the counter, trying to follow her train of thought. Mrs Lewek cleared her throat and sprayed the counter again and the mist hit his arm. Callahan stood upright and wiped his sleeve, frowning.

Giles sucked her bottom lip, her cheek twitched. 'Got family in Scone?' she asked.

Mrs Lewek stopped polishing. Her head popped up and her body swivelled to face Giles. 'I do,' she said.

'And who would that be?'

'A sister.'

'Does she have a name?'

'Deloris.'

'A full name?'

'Pruitt. Deloris Pruitt.'

Gotcha! Deloris Pruitt. The sister with the thoroughbreds and shotgun.

'Did you go to your sister's birthday party in Scone? Maybe give her a gift for her sixtieth birthday?'

'Ah. Yes.'

'What did you give her?'

Mrs Lewek studied her polishing rag for an answer. 'I can't remember.'

Giles jogged her memory, 'A stone and diamond set?'

'Yes. Yes, that was it.'

'What kind of stone, please?'

'Emerald, from our shop. It was one of the sets we had on display.'

'That's interesting, isn't it? Because on your insurance claim, it says that set was stolen.'

Seeking shade, Giles and Callahan sat on opposite benches in the gazebo in Cook Park. Callahan was as excited as a dog with two tails. Robbery, insurance fraud, and two murders – Orange Police Station were going to love their phone call.

'So, what have you got?' asked Callahan.

'Shh.' Giles laughed. 'I'm still playing it out in my head.'

After skipping their stop in Rylestone, they had gone to a bakery in Orange, and Callahan's mood had shifted now that he was finally loaded up with two pies and a vanilla slice. He squeezed tomato sauce from the plastic tube over the pie crust, then licked it from his fingers. 'I've already played it out in my head, but you go first.'

'Just eat your pie,' said Giles, and she bit into her own.

Mushroom and steak. The filling was hot, and she puffed the heat from her mouth then gulped some of her iced coffee. Her mind rolled over like a film reel, the characters all in action, scene one, scene two, scene three. She went back, edited the movements, until she could play out the scenes. *Aaaand cut*, she thought when the last scene finished, a slow fade out with the camera on Ava in the cattle trough, Turner giving Giles CPR, and the killer on his motorbike in the Wollemi National Park. *End scene.*

Giles flicked flecks of pastry from her lap, scrunched the empty brown paper bag into a ball and tossed it at Callahan's head. 'Okay, I'm ready.'

Shoving the last of his pie into his mouth, Callahan leaned back on the bench and put his hands behind his head like he was settling in to watch a movie.

In the heat, Giles let her shoulders sag, cleared her throat, and began. 'So now we know Mrs Lewek put in an insurance claim for the emerald set, but actually gave the set to her sister, Mrs Pruitt in Scone, for her sixtieth birthday.'

Callahan nodded.

'Mrs Pruitt is then robbed, separately, by Kevin Eddy. He stashes the jewellery set in his doghouse.'

Callahan nodded again.

'While bailed up in the doghouse, Kayleen helps herself to the brooch and necklace. The earrings were found in the garbage bag, and Kevin Eddy sold the ring to Sticky Pete at the pub. That's the whole set. Then the mum pawns the necklace, and Kayleen gives the brooch to Sara. Pete sees the brooch —'

'And we know how that ended.'

'Yeah,' Giles grimaced. She turned her mind to the jewellery store. 'I think the shop was hit three times. Ava stepped out to use the public toilets at the end of the alley. While she was gone, the jewellers got hit via the back door, but only in the storeroom. The robber kicks the door in, takes the general stock, but only the stuff they could get to at the rear of the store, like the watches and novelty jewellery. It has to be someone who was watching the shop and waiting for Ava to leave, most likely Jeremy, her boyfriend. When Ava returns her first call is to the Leweks, not the police. Mr and Mrs Lewek tell her to wait for them before doing anything else. That's when the shop is hit a second time, by the Leweks themselves, who figure they'll scoop up some insurance money by claiming some of the merchandise they couldn't sell was also taken – like the emerald set in the front of the shop. But they had to convince Ava to change her story and say she left the door between shopfront and back storeroom unlocked. That wouldn't have sat well with Ava. But for one reason or another, she goes along with it.'

Callahan nearly choked. 'You don't bloody think the Leweks tracked Ava down and killed her? To keep her silent about their insurance fraud?'

'No.' Giles shook her head. 'I think the shop was hit a *third* time, when the engagement rings were swiped from the counter in the back corner. The Leweks didn't check the ring cabinet because they knew the first robber didn't get through the middle door, and they knew *they* didn't take anything from it themselves. Only later did they realise someone had taken the rings and they'd have to revise the statement they initially gave to the officers on the scene.'

'And, what, you think Ava took them?'

'I think a cop took them.'

'Shit, Giles! That's a big bloody leap!'

'The Leweks couldn't point the finger at an officer, could they? Because that would be giving themselves away. How would they know? They can't say to the cops, "Oh, we just nicked our own hard-to-sell shit from the front, but not the engagement rings, so it must have been one of you bastards."'

Callahan rubbed his face, then patted down his shirt and tie. 'Okay, I'm still following.'

'Look, when we were in there, I stood at the ring counter in the back corner – it's in the perfect place to fleece a few rings when no one's looking. If you had access from the back of the counter, say while you were dusting for fingerprints? Just humour me on this: what if Ava witnessed it? The stress of lying and changing her story for the Leweks, *and* witnessing a cop stealing the rings . . . I think she couldn't cope anymore. Her boyfriend getting busted for drugs just tipped her over the edge.'

'Or she suspected Jeremy of stealing from the back of the shop, and that tipped her over the edge?'

Giles tapped her temple with her index finger and gave an exaggerated nod. 'Smart. Couples always talk about their workday – Jeremy would have known the alarm system was on the blink. And so, Ava just ran away from it all. That's why she spent so much time in the bush, she was trying to get away from everyone.'

'And you think the person who killed Ava was . . . the first robber, possibly the boyfriend? Or . . . the cop?'

'Cop.'

'Shit, Giles. That's an even bigger leap – that's a somersault off a 10-metre board!'

'Mrs Emmerson said "police are scary". What if Ava was scared of the police for another reason, not just the uniform?'

Callahan licked his finger and dabbed at a few crumbs left on his trousers. He was silent.

Giles pressed on. 'The cop has the most to lose. Ava wouldn't dob in her boyfriend – loyalty, love, embarrassment for picking the wrong guy – but knew they needed to break up. The Leweks had already got her word to keep silent, so she was involved in their crime. She knew she'd get in trouble for lying to the police. But the *cop* . . . I don't believe Ava was hiding in the bush from the Leweks or her ex. I think she was hiding from a police officer.'

Callahan scratched the back of his head, frowning. 'And how do you think Falkov will react to this new theory of yours?'

'Eat your vanilla slice. When we get back to the motel, we can brief the team. I'll put it out there. We'll know then how Falkov takes it.'

THIRTY-SIX

At The Lord Anson, happy hour was two cocktails and a cheese platter for thirty bucks. Callahan would have preferred a beer, but Giles talked him into a whisky sour while she ordered a dry martini. They found a table that was relatively isolated so they could talk.

They had just finished an hour-and-a-half conference call to the station from the motel. Now, at the pub, they needed a break. Callahan had called his wife to say he was still alive, and then his kids had jumped on the phone and given him grief. Then it was phones off and time to wind down before heading home in the morning. They had struck out interviewing the boyfriend – he was still out of town, kilometres away at Glenwood State Forest, doing some night-time pig hunting and daytime beer drinking.

He'd been there for a week, meaning he was out of town even before Ava's death. The poor prick was still unaware his ex had been killed. Meanwhile the detectives at Orange station would soon be opening a new file with his name on it, establishing his movements on the day of the robbery at Summer Street. Digging deep to see if Jeremy – Jezza – was the one who'd kicked in the back door. Giles wondered – if he *was* responsible for the first break-and-enter, would he be haunted by Ava's death? Fixate on the details, re-imagine the brutality for years to come, knowing he had been the decisive cog, the first wheel to turn, sending Ava towards her fate.

Callahan winced a little on the first sip of his whiskey, the lemon tangy in his mouth, but he knew on the second sip it would slide down easily. He'd dressed in a dark blue Ralph Lauren polo shirt, slim fit – his love of kayaking and weight training had paid off. He had to do something to burn off all those bakery pies and cakes.

Giles was in stonewash jeans, sneakers, and was still wearing the button-up blouse she'd had on all day. She had refreshed with a few squirts of deodorant and a spray of perfume. She wasn't mucking around – she needed a drink and a different outlook. Being in the pub had dramatically changed her mood, and she was more upbeat, but still anxious and buzzing with adrenaline.

'How're the kids?'

'Excited the dog's back home, fighting over whose bed it should sleep in.'

'What kind of dog?'

'Kelpie. Kids hated how it rounded them up all the time like they were bloody sheep, never walked it, never picked up its shit in the backyard. But as soon as I give it away, they swear they always loved the thing.'

'Kids!' Giles rolled her eyes.

Callahan looked down into his drink and frowned. He switched the conversation back to the case. 'So, we'll wait for Falkov to get us the robbery report?'

'We'll have to. Don't want our copper mates in Orange knowing we were at Summer Street and have linked it to Ava Emmerson's murder, but we do need that original report. But if you or I request access, it'll set off alarm bells.'

'Don't envy Falkov having to jump through all those hoops

to keep it confidential from Orange.' Callahan mumbled into his drink. 'You really think it was a cop?'

'Yep. I think Ava saw them – maybe she rang the station once she was back in Muswellbrook? Wanted to report more? And someone made sure she didn't return to Orange to repeat the story.'

'I know these guys. They're mates. We would do anything for each other. We're like family. I just can't see any of them being killers, that's all. Do you think it was a threat that got out of hand?'

'Yeah, maybe. The crime scene was staged to completely bamboozle us. It was someone who knew how to bugger up a scene to make it near impossible for us to find anything.'

'It worked.'

'For a while. But yes, I guess it did.'

'It shook us, Giles. It looked bad at first. Evil.'

'Yes.' Giles fished out the toothpick in her drink and slid the olive off using her teeth. It was salty and juicy. She chewed and nodded. 'We just need to find the officer who did it, the rest don't matter. As soon as Falkov manages to get that file, it will give us the list of officers who were at the scene that day. Our killer will be one of the names on that list. I'm sure of it.'

'Shit.' Callahan sculled half his drink in one hit. 'When all this is over, once we've got evidence to back up your theory, we can come clean, hand over what we've got and tell Orange to bring in Jeremy Liddle for an interview regarding the robbery. He's the only one aside from Ava and the Leweks that knew she was alone in the shop and that their security system was on the blink. And if your cop theory goes arse up, I wouldn't dismiss the boyfriend for her murder. The bloke *is* out pig hunting, with dogs. We don't know 100 per cent that he's been getting pissed and shooting guns with his mates the whole week. Couldn't he have slipped off for a day?'

A table nearby erupted in noise and Giles jerked her head towards the outburst. One of the boys there had slumped down in his seat and rocked the rickety table. Beer had slopped everywhere and foam was still sliding down the sides of the group's schooners. They all jostled to get in their wisecracks and demanded the dickhead buy the next round. It was jovial, light-hearted. Giles laughed. She was jumpier than usual.

Callahan seemed to notice her jitters and opted to change the topic of conversation. There was nothing left for them to do now but get a good night's sleep and head back to the station in the morning.

Callahan asked, 'Where's the cheese platter?'

'Staff will bring it out.'

'You want another?' He tipped his head towards Giles's martini glass.

'Of course!'

Callahan stood, scraping his chair along the floor. 'You've done some good work, Giles. Now we just need the evidence to back up your theory.'

'Ask for two olives in the martini.'

Callahan turned to leave, then hesitated. 'Are you still pissed at Turner? For having a crack at you the other day? He has been trying to apologise, you know.'

Giles shrugged. 'I'm not angry, just disappointed by what I overheard. And you don't have to go out of your way to protect him.'

'He's me mate – I'd do anything for a mate.'

'Would you now?'

'I just hate seeing Turner all mopey.' Callahan winked at Giles. 'Let's see if I can get three olives in the next glass.'

THIRTY-SEVEN

It was an early checkout from the motel. By 6 a.m. the sun was up, and Callahan and Giles were on the road.

Giles was driving and she calculated that they'd be back in Muswellbrook by ten o'clock if they made no stops along the way. She had planned to meet Bray and MacCrum on the corner of Pipeline Avenue. They would give Claire Ellis the respect of leaving their cars parked a little further down the road this time so the neighbours wouldn't peep through their windows and start gossiping.

They agreed Bray and MacCrum would tackle the topic of 'profiting from stolen goods' with Claire, while Giles would chat with Kayleen. Callahan could keep an eye on Mikaela. After the traumatic discovery of Sara's body, both girls were being kept home from school for the time being.

From the front step of the house, under the shade of the jacaranda tree, Giles and Kayleen watched Mikaela transform the footpath into a colourful abstract artwork. With her different chalks, the younger sister was following the tannin-stained patterns left on the concrete by fallen leaves and bark. And Callahan was helping her by idly kicking long strips of stringybark into the gutter.

Giles and Kayleen sat in silence, both of them knowing that, once they started chatting, the conversation would eventually lead to Sara Milligan. So neither was in a hurry to start.

On the front lawn two pushbikes lay on their side. The metallic-painted frames shone rainbow-chrome colours in the sunlight.

Eventually, Giles said, 'New bike?'

'Yeah.'

Giles wondered if the purchase of the bike was as much to help Kayleen get over the ordeal of spending the night in a dog kennel as to help her make new friends.

'Mikaela got one too?'

'Yep, the both of us,' answered Kayleen. 'Mine's the bigger one.'

Giles nodded. 'How's school? You can't keep having time off.'

Kayleen shrugged. 'I did go back for a bit. But at school, everyone kept saying my mum and I kidnapped and killed Sara. That we hurt her the same way the girl was hurt out on that farm.'

'Oof,' sighed Giles.

'I punched a girl for saying it. One of Sara's friends. That's why the school sent me home.'

'They sent you home?'

'Yeah. She said I stole her bestie and then I killed her.'

Giles crinkled her nose. 'That's mean. I'm sorry about Sara, Kayleen.'

The girl rolled into herself and Giles heard the start of sobs. She rubbed the child's shoulder, soothing her. 'It's okay, Kayleen. We know who did it. The kids at school will back off now. People say dumb stuff when they're scared.'

Kayleen wiped her tears with the bottom of her t-shirt. 'Are you angry at my mum?'

'I'm just doing my job, Kayleen.' Giles immediately regretted her blunt answer.

The child twisted her lips. 'What's going to happen to our neighbour, Mr Eddy? Is he in a lot of trouble?'

'Yes. He broke into people's homes and stole their things.'

Kayleen stared at her sister, shuffling her feet as though she wanted to join her, then asked, 'Can kids go to jail?' Her eyes began to well with tears again.

'No darling, that's not going to happen.' Giles smiled down at her. 'But I do need to know if you gave the brooch to Sara. At the park?'

Kayleen nodded. 'Yes.'

'Was she wearing it when you left her in the park?'

'No, but she might have put it on after I left.'

'Did you give the necklace to your mum?'

Kayleen looked up at Giles. She didn't reply. But she didn't need to – Giles could see the answer in her face.

Mikaela now had Callahan on his knees, directing him to join his mural with hers. Callahan had yellow chalk and was drawing swirls shaped like ocean waves that crashed into pink spirals.

'Do you want to draw with your sister? Detective Callahan's not very artistic.'

'Yes, please.'

Kayleen stood and Giles reached inside her jacket pocket, pulling out a handful of mints. 'Here, go share these with Mikaela.'

Giles gave Kayleen the mints and one dropped onto the step.

'You need bigger hands,' Giles said.

Kayleen looked small and smug as she scooped up the mint, then counted them all. There were five. She hid the fifth mint in the waistband of her pants – now there were four mints, easier to divide between herself and Mikaela. Giles held back her laugh as Kayleen skipped down the steps to join her sister. *So that's how she got the jewellery out of the doghouse, the clever little bugger.*

THIRTY-EIGHT

Giles felt a sense of closure as she knelt by the fence line, close to where Sara Milligan's body had been found. The roadside had been turned into a shrine. A half-deflated foil balloon floated in the air, attached to the fence with curly pink ribbon.

There were a few teddy bears slumped against the fence post, and posies of flowers, all wilting in the heat, petals falling off and the leaves drying up. Paper pinwheels spun in the breeze and made a fluttering sound. The cards, both store-bought and handmade, were damp, ink bleeding into the paper from the morning dew and the inscriptions fading.

Tea-light candles, which had all been lit for a night-time vigil, were now snuffed out, just melted pools of wax in the bottom of the foil. The shrine had lost its magic and now looked like a dumping ground. Some of the tributes had blown away and littered the paddock.

Giles dropped her head, feeling the heat on the back of her neck as she carefully read the messages. Most expressed the same heartfelt thoughts – there wasn't anything relevant to their investigation. She stood and stretched, looking away from the dismal shrine and out into the paddock where Sara had been discovered. The police tape floated in the gentle wind, but the paddock was empty, the ERU long gone. Bray was down by the dam somewhere, but she couldn't see him from where she stood.

In the distance she could hear the police helicopter in the sky. It was still on the hunt for Pete.

There was the sudden sound of movement in amongst the dry grass. Giles stayed still, her ears straining to detect the direction the noise had come from. She stood up on her toes, alert, peering through the tufts of grass. She only relaxed when she spotted a baby echidna trudging along the ground.

Giles had never seen a wild echidna this close. She retrieved her water bottle from the car and walked back over to the small animal. Her feet crunched in the dry litter of leaves and dead grass – it sounded like burnt toast being munched underfoot. Giles grinned. *Breakfast for animals, toasted by the sun.*

She kneeled. The echidna had curled up when it first heard her approaching, but now it began to unroll itself from its ball. Its little snout appeared. Giles tipped the bottle over the animal, letting the water dribble along its short snout. She smiled and licked her own dry lips, which were cracking in the heat. At least the echidna's snout was now moist. The weather had been gruelling for the animals, and for the farmers.

Again, the sound of more crunching grass. Giles looked around, waiting for the baby echidna's mother to emerge. Instead, she found Delano standing close behind her, leaning over her shoulder.

'Geez, I'm surprised to see you here.'

'I didn't mean to creep up on you.' Delano looked at the animal and smirked. 'It's a baby echidna.'

'First time I've seen one in the wild.'

'Yeah, same.'

'You here to help?'

'Nah. I saw your car up on the road. Thought I'd stop and say goodbye before heading home tomorrow.'

'Just passing through?' Giles laughed. The road was a dead end – he must have come searching for her.

'Thought it was the polite thing to do. I'm heading back to Dubbo in the morning. Things have dried up on my end – the area of the national park they gave me to search didn't turn up anything. But . . . didn't want to just take off. You know.' Delano shrugged. He looked a little uncomfortable, fidgety. 'Are you here alone?'

'No, Bray is around here somewhere. He wandered off towards the dam.'

'Aha. You on a cycle with him today?'

'Yeah. Spent yesterday in Orange with Callahan, we only got back this morning, so Bray's a welcome change.' Giles forced a laugh, but Delano only grinned.

'Orange, eh?'

Giles nodded. She wished she hadn't tipped all the water out of the bottle. Her mouth was so dry. 'Where's your pooch?'

'In the car, engine running, aircon on full blast. Sprawled out in the dog crate. Sleeping on the job!'

Giles smiled, only it felt forced, so she crinkled her corners of her eyes, 'You never mentioned you were off work on a P902.'

'Who told you that?' Delano looked annoyed. He shifted his feet, and the echidna disappeared into the shrubs.

Giles dusted the dirt from her knees and watched the baby animal disappear, a little sorry that it had ambled off so soon. 'Bray mentioned it this morning. I thought you were in Muswellbrook visiting a friend.'

'I was. Had a few medical appointments at the hospital and some physio down near Maitland. Thought it was a good opportunity to

catch up with an old mate, bring the dog. Crash there instead of
a motel.'

'Who's the friend?'

'Just a mate.' Delano looked over Giles's shoulder, his eyes scanning the paddock, his feet still shuffling in the dry grass.

'What's the problem? For a P902?' Giles asked, not sure if she
was being too nosy.

'Got a bit of a tricky knee, that's all.'

'Tricky knee? Everything okay?' Bad knees were not good news
in the police force. Knee injuries or reconstructions meant a change
of duties – in Delano's case, giving up the dog squad – or taking
early retirement.

'Nah, knee's fine.' Delano laughed it off. 'Light duties for a
while, but then I'll be back in action. Nothing serious at all. I hear
you're still looking for Ava Emmerson's killer, is that right? Are Sara
and Ava's murders related?'

Giles shook her head. 'Related, yes. Same killer, no. I knew
it wasn't the same killer the moment I saw Sara's body. The wire
wrapped around the bodies was completely different. Sara was
clothed, Ava was naked. Sara was hit by a car, Ava was strangled –
post-mortem detected a fractured hyoid bone.'

'Did Rickard have anything to do with it?'

'No.'

'Think you'll catch the guy?'

'Guys.' Giles put stress on the plural. 'Got a hunt on for Peter
Nolan, for killing Sara Milligan. Didn't you get briefed?'

'Nope.' Delano shrugged. 'Busy girl, looking for two separate
killers.'

'I might get lucky. Sometimes the strangest of things make sense
when you connect the right dots.'

'And one of those dots took you all the way out to Orange?'

Giles sniffed and wiped the sweat from her lip. 'I'm so close, I know it. I'm on a bit of a hot streak.'

'Hmm.' Delano shifted in the dirt again. 'Um, do you want to do dinner? Tonight? My treat, as a *see you later, nice to meet you*?'

'Oh, I had plans with Dad. But I can cancel. We see enough of each other.'

'Bring him along! I'd love to meet the great Benjamin Giles.'

'I was going to Merton Court, that's where he's staying. How about I have you both over for dinner at my place? Dad loves to tell his police stories to anyone who's interested. A bottle of red wine and an audience is my father living the dream.'

'I'll pick him up then, bring him around to your place. Say, six-thirty? Seven?'

'Okay.' Giles felt a whip of excitement. 'I'll let the staff at Merton know you're coming to get him. Seven is perfect. Let's barbeque – do you like steak?'

'Bloody love a good steak.'

'If you get to my place before me, I leave a spare key in my hanging basket on the front porch. Dad'll show you which one. Help yourself to a beer.'

'Great. See you at seven.'

There was a moment of uncertainty as Delano leaned in for a kiss, but Giles figured one last hoorah couldn't hurt. Delano opened his lips and let his tongue slide into her mouth. He squeezed his fingers into her shoulder and his thumb rubbed at the edge of her neck. She flinched; she was still sore and bruised from the attack at Rickard's. Delano kept kissing her and his grip tightened, while his other hand curled around her waist.

'Hey, Giles!' Bray called from the edge of the paddock.

Delano released Giles and they pulled apart.

'Delano.' Bray nodded, as he climbed through the fence and approached.

Delano gave a quick nod back and then said to Giles, 'See you tonight.' He turned and headed towards the road, his exit a little abrupt.

Giles rubbed her shoulder where his fingers had pressed and looked away from Bray.

'What's going on there?' Bray asked.

'Dunno. Nothing.'

'Didn't look like nothing.'

'Nothing isn't always something.'

Bray frowned but let it go. 'So, Detective Giles, run me through what you've got.'

'I don't think Pete would return to this spot. I think he'd run back to the arms of his wife before he revisited this place.'

'Me too. Let's head to the station.'

'Can we stop off at the shops? I need to buy some steak.'

'Steak for a dinner date, eh?'

Giles didn't answer, leaving Bray standing by the roadside shrine as she strode off. By the time she got to the car, Delano was long gone, and Bray was still crunching through the dry grass behind her.

THIRTY-NINE

Bray stayed in the car with the engine running, the aircon and music up, while Giles dashed to the shops. She headed through the hot car park of the shopping centre, past the lunchtime rush at the café by the entry.

Once through the automatic doors, the temperature dropped – the air conditioning was a welcome relief. The foyer smelled of fresh bread from the bakery and perfumes and soaps from the chemist. A music shop was playing an unrecognisable tune with bass thumping out the beat.

The shopping centre seemed busier than normal, and Giles had to dodge overloaded trolleys.

'Excuse me,' she said to no one in particular, her eyes on the supermarket entrance beyond the crowd.

No one moved. Instead, the voices dropped, and the gathering turned to look at her. It was the local community Facebook group; Giles recognised one of the ladies handing out flyers from Falkov's media briefing outside the station. They were asking locals to sign a petition to 'save our kids'.

Shit. Giles could see she'd walked into ambush before it even happened. It was the glint of recognition in their eyes. Two of the women stepped into her path, stopping directly in front of her and blocking her access to the supermarket. One of them flicked her ponytail over her shoulder, missing Giles's face by an inch.

'You're one of the officers on the murder case, aren't you?' Her tone was snarky.

'It's a crime to harass an officer. If you'll excuse me, I need to get through. Plus, if this is a protest, you need a permit.'

'It's a community service. It's freedom of speech. We're an awareness and support group handing out information. We're organising a walking school bus to protect our children. What are you doing? Nothing. Shopping. You should be out catching a serial killer!'

'I'm allowed to eat,' said Giles. She stepped to the side, but the woman stepped with her.

'Should the town be afraid?' asked the other woman. Her face was sharp, her thin nose pointed up at Giles, her lips pinched tight.

'Of what?' Giles knew better than to engage, but the hot walk from the car park, the doof-doof music, her thumping head and now this surprise attack – it was clouding her judgement.

'Of *what*? The maniac killing our children! A man *you* can't find. What are you doing? First the jillaroo out on that farm, now a twelve-year-old girl. Who next?'

Giles wanted to say the two cases were not related, but the second woman had moved closer too and lifted her finger towards Giles's face.

'Are you the policewoman who was nearly the second victim? Are you the police officer that got away?'

Giles wished she'd worn her scarf. The bruises around her neck and face were now yellowed. She looked to the left and right, and it seemed the group were converging on top of her.

Another member piped up. 'You might have been able to save yourself, but we're not all trained police officers – and nor are our kids!' The group's bravado was building.

'Do I look like I won the fight?' Giles snapped, and instantly she regretted it. She quickly tried to backpedal. 'We *will* find and arrest the person responsible for the murder of Sara Milligan.'

'And the jillaroo?'

Giles hesitated, looking for a break in the pack.

'So, it *is* a serial killer.'

'No comment.'

But it was too bloody late for that now. The group had already seized the opportunity to confront her on the issue head-on.

'This is a small town. He can't hide forever,' an older member of the group said. This woman stepped through the crowd and grabbed Giles by the elbow, her face only inches away. 'Your father was legendary, surely something has rubbed off on you. Do you think you can follow in his footsteps? Or should you just bring your dad in?'

'*What?*' Giles pulled her elbow free. She clamped her teeth together and hissed, 'Let's hope it's in my gene pool.'

Shit. You always lose the argument when you're angry.

Giles turned and left the shopping centre, ignoring the calls for answers. The customers in the café watched her leave. Even the doof-doof music was now silent.

In the car park, Bray still had the radio up and was tapping the beat of whatever song was playing on the steering wheel with his big fingers. Giles opened the door and slumped into her seat.

'That was quick.' He sat up and turned down the music. 'Did you get your meat?'

'Changed my mind, I'll order in.' Giles fumbled with her seatbelt and snapped it into place.

'Delano likes Thai takeaway then?'

'Just drive.'

She turned her head and stared out the window, wanting to cry. She squeezed her eyes shut and thought of her mother. Giles willed the feeling of her mother's fingertips to gently trace the arch of her eyebrow.

Touch me, please. Touch me now.

She felt nothing.

'You okay?' asked Bray.

'I said just drive.'

A car horn honked – someone wanted their parking spot and was getting impatient. Bray frowned and pulled out, letting the other driver take the space. Giles didn't speak, fearing she would burst into a flood of sobs and snot; she *never* cried in front of her workmates.

Inspector Falkov was scanning Facebook posts in local groups and other social media on behalf of the team. His officers didn't need to read the barrage of incendiary comments aimed their way – they didn't need the negativity or the distraction – but he might spot someone slipping up and posting something that only the killer would know. It was disturbing to think that maybe the killer themselves was reading the posts, enjoying the fame.

He was just starting to get bored with the keyboard warriors when a fresh post hit the screen. The comment was about a quote given by a police officer, outraged that a female cop from Muswellbrook had told concerned citizens, 'What is there to be afraid of?'

Falkov groaned and pinched the bridge of his nose.

The comments pinged immediately below the original, a flurry of choleric posts.

The moment Giles returned to the office, he called her in.

'Shut the door.'

'Yes, sir.'

'Don't sit.'

Giles stood.

'First of all, don't have your online shopping delivered to the station.'

'Shopping?'

'This arrived for you.' On his desk was a parcel labelled with the name of the hat manufacturer she'd ordered from, the dispatch date clearly marked. 'Keep your internet purchases to your own time.'

Falkov kept talking. His mood was dark. 'Did you just give a quote to the Facebook support group those mothers are running?'

'Shit. No – I mean, yes. I got bombarded with questions down at the supermarket, sir.'

'You don't think the community should be afraid? Because we've been running a full-scale hunt for Sticky Pete for almost twenty-four hours, and we still haven't found him. You can't tell a community not to be afraid, Giles.'

'I — I — I'm sorry, sir.'

'Damage is done. No more comments, you hear?'

'Yes, sir.'

'Do you feel you need protection?'

'*What?* No. I've . . . I've got someone coming over tonight.'

'Not really the time for a social occasion, is it?'

'It's my dad coming for dinner. I think the two of us will be fine, sir.'

Falkov's face brightened. 'Say hello for me.'

'Will do, sir.'

Giles was about to turn to leave, but Falkov had not finished. 'I had a confidential chat to the Chief Inspector in Orange. He is going to pull the full case file of the Summer Street jewellery store break-in and email it to me tonight. He wants to wait until it's after-hours before he scans the documents. I didn't fully explain why I needed it kept hush-hush. No disrespect, Giles, but I'm hoping your idea of a cop being involved in Ava Emmerson's murder doesn't pan out. No offence.'

'None taken, sir.'

Falkov flicked his head at the door. Giles was dismissed. As she left his office, he watched her intently.

FORTY

Giles could feel the long day and the long shift in every muscle of her body. If she wasn't having guests for dinner, she'd be soaking in the bath, maybe lighting her candle, and having a glass of sangria – or a jug.

She flicked the lock on her bedroom window and slid it open. The muggy room needed the evening breeze. The shutters had been left open all day and the midday sun had spilled through the timber slats. Even the floorboards underfoot had lost their cooling touch.

She shook off her jacket and hung it over the wingback chair in the corner of her room, unbuttoning the top of her blouse, removing her holster and gun, and emptying it of its magazine and the bullet in the chamber. She laid it gently in her top bedside drawer.

Changing into stonewash jeans, she tucked in the front of her blouse but let the back of the shirt hang free. In the en suite, she pulled the bobby pins from her bun so her hair fell into a ponytail. With a soft brush she added a dusting of powder to her nose and light pink blush to her cheeks, glossed her lips with watermelon-flavoured lip balm and added a smidge of mascara to her lashes. She didn't want to look like she'd made the effort, but she still wanted to look tempting to Delano.

In the kitchen, Giles rummaged around in the bottom drawer and pulled out a bunch of takeaway menus. She flicked through them, unsure of what to order. Would he like a poké bowl, a burrito? Giles kept rifling through the stack of menus and whittled it down to Indian or Thai. In her heart, she knew it would be Thai. Benjamin loved Thai.

Moving from the kitchen into the lounge room, she fluffed pillows and then slid out some bottles from the wrought-iron wine rack, trying to decide between pinot noir or merlot. It didn't matter that they were cheap; she had time to let them breathe, and they would taste better in an hour. Besides, Benjamin would only care that she was serving alcohol with dinner. He believed alcohol consumption improved his cognition.

Every house has its own peculiar creaks and groans as it expands and contracts with shifts in temperature, as well as the sound of the wind as it whistles through certain doors, plumbing that gurgles, clocks that tick, taps that drip, tree branches that brush against Colorbond gutters. But when there is a creak or scrape that is unfamiliar to the ear, when the floorboards groan at a different pitch, the person in the house becomes instantly alert.

Giles lifted her head. She strained her ears. The sound of a scuff. Her eyes locked in on the hallway. No, not a scuff – a scrape or scratching in the study.

She didn't move, just concentrated on listening. Changed her mind – it was a swish on the wooden floorboards in the bedroom. She couldn't determine if it was coming from the bedroom or the study. But it was a sound that didn't belong.

Giles quietly inched forward, her head cocked to the side, straining to hear. She stepped gently and slowly down the hall, sticking close to the wall, where the floorboards didn't squeak. She paused and stared at the closed study door, taking in a deep silent breath. She could almost feel the presence in the house. Slowly, she inched along the wall, moving closer to the end of the hall, towards her bedroom where her gun was in her bedside table.

She was almost there when Sticky Pete stepped out in front of her. He stood in the door to her bedroom. He was holding Giles's gun, raised and aimed. Ready to shoot her straight in the head.

FORTY-ONE

They locked eyes – Giles shocked, Pete vengeful. Neither moved or spoke, not until Pete's face dropped into a joyless smile. His lips were pale and cracked.

'Hello, Detective. I think you forgot to call me.'

'Pete,' Giles whispered.

She swallowed as her mind raced. She needed to establish rapport, fast. But how do you form a connection with someone who is a hair-trigger away from connecting you with a bullet?

'Shut the fuck up, Detective. I killed a kid because of you. This is *your* fault. I'm not a fucking kid killer. I'm not. Do you understand, Detective Rebecca Giles?'

Giles nodded. *Make sure every movement is deliberate and measured, nothing swift or reckless. Concentrate on every gesture, do not startle him.*

If Pete was trying to work out if he should actually shoot her, his bloody rickety hands were going to make his mind up for him. The Glock-23 was trembling, wobbling all over the place, moving from her nose to her chest to her neck to her forehead. The bastard would kill her. Pete had his finger on the trigger already, if he put just a little more pressure on it the hollow-point bullets would pierce a neat hole in her skull and blow out the back of her head. She'd be dead before her knees even buckled.

Giles slowly raised her hands in surrender. She struggled to find her voice; even with all her training, she couldn't suppress her fear. She muttered in a soft, slow voice, 'Now, Pete —'

'I said shut the fuck up! You *bitch*. You've ruined me.'

Giles let Pete rant. There was nothing heroic about his confession – he was a weeping, trembling man, wailing and trying to stay out of jail: because *you made me do it, you were sending me back to the clink, it's all your fault.*

Pete pointed the gun left and right, at Giles and at himself. She watched Pete's hands, the tension in his fingers. The more worked up he got, the more erratically the gun moved. Still, it was mostly directed at her chest. He was going to pump her one in the heart.

'You fucked *me*, so now now *you're* fucked, Detective.'

He was talking with his hands, tapping his chest with the muzzle when he spoke of himself and pointing it at Giles's face when he was cursing her. If he didn't shoot her, the stupid prick would end up shooting himself.

'Maybe they call me Sticky Pete because I stick to my word. Ever think of that? And I promise I'm going to fucking kill you. That's right, Detective. I stick to my word.'

Pete's face was sunburned, red and inflamed. There were small lumps on his cheek from insect bites, and as he spoke white foam spat from his mouth.

'Fuck you,' he said, swinging the gun towards her again. 'Fuck. You. You . . . you fuckin' —'

Giles heard a thwacking noise, a sharp crack like someone had just smashed an egg next to her ear.

For a second, everything was pitch black. She flinched and squeezed her eyes so tight that, when she opened them again, they were dry and blurry. Tears were stuck to her eyelashes. It felt like someone had flicked warm water into her face and, when she looked down at her chest, she saw blood splattered across her blouse.

Giles looked back up. In front of her, Pete was falling forward, his chest turning red as blood seeped into the material of his shirt.

The old man dropped to the floor – and there, standing behind him, was Turner. His gun was still pointing forward and now at Giles.

Turner! Why is he in my house? Fuck! Is he friends with the cops in Orange?

Giles winced again, anticipating Turner firing off another round. Instead, he dropped his gun to his side and rushed to Pete's aid.

Turner was on his knees, his lips moving, but Giles couldn't hear a thing. He was performing CPR on the old man, pumping Pete's chest.

Giles didn't move. It was like her feet were stuck to the floor. An intense ringing had filled her eardrums.

Turner was yelling. His eyes darted up at her, then back at Pete. Giles had to focus to hear anything over the hissing in her ears.

'Giles, *Giles*, call it in! We need an ambulance.'

Giles blinked and started to come back to the room. She was okay. She sucked in a few sharp, rapid breaths. *Fuck*, she was okay. She slapped her empty pockets. She couldn't think where her mobile phone was, then she just grabbed the landline and summoned an ambulance and police.

Turner was clearly tiring fast, so Giles took over, dropping to her knees and resuming compressions. Pete was going into cardiac arrest. With her palms pressed flat and her fingers interlocked, she kept pushing deep into his bloody chest.

After a few minutes, she felt fatigued and Turner took over again.

'Apply pressure, stop the bleeding,' he said.

'Where's the wound?'

'I think it's the shoulder – the collarbone. That's where I was aiming.'

'How did you —'

'You left your bedroom window open.'

'No, how did you know about Pete?'

Giles found the entry point. She applied pressure and Pete moaned.

'I didn't.' Turner kept pumping Pete's chest. 'I thought I'd find Delano here.'

'Delano?'

Turner was panting with the effort of compressing Pete's chest. 'Bray said Delano was coming to your house for dinner.'

'He is. So what?' Giles's mind flashed. 'Oh shit, Turner! I think I heard something in the study before.'

Turner jumped back to his feet, and Giles took over the compressions on Pete. Her hands were bloody and shaking.

Turner was taking no chances. With his gun at the ready, he sidled down the hall, staying close to the wall. Small steps, quiet steps, inching towards the study.

He stopped and called, 'Armed police! Answer and make yourself known.'

A moment of silence, then he swung the study door open, his gun raised. The room was empty. The ceiling fan whirled on high and loose papers on the pinboard fluttered.

Turner ran back down the hall, passing Giles, into the lounge, the kitchen, calling out 'Clear!' as he swept each room of the house.

He yelled from the laundry, 'Did you leave the fan on in the study?'

'Huh?' *The key's in the flowerpot.* 'Maybe Delano stopped off here first, before picking up Dad.'

'Oh Christ, Giles.' Turner bounced back into the room. 'Michael from the vet rang. The animal hair you spotted at Rickard's property? It's from a German shepherd. I called Rickard and he couldn't recall a German shepherd ever being on his property. That's when I made the connection. I looked into Delano's service history and,' he took a big breath to finish his sentence, 'that prick was stationed at Orange three months ago.'

'*Shit.* I sent him to collect Dad!' Giles paused the compressions, blinked. In her mind she saw a flash of a dark face above her. The clear eyes. Delano's eyes. 'Ring Merton Court. Tell them not to let dad leave. No matter what.'

She left Pete's side, snatched up her car keys and gun, and was out the front door.

FORTY-TWO

An email notification popped up on Falkov's computer. He had been sweating on this message, staring at his inbox and refreshing it for the last fifteen minutes. Finally his computer pinged to let him know it had arrived.

He was quick to click the email open. The inspector in Orange had discreetly scanned the full police report from the Summer Street jewellery store burglary. The attachment took a moment to download, then opened on his screen. Falkov scrolled, his finger rhythmically flicking the mouse wheel. When he found what he was looking for, he squinted at the screen to be sure. He dropped his pen on the desk and it rolled off the edge.

The officer who had signed off on Ava's statement was Sergeant Andrew Delano.

At the bottom of the scanned documents were Delano's police details and photo.

Falkov's voice bellowed from his office, '*Turner!*'

Bray hesitated before answering. Falkov rarely raised his voice. 'He's picking up some dinner, sir.'

'Where's Giles? Did I hear you telling Turner she was seeing Delano tonight?'

'Yeah, who knew they were —'

Falkov was out of his chair and clutching his door frame. 'If Giles's theory is right, Delano is Ava Emmerson's killer.'

At that same moment Constable Griffin ran into the room. 'Sir, there's a dispatch call for ambulance and police. It's just come through. It's from Detective Giles's house.'

Bray and MacCrum grabbed their jackets, but Bray was the first out the door.

FORTY-THREE

The two aged-care nurses thought Delano was delightful. Perhaps even imagined him in his blues, swinging a pair of handcuffs, wishing they could witness a display of his valour. They'd given him a brief tour of Merton Court, pointing out what they considered to be the highlights and best features of the facility. They had talked up Benjamin's exercise regimes and how well his occupational therapy was progressing – how quick-witted he was, one of their favourite residents.

When they finally reached his room, smiles still plastered on their faces, Giles's father was already outside, leaning into a pair of forearm crutches, ready for his outing. Five minutes later, his walking braces were in the boot of Delano's car and he was strapped into the front seat.

'Let's take the doggy view,' suggested Delano.

'Doggy view?'

'Tree route.'

'Oh, good-o,' Benjamin agreed.

Delano kicked over the engine, gave the flirty nurses a goodbye wave and a handsome grin, then pulled onto the road. They cruised down the main street of Denman, passing the pub on the corner and taking a left turn.

'Been reading about your wife's death, Benjamin,' Delano said matter-of-factly.

'Eh?'

'Yeah, your daughter has heaps of files about it on the desk in her study. Newspaper clippings, coroner's report, statements – all about your wife's drowning. The flood and the damage and destruction. Stacks of photos. She's been doing her research.'

Benjamin swallowed. 'Is that right?'

Delano stopped at an intersection, looked left and right. The roads were empty. 'Yep. I've spent all afternoon having a right old read.'

'Don't think it's right, you snooping around my daughter's personal effects.'

'Just trying to get to know you and Rebecca a little better.'

Delano didn't indicate. Instead, he drove straight through the intersection and continued down the road.

Benjamin shifted in his seat and stared out the window. 'You missed the turn-off, the doggy view to Muswellbrook.'

'Yeah,' said Delano. 'I did, didn't I?'

FORTY-FOUR

Giles hit the button on her steering wheel, hanging up the call to Merton Court's front desk. The nurse had said that, just like she'd explained to the other detective who called, Delano and Benjamin had already left, she'd just missed them, but that they'd both been in high spirits. Benjamin was looking forward to his evening out.

I bet he was. Giles shuddered at the thought of her father with Delano. His lack of mobility meant he had no hope of getting away. The stubborn bastard didn't even have a mobile phone she could ring. *Shit, shit, shit.*

Giles pulled the car up to the kerb. Her hands were shaking and covered in Pete's blood. She grabbed her gym bag from the floor of the car, rummaged inside, then reefed off her blood-soaked blouse and put on a wrinkled gym t-shirt. She washed the blood from her hands as best she could with the few dregs left in her water bottle, then snatched up her mobile. Her fingers trembled as she hit the dial button.

Delano's voice. He was quick to answer. 'Hello, lovely.'

She smiled, forcing the friendliness into her voice. 'Where are you guys?'

'Visiting your roots. The place where you were crucified.'

Rattled, she hit the end-call button, tossed the phone beside her, then slammed the accelerator, spitting gravel as she made a U-turn and headed to the Hunter River.

Giles knew Delano would have seen her car pull up at the edge of the paddock, probably heard the door slam. She took a breath. *Easy girl, stay calm.* She climbed through the fence and then cut across the open paddock.

'Dad?' called Giles.

'Over here, Giles,' Delano shouted back.

Giles ran her eyes along the banks of the river and spotted them under a tea tree. She saw Delano grab Benjamin by the shoulder, yanking him back up onto his feet. She slowed down, forcing herself to walk at a normal pace, trying not to look panicked. She didn't know if Delano was aware she had worked it out – she had no idea what cards she was playing, but she had her gun in its holster. She'd take down Ava's killer if she had to.

It was the look on her father's face and the way Delano was holding him up – like a dirty sack of potatoes – that let Giles know she could give up the facade, drop the poker face. Benjamin was being held up like a human shield, covering Delano's chest so only the side of his head and arm could be seen.

Giles thought quickly. She could pull her gun out now and try a shot at his head, but from 20 metres she'd have to be a crack shot and, if she missed, she might hit her father instead. She opted not to play quick-draw.

'Stop there,' commanded Delano.

Giles stopped. The late afternoon sun was in her eyes. It forced her to squint, and the longer she stared at Delano and her father, the more they became shadows, dark outlines of themselves. They blurred into the trees and shrubs.

'Not coming back to mine for a steak then?'

Delano didn't answer.

'Are you going to do the same job you did on Ava Emmerson to my dad?' Giles asked. It was time to cut the shit. The sarcasm was gone from her voice: this was deadly serious.

'Now, Giles, don't get all cunty with me. We can sort this mess out and both walk away.'

'And how would we do that?'

'Do you like diamonds? I offered some to the jillaroo, but she wasn't a bling kind of girl. What use are diamond rings to a girl who's got her hands in cow shit all day?' Delano laughed, and Benjamin wobbled. He moved his crutches in the grass to steady himself.

'Why'd you take the rings?'

Delano shrugged. 'I don't know. Golden opportunity? My knee's fucked – I need a full reconstruction. Which means I've got to give up my post, my dog, my career. I'm not sitting behind a desk. A fucking has-been cop. I did that shit after my first operation – general duties, small crimes, dusting fingerprints. Bullshit. Boring. Realised if I couldn't go back to the dog squad I'd lose my fucking mind with the mundanity. The jillaroo would never have understood that. I wish she'd had her dog with her that day, I would have popped it one, then she would have understood what losing *my* dog, *my* career means to me.'

'Ava. Her name was Ava.'

'Sure – Ava, Ava, Ava. I'll tell you what, she was scared of my mutt. Powerless against a menacing police dog. Two against one. But . . . I got a bit carried away, I have to admit. I was losing my career. That's the problem with kids these days, they've not *sacrificed* anything. I worked hard for my rank, Giles. You would understand that.'

Giles inched forward, trying to move into the shade. She needed to get her eyes out of the sun.

'Police pension isn't enough to carry me through an early retirement. Thought the bling would soften the blow. I was going through a shitty time in my life. I just thought, what's the harm? Fuck me, Giles. *Faaaark!* I was in a different headspace at that time. But that *bitch* was going to turn me in, I was going to lose everything – more than my job. So I just got there first.' Delano scoffed. He had his gun in his hand, although his arm was slack and the weapon was hanging by his side. 'Funny how I was right there under your nose the whole time.'

There was a tight squeeze in Giles's chest that caught her breath. Yes, the killer had been in front of her the whole time. 'Fuck you, Delano. You thought buying off a witness with a couple of rings would solve your problem?'

'These are not just any rings, Giles. It's all about cut, clarity, colour and carats.'

Giles shrugged. 'And now you think a few rings will buy *our* silence.'

'It will buy your life, Giles. And your father's. I heard you on the phone the other morning. You found a boot print. Big whoop. But twigging that Ava had been silenced . . . that's when I realised you were getting close. And then your trip to Orange. Geez, you've had me sweating buckets! Look, we can square a deal. You stop following the lead, prevent this getting to the end. I get on with my life, you get your dad. You can let the lead fizzle out. Fuck me, *please*. Just do this for me.'

'I've seen what you do with loose ends, Delano. Have you got a dead wallaby and a coil of barbed wire ready for us too?'

Delano frowned. 'I'm not spending any time in prison. You know what they do to cops in there. If I go down, I'll make sure I leave the force with a bang.'

'How did you know where to find Ava?'

'Pot luck! After I told that bitch if she opened her fucking mouth I'd cut her tongue out, I got transferred from Orange to Dubbo. But I'd check in on her every now and again, walk past the shop in my uniform, do a bit of window shopping, let her see I still had my eye on her. Then one day, she'd upped and gone.'

'You harassed her? Intimidated her?'

'Just ensuring her silence, that's all. But no one would be afraid of an *ex*-cop, would they? So I had to make sure I ensured her silence before leaving the force for good.'

Giles thought perhaps Ava might have actually loved her boyfriend, but when he got pulled over and busted for a few party pills, she worried the police harassment was spilling over and affecting those she loved.

'But the bitch went missing on me. She skipped town. That's when I got lucky. I was on my way to Newcastle to see my surgeon, start planning my *new* future. Happened to stop in Muswellbrook for a bite to eat and, fuck me, there she was! Fucking fate. Followed her for a few days, saw where she worked. Got myself a map, borrowed a mate's trail bike, easy as!'

'Did you plan on killing her?' Giles was afraid of the answer.

'Fuck no, it just got out of hand. The dog was going off. She was mouthy, and just — I didn't trust she'd keep her trap shut. She looked like she was going to crack. Maybe if I hadn't hunted her down, she would have said nothing. But I just snapped. I guess I fucked up. Got myself into a right clusterfuck.' Delano was starting to sound agitated. He was annoyed by his own mistakes.

'I think you have.'

'But we're in the same shit-storm now, ain't we, luv? If it wasn't for that fucking emerald set and useless dickheads like Kevin Eddy and Sticky Pete, you would never have made the link. You'd still be scratching your arse.'

Calm him down, don't piss him off. Get him feeling like he's in control. Giles had to get Delano to release his hostage. To get her father to safety, she had to earn Delano's trust, not let her ego insist on one-upping him.

Delano was rambling. 'You know, us cops always laugh at killers leaving behind dumb shit, clear evidence. Oh, the wire and wallaby was a good move on my part – cracker thinking there. But going back to plant the hat to point the finger at that old cunt Rickard, that was fucking stupid. I was in panic mode. You don't understand it until you're in it. God, I couldn't sleep. Paranoid. Then the barman told me the story of Rickard and his wife, drowned and found caught up in barbed wire. I thought I could be a clever bastard, use that detail to my advantage. Went back thinking I could make the case even harder to solve. Frame the old codger, chuck in the hat and flowers. Then you and Rickard turned up while I was there. Fuck! That was fucking stupid.'

'You tried to drown me.'

'Tried, but didn't.'

Benjamin was struggling to stay on his feet. Delano hitched him up.

'So what do you say? You slowly unclip and toss me your weapon, we go back to yours for that steak, I skedaddle.'

'I'm not giving up my gun, Delano.'

'Even if you manage to shoot me, Giles, your old man falls back into the river with me. *He* could drown if you don't get to him in time. Don't think he's much of a swimmer.' He paused, gave a sly grin. 'Nor was your mum, was she?'

Giles tensed. She clenched her teeth to temper the quivering in her jaw.

'You've not worked it out yet, have you?' Delano laughed. 'Tell her, Benjamin. Go on, old man.'

Delano jiggled Benjamin's shoulder and the old man looked pained. He stared down at the grass then back up at Giles. 'Just shoot him, luv. Take your best shot. I'll forgive you.'

'Nah, nah, she's not going to have a crack with you in front of me, Benjamin. You see, Giles, your father and I have had a lovely chat. A nice little natter. Did you know why your mother was swept away in the flood? She was trying to get away from this old prick.'

'Rebecca, listen to me, your mother was ill,' Benjamin said immediately. 'People didn't really talk about it back then. She was depressed – postnatal depression.' His voice warbled as he spoke, a last confession from someone who knows he's a dead man. This was her father's final chance to unburden himself, ask for forgiveness before the lights went out.

Giles swallowed. 'Suicide?'

'Attempted homicide.' Delano lifted his chin. He looked so pleased with himself now. 'She tried to commit suicide and drown you with her.'

'You're a fucking liar, Delano.' Giles blinked away the hot tears rising in her eyes. Both Delano and Benjamin were silhouettes against the riverbank, the sun burning her eyes. She couldn't see their faces clearly; she couldn't read their expressions.

'No. I'm not. Tell her, Benjamin, before I pop you one.'

'I tried to save you both,' said Benjamin. He sounded defeated. 'I pulled you from her arms, but I lost her to the river. I didn't . . . I didn't want people to think your mother was mentally unstable.' Benjamin sounded short of breath. Giles wanted to see her father's face clearly. She wanted to see the expression that came with the truth. She inched closer as Benjamin, drawing in a rasping breath, continued. 'I didn't want the town to remember her for trying to kill her baby.' Giles's hands quivered, her jaw ached. But she failed to answer, lost for words. 'Rebecca, I typed up the report to make it read like a tragedy. Told Falkov to make no mention you were there. That it was an accident.'

Giles choked and her fingers were beginning to tremble. 'That's not what happened, Dad.' Her breathing was rapid. Her chest ached with the urge to scream. But then, it had been the lack of detail in Falkov's report that had made her suspicious in the first place . . .

Giles shook her head. 'No, Dad.'

'It's true, sweetheart,' said Benjamin. 'She . . . she tried to take you with her. I had to fight to unhook her from around you. She was like an octopus, the strength, her arms everywhere, clutching you, trying to take you under with her . . . I ripped you from her grip, and then she was gone.'

Fuck, thought Giles. *My* mother *was the Kraken.*

That gave Giles the strength to pull her gun from her holster and point it at Delano. He disappeared behind Benjamin immediately – she could see just the edge of his head and one ear.

'Detective Sergeant Delano, I'm arresting you for the jewellery theft at Summer Street, the murder of Ava Emmerson, the kidnapping of Benjamin Giles, and for the threat with intent to harm Rebecca Giles and Benjamin Giles.'

'*Threat?*' laughed Delano.

Giles continued, fighting back her rising anxiety, trying to will the weapon in her hands to steady. 'You are not obliged to say or do anything unless you wish to do so. But it may harm your defence if you do not mention when questioned something which you later rely on in court. Anything you do say and do may be given in evidence. Do you understand? I need to hear you say it.'

'Yes, I know the caution. Yes, yes, Giles, ye—'

Giles pulled the trigger.

The first shot hit his ear, taking off the tip. Delano instantly raised his hand to the side of his head. Her second shot pierced his shoulder. The third shot hit him in the abdomen as he spun away from Benjamin, arms outstretched. The fourth shot hit his chin, cut through his jaw and blew out the back of his skull.

Delano dropped back towards the river with his arms flung wide. Then she heard his body hit the water.

Crucified, Giles thought.

She ran towards her father as he too began to topple backwards. Arm stretched out, fingers fanned. She just about managed to snatch his shirt and pull him towards herself, for a teetering moment feeling like she'd go over the edge with him before her feet found purchase and she managed to haul him back to safety.

'Fucking hell,' Benjamin croaked as he lay on his back on the riverbank. 'A bit of a bloody overkill, luv.'

Giles stood at the edge of the bank, looking down at Delano's body floating in the river below. She pulled the trigger of her gun one more time, expelling her rage with one final bullet that went straight into his chest, knowing as she did so that this action alone would have been enough to spark a full-scale inquiry.

'*That's* overkill.' Giles dropped to her knees and helped her father sit up. 'You okay?'

Benjamin nodded and looked deep into her eyes. 'I guess now we've both saved each other from a watery grave.'

———

As the evening sun began to set, Benjamin and Giles sat with their arms around each other and foreheads pressed together.

From a tree branch above came the long, eerie wail of a bush stone-curlew. Then the bird was drowned out by the sound of police sirens screaming down the road.

Giles knew Bray, Turner, MacCrum, Callahan and Falkov were all coming for her. She gently squeezed her father's hand and said, 'The cavalry is here.'

Benjamin grinned. 'A bit fucking late.'

FORTY-FIVE

In a guarded hospital bed, Sticky Pete stared at the pale lime-green wall. He was high on morphine and contemplating all the ways he would fuck Giles over for ruining his life. The only thing that gave him joy – the only thing that would give him a reason to behave himself in prison and get an early release – was the desire to hear Giles's shoulder splintering the way his had done.

He hoped she would go into cardiac arrest from the shock of it, just like he had done.

Detective Giles had made herself an enemy alright.

FORTY-SIX

Sitting by the river, Giles sipped on a bottle of chilled James Squire while she tossed pebbles into the water below. She watched the ripples, varying in size, and felt a strange satisfaction when the edges of the little waves crossed each other's path.

Sergeant Delano had now been dead for six days. The ERU had finished with the scene, although the police tape was still tied to the trees and flapping in the breeze.

Yet Giles was far from closure. When she hadn't been helping with wrapping up the initial investigation, her time had been swallowed up by the internal inquiry that had been opened – inevitable after she had drawn and emptied her weapon. Maybe she could give David Hemmings a call, see if he was as good as he said he was. Internal investigations had a reputation of being gruelling; if Hemmings couldn't help her with the legal side of things, he seemed like he could help her with the emotional side. She had kept his card.

Since the shooting – when not at the station – Giles had spent the mornings with her father and the afternoons with her mother, here on the riverbank.

The sound of her phone ringing hurt Giles's ear. She had trauma in her right ear from the bullet that passed through Sticky Pete's shoulder. It had buggered her eardrum – not to mention her lounge room wall.

'Morning, blossom.' It was Bray. 'This is your friendly check-in call.'

'Morning.'

'I've got a final update on Sticky Pete,' he said. 'Want to hear it?'

'Sure.'

'Peter Nolan has given a full confession about abducting and then running over Sara Milligan. Now, we all know a confession in a police interview is not the same thing as a conviction, but Pete says he's happy to repeat it all when he's out of hospital and appears in front of a judge. We did it, Giles. You can put both cases behind you.'

Giles nodded, forgetting Bray was on the phone and couldn't see her response.

'You there?' he asked. 'Did you hear me?'

'Yes, I heard. That's good news, Bray.'

'Too bloody right it is. Are you smiling?'

Giles's face started to cave in. She couldn't stop shaking. The sound of the river and Bray's voice, the thought of Delano in her bed, of Sara and Ava's bodies, of her father being held hostage, the idea of her mother wishing them both dead – it all started to flood through her body.

'Giles? *Are you smiling?*'

The air was still. The birds were quiet. Even the sun lowered its simmer.

Giles drew in a long deep breath, squeezed her eyes shut and answered, 'Yes, I'm smiling, Bray.'

'Good. I'll pop in after work with a brewski snack-pack. You and I can have a beer together to celebrate. Bloody Falkov brought in a homemade hummingbird cake this morning – it took half a tub of butter and two cups of tea to help get it down. I'm seriously thinking of having a word with his wife, she's killing morale.'

Giles sniffed and licked her lips, wiping away her tears with the bottom of her t-shirt. Only Bray could make her smile at a time like this.

'Oh, and did you send a box of Arnott's biscuits to Mr Rickard?'

'Maybe.'

'A *box*? That's over three hundred biscuits, Giles. He rang to see how you were recovering, called you a bloody boofhead and said when you feel up to it, pop in for a coffee and help him get through a packet. He wants to know just how big of a biscuit tin you think he has.'

Giles grinned. There was a moment of silence as she swallowed down her need to cry.

'You okay?' Bray asked.

'Yep. All good. I'll see you tonight.'

Giles's finger shook as she tapped the phone. She took a swig of beer to calm her nerves, then kept drinking until the bottle was empty.

~

It takes three beers before Giles finds the nerve to confront the river. She tosses the empty bottle by the trunk of a willow tree, stands, and then thrashes through the waist-high buffel grass. At the edge of the water, she slides down the dirt embankment and into the Hunter River. The water is cold. She trudges out waist high, her clothes trying to drag her down. In the centre of the river, she flops on her back and floats on the surface.

The water laps around her and she drifts, splayed on her back, and stares up through the overhanging trees, into the blue sky.

She tries to find forgiveness for her mother's actions. Finding none, she instead rolls on her stomach and screams with all her might under the water, hoping to raise the ghost of the Kraken so she can have the final word.

ACKNOWLEDGEMENTS

In December 2021, I entered *The Fall Between* into the 2022 Penguin Literary Prize with fingers crossed and a head full of fanciful dreams. Some months later, I was ecstatic when I saw my name on the shortlist of six. If nothing else, I felt this was affirmation enough that I could write something that made someone say 'huh, not bad' – and my cup was full. Whilst I didn't win the prize, the dream didn't end! Thank you so much to Bev Cousins and Meredith Curnow for your phone call that morning and belief in my manuscript. My appreciation to the judges, and deepest congratulations to Annette Higgs, who did win the 2022 Penguin Literary Prize. I look forward to seeing you around on the writers' circuit.

Thank you to the dedicated team at PRH, you're the dream team.

Huge thank you to Johannes Jakob for your fresh eyes on my manuscript, you have taught me to scratch deeper for the gold, and to Bev, my editor, I'm in awe of you. Thank you for your wisdom, skill, and expertise – you're the bestest ever – and no, you are *not* highlighting that line for me to reconsider!

I also wish to thank Pat Griffith and Renee Nieass for your unceasing thumbs up during my writing journey. Cassandra Chan,

Jenni Beaumont-Hunt, Ray Harding and Sally Ruston for reminding me that I think outside the box and that's okay. To my girl pals, ANGELA JEAN (because she wanted to be in capital letters and first), Debbie Wainkauf, Julie Judd, Trudie Lee Tulloh, Annette (no-middle-name) Price, and Billie-Jo Nicholson. You make life awesome in every way.

Craig, Vanice, Molly, Mum, Dad, and Ethan. I couldn't wish for a more supportive family. Thank you for all the love.

Mikaela, my goddaughter, whose only similarity to the Mikaela in the novel is through name, beauty, and sweetness.

Thank you to the community of Muswellbrook for always welcoming me with open arms to poke around, and the surrounding Upper Hunter areas. You truly have the perfect backdrop for a novel. All characters and events in this book are fictitious, with a little creative licence in setting and place names. To the police at Singleton station – I think I might owe you a Nespresso machine?

Lastly, thank you to Mel and Jason. No amount of red wine and steak dinners could ever thank you enough. Detective Giles and I will forever be grateful.

Mel, you really are an inspiration with an eloquent understanding of human behaviour, motivation, and psychology.

A mammoth thanks to Jason of the NSW Police Force's State Crime Command for your utter patience, laughing at my first drafts and endless insightful information. All mistakes in this novel are mine and mine alone.

Darcy Tindale is an actor, author, theatresports player and director, and has appeared in television commercials, film and on stage. She has written comedy for radio, stage, media personalities, comedians, and theatre restaurants. Her short stories, plays and poems have been published in anthologies, journals, and magazines. Darcy lives in Sydney and has a BA in Creative Writing. *The Fall Between* is her first novel.

Discover a
new favourite

Visit **penguin.com.au/readmore**